Heading toward Tampa, Tony Lo[...] mirror again. Still no pursuit. He spotted two troopers parked in the meridian a half mile ahead, strobes flashing like beacons. Dropping behind a pack of trucks, he killed his lights and yanked his wheel sharply to the left. Skidding into the meridian, he spun across the grass, and pulled in front of a southbound pack of trucks before the cops ahead were even aware he'd come and gone.

He stepped on the gas and sped south. He'd have to take an alternate route. At least there were no more signs of police or possible pursuers. Only ten angry truckers on his trail, reminding him to put on his lights, for Chrissake, before his ass became road roast.

As Lowell drove, the white lines flicking past hypnotically, he couldn't shake the vision of that poor woman, which continued to hover in the forefront of his consciousness...

HOUR of the MANATEE

MANATEE

E.C. AYRES

ST. MARTIN'S PAPERBACKS

HOUR OF THE MANATEE

Copyright © 1994 by E.C. Ayres.

All rights reserved. No part of this book may be used or reproduced in any manner whatsoever without written permission except in the case of brief quotations embodied in critical articles or reviews. For information address St. Martin's Press, 175 Fifth Avenue, New York, N.Y. 10010.

Library of Congress Catalog Card Number: 93-11469

ISBN: 0-312-95406-9

Printed in the United States of America

St. Martin's Press hardcover edition/February 1994
St. Martin's Paperbacks edition/January 1995

10 9 8 7 6 5 4 3 2 1

HOUR of the MANATEE

1

The great blue heron's cry pierced the morning air along the bay front, sending a flock of snowy egrets scurrying to wing from the shoreline, where they had been scouting the tidal flats for crabs.

Another sound echoed across the waters as the air suddenly began to vibrate with a swelling, thumping, grinding rhythm. It grew, alien to the landscape, more intense. More birds took flight. Even the ever-restless mullet seemed to hesitate, then seek cover, leaving the surface waters still as glass.

Twenty feet above the high-water mark lay a hulking wooden schooner, in homemade dry dock at the edge of a pine wood that bordered the mangroves along the water's edge. Forty-five feet of half-rotten planks, a solid twelve-by-twelve keel, and broken spars jutting skyward like the vestiges of a burned-out forest were all that remained of the once-stately vessel.

A heavy yellow power cord ran from the boat across an open marsh toward a clump of trees. Beyond stood a small, dilapidated bungalow, barely visible in the woods. The boat shuddered on its cradle, sawdust drifting in thin streams from cracks in the planking forming tiny cones on the sandy soil below.

Someone began to sing: a voice from the past, captured for decades on brittle mylar; thin and Caucasian, rendering a kind of folk-blues fusion. The air trembled next with the roar of an electric bass and guitar, blaring across the water from twin Altec-Lansing speakers, long ago salvaged from a condemned movie theater, and now set up on the boat deck in defiance of man and nature alike. The music was old—vintage sixties rock and roll, a cut from an album by Donovan called *Mellow Yellow*. From a time that was certainly not mellow, despite myth to the contrary. The song was "Season of the Witch." And such a season was about to begin.

As the music began to swell, the bird cried out again, as though provoked by something unseen. It could have been from sheer pleasure. It could have been in pain. It finally spread its great wings and lurched away, in search of more tranquil waters.

"Yeah, that's good. Real good." A man's voice. Mature, like tires crunching on loose gravel. Confident. Possibly just slightly bored.

A woman spoke out, in mild protest. Whoever she was, she was young. Too young to know who Donovan was, or to care.

"Beautiful!" said the man.

Other sounds began to invade the normally peaceful atmosphere along the shoreline. There was a kind of grinding noise. And a series of muffled clicks.

"Was that good?" The young woman spoke again, her voice slightly plaintive. Or maybe just winded.

"Great," was the reply. "You're beautiful."

Up on the pilot deck of the boat stood a man in his forties—long, sandy hair pulled back in a ponytail, face weathered and tan—both permanent features in the hot Florida climate. He had not recently shaved. Armed with an antiquated Nikon F-1, he took one final frame and was finished. Switching off the ancient reel-to-reel tape deck that sat on a nearby hatch cover, he unscrewed the 50-millimeter lens, and put it away. He then unloaded a roll of black and white 35-millimeter Tri-X from the camera and tossed it to the girl.

"You'll have to do your own lab work," he informed her. She caught it deftly, with an uncertain grin. She was wearing a "Florida" T-shirt and faded cutoff jeans, and had been exerting herself cranking an old-fashioned carpenter's brace and bit. Hence the sounds.

"Sure, Mr. Lowell. They're gonna look good, aren't they?"

"Long as you use the right mix of chemicals, and don't rush the timing."

She really seemed worried about it. Lowell laughed. Sheila Balfour was nothing if not stunning. If she felt she was nothing, that was her problem. She was one of the students at the local junior college where Tony Lowell taught photography in his spare time. She wanted to be a model and would probably succeed. He was taking a portfolio of stills for her, as a favor, and had made no demands for compensation. She found this peculiar and a little disquieting. She had offered him money, which he'd refused; then hinted at more sensuous rewards, which he'd tacitly ignored. As he explained it, if he liked someone he would gladly help them, and that was that.

Tony Lowell had other things on his mind than the opportunities that inevitably arose from contact with attractive female students. There was his boat, a longtime restoration project. It needed a million things done, and life was short. There was his business, such as it was. He could use a client—and soon. And sexual involvement, however fleeting, with a student, however stunning, was something he could do without. Now, and always.

They climbed down from the deck, breathing in the humid, salty air. It was October, and the heat was finally beginning to break. It was going to be a gorgeous day.

Lowell turned his gaze to the bayou and bay beyond. The mullet weren't jumping today. Probably because of the cooler weather. No one knew exactly why mullet jumped. The most accepted theory was that hot weather depleted the oxygen in the water, and the jumping was supposed to have an aerating effect—sort of like shaking a soda bottle. But Lowell believed the small vegetarian fish jumped for no other reason than sheer terror—a desperate attempt to escape the relentless jaws of dark predators that slid through the glassy water like hollow daggers.

"I'd offer you a beer but you're underage," he told her. "If you like tea I got Red Zinger, Constant Comment, Chamomile, Lemon Sunrise, Tangerine Dream, and some kickass Jamaican Blue Mountain Java."

"That isn't something you smoke, is it?"

3

Lowell laughed appreciatively, enjoying her naïveté. He started up the crushed oyster-shell path leading through the bromeliads—succulent and blooming now—past the clumps of red and pink hibiscus and spring gardenias, to his bungalow. It was an original crab fisherman's cottage, Queen Anne–style single story, with a peaked, red shingle roof overhanging the large veranda in front and smaller porch in back.

Sheila adjusted her hair and clothes, and hurried to catch up with him.

"Mr. Lowell?"

Stopping by the back door, he turned his gaze on her. "Yeah?" His eyes were that rare variety that changed color in the prevailing light: sometimes gray, sometimes green or brown. Today they were pale, smoky blue, and fixed on her like twin Nikons. She felt almost naked.

"I was just wondering if you were busy this afternoon?"

"Why?"

"Well." She faltered, then went on. "There's a rally over at the campus today. To stop the drilling?"

He paused. "What about it?"

"The wading birds are dying," she explained, defensively, misconstruing his response as disapproval. "You live right by the water. It impacts on you."

Lowell shook his head. He knew about the drilling and the birds, and cared plenty. A small oil slick was licking against the shoreline at that very moment: the price of economic development further south along Manatee Bay. So-called progress consisting of dredging for yet another shipping channel. More ships, more spillage and bilge, all to feed the endless outward spread of industry and commerce. Soon, the spectacular west coast of Florida would be no different from the long since devastated bays of Mobile, or Galveston. Or for that matter Wilmington.

Just yesterday, the parasite-ridden carcasses of two spotted terns and a snowy egret had washed in on the high tide. Fewer and fewer shore birds could be seen, even here on the backwater. Ninety

4

percent of Florida's bird population had died off since he'd been born. The rest would go soon enough. There'd been manatee once, as well. But no more. The last had been shredded by a cigarette boat five years before, and no others had ventured into these waters since.

"We really could use some faculty support on this," Sheila persisted. "And you're from the sixties. You know about protests and stuff."

Lowell's eyes narrowed. She watched him, sensing some inner disturbance, and correctly intuited her mention of ancient history to be the cause.

"I—I'm sorry, I know how busy you must be—" she stammered.

"Forget it. What time is it going to be?"

Her eyes lit up. God, she is beautiful, he realized. He suppressed the thought immediately.

"Three o'clock. At the main quad. That'd be so fabulous, if you could make it."

Lowell knew he wouldn't go. There was no point. The growth and development people had long since won out: here in Florida and everywhere else, too. They were going to do what they wanted, exploit and pollute some more of what was left of the Earth's natural resources, bankrupt a few more lending institutions in the process, and stash the profits in the Cayman Islands or somewhere. That's the way the world turned now. And he, Tony Lowell, wanted no part of it. Of course, things might change with the new generation—his own generation coming to power up in Washington. But somehow, he doubted it. As the forgettable Alphonse Karr once observed, *"Plus ça change, plus c'est la même chose."*

Sheila saw his eyes cloud over, and turned away.

"Well, thanks for the pictures."

"Any time."

Ducking under the canopy of live oaks, palmettos and spreading magnolias that lined the oyster-shell drive, she headed back up the drive to her recent-model cherry-red Honda Civic, parked on the thick, uncut St. Augustine grass out front.

With detached approval, Lowell watched her tight buttocks flex.

5

as she went. Nice girl, he thought to himself. But the encounter depressed him. He rarely had visitors. Nobody bothered him here on the bayou unless it was business. And the feeling was mutual. His nearest neighbor was two miles away across the water, five by road. Which was exactly the way Lowell wanted it.

Tony Lowell was a private investigator. So private, few even knew of his existence here on Manatee Bay. Again, that was the way he wanted it. When work came his way, it was by word-of-mouth. A former press photographer, Lowell had once had access to many exalted persons and places. Those connections, and memories, had served him well over the years.

When work didn't come his way, that was fine with him, too. He had a few shekels stashed away that he could fall back on, and a modest income from a couple of bond funds—enough to cover bare necessities. He'd just as soon work on his schooner as poke his nose where it wasn't wanted, into other people's business. His boat restoration was clean, neat, predictable, and completely under his control. Other people's business was none of those.

Lowell watched his pupil drive away and decided to take a break. It was getting hot. And after all, there was no deadline. He carefully packed the rest of his tools into their handmade wooden box—an old habit from his photographer days—and headed for the bungalow that he called home.

Lowell had lived here on the Gulf Coast since he left his job at United Press International, just after Watergate. As he'd jokingly told his surprised colleagues, it just wasn't any fun anymore without "Tricky Dick" to kick around. He'd bought the deteriorating fishing shack for $5,000 cash. It was probably worth $60,000 now, or more. But it hadn't improved with age.

He entered his thirties kitchen, with its cast-iron double sink, yellowed cupboards, and ancient Frigidaire—the kind with the cylindrical compressor on top. Checking the fridge, he found a pitcher of sun tea, made yesterday. It smelled slightly of rotting hamburger. He poured himself a glass anyway and gulped it down.

He sauntered into the living-dining room area. His one alteration

6

had been to tear out all the walls on the ground floor, creating one large room. He called it his studio, in deference, mostly, to his bygone days as a photo journalist. Now it served more as a gallery of sorts, a tribute to some of his more memorable works. The ceiling had been raised to the rafters, punching through to the second floor across the front part of the house. To the rear, a second-floor balcony ran across the back half of the room, with a polished oak staircase curving up from the studio below. Lowell's bed and bathroom were upstairs. There was also a guest room (although he never had any guests), filled mostly with boxes of old prints and records.

The studio was white, with simple oak cabinets and a white laminated drafting table in the center, a white leather couch and love seat, a black reclining chair, and an ebony desk, bookcase, stereo and work area in what used to be the dining room.

A huge blowup of a photograph hung from the balcony. The photo was of John Lennon with a triumphant Yoko clinging possessively to his arm. He looked surprised, staring defiantly at the camera. The walls were hung with startlingly familiar news photographs from the late sixties: Martin Luther King in Memphis; Lyndon Johnson and Hubert Humphrey; People's Park in Berkeley; Ken Kesey and his Merry Pranksters in their bus; Timothy Leary at the Hitchcock twins' painted mansion in Millbrook; Mama Cass at the Monterey Pop festival; the Beatles at Shea Stadium; the triumphant Mets of '69; Nixon flashing his victory sign; the '68 March Against the War in Washington; Tiny Tim's wedding; and oddly enough, the America's Cup races at Newport, Rhode Island. From before the time the cup was wrenched away by corporate Philistines, never to be returned.

Three doors led off the back of the studio: one to the former den, now darkroom; a second to a closet; and the third to the kitchen and eating area.

Lowell went over to his ancient eight-track and put on a tape: the Stones' "Beggar's Banquet." He had just seated himself comfortably on his settee to reread *Piloting, Seamanship, and Small Craft Handling*, when the phone rang.

7

There was only one phone downstairs—an ancient black model with a rotary dial on a small table at the foot of the stairs. Lowell got up with a sigh, and took his time getting there. There was nobody he wanted to hear from. Or talk to, in particular.

The voice on the other end of the line sounded as though it were coming from the end of the world. Old, tired, frightened, and female. The hair on Lowell's forearms prickled when he heard it.

"Hello? Anthony? Anthony Lowell, is that you?" She had an Irish accent.

A ghostly flicker of an image from the distant past flashed through Lowell's mind like the dizzying red haze you get when you stand up too fast. "Who is this?" he demanded, his memory cells reaching, reaching, and resisting at the same time.

"You wouldn't know me, Anthony," crackled the ancient voice. "But I got your number, you see. From Caitlin."

Caitlin. Another ghost. Lowell dragged the twenty-foot cord across the room and dropped down hard on the nearest love seat. The leather felt cold, and so did the back of his neck.

"Do I know you?"

"No, no, we were from the same town, though. Long, long ago. My name is Maureen Fitzgerald. But I knew Caitlin, you see."

"But how the devil did she—?"

Maureen anticipated his question. "She knew, Anthony. She always knew."

"Jesus," he muttered, mostly to himself. But the old woman clucked in disapproval.

"I need your help, Mr. Lowell. It's a favor for an old friend."

"Caitlin?" that came out more sharply than Lowell had intended.

"No. I'll explain it all when I see you. Could you possibly come tomorrow morning, for tea? Say around nine?"

"I guess so. Where are you?"

"I'm at the Sun Coast Motel. Do you know it?"

He knew it all too well. A rat-trap known mostly as a place where fraternity boys from the college took their girlfriends, in hope of

8

getting laid. Usually, they just got drunk, made noise, tore up the place, and passed out. It wasn't far, maybe four or five miles down the coast road.

"All right," he sighed. Mornings he usually reserved for work on his boat. But there was something about the old woman's tone that gave him a profoundly uneasy feeling.

"Is this a personal matter, Mrs. Fitzgerald? Or are you looking to engage my services?"

"Oh good heavens, I wouldn't think of asking what I'm going to ask of you as a favor. No, please, I intend to pay. This is business!"

"Do you know my fee?"

"Don't worry, I'll pay you well," she said, firmly.

Lowell hesitated. He hadn't seen any significant income in almost a year. "We'll discuss it tomorrow," he decided. "It all depends," he added, "on what it is you want me to do."

"Exactly. Nine o'clock, then? I'm in room one."

That was it. She hung up the phone.

Lowell put down the receiver slowly, his pulse racing. The old woman had mentioned a name he hadn't heard in years. One that brought back a flood of remembrances, most of them painful.

Going over to his cluttered desk and office area, he searched through the bottom file drawer. Tattered earmarked yellow folders were stacked in erratic heaps, with such arcane labels as: "Msc. Unfin." and "Old Bus." and "Dead File."

The letter was still there after all these years. Relegated, appropriately enough, to the Dead File. It was addressed to "Miss Caitlin Schoenkopf, 1001 Bayshore Drive, Palm Coast Harbor, Florida." The stamp was mint, never canceled because it had never been mailed. First class, seven cents.

Lowell stared at the letter a long moment, pondering. Then, yanking open the top drawer of his desk, he fished out a tattered old brown leather address book and tore through the pages: name after woman's name, most crossed out with angry red X's. The name was there, prominent among the banished. "Caitlin." Under the "C's." With a phone number. He picked up the telephone, hesitated a long moment, and put it down again. This was a call he'd tried a thousand times before and never made. He wouldn't make it this time either.

2

Morning came with a stabbing shaft of early tropical light, invading Lowell's uneasy sleep through a gap in the old beige muslin curtains. There was a sound somewhere out on the bay. He sat up abruptly, with a thudding headache and a vague conviction that something was wrong. It was as though somebody had slammed a door or dropped a hammer. He listened, but the sound was not repeated. Maybe it hadn't occurred. Maybe it was distant thunder. Or the sounds of construction—pile driving—across the water. One never knew. More likely it was something he'd dreamed. His dreams had been getting increasingly disquieting of late.

Lowell groped his way out of bed, vaguely bothered by an innate sense of impending doom. Stumbling down the staircase trying to clear his vision, he avoided the accusing glare of John Lennon, whose eyes followed him wherever he went. I have to get rid of that, he thought to himself, for the thousandth time. John Lennon had destroyed the greatest rock and roll band of all time with his hubris and stupidity. If it hadn't been for that—but he shook the thought off. No use rehashing old history. Man, he sure used to love that John Lennon, though . . .

Rolling up the blue cyclorama he used instead of a window cover, he let the day in. The light was already brutal—the way only tropical sunlight can be. The brief cool spell had been premature. Indian summer still had some drums left to beat. Outside, the palmettos, mangroves and surrounding woods, and the glassy surface of the

11

bay, were deathly still. Sometimes it could be almost too quiet here in this rural tropical paradise-that-was. He hurried to make some coffee.

Lowell filled his battered aluminum camping percolator, and had just struck a match to light the old crowfoot gas range when he remembered his client. Maureen Fitzgerald. He glanced at his watch. Nine o'clock. Damn! He'd have to hurry.

Fifteen minutes later he was somewhat shaved and wearing his one and only tweed sports coat and polyester tie in a sorry concession to social convention. Backing his rusted-out '65 Chevy Impala out of the driveway, he headed east on the two-lane road innocuously identified on state maps as SR 650. Better known to Lowell and other longtime locals as Mangrove Road.

The macadam wound its way along the bayshore and estuaries, through thick scrub pine and over two low wooden river bridges. Just over an inlet it turned south through the village of Gulfbridge (which consisted of a post office, gas station, fish restaurant and two motels) his legal address. It then headed due east along the river, toward Manatee City and the Sun Coast Motel.

Lowell couldn't shake this gnawing feeling in the pit of his stomach, which a continuous supply of Maalox tablets did nothing to appease. There was something unsettling about an old woman for a client. Most of his work revolved around nasty divorces, and the occasional workmen's comp fraud, or missing person. Old women never hired private detectives. Not unless something was very wrong.

In unit #1 of the Sun Coast Motel, Maureen Fitzgerald—a slender elderly woman with white hair tied back in a neat bun—busied herself getting ready for company. Oblivious to the odd bits of luggage and clothing scattered about, she was very carefully, very meticulously setting a tea service for two on the cigarette-burned, coffee-stained pressboard motel coffee table. She studied the table a moment, decided it wouldn't do, and quickly stripped the sagging double bed. Taking the white top sheet, she deftly folded it in quarters, and fashioned what she decided was a passing fair table-cloth. Now for the cutlery and china. She opened a wicker box that sat on the dresser next to an ancient leather suitcase, and removed three purple velvet bags tied with ribbons. Next came a full Wedge-wood tea service—each piece carefully stored in its own wicker compartment.

"Ah, my lovelies, and you thought we'd never have tea again, I'll bet, eh?" She arranged the dishes on the table, each with a carefully polished sterling silver spoon, fork, and butter knife. The tea caddy stood ready, oblivious to the fact that there was no water in it, nor any way to heat it had there been any.

A small, battered early-edition radio-cassette player sat on the floor, playing an equally ancient cassette recording of a Verdi opera, *Otello*. It sounded as though it had been hastily dubbed from an even more ancient, scratchy LP. The old woman sang and hummed to herself, fussing and fiddling about the dreary room as though it were the parlor of the Queen of England.

"Do sit down," she said to no one, pulling one of the two vinyl-backed chairs up opposite her own. Gesturing at the chair as though to a phantom visitor, she poured invisible tea from the pot. "So many memories, so little time," she chattered. "Oh my heavens. I forgot the crumpets!"

Rushing to the dresser top, the sand-colored veneer of which was already peeling away, she opened a brown paper bag and quickly removed a large square tin of English tea biscuits.

"Now then, Henry," she went on to her unseen guest. "You mustn't let on that you've seen me. Because company is coming. A detective person, isn't that lovely? We'll tell him everything, you and I."

Outside the cabin someone approached from the woods in the rear, sheltered from the sight of passersby by a clump of scrub pine between the cabin and the road. A foot creaked on the steps outside the bungalow door. The old woman turned expectantly toward the door.

"Be right there!" called Maureen, checking her faded image in the mirror above the dresser. The red lipstick was nice. She'd bought that at Wal-Mart on the way from the bus station.

"Coming, Mr. Lowell!"

Lowell, however, had not yet arrived. He was at that moment just turning his car into the gravel parking lot at the far end of the faded fifties-style motel. The place consisted of a row of unpainted bungalows scarcely more than quonset huts. Sun in his eyes, he drove slowly along, trying to make out the cabin numbers. Unit #1 was the last one at the end of the curved drive, and as he rounded the bend he glimpsed movement in the shadows on the bungalow porch. But as he drew closer, whatever it was vanished. He dismissed it as another symptom of the jitters, like those noises this morning. His mind was on other things.

Lowell pulled in front of the end unit and shut off the engine. The cabin door opened and a tiny, ancient face peered out. The eyes seemed inordinately large and alive for someone of such advanced age. She waved, beckoning him in. He followed, wondering what to expect. His collar itched under the weight of the tweed jacket. At nine-thirty in the morning, the temperature was already in the high eighties, humidity in the nineties.

He had seen enough over the years that nothing much surprised him anymore. But even he was taken aback by the sight of a formal English tea, served on blue and white china. A distinctive crest—a falcon poised to fly—was engraved on the silver. He watched her fuss and coo, wondering what had brought her to this filthy, roach-infested excuse for a motel.

The old woman sat him down and poured tea. Except there was no tea. She was a child, playing make-believe. Only the biscuits were real. Lowell nibbled one and watched, waiting. The cassette finished the first act and she hurried to turn the tape over.

"Everyone's forgotten how good she was, haven't they?" she called from across the room.

Lowell looked up, puzzled. "Excuse me?"

"I adore the opera. I think this was one of her best recordings, don't you?"

The singer's voice sounded adequate, if somewhat thin—even reedy at times. He had no idea who the soprano was.

"What can I do for you, Ms. Fitzgerald?"

"They let me out, you see," she explained, simply.

He could guess what she meant, of course. He studied her, still waiting.

She pursed her lips, a child's pout, red lips forming a flower. To please her, he took a sip of his invisible tea.

"I saw what happened, that night," she said, sulking. "It wasn't like they said."

"What night?"

"The night Henry drowned, of course. Henry Hartley."

Alarms went off in Lowell's head. Loud, clanging four-alarmers. He should have anticipated it would be something like this. Buying time to collect his thoughts, he glanced over at the cassette player. "Could we turn that music down, please?"

She shook her head. "The walls have ears, you know!"

He looked at the peeling walls, incredulously. There was a sudden chill in the air, despite the heat.

"What exactly did you call me about, ma'am? That's all ancient history." His troubled sleep had been a premonition of this. He wished he hadn't agreed to come. The woman was certifiable. Whatever demons she carried with her from the past were her own. He wanted no part of them—especially when they were so close to home. He had enough demons of his own.

"I was a witness," she explained, almost cheerfully. "I was as close as you are to me when it happened."

The alarms went off again. "When what happened?"

Maureen shook her head. "When—when he was pushed. Henry Hartley was pushed. Murdered! And I saw it happen."

Something had happened many years ago at Palm Coast Harbor, where he'd grown up, a working-class local in an atmosphere thick with money. It was one of those tony towns over on the other coast,

15

just north of Palm Beach. The so-called Gold Coast. There'd been a drowning, of a fabulously rich playboy, and a lawsuit. The grand jury had ruled it an accident. It had been in the news and he had covered the story as a cub photographer. He'd been working the neighborhood at the time covering social events. This was one that had gone awry. But why had she come to him now? And why him? Surely there must be a private investigator closer to home who could handle her case. He wondered what else she knew. He went to the window and stared out through the unwashed pane at the glimpse of marsh and inlet beyond.

"Why did you want to see me, Mrs. Fitzgerald?"

"They wouldn't let me speak, don't you see? They took me away before I could talk to the police, or tell anyone."

"I'm afraid I don't follow. You saw someone push Henry Hartley overboard, you say?"

"Yes, and more than that. He was kissing her."

"Who was?"

"I panicked so badly I fear I never did quite recover," sighed the old woman. "It was all such a blur. And poor Henry, he used to turn to me when his mother would fly off the handle, the way she sometimes did—"

Lowell remembered now. She'd been a notorious bitch.

"She was very—strong-willed, you see."

"Yeah. So I heard. But I don't see—"

"There are things you don't know about Lucretia, Mr. Lowell. And about Henry. That nobody knows but me and—them. Which is why I must tell someone. Would you like some more crumpets?"

They weren't crumpets, but then this wasn't tea.

"No, thanks. Please get to the point."

She went back over to the cassette player and turned Desdemona up louder. Lowell winced.

"OK," he said. "You claim you were witness to a murder that, according to the grand jury, never happened. Why didn't you come forward back then?"

"I told you. They wouldn't let me."

16

He frowned. "What do you mean? Who's 'they'?"

"They said I wasn't competent." She shrugged, matter-of-factly. "But I saw what I saw."

He shook his head. "So what exactly is it you want me to do for you? Seems to me what you want is a district attorney. Or a cop."

"Oh no, they'd be no help at all." She looked at him straight in the eye for the first time, and oddly enough, he knew she wasn't crazy. "I know what's right and what's wrong. What happened to Henry," she said. "And to his mother too. It was wrong. I know. I was there."

Lowell stood up and paced the room. He resisted an impulse to stomp on the still-blaring cassette player. "Mrs. Fitzgerald," he said, finally. "You say you saw a murder. Did you happen to see who perpetrated this crime, because that's really the crux of the matter, isn't it?"

"Yes," she said, a note of uncertainty creeping into her voice. Or was it fear? "Yes. You're right. No one will believe me anyway, of course, and it was so long ago, but I saw her. And him. They did it together, with that other one."

"Who did it together? What other one?"

"The one who took me away. I didn't want to go and they made me. And I've seen him since then. He's very important now. But then, so are both of them, aren't they?"

Lowell hated conversations like this. "Both of whom, ma'am?"

"Those murderers! Those politicians!"

He sighed. "Politicians. I should have guessed." He got to his feet. "I'm sorry, but I can't just go out there and bust some un-named alleged perpetrator based on your word, twenty-five years after the fact, can I? God bless you, ma'am, but unless you have some new evidence about what you say about this Hartley case, I don't think you've come to the right—"

"Ten thousand dollars, Mr. Lowell. That's what I can pay. It's my life savings, but money no longer means much to me."

"Ten thou?" Lowell's ears prickled and paid close attention. Money meant plenty to him. He didn't like the idea of taking money

17

from old women. And this one was certifiable, by her own admission. She probably didn't have ten cents, let alone ten thousand. But she had named a name, and struck a nerve. Odd that she'd gotten hold of some of the Hartley cutlery. He felt certain that was the origin of the crest, which meant it was probably hot. Still . . . just in case she did have some hidden asset in some old coffee can, work was work and opportunities like this were hard to come by. Ten thousand dollars would finish the schooner, for one thing. If the money existed, of course.

"All right. I'll bite. You were there. At the hottest New Year's party south of Newport. And you saw someone push Henry Hartley overboard."

"That's right. And the person I saw was with—" She was interrupted by a creaking sound outside on the stoop. Lowell caught it. The sound reminded him of something. From a dream he couldn't remember, and didn't want to. There was a soft knock at the door.

Maureen reacted, startled.

"Did you tell anyone I was here?" she asked, nervously. He shook his head. "It's probably the manager. I promised I'd pay him later when I cashed my check." She reached for her purse. "Just a moment!" she called.

Lowell stood and moved into the shadows as Maureen went to the door. As a precaution, she chained the lock before opening it.

"Maybe you should find out who it is," Lowell suggested in a low voice, almost as an afterthought. She had described herself as a material witness to a major crime, after all. She didn't hear him. The opera was too loud.

Maureen opened the door a crack. "Yes, what is it?" She demanded. There was no answer. She leaned closer to peer out.

There was a simple pop, like a small firecracker. Or a stick breaking. She fell backward, onto the floor. A small, thin trickle of blood seeped onto the carpet. That was all.

Lowell stood in shock. Then he sprang for the door and received a second shock: The shooter was still there, shadow filling the narrow opening. He ducked out of the line of fire, and a moment

18

later whoever it was, was gone. He tore at the latch, but couldn't open the door without first closing it to unfasten the chain. Maureen's foot was in the way, blocking the door. She had to be moved. Cursing himself for answering that telephone call yesterday afternoon, he dragged her aside until the exit was clear. Then he opened the door cautiously, muscles tense, keeping low and close to the wall.

The parking lot was empty. No one was in sight except a gardener riding a Lawn Boy two hundred feet away, oblivious. He ran back inside. Maureen was still alive. He knelt at her side. She groaned softly, and a hand reached for him, trembling.

"Anthony!" she moaned, voice fading. "It was my—kill—an—jewel. Get—Lucretia!"

"What? What jewel? Who was it?"

"No. Not . . . j— . . ." Her hand went limp. Blood and spittle foamed from her mouth and she expired.

He went for the telephone and dialed 911. The line was busy. He dialed again. Still busy.

"Come on, come on," he muttered, cursing his luck as well as the old woman's. Ten thousand—here one moment, gone the next. He chided himself for even harboring such a thought at a time like this. But what was that about a jewel?

Bewildered, Lowell slammed the phone down, turned and surveyed the room. A brown manila envelope sat on the coffee table. He'd noticed it when he'd entered. It had his name on it, clearly written, presumably in Maureen's handwriting. Hesitating a moment, he picked it up. If it was his fee he was still employed, dead client or not. Now he definitely had a murder to solve. He reclosed the door and opened the envelope.

There was no money or jewelry. The envelope contained a yellowing 8 × 10 photograph, and nothing else. It was a candid shot of a young couple kissing on a crowded city street, possibly New York. The woman was brash and beautiful, cheaply but flashily dressed. She wore a short skirt and long hair that fell in two braids. She had a campaign button on her cashmere sweater, the inscription on which he couldn't quite make out. The man embracing her was partly turned away from the camera, she toward it. He looked oddly out of place. He was wearing a suit, slightly too large, while everyone around them was sporting far flashier attire.

The photograph looked familiar, somehow, but he couldn't quite place it. Stuffing it back into the envelope, he shoved it into his jacket pocket, and picked up the telephone once more. This time the call went through.

3

Flashing police strobes lit up the vicinity of the Sun Coast Motel like red lightning: rhythmic silent echoes of a violent, passing storm of human origin. Because the motel was on the edge of town, there were only a few bystanders in the area. Most of them were tourists secretly hoping something exciting would finally happen on their vacation.

Detective Sergeant Lena Bedrosian of the Manatee City Police Department got out of her unmarked squad car and surveyed the area, bracing herself for the onslaught of male hostility her recently acquired rank and position had taught her to expect. She'd worked hard, and won honors. There was no question that she was smart, capable, and tough. Tougher than any of the men she'd beaten out for the job. Not physically stronger, of course. But mentally tougher, more resilient, more intuitive (yes, she'd taken plenty of guff for that, too) and in test after retest, had shown more stamina and persistence than any ten of her male colleagues combined.

Still, to be the first female detective in a major police department in the state of Florida was no small thing. Bedrosian had to watch her back at all times, she knew. Especially for friendly fire.

Sheriff's Deputy Joel Pilchner and Police Sergeant Bill Allenson were already there, along with a couple of patrolmen whose names Bedrosian couldn't remember. The area was cordoned off, and they were waiting for her with nervous expectation. Procedure called for the Sheriff's Department to handle routine situations in the unin-

21

corporated county, including Gulfbridge, which didn't have a police department of its own. When more serious matters arose, such as murder, Manatee City was called in. This tended to cause resentment. The fact that a woman detective had shown up to take over caused even more resentment. But the cops were careful not to show it too openly. It would come with reproving glances, cutting little remarks, and a generally patronizing attitude.

The fact that the victim was an old woman gave Bedrosian immediate authority, in this case. The male cops on the scene seemed embarrassed, almost, at having to witness this ultimate indignity inflicted on someone who, in all likelihood, reminded most of them of their grandmothers. It wasn't that uncommon, in Florida, for a murder victim to be elderly. Older people were prime targets for every sort of abuse—especially female ones. Usually just scams and cons, but sometimes worse. Like now.

"Small-caliber bullet, right in the heart," muttered Allenson. A veteran police sergeant of twenty years, Bill Allenson was beefy and sweated profusely, especially in the relentless heat of the Gulf Coast. He prided himself in having been around the bayou a few times. In this case it hadn't helped. "Clean as a whistle." he added mournfully.

A chill swept down Bedrosian's spine. She was still young, thirty, and had moved up through the ranks with incredible speed. Her promotion to detective, however, had come primarily on the strength of a dramatic series of relatively peaceful drug busts. Violent crime was not her forte, and the things people seemed capable of doing to other people still appalled her at times. This was one of those times.

Joel Pilchner came over. "We can't find the weapon, but it looks like the shot came from outside. We think she had the door chained when she answered it, and they got her anyway. Jesus."

Bedrosian looked around at the solemn faces.

"Who was she?" she demanded.

"No I.D." offered Allenson. "All we got is the name on the registration. Maureen Fitzgerald. No other address."

"Christ," sighed Bedrosian. Why couldn't it ever be easy? "Get these people out of here, and let's take a look."

While the policemen shooed the onlookers away, Bedrosian climbed over the rope, careful not to muss her meticulously pressed gray suit—jacket and long pleated skirt, with white blouse and boots. She stepped carefully over the small, forlorn puddle of blood, and into the motel room. She stooped by the body for a moment, lifted the sheet covering it, and examined the victim's face. Frozen in surprise. And defeat.

She became aware of a popping sound in the room, repeating over and over. It made her scalp crawl. "What the hell is that noise?" she demanded.

One of the cops pointed at the cassette player. The tape had long since finished, but either the machine had no automatic shut-off or the mechanism was jammed. The spindle was trying to force its way onward into musical oblivion. The tape clung stubbornly to the hub with its last thread of tension. One would give soon. If not both. Meanwhile, for fear of tampering with evidence, nobody had dared turn the thing off.

The tension in the room was palpable. "Somebody find a handkerchief or something and turn it off!" she snapped. "Dust it later if we need to. Christ!"

The cop grudgingly complied. The noise was getting on his nerves too.

Lowell sat waiting at the coffee table, eyeing her with some interest, flanked by two more cops—Peters and another Sheriff's deputy. Detective Bedrosian knew Peters from church. That was about it. She gave Lowell a glance, then a double take, followed by a glare of instant disapproval. "Lowell?" She spun on the officers. "What the hell is he doing here?"

"Sorry, sir. I mean, ma'am. He's a witness," volunteered Peters, with a nervous glance at his partner.

Bedrosian froze Allenson and Pilchner with a withering look. "Is this a joke? Nobody mentioned a witness."

23

"We thought you might want to get here first," explained Allenson, with a knowing grin to his partner.

Bedrosian turned back to Lowell. Tony Lowell was the living epitome of everything she despised. Lena Magdalen Bedrosian had grown up in Tarpon Springs, raised in the Greek Orthodox Church by devout, God-fearing Republican parents, first-generation immigrants from Armenia who had taught her to fear God and love Country, in that order. To her father, pride had meant having a full table, a clean face, your-own-home-however-humble, and a reasonably new car. Her own improvements on that legacy had been to dress as well as one could afford, and then one better. Like now, she was wearing a brand-new Halston suit. Off the rack, but then adjusted by the dry cleaner's tailor. And Italian shoes. OK, so the blouse was J. C. Penney's, but it was all cotton, which was the most comfortable. Lena Bedrosian wore her pride like a badge of honor, reflected in her personal appearance and hygiene as solid proof that she worked hard and lived clean.

As for Lowell, he was dead opposite her in every way: unshaven, hair long and unkempt, sloppy, involved in bleeding heart liberal causes, a goddamn reprobate who called himself a detective! She'd had dealings with Lowell before, never pleasant. He'd handled a couple of particularly messy civil cases between retired Sunbirds that had led to violence; and had worked to free a student leader she'd been damn certain was involved in drugs.

They hadn't mentioned whether he was a suspect or not. Bedrosian chose not to assume she could be so lucky.

The police detective's eyes narrowed as she regarded her rival one more time.

"So, what's the story this time, Lowell?"

Allenson and Pilchner exchanged looks.

"He's the one who placed the call, Detective," said Pilchner. "He was here when we got here."

Bedrosian didn't like the sound of that. Bad enough she had competition. Worse, competition that had beaten her to the scene.

She was damn sure Lowell had an angle here, somewhere. She scanned the room once more.

"Anything missing?"

"Hard to tell," Allenson wiped his brow. "We don't know what she had. But there was two hundred and change in her purse."

Bedrosian sighed. It was never easy. She took a seat opposite Lowell and looked at him squarely. He gazed back calmly. She smelled of jasmine.

"You placed the call?" she asked, simply.

"Sure." Lowell thought he could read Bedrosian like a stop sign, and didn't try to conceal his smile. He knew full well that she despised him mostly for his image. Which Lowell had created by device and cultivated every bit as carefully as the police detective had cultivated hers. Plus, she probably had a lot of baggage to carry about men. It would be inevitable, with the job she held.

"What were you doing here, Lowell?"

"Interviewing a client. We were having tea," Lowell explained.

"Tea." Bedrosian looked at the silver service and china, and the empty teapot. "What is all this shit, a rummage sale?" She examined one of the cups more closely. "This looks expensive. This too," she added, picking up one of the spoons. She looked around at the waiting cops. "Anybody check to see if this stuff is hot?"

Allenson shook his head. "We didn't have a chance, Lena," he replied, defensively. "You want, I'll run a check right now."

"You do that."

Allenson gingerly scooped up a cup, saucer, and spoon with his handkerchief, placed them in a plastic bag, and left hastily. Bedrosian looked around the room, in exasperation. Nothing fit right. People just didn't go around killing old women if there was no sign of robbery or (in the sickest cases) rape.

"Is somebody gonna tell me what's going on here?" she barked.

Nobody seemed anxious to volunteer an explanation. Lowell would have enough explaining to do if they searched him and found the envelope. On the other hand, it had his name on it, and there's

25

no way they could prove it hadn't been his in the first place. Bedrosian turned back in Lowell's direction.

"OK, Lowell. So you were having tea with the old lady on some fancy china that just happened to be here in this sleazeball dump of a motel. You gonna tell me why there's no tea in this pot?"

"I was wondering about that myself."

"What did she want to see you about?"

"She didn't say. All I know was she called me yesterday and asked me to come over and talk."

"I see."

"She wanted to see me first thing this morning, so I came over. Then somebody knocked at the door, she answered, and—they got her."

There was a moment of silence in the room. Bedrosian knew with the certainty of her five years experience that Lowell was holding back on something.

"So she went to the door. Did you see who was there? You musta seen somethin'!"

"It was only open about four inches, and Maureen was between me and whoever was there."

"You couldn't tell if it was male or female, even?"

"No."

"Jesus," muttered Pilchner. Bedrosian gave him a look, then turned back to Lowell.

"What about her? She say anything before she died? You're not giving me a whole helluva a lot."

"It happened fast. By the time I got her out of the way and the door opened, they were long gone."

Bedrosian turned to the other officers. "Anybody see *anybody* leaving the area?"

"No, ma'am," said Pilchner. "There was a gardener, but he was running a power mower and didn't see or hear a thing."

"Great," growled Bedrosian. "Nobody saw nothin', and nobody heard nothin'."

By this time, Lowell had also decided not to mention Ms. Fitz-

26

gerald's last words. Not until he knew what they meant. Nor was he about to mention the ten thousand. It might still turn up, for one thing.

Allenson came back in. "I called in to Manatee, Sarasota, St. Pete, and Tampa. Nothing matching the description's been reported missing, Lena."

"Figures," muttered Bedrosian. It was never easy.

"Can I go now?" asked Lowell, mildly.

Bedrosian gave him a calculating look, and turned back to Allenson. "You get his statement?"

"Yeah. Nothin' useful. As usual."

"I'll decide that." Bedrosian pivoted back to Lowell once more. "I could hold you as a material witness, Lowell. The killer is still at large, obviously, and maybe knows who you are, too. I know damn well you're holdin' back on me. Maybe they think so too."

Lowell didn't much like that train of thought, but kept it to himself.

"I'll take my chances. They have no reason to be after me."

Detective Bedrosian decided not to press the issue. But knowing as she did that the P.I. was being less than forthcoming angered her no end. She took it personally, as an affront to her profession and her gender.

"People do weird things for even weirder reasons in this world, buster," she snapped. "You ought to know that. Being one of the champion weirdos."

" 'To consider oneself different from ordinary men is wrong. But it is right to hope one will not remain like ordinary men.' "

"Spare me the college Shakespeare."

"Actually that's Japanese. Zenshu, volume two. I recommend it for expanding one's perspective."

Bedrosian folded her arms, and leaned back, against the door frame. "Look, I don't need your philosophy. I need a suspect. If you come up with one, you will let me know?"

"Of course."

27

"OK, you can go. But stay in touch. If that's agreeable, of course."

"Of course."

Lowell headed for the door, aware of five pairs of eyes aimed at him like dart guns.

"I'm serious, Lowell," Bedrosian called after him. "I'd watch my back, if I were you. Have a nice day."

Lowell got into his Impala and drove away in a cloud of blue smoke. I'll have to do something about this car, he thought to himself. Bad for the environment. Fat chance of that ten grand turning up, of course. Or any missing jewels, whatever she'd meant by that. The dame didn't have two buttons to rub together, let alone bucks. Too bad. He could have used it. He'd been thinking about a methane converter for the old clunker. Economical, simple, and incredibly effective. Parts hard to come by, of course. Not to mention methane. He could make his own, possibly. He could do a lot of things. All it took was time and money. Time, he had plenty of. He'd been wasting it in vast quantities for years. But money? There was the rub. He'd have to start thinking about that. He might need some, one of these years . . .

4

Lowell pulled into his driveway, drove down to the falling-down shed at the back of the property that served for a garage, and sat in the car for several minutes to collect his thoughts. The wind was picking up outside—a late-autumn storm blowing in from the Gulf. The palmetto leaves rustled in restless anticipation. He could hear the hollow twang of rigging, steel stays on the sailboats moored out on the bay, snapping against aluminum poles.

A county sheriff's patrol car came slowly down the road, past the Lowell property, from the direction of Gulfbridge and Manatee. Tony saw it glide by in his rear-view mirror. Just checking, he figured. As though they didn't have better things to do.

A black Cadillac Seville with tinted windows passed by, from the opposite direction, and slowed perceptibly as it approached Lowell's mailbox. As it passed the patrol car, Deputy Pilchner glanced up and tried to catch the license number but it was impossible. The car was new. The license frame was an ad for an unfamiliar dealership, and the tiny sticker in the window was less than useless.

The Caddy continued on around the bend and out of sight.

Two hundred yards away in his shed, Lowell suddenly felt a chill of vulnerability, sitting in the dark, lit only by an occasional stab of sunlight filtering through the trees and the shrinking planks of the leaky roof.

The old shed was cluttered with unused garden tools and some ancient farm equipment from another era. As far as he knew, it had always been here, sort of an appurtenance of the property itself. There was a horse-drawn harvester, a mowing attachment, and a huge rusty scythe. The shed was starting to give him the creeps. He opened the car door and stepped out, nerves taut. He kept seeing that poor woman's face. He'd seen too many faces like that in his day and they all still haunted him: each and every one.

Down by the water, the schooner sat on its stilts patiently awaiting his infrequent ministrations. Maybe he would work on it today, to cleanse himself of the psychic stain of this morning's events. If the weather cleared. But first, he had to see about more immediate problems.

He crossed the yard and entered his unlocked house through the kitchen door. Remembering the detective's parting words, he wondered if it wouldn't be a bad idea to take precautions. Just in case. He decided the hell with it. Whoever killed the old woman had no interest in him. Why should they? Besides, Lowell believed in karma. If it was your time, so be it. No point fighting karma.

He went to the refrigerator, now rattling and railing angrily against years of forced servitude in the tropical Florida climate. Fetching himself a glass of herbal sun tea, he dropped a couple of ice cubes into his drink and walked into the studio, to his designated living area.

He'd left the stereo on from the night before. Annoyed with himself, he removed the old copy of *Beggar's Banquet* and slid it into what was left of the sleeve. Then searching through his vast and ancient record collection stored mostly in a stack of orange crates in the closet, he spotted an album he'd almost forgotten about these past twenty years. Paul Butterfield's *Resurrection of Pigboy Crabshaw*. Heavy Chicago blues suited his mood right now, and he laid on his favorite track: "Driftin' and Driftin'."

The cracked white leather sofa that dominated the room represented a singular material splurge a few years earlier. Settling down into its familiar depths, he kicked back and washed the bile from his throat with a long swallow of cold herbal brew. Then he took out the envelope he'd managed to spirit away from Maureen Fitzgerald's motel room.

Pondering the photograph, Lowell tried to glean some meaning from it. Its vague familiarity nagged at him: a young couple embracing, in an urban setting, celebrating. Who? Celebrating what? More to the point, what did they have to do with the Hartley case? The girl he thought he recognized. But twenty-five years and untold events had passed since that infamous night.

"Shit," he muttered to himself, savoring the tea. The salty air made him thirsty. It was lunchtime now, and he was also feeling pangs of hunger. He went to see if there was anything not too moldy in the ice box. Maybe those fried clams he'd picked up the other night at The Oyster House (Gulfbridge's lone eatery) were still edible.

Paul Butterfield's famed lead guitarist, Mike Bloomfield, wailed into a long solo: filled with the pain of lost souls, lost love, and empty tomorrows. Like Lennon, like Joplin and Hendrix, like Jim Morrison, Paul Butterfield was dead now. And small wonder, from the tortured sound of his music.

The clams were bad, which didn't improve his mood. By the time he found the box of Ritz crackers and some hardened yellow cheddar wedged behind a rusted can of old tomato juice, the weather had changed. The sky darkened, and a sudden gust of wind blew the curtains back. It started pouring as only a Gulf cloudburst can pour, and like a true native son, Lowell made no attempt to close the windows. The jalousies kept most of the rain at bay, and the breeze felt good. But as he glanced out the window—the one facing the driveway—he thought he heard a loud scraping noise just outside. The gray muslin curtains were dancing and weaving fretfully, and as he looked out between them through the driving rain and waving palm fronds, he saw the dead woman's face again, staring at him accusingly.

He jumped up; jolted for a sudden moment back to the South China Sea, where death had stalked him every moment. Forcing himself to go to the window, he saw that it was just a knothole in the

31

magnolia tree outside. Mocking him, balefully. Framed by the curtains and wet with rain, it had come malevolently alive, for that one unsettling moment.

Lowell shook it off and returned to the sofa. He finished his tea, and studied the photograph again. The woman definitely looked familiar. The singer, from Maureen Fitzgerald's tape? He knew who that was, of course. Julie Barnett Hartley. Henry Hartley's young widow and would-be opera ingenue. Still no clue about the man, though. He contemplated making a duplicate negative. Maybe he could enhance some of the darkened areas, and get a better look at his face. Maybe tomorrow. Cursing whoever it was who'd taken this shot that long-ago night without getting a decent focus, he tossed the photo aside and sipped his tea. Maureen Fitzgerald's brief unwelcome arrival into his life, and her mention of the drowning of Henry Hartley, brought memories flooding back to him of the infamous slander suit that had rocked Palm County so many years before: the celebrity, the notoriety, and the fleeting dreariness of it all. It had been another lifetime, another era ago. Until today. Oddly, he had no recollection of Maureen Fitzgerald. He realized now that he had followed the case closely, at the time. And it seemed to him he would have at least remembered her name.

Caitlin. She had mentioned Caitlin! He had been putting off calling Caitlin for more than twenty years. Maybe the time had finally come.

Getting up, he replenished his tea for reinforcement and went over to the telephone stand, where he kept his phone books. The tattered brown book was where he'd left it last night. Still open to the same page. Come on, he prodded himself. Time to show some resolve. After a long hesitation, like a boy on a high rock staring down at the chill waters of a cold, deep lake, he took the plunge and dialed the ancient number, knowing with an instinctive certainty that somehow it would still be good.

After the usual clicks, pauses, and hesitations of an overloaded technology, came the familiar ringing sound at the other end. It rang three times, then someone answered.

"Hello?" The voice was female, and breathless.

"Hello. Caitlin?"

Then it struck him. This was the voice of a girl. Caitlin would be a woman in her forties. Feeling foolish, he hung up, quickly. And yet whoever it was had thrown him for a moment. The voice sounded strangely familiar. He stared at the receiver in wonder.

By early afternoon the rain stopped and it cleared up the way it does in the subtropics, drying out as though the rain had never come at all. It was the quick evaporation caused by the intensity of the sun that made it so humid here. But with humidity came the lushness of greenery that Lowell loved so much.

He decided to work on his boat. It was good therapy. The physical movement of manual labor, the necessary concentration required for precise carpentry and finishing work emptied the mind of all but the intricate details of the job at hand. It was just what he needed.

The restoration of the old schooner he'd salvaged from this very bay was a long-term project. He'd been at it for a long time. It was going to take a lot longer. Plank by plank, rib to stringer, he had to take it apart, replacing each board and fitting, until only the solid oak ribs and keel remained of the original boat. Thank God that keel was still good, because finding, let alone warping and shaping, a twelve-inch-by-twelve-inch-by-fifty-foot piece of solid white oak— the strongest, heaviest, and most resistant fine grained timber in the world—was next to impossible. There just weren't any such trees available anymore. Not of the age, size, girth, and height necessary to produce such a beam. Up until now he had been concentrating on removing, matching, and splicing in the new hull planks one by one. Making each by hand, with nothing but an adze, a hammer, an awl, assorted wood files, several saws, and the hand brace and bit he'd been using only yesterday. Which seemed now like ages ago.

The hull planking was about half-replaced now. Next would be the decking and cabin. Then would come the hardest part of all— the finishing work—countless cleats and fittings, cubbies and cabinets, brightwork and brasswork. Then, like a house, such fundamentals as wiring and plumbing would have to be done. Finally there would be the spars (endless finishing and refinishing), rigging, cutting and stitching the sails, and installing the rebuilt engine. It was a massive project. A lifetime project. But doggedly he pressed on. Often merely because, as he would tell himself, he enjoyed the simplicity of working with his hands.

A portable turntable and hundred-watt amplifier to drive the massive Altecs were plugged into the long, oft-spliced yellow extension cord stretching from the kitchen. Lowell put on another ancient recording of the blues—this time what purists would consider the real McCoy: Howlin' Wolf's *The Real Folk Blues* from 1957, on the Chess label. The Wolf, another voice from the dead, began growlin' and howlin' as only he knew how: "I Ain't Superstitious."

Today, for a change of pace, Lowell decided to shape a toe rail for the bow deck out of solid teak, using a semiround file. The rough shaping was done with the rasp, then the coarse file, then the fine file, followed by fifty-grain sandpaper, then one-hundred grain, then two-hundred. Then would come the first of six coats of spar varnish, followed by fine sanding, then another coat. Then the same again. It was endless. And yet rewarding because the kind of craftsmanship that went into this work was an almost lost art that once gone, would never be seen again. He didn't even care if the boat never tasted the salty brine or felt the wind in its sails. He knew it would be a work of art—a homage to Nat Herrshoff himself, the original builder. And so he was determined to finish it one day. But there was no hurry.

As the music blared and the file rasped, Lowell didn't notice the gray government-style Ford sedan roll down the drive, new radial tires crunching on the oyster shells, until it had almost reached him. Two men got out, dressed in gray summer suits. They could have been Wall Street or Washington. Or hoods. They didn't look like cops, whose blue-collar sensibilities usually scorned suits. Whoever they were, they weren't here to admire the scenery.

Lowell stood up from his hewn-plank workbench and waited as they approached. One was large, coal black, and looked as though he'd be equally comfortable in a football lineman's jersey. The other

34

was white, small, and looked to be the meaner of the two. Both had close-cropped government haircuts.

"Sorry to bother you," said the small man. "Your name Anthony Lowell?"

"According to my mother."

The large man grinned. He had a sense of humor. Too bad his friend didn't.

The small man didn't even blink. "We have a few questions for you, if you don't mind."

"Depends who you are, and what the questions are," replied Lowell evenly.

The big man smiled again. His partner produced a heavy black wallet, flipped it open to reveal a gold-tone metal badge with a silver border.

Lowell looked. "I can't read that from here. For all I know it says Mickey Mouse Club. You mind if I take a closer look?"

The two men exchanged the briefest of glances.

"Help yourself." The small man tightened his lips in obvious annoyance and slipped the badge out of its plastic holder. He handed it over. "I'm Bud Werner, this is Cecil Lefcourt, and as you can see in nice big letters there, we're Special Agents, Federal Bureau of Investigation."

Lowell gave it back. "You got any other I.D.?"

The small man who called himself Werner hesitated. With a slight shrug he fished out a driver's license, Master Card, and a voter registration card from Reston, Virginia. The photo was a good likeness, and Lowell knew if they wanted to con him with fake I.D. he might not catch them anyway. He returned the cards cheerfully.

"That's OK, don't bother," Lowell said to the other man, Lefcourt, who was just getting into the swing of things and had his own stack of I.D. ready. Lefcourt put them away without comment and glanced around the area. As though nervous about something. Lowell wondered what.

Werner gazed at the schooner. Lowell decided to move things along. "OK," he said. "So what do you want?"

35

Werner tore his eyes from the schooner and fixed them on Lowell. Down to business. "You were a witness to a murder this morning, of one Maureen Fitzgerald." It was a statement, not an inquiry.

"Yeah. It's been a fun day. But last I heard, murder wasn't a federal offense. So what's it got to do with the F.B.I.?"

"Just routine, sir," answered the agent smoothly. "A key member of the U.S. Senate will be vacationing in the area next weekend. And we get nervous when there's a killer on the loose."

"Yeah, so do I. But I thought that was the responsibility of the Secret Service."

"This is an interagency matter, sir." The agent changed his inflection, ever so slightly. "You have any theories about the shooting this morning?"

"Can't say I do. Have you?"

"I couldn't say." Werner looked as though he didn't care for the question.

Lefcourt glanced back at the house again. He looked at his partner, who was once more admiring Lowell's boat.

"That isn't a Herrshoff, is it?" asked Werner.

Lowell was impressed. "It was. The keel and ribs are all that's left of the original, that's any good. You know your boats."

"A little. I used to sail the Chesapeake in my spare time. Back when I had some. Had a replica Skipjack, built by a guy over in Oxford who knew what he was doing. Nice lines, though. Sleep six?"

"In theory," said Lowell. "Someday I might even put it in the water."

Werner revealed a slight smile. "Mind if I take a look?"

Lowell smiled back. "Depends. You have a warrant?"

The smile vanished. "Take it easy, Mr. Lowell, I just like boats, is all."

"Well, then maybe another time," said Lowell, smoothly. "But since we just met, I'd rather wait till we know each other better." He wasn't usually so inhospitable. But in keeping with his sixties traditions, he had never been that fond of cops. Especially Federal ones. And there was something about these two that gave him the

36

creeps. He knew damned well they had a hidden agenda. They were after something. He wished he knew what.

The small man merely shrugged, contemplating the boat. Almost wistfully. He turned away to the bay beyond. "I see a storm warning, Lowell. Better batten down."

Lowell grinned at the metaphor. It was one he could relate to. "Yeah? One flag or two?"

"One. Right now it's just a small-craft warning. But you stay in these waters there's gonna be rough sailing ahead. I'd find a safe harbor and drop anchor fast if I were you."

"I'll keep that in mind."

"You do that." Werner nodded to his partner, and they turned to go. The agent stopped and turned back, once more. "By the way," he said. "Do you own a weapon?"

The question caught Lowell off guard and stood the hair on the back of his neck on end. Upon his return from his tour of duty in Southeast Asia he had vowed never to handle a lethal weapon again, no matter what. He had remained true to this vow despite the hazards of his profession. Recovering quickly, he reached for his Nikon, sitting on a tree stump nearby. He picked it up.

"Yeah," he replied. "Right here."

He aimed the camera at them and cocked the shutter. Before he could snap off a frame, Lefcourt moved with a linebacker's speed and wrested the Nikon away.

"No pictures!" he ordered. Deftly removing the film, the linebacker returned the camera. The two men turned back to their car.

"See?" shouted Lowell, waving the camera as they got in. "Powerful, isn't it!"

"That won't stop a bullet," Werner answered as he got behind the wheel. "You're a sitting duck out here, I hope you know that."

"I appreciate the warning."

Lefcourt got in the car and Lowell watched them go, wondering why everyone was suddenly so concerned for his welfare.

As the two Federal agents backed out of the driveway and drove away, silence settled over the bayou. The evening mist was closing in, creeping through the scrub pine and mangrove woods, and the sudden chill was tangible. The isolation that had been Lowell's longtime friend and ally suddenly seemed threatening.

The late-autumn darkness came on fast, and a rare night heron let forth its strangled, hoarse cry, from deep in the mangroves. Another cry echoed back across the water—an anhinga, from the sound of it—lonesome for its companions still out on the bay. With a shiver, Lowell quickly put his tools away and went inside the house. The interview had left him with a very uneasy feeling. The Feds, or whoever they were, had hardly asked any questions.

5

Nighttime settled in along the bayshore. The last streaks of orange and purple glowed dimmer on the underside of the distant clouds, hovering ever present out over the Gulf.

As soon as his visitors had left, Lowell made a decision: He had to get out. Moving to the stairs, he took them two at a time. In his room he dug his ancient leather shoulder bag out of the closet and began jamming things into its spacious interior. Underwear, all he could find of clean clothes, toilet kit, money—he always kept a stash in the unused inner pocket of his camera bag. He quickly counted. Two hundred twenty-five dollars. It would have to do. He tucked it back into the bag, and added six rolls of film.

Downstairs, he went quickly to the kitchen. Grabbing a box of Wheat Thins and what was left of his rock-hard cheddar cheese, he threw those into the bag as well, along with a jug of apple juice. He considered making a thermos of coffee. He was going to need it. But there was no time, he'd have to find some on the way. He got his rechargeable flashlight and Swiss army knife.

Then he remembered the photo. The one Maureen Fitzgerald had given her life to bring to him. Rushing back to the living area, he grabbed the envelope and jammed it into his bag.

Moving swiftly but cautiously, he moved out to the shed, shining the flashlight into every corner. It was empty. He checked the car as well, front seat and back, taking no chances. No doubt about it—those Feds had given him the willies. He threw the bag into the back, jumped in, and started the engine. The old V-8 grumbled crossly about the night humidity, bad gas, and being awakened so abruptly. Then finally, it slowly rumbled to life. Lowell didn't bother waiting to warm it up. He blew some oil out the tailpipe with a couple of angry revs, and backed out, tires spinning on the broken shells. Hurling the car into low, he sped up the drive, and turned east on Mangrove Road.

He checked his mirror. No one was following him. So far so good. He kept his foot on the gas.

A mile ahead was the turnoff to Baker Road, which was a shortcut to the Smithfield on-ramp and Interstate 75. Lowell pushed the big "8" to eighty-five. A car pulled into the highway behind him. He accelerated, and the car behind him did the same. He slowed down to thirty. Anybody in enough of a hurry to race him would certainly speed up and pass him given the opportunity. The car did so, a couple of sullen teenagers out looking for trouble.

The green sign marking Baker Road was just visible, a quarter mile ahead. Lowell turned onto it. He could just make out the Interstate overpass now. North was the way to Tampa, connecting with Interstate 4 to Orlando, and the east coast of Florida. South meant Sarasota, Fort Myers, the Tamiami Trail across the Everglades to Miami, and the Keys. Lowell made a left, crossed the highway, and onto the northbound on-ramp.

Heading toward Tampa, Tony Lowell checked his rear-view mirror again. Still no pursuit. He spotted two troopers parked in the meridian a half mile ahead, strobes flashing like beacons. Dropping behind a pack of trucks, he killed his lights and yanked his wheel sharply to the left. Skidding into the meridian, he spun across the grass, and pulled in front of a southbound pack of trucks before the cops ahead were even aware he'd come and gone.

He stepped on the gas and sped south. He'd have to take an alternate route. At least there were no more signs of police or possible pursuers. Only ten angry truckers on his trail, reminding him to put on his lights, for Chrissake, before his ass became road roast.

As Lowell drove, the white lines flicking past hypnotically, he couldn't shake the vision of that poor dead woman, which continued to hover in the forefront of his consciousness. . . .

6

Palm Coast Harbor, nestled on the ubiquitous barrier islands of South Florida's Atlantic coast, was a semisecret enclave like so many that tend to emerge on the sands and shores of the world's preeminent geographical destinations, where only the truly rich can afford to congregate. Few others even knew about this particular moneyed Mecca, or were given access—aside from the "necessaries" (domestic help, service people, etc.) and a select number of tourists, who were permitted entry only by the ferry to Harbor Village proper. "The Harbor," as it was known, was preferred by those who chose to eschew the limelight of previous fame, or who simply detested cohabitation or contact with the great unwashed and wished to enjoy the fruits of their good fortune in relative seclusion.

Palm Beach, just to the south, was far too visible, crowded, and popular for such people. And its elegance and glamour were badly tainted, in the eyes of society's true blue. Especially by the overwhelming influx, in recent decades, of the newly rich and notoriously famous, not to mention more than a little drug and syndicate money.

People with what was left of "old money" had abandoned Newport eons ago in a Diaspora that had scattered them—and their once tight-knit sodality of culture and comfort—like gold dust before the winds of the Sierra Madre. Of course most of the old families still maintained their New York co-ops and cottages in Newport or the Hamptons, "farms" in Millbrook, ranches in Texas or Louisiana, bungalows at Pebble Beach or Montecito, and retreats in Jamaica, St. Moritz, and the Riviera. But no longer could one place be called home to the descendants of the "Four Hundred." Unless that one place might be Palm Coast Harbor.

Tony Lowell had driven through the night, stopping to sleep briefly at a rest area east of Orlando. The crisp morning air found him looking and feeling like hell as he approached the island. As his rusted-out, smoking old Impala creaked and rattled its way over the causeway that linked The Harbor to the mainland and all its déclassé iniquities, he was delayed, temporarily. The drawbridge was up, to permit passage of a stunning white three-masted frigate flying the Norwegian flag. The splendid tall sailing ship was cruising north on the Intracoastal Waterway, all classic lines but spanking new and high-tech from crow's nest to keelson. Following in its wake was a flotilla of scavengers—sea birds and small sightseeing boats alike. Probably a Naval exercise of some kind, figured Lowell, watching in admiration.

The drawbridge finally lowered itself, and he continued on his way, his approach now duly noted. From his appearance, he would not be very welcome when he arrived at the guarded gate that protected Palm Coast Harbor from the less-deserving rest of the world.

Sure enough, as the smoking Chevy pulled up to the guardhouse, he was regarded with predictable disdain. Throughout history, no one could show disdain better than the flunkies of the rich and powerful, and gate guard Harry Martin was no exception. Harry made two-fifty a week—less than the average resident of Palm Coast Harbor spent for dinner. But it served to pay the rent on his modest little trailer across the bay behind Albertson's, and for the necessities of life. Including the three beers he carefully allotted himself at Pete's Tavern on days off, and occasional evenings. Such as for "Monday Night Football." As it often was with such people, Harry considered himself to be every bit as elite as his employers, which opinion was daily reinforced by the camaraderie with which the residents expressed their greetings. It was always " 'Morning,

Harry," and "How're ya doin', Harry?," and "Nice day today, eh, Harry?" And he would always tip his hat, smile professionally, and reply "Yes sir, Dr. Peterfreund," or "You betcha, Mrs. McGregor."

Harry Martin had been on the job for seventeen years at the only land entrance to The Harbor and was rightfully considered to be a local institution. His job was to keep strangers and tourists at bay, without prior appointment or something equivalent to a letter from the governor.

In keeping with his professional duties, Harry would make quick work of this obviously lost deadbeat in the smoking clunker heading his way. For one thing, no cars were allowed on the island, except for residents and people with legitimate business. For which unquestionably this pile of junk and its unkempt operator didn't qualify. But, as he was trained to do, he would get rid of the guy politely. Any trouble, all he had to do was press the red button on the gate console, and an alarm would sound at the police station. He kept his finger ready. Just in case.

"May I help you, sir?" Harry always tempered his courtesy with just the right amount of scorn to remind unwelcome arrivals that they'd made a wrong turn somewhere. By the looks of this guy, he'd probably made a lot of wrong turns.

"No thanks," replied Lowell, evenly. "Personal business."

The guard's eyebrows inched upward a few centimeters. "What kind of business?" he inquired, still polite.

"My own," said Lowell. "I'm here to see Ernie Larson at the boatyard."

"I see." Harry Martin frowned, darkly, not liking this development one bit. Ernie Larson was the Harbor's resident black. This could only mean trouble. With a reluctant sigh, he checked the directory for Larson's number, picked up the phone, and dialed. It rang.

"Hello, Mr. Larson? This is Harry Martin at the Main Gate. There's a guy here wants to see you." He turned back to Lowell. "What's your name, bud?"

"Lowell. Anthony Lowell."

43

Harry Martin nodded vaguely and turned back to the phone. "Name's Anthony somethin'."

There was an irritated grumble over the line. Harry scowled, and gave Lowell a dubious look. "What's it about, bud?"

"Tell him I want to buy an anchor hoist for a forty-foot Herrshoff topsail schooner. And tell him I want the one off the *Laurie D*, if it's still in dry dock."

Harry sullenly relayed an abbreviated version of the message. Another, more puzzled grumble came over the line.

"OK, if you say so. He gives you any trouble don't blame me, though." He raised the gate, and grudgingly let Lowell into the presence, as it were, of royalty.

"You know the way?" he growled, as Lowell pulled forward.

"Yep."

Lowell drove along Ocean Avenue past the seaside palaces of America's financial kings—huge rambling structures in guarded compounds surrounded by stucco walls or iron fences, of every possible architectural style, but leaning for the most part towards Moorish or Spanish. Not surprisingly, there'd been a few new additions since Lowell had left a quarter of a century ago. Most of them were the usual hideously massive declarations of ostentation. But more surprising was how little had changed. The grand old "cottages" still prevailed along the shoreline, much the same as they'd been since the turn of the century. Condominium fever had not struck here, at Palm Coast Harbor.

Lowell slowed down at the largest house of all, set back nearly a quarter mile from the road. A vast Georgian mansion behind rusted gates, the house seemed sadly decrepit, grounds and gardens overgrown and untended. He gazed through the gate a long moment before speeding on.

A few blocks further, the island narrowed where a storm-cut harbor (the town's namesake) extended like a thumb from the sheltered bay. One day, a full-fledged Atlantic hurricane would blow through, cut a new channel from the beach to the bay, and Palm Coast Harbor would be no more. Meanwhile, with typical Floridian scorn for the vagaries of mother nature and her environment, here was where the village center had been built. And this was where Lowell received his first shock of change. What once had been a simple collection of rustic shops, there for the use of fishermen and the supply of provisions to the "cottagers," had gone upscale. It now consisted of a cluster of "quaint" adobe stores and businesses (many of them small branches of the posher chains such as Bergdorf's) built above a small, brand-new terrazzo "strand" that ran along the water's edge to a series of modern marinas at either end. Lowell would not have recognized it as being any different from a hundred similar high-end tourist colonies, up and down the coasts of North America.

Turning right on Pelican Street—which ran behind the new shopping center and which he dimly recognized—Lowell rumbled down a small hill onto the sandy road that led to the entrance of Larson's Boatyard.

This, at least, had not changed. He felt a twinge of nostalgia as he watched the old man shuffle from the tin shed that served as an office over toward the dock. A sports fisherman and a couple of bellicose buddies were just gearing up for a probably futile day chasing marlin. They were already running about two hours late, which wasn't helping.

Ernie Larson knew better than to try to placate them. He was therefore glad for the distraction when the old Chevy pulled into the parking lot, and a strangely familiar voice called out his name. "Hey, Larson!"

Ernie squinted toward the shed. His wife, Estelle, had been badgering him since longer than he could remember to get glasses. But he was damned if he was gonna encumber his face with a goddamn contraption hanging from his nose. Besides, he could see just fine. No trouble making out the outline of that tall figure standing there next to an old Buick. He was suddenly bothered, trying to remember what or who that car reminded him of.

Ernie edged his way past two of the charter clients—arguing about who was going to drive—and strode toward the car and the man standing next to it. He squinted again. He still couldn't see too well, the sun was behind whoever it was.

The engine was running on the Chevy, pumping blue smoke into the ocean breeze. Larson frowned.

"Looks like you need rings, Mister."

" 'Mister,' my ass, Larson. You're the one who put that engine in. Used to be in that runabout over there."

Ernie involuntarily glanced where the man was pointing—at a derelict Chris Craft rotting next to the gas pumps. He gaped and came closer. It couldn't be.

"Do I know you?" Now he wished he could see better.

"A long time ago. But you needed glasses back then too."

Larson let out a gasp of disbelief. "Tony?"

"Who the hell else?" Lowell stepped forward with a grin.

Larson stared. "I'll be damned. Tony Lowell. It is you!"

The Tony Lowell had been a near-legend in these parts and a personal protégé of sorts. And his abrupt departure from The Harbor so long ago had left a gap in Ernie Larson's life that, like a storm-cut inlet, had taken a long time to close and heal. But that was ages ago.

Lowell clasped the old man around the shoulders. "Jesus, I told the man my name! What does a guy have to do around here to get a hello?"

"Hot damn! Tony Lowell. He said 'Tony Somethin', but how would I know it was you, y'know? After all that time, what's it been, twenty years? Thirty? A lotta people come through this boatyard since then, boy. And I gotta tell you, you're the last person I ever expected to see around this place again."

"Things change, as the saying goes."

"Hot damn! How you been, boy?"

"Not good, Ernie. A lotta miles."

"Yeah." Larson stepped back to look Lowell over, and shook his head disapprovingly. "Jesus, you look like hell. Where you been, anyway?"

"Over on the west coast."

"California?"

"Not that far, actually."

"No. The Gulf Coast. Up north of Manatee City."

Larson shook his head in wonder. "Manatee City? That's not so far. You coulda come around once in a while. Hell of a change from The Harbor, though. What brings you back here after all this time?"

Lowell had come to Ernie Larson because Ernie was one person he could probably trust—even after twenty-five years. But he didn't want to endanger him either. It was a delicate balance that would require some thought.

"I've got a problem, Ernie. I can't tell you too much, right now. But until I figure it out, I have to avoid some people looking for me. Unfriendly people."

The weather-etched lines around Larson's eyes hardened. "You been running with them druggies, boy? 'Cause if you have, I don't care how fond I was of you, you don't just show up here after two decades an' expec' me to cover for you 'cause if that's what you got in mind you can just turn around and get right the hell back off this island, before I—"

"Easy, Ernie. It's nothing like that. It has to do with a couple of visits I got yesterday. I'll tell you about it later."

"All right then. I believe you. I'm glad to see you anyways, you know that."

"I know," said Lowell, gently. "Me too. Thanks, Ernie."

"Forget it. You here to see your old man?"

"No. You know how it was, Ernie, I don't want to go over there unless I have to. He may not even know me now anyway, and it's just as well."

Larson shook his head disapprovingly. "Family is family, boy. Didn't nobody ever explain that to you?"

"Nope. Nobody from my family, anyway."

"That's white folk for you."

They both laughed. Larson looked over his shoulder. The marlin hunters were just heading out to sea, quarreling contentiously. Good riddance for the next six hours, anyway.

"What kind of trouble you in, Tony? You always did have a nose for trouble," Ernie went on. "Worse'n a stray dog in a dump."

Ernie Larson hadn't been that surprised when Tony Lowell finally up and disappeared one day. But he had missed him.

"I need a place to stay, Ernie. Any chance you still got that loft available, above the boathouse?"

Larson glanced over his shoulder, once again. "Still there, don't ask me how come. Twenty-some years more dust, is all. But you're welcome to it. You can park over by the shed. Fetch your gear, and come on into the office outa the heat. Then you can tell me all about it."

Lowell went to move the car and get his bag, wondering at how much his old friend had aged. It was more shocking than he would have anticipated. Twenty-odd years was a long time.

Ernie sat waiting for him in his musty, overcluttered office, with the same metal desk and black dial phone Lowell remembered. With the same papers scattered around, or so it appeared. At least the calendar was up to date, Lowell noted, with a wry smile. A full-color poster of the singer, Sade. Nice. The same ancient window air conditioner rattled away, noisy as ever. To Lowell, it almost felt like home.

"Care for some coffee? I don't drink it no more on account of ulcers, but I got some somewhere." Ernie offered, nodding at an ancient percolator sharing a double-stacked wall socket adapter overloaded with half a dozen other frayed plugs and wires—not unlike Tony's own circuitry, back home.

"Maybe not, thanks. Got anything cold?"

"We'll take a look. Don't take nothin' much but milk, myself." Ernie opened the small motel-sized refrigerator, which emitted a familiar odor of decay. It contained an assortment of half-eaten sandwiches, rotting fruit, sour milk, and forgotten, opened soda cans.

"Don't look too good," admitted Ernie.

"That's all right. You mind if I pick up a few things for you?" Tony offered, with a wince. The sight reminded him a little too much of his own home, bachelorhood, and passing years. "You used to drink grapefruit juice by the gallon, didn't you?"

"Not anymore," sighed Ernie. "Can't handle that no more, either. Don't seem fair, the older you get, the less you get to enjoy for all the years you put in."

"You got that right. Times been hard for you, Ernie?"

Ernie managed to rummage up a can of apple juice and they shared it. "Glad to see you still got some memory left, considerin' all that pot you kids smoked," he teased. " 'Course times are hard. Ask your old man. Nobody buys boats no more, ain't you noticed?"

"Can't say I have." Lowell tasted the juice and made a face. It tasted like zinc. Shoving some papers aside, he sat back on the cracked, black-vinyl chair that also served Ernie as a filing cabinet, when there were no guests around. Which was usually. "I was serious about that anchor, by the way."

Larson sat behind his desk and gave Lowell a dubious look. "I thought you didn't go in for all them trappin's and trimmin's of the big money crowd. And what you doin' with a forty-foot schooner over there on the Gulf, anyway? A boat like that needs deep water and room to run, or what's the point?"

"The Gulf is plenty deep enough. Anyway, it's a restoration project. Which reminds me, did you ever get that old cutter to hold water?"

"Nah. Them planks dried out before you was born. She'll never float again, I'm afraid."

"Never say never, Ernie. A man's gotta believe in order to get up in the morning."

"Not me. I can't hardly get up in the morning no more anyways. How'd you find her?"

Lowell flinched involuntarily. "Find who?"

"The schooner, boy! You feelin' all right?"

"Yeah, sorry, I was driving most of the night. She capsized out off the Manatee River during Hurricane Ella a few years back and broke up. Damn fools were heading for Panama City and thought they could outrun the storm. The owners wrote her off so I got

49

salvage rights and towed her in. She's a beauty, Ernie, what's left of her."

"Wood still good?"

"No, that's the problem. Most of it shrank or got dry rot, same's yours. But I'll bring her back one of these years."

"Yeah? I hope to live that long." Larson gazed thoughtfully out the window. Or at the window, since it hadn't been washed probably since Lowell's last visit. "So, are you gonna tell me what brought you back here, after all this time?"

Lowell took a swallow, deliberating. Ernie Larson was his oldest friend—as honest and reliable as they come. He also knew how to mind his own business.

"Ernie, you remember a woman named Maureen Fitzgerald, back from the old days?"

Larson thought a while. "She was some kind of domestic around here, somethin' like that. Irish woman, wasn't she?"

"I think so. You remember what happened to her?"

Larson thought some more. "Now't you mention it. Seems like she disappeared 'round same time as you. Word was she got sick, or hospitalized, or somethin'. Was that right?"

"I don't know. Could be. I believe she was institutionalized at the time of the Hartley lawsuit. You remember hearing anything at all about that? Any kind of local scuttlebutt?"

"No, except that she got sent away, all kind of hush-hush. After it was over the whole story disappeared from the news faster'n a summer squall, that was kinda strange. You was already gone, wasn't you? It was almost like, all of a sudden you didn't exist no more. Why you ask?"

Lowell frowned. He didn't want to discuss the murder just yet. Not even with Ernie. He still had some very strong misgivings and needed to know more, first. "So you never heard where she went?"

"Sorry." Ernie studied the wall. The case had been sensational, but it was the kind of sensation this town had no use for. It was of little surprise that the whole lousy affair got swept under the rug as soon as possible. "Somebody told me she mighta took some hush money. I don't know what for, though, or who from. Though I could guess."

"Yeah." Lowell pondered a moment, contemplating the next move.

Larson finished his Coke and stood up. "C'mon, I'll open up the loft. Pretty musty up there but it's all yours. Ain't nobody else would want it anyways. Nobody's hardly been up there since you, come to think of it."

"Thanks. You're a real pal, Ernie. I ever tell you that?"

"Since when was a white boy like you ever a pal to an ol' black man like me?"

"Since the day you and I met."

Ernie smiled, in spite of himself. "Go on, get outa here."

Lowell followed his old friend out the door and across the boat-yard lot to the boathouse. As they passed an assortment of wooden boats in dry dock—many not dissimilar to his own—he felt another pang of regret. Almost half a lifetime had passed since he'd walked through this yard. And so little had changed, other than Ernie himself. It was almost like stepping back in time. But this was no time for reminiscence. Not here. Not now.

They climbed up the rickety wooden stairs—hung precariously onto the outside of the building like a fire escape—and Larson unlocked the door to the loft. Swinging it open, he gestured in mock grandeur for Lowell to enter.

It was dim, hot, and more than a little spooky inside. There were two skylights, each too caked with dirt to let in much light, and what little illumination there was mostly came from small shafts of sunlight that managed to slip through the cracks in the roof. The loft was a single large attic space, running the entire length of the building, cluttered with a variety of musty sailmaking apparatus and stacks of nautical gear of all kinds, from oars to lobster traps to hardware. Three floor-length dormer windows faced the harbor on one side, and clustered around the nearest was an eclectic collection of old furniture creating a living space of sorts: a pine dresser, a writing table, a couple of old chests of drawers, and a bed set in the

51

dormer itself. There was even a small, primitive-but-serviceable bathroom built into the dormer at the far end: sink, toilet, and sheet-metal shower stall.

"See?" beamed Larson, waving his hand. "Same's you left it. We quit sailmaking when Louie died, back in '71. Ain't nobody's stayed here since you."

"Sorry to hear about Louie. He was a good guy."

"Aah, he smoked too damn much." Lowell could believe it. The musty smell still pervaded the room, like a bad memory. Ernie blew some dust off the nearest dresser and poked at some old papers and photographs on its top. "You can nail up some sailcloth for a shade, if you want." He looked around. "Hot damn. Looks like there's still some of your old junk up here."

Aside from the layers of dust, the loft was almost the way he'd left it when that draft notice had come. How incredibly long ago that seemed now. And how little of importance he had accomplished since then! The thought was sobering. Like so many of his generation, Tony Lowell had clung to selective memories of that now-ancient decade as though to hang on for dear life to his youth. Never noticing that it had jilted him like a one-night stand, and left him pining ever after.

Lowell had moved out of his father's house when he came home from the University of Florida that first summer out of high school, unwilling to accept the old man's terms and not yet ready to face life on his own. Ernie had been kind enough to give him a place to stay and keep him busy in the boatyard doing odd jobs. From this base he had learned to sail, crewing on many of the boats that took part in the Palm Beach regattas, even as far north as Newport, where he'd spent a memorable summer with—but he didn't want to think about that. Not yet.

And then—up until the draft—the job at the *Sentinel* had come through. The job that had given him the confidence to make a positive decision he had never regretted. Until yesterday.

"Looky here." Ernie was poking through another chest of drawers. "Some of your old pictures when you worked for that sorry excuse for a newspaper." Sure enough, there inside the top drawer was a stack of dusty old clippings and photographs. Job assignments from the *Sentinel*.

The *Sentinel* was little more than a local society clarion. But it had served to get Lowell started as a photographer. Which, in combination with his military experience, had led (eventually) to his current career. If it could be called that. He hadn't told Ernie he was a private detective yet, either. All in due time.

Larson turned to go. "Well, make yourself at home. And welcome back, Tony. You need anything, I'll be in the shed."

Lowell looked up, tearing himself away from his recollections. "Thanks Ernie. Thanks a million."

Larson turned with a sigh, and made his way back down the stairs, choosing not to press Lowell any further about his reasons for coming home. If there was one thing his sixty-odd years of struggling in the slipstream of white society had taught him, it was that when they made a mess in the road, it was best to hold his nose, shut his eyes, and keep his shoes clean. Which is exactly how he'd managed to get along in Palm Coast Harbor for so long.

As soon as his old friend was gone, Lowell began searching through the clippings and photos. Mostly society crap—cotillions and engagement parties, charity balls, local fishing lore, so and so's new yacht, Mrs. such and such's string of thoroughbreds doing just fine in Green Spring Valley or Easton, thank you very much, and so forth. Nothing on the trial. But then, he remembered in disappointment, that had taken place after he'd left for the Navy.

He'd come back here on leave more than once. Maybe, just maybe—he dove into the dresser, and there in the bottom drawer was his old dress uniform. Angrily discarded that stormy summer night when he got his discharge. He'd come home, fought with the old man for the last time, and moved away for good. Good old Ernie, he thought. The old son of a gun had actually folded it up like a flag and stored it away all these years. As if I'd want it again some day . . .

An hour later, Lowell stood in the washroom, glaring in the

mirror. He'd showered, and using a rusty pair of scissors from the sailmaker's gear, had managed to get most of his remaining beard and mustache off. The ponytail lay in a heap on the floor. His razor hadn't been much help. He'd have to pay a visit to a barber for the finishing touches. He piled his usual attire—grubby jeans and shirt—in the corner, and tried to squeeze into the Navy pants and shirt without bursting any buttons. Too many years and too many beers, he thought, grumpily. And all for what? Time to get back into a conditioning regimen, starting today. Make that tomorrow . . .

He slipped out while Ernie was busy hosing down the dock, and decided it would be better to walk to town. Driving around Palm Coast Harbor in a car like his would be asking for trouble. At the very least, it would instantly identify him to any pursuers.

The old barbershop was still in the same place, upstairs from Fleishman's Deli—famed for the somewhat hyperbolic "Fresh Truffles No Matter What!" But Leo, his favorite barber from his childhood, had died years ago. The place had been redecorated about three times since, and the newest guy was New York blunt and uninterested in him. Which was just as well. Lowell didn't want to have to answer a lot of questions.

He got a suitably short haircut and a straight razor shave, ignoring the barber's barbed comments about having to fix up the butcher job Lowell had just inflicted upon himself with the scissors. He hated the new look and all its connotations, but paid the ten dollars (not bothering with a tip), then studied himself once more in the mirror.

"So long, old buddy," he said to the stranger staring back at him. "It's graduation time."

The barber glanced up from where he was busy sweeping and muttering veiled derogations. "You talkin' to me?"

But Tony Lowell was gone.

7

The Harbor Racquet Club was modeled after the famed Newport Casino, but with a more tropical emphasis—more outdoor seating in the restaurant, for one thing. But the attitudes, and the players, were much the same. Guest celebrities shared center court with local hackers, while the socially exalted held sway on the overlooking veranda beneath green-and-white striped awnings. As a teenager he'd imagined them sitting there, sipping Crystal champagne from Baccarat flutes and nibbling beluga and blini from sterling-silver trays. Of course in reality they probably just drank beer and munched on chips like everybody else.

A newly purchased blue Navy duffel bag over his shoulder (containing his camera and other essentials), Lowell approached the green awning proclaiming the Club entrance. This venerable edifice, too, had not changed over the years. Other than a few more coats of paint. It was only a short walk along Ocean Avenue from the new village center, and as he drew nearer, the profile at the entrance looked familiar. An aging doorman stooped over the gleaming carriage of a black Rolls-Royce Phaeton Saloon to open the door for a Mrs. Barrington and her obnoxious daughter, Stephanie. As a local street urchin, Lowell had had run-ins with the Barringtons, not that they would remember him now.

Lowell slowed his step while the Rolls passengers climbed laboriously out. Mother and daughter between them probably outweighed the car, he decided. He pretended to study a selection of tuxedos

55

with neon ties and cummerbunds—the latest rage among the wannabes—in an adjacent shop window until the Barringtons were safely inside.

A reflection in the plate-glass caught his attention, and he ducked his head just as a plain blue Ford sedan cruised by. It had "government" written all over it (virtually nobody else bought or drove such cars that he knew of). Inside rode two men, searching the streets. The two men who had visited Lowell at his home the night before. What were their names—Warner? No, Werner. And the black one had a French name. Creole, maybe. Their gazes fell on his back, hesitated a brief moment, and moved on. A crew-cut sailor in dress uniform was not what they were looking for. Not yet.

As the Ford continued past, Lowell risked a glance up and caught the eye of the doorman, shrugging off some harsh parting words from the Barringtons. They hadn't cared for his smirking demeanor upon their arrival, thank you very much.

Incredibly, it was the same doorman Lowell remembered from his youth. Fred something, now long in the tooth but still recognizable. Amazing, to have kept such a dead-end job for so long. But ambition had never been Freddy's strong suit.

Freddy scrutinized the man walking toward him, trying to place him. Lowell offered no hint, until they were face-to-face.

"How's it goin', Fred? Long time no see."

The doorman stared, suspiciously. His hair was white around the temples now, the few strands that hadn't yet receded over the horizon. But he was much the same old Freddy. He scratched his bald spot, trying to recall.

"Wait a minute. You're one of the Fromberg kids, from—"

"Wrong."

"Wait a minute. You're a little old for seaman first class, buddy. What is this, a gag?"

Lowell glanced around. "Still dealing Panama Red, Fred?"

Freddy's eyes widened. "Hey, you got the wrong man—"

Lowell smiled. "Relax, I'm just pulling your anchor chain, man. It's been a long time, I don't expect you to remember that far back."

Freddy the doorman had been an ally then, having assisted Lowell in sneaking into this same club more than once back in his impetuous youth.

Freddy studied him, more closely this time. He had always prided himself on remembering faces and names. It was part of his job, and a major reason he'd kept it so long. Not to mention the fact that the money—mostly tips—was damn good. A lot better than most people, including the IRS, knew. Not to mention the other services he provided on the side. Then it hit him.

"Tony! Tony something. Wait a minute—"

Lowell grinned and waited. A Mercedes pulled up, and Freddy rushed to open the door. Two young jet setters got out, dressed to kill. Freddy dispensed with them, pocketed a fiver, and rejoined Lowell by the curb.

"Tourists," he snorted, with disdain.

"You mean they let those in now?"

"Yeah. The businesses need the money, and a lot of the locals don't throw it around the way they used to. Like those Barrington bitches, if you'll excuse my Turkish."

"No problem. You figured it out yet? I'm kinda in a rush."

"Wait a minute." Freddy glanced around. "I know who you are. You're the old police chief's kid, I remember you."

"I'm impressed."

"It's my job. How you been?"

"OK. How 'bout you?"

"Can't complain. You used to run around with what's-her-name—she's here, by the way."

Lowell's pulse skipped a beat. "Here? Now?"

The doorman nodded, studying him.

"How's she look?" Lowell managed, after a moment.

"Fantastico, as always. She's on the courts, check her out. But what's with the sailor suit, don't tell me you're still swabbin' decks after all those years?"

"In a way. I'll explain later. Can you get me in?"

57

"Just walk in. They don't check like they used to, the restaurant is open to the public now."

"Oh. Thanks, Fred. I'll catch you later."

"No sweat."

Freddy opened the door. Lowell walked in, feeling very exposed.

The Racquet Club's restaurant was called The Casino, in homage to its famed Yankee predecessor, with the de rigueur black and white checkerboard floor tiles and potted indoor palms. The room was brightly lit by wide skylights above and opened to the courtside patio and veranda beyond, with a wall of French doors that ran the full length of center court.

White Naval uniforms had always been acceptable in upper-class resorts. On the other hand, officer's epaulets and stripes were a lot more socially acceptable than the plain whites of a lowly seaman. Lowell couldn't worry about that now, as the maître 'd bore down on him.

"May I help you, sir?" came the polite inquiry.

"No thanks, I'm looking for someone."

"Very good, sir."

The maître d' wasted no more time on him, which suited Lowell just fine. He made his way through the restaurant to the veranda and stepped outside. Center court was vacant, but the pock of tennis balls striking gut could be heard clearly from the courts beyond.

Lowell walked the length of the veranda and down the steps to the asphalt footpath that ran between the courts and the clubhouse. He could hear voices now. Female. One, a younger voice, he didn't know but it sounded oddly familiar. The other was a voice he'd heard a thousand times before, in a long-past life and countless restless dreams since. Aged, perhaps. But still the same.

Caitlin.

"Out!" cried the younger voice, triumphantly, as Lowell rounded the far side of the chain-link tennis enclosure, hidden from sight by the canvas wind breaks.

"Oh, you. Why did I ever teach you this game!" protested the other, older voice, in mock anguish.

He could see them now on the clay courts, in their traditional short white tennis skirts. They were both blond, and stunning. One was a girl of around twenty who reminded Lowell of many of his female photography students. But the other—my God. She's as beautiful as though it were only yesterday. Long legs still lean, no sign of varicose veins or cellulite, waist still trim, breasts still firm. She's a year younger than I, let's see. She's forty something and looks not a day older than twenty-five! He felt sick at the loss—the sheer waste of those prime intervening years. And what obscure, forgotten principle had it been that had caused him to walk away so long ago?

"That's game," announced the younger of the two women. They headed for the bench, just as he reached the gate. They were busy putting their gear away and didn't look up as he opened it and stepped onto the court. They didn't even glance his way as he opened his duffel and took out the Nikon, focusing it in their direction.

He snapped a frame, almost as though for proof that this moment had actually occurred. But even the click of the shutter was not enough to attract their attention. Beautiful women were always being targeted by shutterbugs. It was just one of those things they learned to put up with.

"Hello, Caitlin."

That caught their attention. They looked up together. The young woman gave him a cursory glance, a quick dismissal, and turned back to the other with a questioning look.

The older woman, Caitlin Schoenkopf, stood rigid, staring at Lowell, eyes wide with wonder. Her towel slipped out of her hand and fell forgotten to the ground. She let out a gasp.

"Tony?"

It was more a statement than a question. The girl gave Caitlin a quizzical look and decided her place was elsewhere. "I'll see you later. Thanks for the game." And she was off, in long strides heading quickly for the locker room on the opposite side of the courts.

Now they were alone. Anthony Theodore Lowell, P.I., and the

59

only woman he had ever loved. It took a supreme effort on his part to flash his patented flippant grin.

"Still got that dynamite backhand, I see."

She stared, still too stunned to speak.

"C'mon, you can't be that surprised."

Her look said otherwise. . . .

Ten minutes later, after a quick shower and change, she joined him at a table on the veranda, away from the noontime crowd. She had regained her characteristic composure and sat down opposite him as though they did this every day. She wore a simple white blouse and shorts now. If anything, she looked even better than before. Her hair was still wet, and hung in loose curls around her face. Caitlin was one of those women who looked great no matter what.

"Well, look at you!" she remarked, in an offhand manner, green eyes flashing. "The same as the last time I saw you. Right down to the uniform!"

"Jesus, I'd forgotten about that." About how she'd faced him, hurt and angry at the restaurant, as he stubbornly refused to explain why he was leaving her, why he had decided to go when surely he could have found a way out of it. Like so many of his friends and peers had done. He'd been wearing this very uniform that day. It had been the last time he ever saw her. Until now.

"You mean you weren't just trying to be ironic?" she demanded. The pain was clear in her eyes. Of course she wouldn't have forgotten. Lowell cursed himself for his stupidity, but there was nothing he could do about it now.

"I know you're not going to believe this. But it was the only thing I could find to wear."

She let out a bitter laugh. "My God. You sound like me!"

"Yeah. Sorry."

"Forget it. So what brings you back to these sunny shores, Anthony? After all these years."

This was proving to be no easier than he'd anticipated. But then,

60

why should it be easy? After all, for the past two decades he hadn't even been able to dial her number, let alone sit down with her.

"I know, I know, time flies," he finally said. "But what's twenty years, when you're having fun." She wasn't amused. He tried changing the subject. "So, how have things been for you? I assume you're married, or have been."

"You can spare me the sarcasm, if you don't mind."

"Sorry. All I meant was—"

"I got engaged a couple of times, not that it's any of your business. It didn't work out."

"Oh." He went silent, trying to regroup his thoughts.

"I hear you've become a private detective," she said, after a moment. "So tell me. What in God's name inspired you to do something like that?"

So, she knows that much, he thought. But then she had sent that woman to him, hadn't she? "Maybe it had something to do with my old man," he replied, guardedly. "Maybe it had to do with wanting to make things right."

"Well, some things you just can't!" she snapped.

He sensed the whole conversation rapidly going down the proverbial tube.

"I heard you had a message for me." No, that didn't come out right either, you're putting it all on her, fool!

Her pale smooth brows drew together. "Is that why you're here? Because you heard I had a message for you?"

"You don't?" He was sinking deeper and deeper, unable to help himself. Was love always like this? He'd forgotten.

"Look, I'd better go, it's been very nice seeing you again, but—" she got to her feet.

"Wait!" he reached out and put his hand on her arm. She drew it away, instinctively. "Caitlin, a woman named Maureen Fitzgerald came to see me. She mentioned your name. You know about that?"

She hesitated. He could tell she knew.

"Sit down. This isn't easy for me either. I've been trying to figure

61

out how to have this conversation for twenty years and it obviously hasn't helped one lousy iota."

She gave him one of her inscrutable looks, and sat down again. She smelled of hyacinth. "All right. I did talk to Maureen. She didn't tell you?"

"She didn't have a chance."

She frowned again. "What do you mean?"

"I don't know how else to put this. She's dead."

She let out a small gasp. "Dead? What happened?"

He decided to get straight to the point. "She was murdered. She wanted to—to hire me—about the Hartley case. And some jewels or something. Then somebody killed her."

"My God. Oh my God."

Lowell didn't know what to do or say, except to press on, like a runaway train. "Caitlin, you obviously know more than you're letting on. What did she want?"

She glared up at him now, tears tinged with fury. Then she looked beyond him, and her anger changed to something else. Worry? Apprehension even? Lowell followed her gaze. A tall, white-haired gentleman in a Navy blazer had just entered the veranda from the clubhouse, chatting with a couple of uniformed Navy brass. Probably visiting dignitaries from the naval base just across the bay at Punta Blanca. As they watched, the man swept his gaze around the room like a radar scope, and it fell on Caitlin. He hurried toward them with a quick smile.

Lowell braced himself. Caitlin's father and he had never gotten along. In fact, that would be putting it very mildly. Admiral Robert Schoenkopf had taken a considerable dislike to Tony Lowell from the moment they met. And it was more than just rank, or social status.

"Ah Caitlin, I was looking for you. Are we sailing this afternoon?" The admiral's voice was deeper and hoarser now than Lowell remembered. Probably from all those cigars. But it still boomed with authority.

"Hello, Father," she breathed, so tense she could barely speak. "Yes, I'll be there."

The admiral nodded, and his glance fell on Lowell. Caitlin held her breath. Lowell looked back, eyes steady. Awaiting the reaction. It didn't take long. The admiral's eyes widened in recognition, then narrowed to slits of anger.

Lowell decided to beat him to the punch. "Hello, Admiral. How's the fleet?"

"Lowell." The admiral's tone said it all. He straightened up and turned to Caitlin, who, to her tremendous credit, kept her composure. "How long has he been here?"

"Father, he doesn't know."

The admiral faced Lowell, with acid civility. "Lowell, I am going to assume you haven't remained in the service all these years at the same lowly rank, which tends to suggest that you are impersonating a member of the U.S. armed forces, which is a federal offense. I would therefore strongly advise you to remove yourself from our presence and these premises, after which I am inclined to call the police. Now that your besotted father has retired on undeserved disability, you have no friends there to bail you out this time. Have I made myself clear?"

Lowell held his ground. "Gee, Admiral, that's pretty harsh for just dating your daughter a few decades back."

"It was more than—"

"Father, don't!" Caitlin cut in, sharply.

Lowell looked from father to daughter, trying to pick up a clue as to what was going on. There was none. They were impervious, a single barrier erected against him. He shrugged. "All right. Sorry to bother you." He started to go, then turned back to Caitlin, intently: "Caitlin, remember when we crewed in the America's Cup trials back in '66? We damn near won that one time! Pretty strange, you and me living it up like that, while some of my buddies were already getting shot down over Canh Ram Bay, trying to protect certain highly placed people's China Sea petroleum interests. Don't you see why I had to go?"

63

"Times up," said the admiral. "Get out."

"Well," sighed Lowell, ignoring him. "That's all just another oil slick lapping on history's forgotten shores now. You were right, kiddo. Some things you just can't change. But we live and we learn, and sometimes we even grow up." He saluted the admiral, in a mock salute, and continued. "Goodbye, nice seeing you." He shook her stiff hand, wishing he could brush the old man aside like a swamp fly and carry her away with him now. Knowing it would be impossible. That reality would stop him in his tracks.

She looked away. He hesitated a moment and walked off, shoulders square. Taking his time.

8

The Palm County Courthouse was in Collinsville, across the bay from Palm Coast Harbor and five miles to the south. The town had been named for the visionary nineteenth-century New Jersey farmer who had purchased huge tracts of land between Jupiter and Key Biscayne to pursue his dream of developing citrus farming as a viable form of agriculture. He'd created numerous new strains and succeeded hugely. He'd then gone on to construct bridges and canals for better access to his vast coastal lands, including the first bridge across Biscayne Bay—paid for out of his own pocket. Then the great developers had come—Henry Flagler and others, bought him out, and built what were now Miami, Ft. Lauderdale, and Palm Beach. John Collins's name had long been forgotten, but for an avenue here, a bridge or canal there, and the county seat of Palm County.

The town of Collinsville was as different from "The Harbor" as reality from dreams. It was a working-class town whose main business was county government, surrounded by blue-collar industries and sugar plantations. The latter, run by insular Florida "cracker" families, enjoyed federal agricultural subsidies in the billions, and their owners were often far richer and more influential than "The Harbor's" monied northern immigrants. The landscape in the town itself consisted primarily of trailer parks, shacks, and slums of the "po' folk": a local euphemism for the blacks and Hispanics who worked the farms, factories, and sculleries of Palm County.

Checking to see that he wasn't followed, Tony Lowell slipped out of Palm Coast Harbor by taking the bus—usually reserved for the day help from the town's mansions and "cottages." After a steamy forty-five-minute ride he was unceremoniously dropped off two blocks from the courthouse on Osceola Street.

Osceola was another forgotten name from Florida history, Lowell recalled with irony. Osceola had been a Seminole chief who had gone to politely ask the commander of the occupying United States Army to please unoccupy his homeland. The army had obliged him by commandeering his mulatto wife as "contraband property." Then they tried to arrest him. He'd escaped, and after she was sold into slavery, had led a daring and successful raid to rescue her. After that, the United States government wasted no time disposing of Osceola and the irksome Seminoles in the same manner as the rest of their Native American brethren.

Lowell entered the courthouse unobserved and made his way to the Records Department. There he got access to the microfilm files without difficulty. That was as far as he got. The trial transcript he was interested in, from 1968, was "Hartley vs. Hartley": a well-known celebrity slander suit that had cost a wealthy dowager, and now more recently an elderly woman, dearly. So where was the transcript?

He rousted the records clerk, a prim female New England transplant who was surreptitiously reading a large paperback book, carefully concealed by a copy of yesterday's *Miami Herald*. She quickly covered the book as he approached and regarded him with pursed lips.

"It must be there, sir."

Lowell restrained his annoyance. "But it isn't."

"That's impossible. Our records go back to the earliest settlers of this county. They have to be there."

"Then maybe you could help me locate them because they aren't where they're supposed to be."

She looked at him like a school teacher at a boy who's been making farting noises. Her lips tightened further.

"Wait here a moment, please."

With a haughty toss of her head, the clerk lifted the countertop, stepped out, and marched off to the microfilm section. Her long, chaste skirt swishing angrily about her heels. It didn't take her long to return, looking somewhat sheepish and more than a little annoyed.

"Some people just can't put things back where they belong," she sniffed.

"So it's not there?"

"That's correct, sir. If you'd care to fill out the form for a file search, I'll put in a request for you."

"How long would that take?"

"About two to three weeks."

"You're joking."

The eyebrows rose, in a long thin line. "Do I look like I'm joking?"

That she didn't. Lowell said as much and left.

He exited through the heavy bronze double doors of the Records Department into the rear of the main Courthouse, and headed down the long marble hallway to the rear exit, closest to the bus stop.

The whole trip had been for nothing. Lowell had wondered about Maureen Fitzgerald's claim to be a witness. No charges had ever been filed, and he'd been fairly certain she'd never been called to testify on behalf of the defendant, whose charge of murder had brought about the suit. But he'd wanted to make certain. Someone had gotten there before him—someone who didn't want those records or that file reopened. Why? The Hartley slander trial had been a famous case in its time. It didn't make sense. Unless . . .

As Lowell rounded a corner to the exit, two men stepped out of a doorway in front of him and blocked his way—the same two alleged Federal agents. They'd done a better job following him than he'd done avoiding them. He hesitated, considering whether to exchange pleasantries or run for it. The big one, Lefcourt, laid that question to rest by quickly stepping behind him and putting a gun to his back.

"You look like you need to take a leak, Lowell," he suggested cheerfully. Lowell didn't need to take a leak.

"You're wasting your time. I am in a peaceful transcendental state, and you do not exist."

Lefcourt jabbed him hard in the back with the barrel of the gun. Lowell winced. Thoughts of mayhem crossed his mind. He banished them at once. "All right, so you exist. What do you want?"

Werner nodded at the men's room door across the hall.

"Like my man said, you need to take a leak."

Lowell yielded. Once inside the men's room, he turned to face Werner. Lefcourt kept to his back, with the gun.

"OK, what's this all about?"

Werner looked thoughtful. "It's like this. There are things that happen that are very unfortunate. Such as your old lady friend. We know you feel bad about that and we feel bad about it, too."

"It's gratifying to know the government feels bad but—"

"Quiet, please," urged Lefcourt, with a gentle reminder to his kidney. "Let the man finish."

"Thank you. If I may continue," continued Werner, "certain issues were laid to rest a long time ago. A lot of people wanted it that way, and still do."

"What people?"

"Shut up, please," reminded Lefcourt. This jab wasn't quite so gentle.

"Names are not important. What's important is that you feel satisfied that the best interests of you, personally, and your country, particularly, would be served by you dropping this misguided mission of yours, getting your car, and going directly home. Where your students need you, and you can finish your boat. It's a beautiful boat, you shouldn't leave it untended, you know?"

"That's real thoughtful of you."

"That's our job. I believe you have a class scheduled for ten A.M. tomorrow. We'd be happy to run you back over to pick up your car, so you can be sure to make it on time."

While Werner talked, in his smooth, lilting voice, Lowell was only half-listening, calculating. Suddenly a few more of the pieces clicked into place.

"Which agency did you say you were from?"

"FBI. Why?"

"Just wondering. Such as why this all is so important to you clowns."

"Look, Mr. Lowell, we're trying real hard to make you see reason. Enough damage has been done already over this thing and—"

He didn't finish because Lowell suddenly spun, knocked Lefcourt's gun away with his elbow, and trip-kicked Werner in the left ankle, toppling him to the floor. He turned and ran for the exit. Unfortunately, they were trained better—and much more recently—than he was in martial arts, had no inhibitions against violence, and were in better shape. He almost reached the door, yanked it open, when Lefcourt was on him. A quick chop to the neck, a kick in the solar plexus, and the fight was over. But not ended. As Lowell doubled over, Werner got up and hit him in the mouth with an uppercut, and then twice more in the eye and nose, drawing a fair amount of blood.

Lowell lay on the floor trying to breathe, blood filling his throat and nasal passages. The pale, green-painted ceiling swirled above him. The stench of urine burned his nostrils. Two faces bent over him, swimming in and out of focus. There was a sharp pain in his ribs. That was Werner, kicking him again.

"Son of a bitch," somebody very far away was saying.

There was a scream, off in another universe, somewhere down the hallway. A secretary, returning from the nearby ladies' room after a late lunch with her boyfriend, had heard the sounds of violence and was hollering, on her way to get help.

Werner quickly checked the door, watched the secretary's back disappear around a corner, and nodded to his associate. "Let's go. I think he got the message."

They left the building quickly.

Outside in the hallway, a security guard and an attorney on his way to a pretrial hearing came running. The secretary was with them, scared half to death. She pointed at the men's room. "In there!"

The guard and the lawyer looked at each other, hesitating. They weren't too sure they wanted to be heroes.

"Hello," called the lawyer. "Anybody there?"

"What's going on?" called the security guard.

Finally the security guard reached for the door handle. At that moment, the door flew open and Lowell stumbled out, his face a bloody mess. The secretary screamed and fainted. The lawyer turned as pale as a snowbird and had to struggle not to throw up. The security guard—a retired cop—was shaken but not seriously. Checking the lavatory, he determined with some relief that the perpetrators, whoever they were, were gone.

The two men assisted Lowell in cleaning up somewhat, but he refused further aid, such as calling the paramedics. The security guard wanted to call the police, who were just across the street. Lowell insisted no, he was fine, he'd just stumbled into somebody's drug deal at the wrong moment is all, and they were long gone, so what was the point?

They didn't like it much and didn't think it was right. On the other hand, like most citizens, they didn't want to get involved.

Within half an hour Lowell was back on the bus, daubing his bloody mouth and nose, avoided by the other passengers like a leper. The lawyer had walked him that far—the least he could do and the most Lowell would permit—and talked the driver into letting him on. It was assumed by the other passengers (and the driver, for that matter) that Lowell was just some old drunken sailor who'd probably fallen in the gutter. They let him alone, and that was fine with him.

It was nearly dark when the bus pulled up at Pelican Street. Lowell got off, unobserved by any of the well-to-do islanders or their Praetorian guards, and started down the sandy road to Ernie's boatyard. A stiff breeze was blowing off the bay, laced with the smell of salt marsh and dead fish. Something moved in the shadows, off to the left. He stopped and crouched, trying to see in the cloud-shrouded moonlight. A twig snapped. A bush crackled. He looked in the direction of the boatyard. It was dark down there, the workers long gone. Ernie was too old to be of much help even if he hadn't left. Lowell was on his own. He searched the ground for a rock or stick. The bush moved again. There—a broken conch shell. It would have to do.

A car approached along the road above. A long beam from a spotlight shone on the trees and along the periphery of Ocean Avenue. The local police patrol. Lowell was torn. He didn't want to advertise his presence. But he might also be in danger. Whoever was after him was in all likelihood fully familiar with this area. This, after all, was where it all began, long ago.

There was also the problem of the two Feds. He wondered if any of his father's men were still on the local force—if any would even remember him. He decided they wouldn't, which was just as well. Buddy Lowell had not been a well-liked man in these parts. Especially by his own family. The fact that he lived alone now, with a bottle for a nurse, was a fate of his own making.

Lowell ducked down behind a hummock as the spotlight swept overhead. The bushes across the road became still. Whoever or whatever had been there was gone. The patrol car moved on down the avenue. Gathering his strength, Lowell ran for it. Stumbling blindly in the dark, he somehow made it to the yard, with its protective circle of security floodlights. There, he collapsed at the foot of the steps to the loft. Which is where Ernie Larson found him, on his way to a late supper. . . .

9

Lowell came to in the morning, flat on his back in the loft. Ernie Larson had managed to get him up the stairs somehow and put him to bed. Now Ernie hovered over him, urging him to sip tea that smelled like boiled dirt.

" 'Bout time," grumbled Larson, as Lowell opened his eyes and tried to sit up. He couldn't lift his head very far, due to the fact that it felt like a large hippopotamus was sitting on it. Ernie cooed and fussed, and brought a chipped Garfield coffee mug to his lips.

"C'mon, drink up. My momma used to make this stuff when I got beat up by the local white trash. Tastes like shit but it works real good."

Lowell forced a grin. "No problem. I read somewhere Albert Schweitzer's patients always complained that if it wasn't bitter it couldn't be medicine."

He took a gulp. It tasted worse than boiled dirt. But it seemed to help. He tried once again to sit up.

"Take it easy. Maybe I should call Doc Felker to have a look at that," said Ernie.

"No doctors. And no cops."

The old man shook his head. "Still got a nose for trouble, don't you, boy? What happened, anyway?"

"Can't tell you. Not yet."

Larson suppressed his annoyance, picked up a wet washcloth from the night stand and wiped Lowell's brow.

72

"You know that old story—this boy come home after a fistfight at school, and he's a bloody mess? So his daddy says, 'Son, you look like hell.' And the kid says, 'Yeah, Dad, but you shoulda seen the other guy!'"

Lowell flinched as the cloth brushed his swollen lip. "So?"

"So, you looks like the other guy."

Lowell struggled to his feet.

"Thanks, Ernie. I really appreciate your humor, but I've gotta get outa here."

"Where? Where you gonna go like that? They'll spot you in a minute. You look like a goddamn hankie after a nosebleed!"

Lowell laughed even though it hurt. He walked with wobbly knees to the bathroom. He looked in the mirror and winced.

"You're right. I look like shit. Just help me get into the shower, so I can clean up."

Clucking like a mother hen, Ernie grudgingly complied. He got the water running, and helped Lowell peel the ruined sailor suit off.

The hot water stung the cuts, but the shower helped a lot. Lowell managed a shave without inflicting any serious further damage, and almost felt human again when he got out. Ernie had gone downstairs to open up the yard for the day. But he'd left the tea on a hot plate he'd dug up somewhere. Along with a Styrofoam platter of grits and a huge ham steak from Eddie's Deli up the road, which Tony gratefully wolfed down. There was also a clean pair of jeans—somewhat torn—and a workshirt. Lowell recognized them at once. They'd once belonged to him.

After putting on clean bandages, his face looked almost presentable. He dressed, thankful for Ernie's thoughtfulness, and checked the mirror. He had to laugh. "Whaddya know," he grinned to himself. "You wait long enough, you're right back in fashion!" He looked like a yuppie pretending to be hip—the current rage. People nowadays spent big bucks for pretorn jeans just like these.

Feeling smug at his unintended savvy, Lowell ventured out into town, silencing a nagging inner voice that demanded to know what the hell he was doing here when there was no longer a client, no fee in sight, and where he so apparently wasn't wanted.

The *Harbor Sentinel* had moved since Lowell worked there in his late teens. It used to be in a wooden frame house on Peach Lane next to the post office. Now it occupied a small stucco block on Jupiter Street, just back of the village center. Jupiter Street was the closest thing to an industrial area the town had. In addition to the *Sentinel,* there was a sailmaker, a surfboard shop, a marine supplies store, the local cable franchise, a candle factory, a coffee mill, a computer mart, and an actual chocolate factory that specialized in chocolate monstrosities for the rich and addicted. Most of these had existed for a long time, in one guise or another, and Lowell had no trouble finding his way.

Blending right in with the island's daily quota of tourists, he worked his way through town, watchful for blue Ford Fairlanes and other signs of surveillance. The local police also seemed to be out in unusual numbers. Worse came to worst, he figured he'd be able to deal with them if necessary. His father's name probably still had enough clout to do that. If not, there was always his P.I. license.

Lowell reached the *Sentinel* office without any problem, other than that he ached all over and felt like shit. His old editor, Ted Weissberg, had retired and moved to Maryland back in '75. The current editor, one Shirley Templeton Fessinger, was a social climber from New York who imagined herself to be right at home among the Harbor's hoity-toity. She didn't have time to talk to a stranger in torn jeans—fashionable or not. But the receptionist was sympathetic. She was in her late thirties, with dark hair, was border-line pretty, wore heavy glasses and no makeup. Lowell liked women who looked like that, and had a way of making them comfortable.

"You used to work here?" she asked, curiously.

"Freelance photographer and local stringer. I used to cover all the big stories, like the time the rats came ashore from the Panama freighter and the day Billy Barrington almost got drafted by mistake."

The receptionist wasn't sure whether to believe him or not. Her name was Samantha Scattergood, a native of Ocala in central Florida, and she seemed unaccustomed to the ways of the worldly wise. But she was sweet, and bright, and eager to help.

"We do have some old files but only back fifteen years, and most of those are in storage," she informed him.

"Only fifteen years?"

"Yes, I'm afraid that's as far back as they go."

Lowell was increasingly certain there was something to what Maureen Fitzgerald had alluded to. Something malevolent that the wheels of justice had somehow overlooked. That the old housekeeper had stumbled into, or known all along. Something that was revealed in that photograph she'd given him. Old Ted Weissberg—a veritable pack rat—used to keep everything that ever crossed his desk. So there was an outside chance something from that night, or at least pertaining to the trial, might still exist. But only fifteen years back? If that were so, the newspaper files wouldn't help at all.

"What happened to the old building?" he asked, while Samantha tried to ring through to Ms. Fessinger's office. The whole paper consisted of the production room, the reception room, and the editor's office. The office door was closed. Ms. Fessinger, as Samantha had tried to explain, was busy on the telephone to the Yacht Club, trying to solicit advertising revenue without which a newspaper, as it was well known, could not survive.

"The old building?" Samantha pondered a moment. "Oh, that was a long time ago. It burned down."

"Burned down?" Lowell's pulse quickened. "Burned down when?"

"Right before Mr. Weissberg left."

She saw his frown and continued quickly. "Oh, nobody blamed him, it was an electrical thing. It broke his heart, everybody said. At least that's what I was told. It was before my time."

"Oh." He didn't have to ask, but would anyway. "What about the records?"

"Everything went in the fire. That's why they only go back fifteen years. It was a terrible shame, really."

"Yeah."

"Do you still want to see Mrs. Fessinger?"

"No, it won't be necessary. Thanks anyway. I like your dress, by the way."

She was wearing a simple gingham dress, blue and white checks. As American as Wyeth, and as plain. She blushed and glanced down at herself with intense embarrassment. As Lowell left, bad as the news was he took some small pleasure in knowing that at least he'd made one person's day.

He stepped outside. The sun beat down, clouds white and puffy, the ocean breeze gentle and cool. It was a perfect day. Wednesday? Or was it Thursday? Either way, fat chance he'd have enjoying any of it. Fortunately, the sun provided a good excuse for sunglasses, and he'd added a light blue tennis hat to complete the new disguise. But he had no illusions about fooling anyone for long.

The blue Ford—or another one?—passed by on Ocean Avenue at the end of the block. They were still watching him. They and who else? Time was running short. He was going to have to face Lucretia Hartley soon, and he wasn't ready yet.

Lowell hurried across the street, cut behind the surfboard shop, and through the parking lot in back. There was a small park beyond, between the Avenue and Harbor Street. There were a couple of tennis courts for the kids, a mosaic tile fountain, and gardens for the tourists. None of which had existed twenty years ago. At the far side of the park, on Ocean Avenue, was a small Queen Anne cottage, not unlike Lowell's own house in Gulfbridge. Except this one was meticulously maintained, with an explosion of manicured year-round blooms in the front: marigolds and petunias, rooster tails, and bachelor's buttons. Also shrubs of riotous purple hibiscus, much like Lowell's own. Fresh white paint with peach trim covered the walls and shutters, and peach and white roses adorned the lattices at either end of the veranda. There was a small, hand-carved wooden sign above the entrance, white with discreet peach letters bordered with blue that read: PALM COAST HARBOR HISTORICAL SOCIETY.

With a flash of inspiration, Lowell crossed Center Street, cut through the park, dodged a group of local kids on skateboards, and headed across Ocean Avenue.

A smaller sign by the entrance to the Historical Society proclaimed the hours: "10:00 A.M. to 6:00 P.M." Lowell opened the door, which set off a chain reaction of clamoring little brass bells to announce his arrival. He vaguely remembered this building as being a rundown derelict that had seen better days. Apparently better days had returned, at least for the museum set.

The museum was a carefully studied paradigm of decorative monied traditionalism, full of tributes to bold Spaniards and brave clipper shippers and colorful Seminoles. There were even a few relics of space flight, since Cape Canaveral was just up the coast. The space stuff probably fell out of the sky, mused Lowell, looking around. The rest of it had been donated by the families who inhabited the island—a painless tax-deductible contribution, no doubt, to society—thereby assuaging any guilt as might exist about one's privileged past. And also an excellent way to get rid of Auntie's old bric-a-brac at the same time.

The curator, Elliot Dupree, was a pasty-faced thirtysomething intellectual sort, whose aversion to Florida sunshine was such that he may as well have lived in Minnesota. Despite being a native, his list of tormentors included some, or all, of the local flora and fauna. He was obviously at this particular moment enduring one of the worst cases of hay fever in modern medical memory.

As Lowell entered, he was greeted by a sneeze that almost blew him back out the door. Dupree had been attempting to repair a broken scrimshaw clipper ship with a tube of highly toxic, volatile, and allergenic superglue.

"Aargh! Sorry," sniffed the curator, groping for a tissue. "It's this damn pollen. Be with you in a minute."

"No problem, Elliot," said Lowell. Dupree raised his head, startled, and gave Lowell a puzzled scrutiny. He couldn't place him at all. But it was unusual to be addressed by name. Nowadays, most people didn't even look at you, let alone bother to know who you were.

Lowell knew who Elliot Dupree was, though, as soon as he saw the name plate on the desk by the door. They were cousins. Elliot's mother and aunt were his mother's two half-sisters, from the educated, more successful side of the family. But like so many modern American families, the various relatives scarcely knew one another and made no effort to communicate. Lowell mostly remembered Elliot as the town nerd who he'd been ashamed to acknowledge as a relative.

Lowell and Elliot had another thing in common. After Lowell's mother had died, Mrs. Dupree had frequently cared for them both—Tony as a rebellious teenager, and little Elliot, he recalled, as a runny-nosed pipsqueak who couldn't even ride a bike.

Well, thought Lowell with grim amusement, the poor guy still has a runny nose.

"Do I know you from somewhere?" queried Dupree, blowing his nose as though in response to Lowell's thoughts.

"Long time ago. You probably wouldn't remember. Or want to."

Dupree looked at him a long moment, and shook his head. "Sorry," he finally shrugged. "I can't place you."

"How about in the backyard at 1215 Perch Lane?"

Dupree thought a moment, then his eyes widened. He got up, sneeze attack forgotten, and came closer. He cocked his head, studying Lowell's face and profile. Like a sculptor, thought Lowell, amused. Then the curator's jaw fell open, his eyes widened, and before he could stammer "T-T-T-Tony!" he let loose with the worst sneeze yet. Lowell ducked and handed him a tissue, which he accepted gratefully.

"Still got all those allergies, huh, kid?"

"Those and a few—aaaachooooo!—dozen more." He waved his hand in the general direction of the town. "Actually, I think I'm allergic to money." He noticed Lowell's cuts and bruises. "Jeez, Tony Lowell. What happened to you?" He paused, and added, for emphasis, "And whatever *happened* to you?"

"Long story, Elliot. Way too long. But it's great to see you again."

78

Dupree seemed genuinely surprised. And touched. "Thanks. Most people don't remember me from one week to the next."

Lowell could believe that. Elliot had been the youngest of three brothers, both of whom had harassed him mercilessly as a child, and then gone on, no doubt, to harass him as adults. And, he remembered with a twinge of guilt, he, Tony Lowell, had been almost as bad himself. Jesus, he thought. People don't just grow up to be shits. It takes training and practice. And they start young. He sure as hell did.

"I kinda followed your career from a distance," said Elliot, shyly. "I got copies of all your *Times* and U.P.I. photos here, somewhere." He waved at a disorderly stack of file boxes, visible in the kitchen/ storeroom in the back.

Lowell's pulse quickened. That was better news than he had hoped for. "Hey, that's great." But those weren't the photos he wanted.

"Yeah. I gotta tell you, Tony. You did well getting out. You're probably the only person from here who ever amounted to anything. On their own, I mean. But what happened to you, after Watergate?"

"I quit. Got a new business now. Private investigator."

Dupree's eyes widened once more, in surprise. "No kidding? I didn't think people actually did that stuff. Is that what brings you back here?"

"In a way."

"Makes sense, I guess. Son of a policeman and all that."

Lowell winced, fingering a Norwegian crystal goblet that, as far as he could tell, had nothing whatsoever to do with Florida history. Except that some time in the past, some local plutocrat had probably paid a bundle for it. "Look, Elliot. You wouldn't happen to have any of the—"

"That came from the Quincy estate. Remember them?" interrupted Elliot, more in his element now.

"I'd rather not." Lowell hastily put the goblet down again with a wry smile. The Quincys were nice people, he recalled. But they had all died off of some dreaded rare disease. Terminal wealth, or something.

"Elliot, I'm trying to get my hands on some of the photo archives from the *Sentinel*. Any chance you have any stashed away?"

Dupree frowned. "That was just weddings and social stuff, wasn't it?"

"Yeah, mostly. But they—we—also did some coverage of the Hartley trial. And before that."

Dupree frowned. "I don't know. We got a lot of old files in the garage out back, but—"

Lowell decided candor would be the best approach, with this fragile cousin of his.

"Listen, Elliot, I need a favor."

The curator's face clouded over, warily. "Last time I did you a favor, I loaned you my boat and you sank it."

Oops. Wrong tack. "Oh. Yeah, I'm really sorry about that. But I did get it fixed, didn't I?"

"No, you didn't. You said it was my own fault! You said it was already leaking, and it wasn't!"

"Oh." This wasn't going well. "I'm sorry, Elliot. I really wasn't very nice to you growing up, was I?"

Elliot softened a bit. "Well, you weren't the only one."

How true. "I want to make it up to you. Beginning now. Let me buy you lunch, for starters."

Elliot seemed genuinely pleased. Lowell doubted that many people had ever offered to buy him lunch.

"Well, I guess I got time. Thanks," he said, simply.

"My pleasure. Anyplace around here not too pricey or touristy?"

Elliot thought a moment. "Is seafood OK?"

"Now you're talkin'. Seafood is my middle name. Didn't you know that? Anthony 'Seafood' Lowell. It gets tiring, always being chased by babes with little forks."

Dupree half-smiled and sneezed again. This was going to be a memorable day.

"There's a little place down on the dock where the commercial boats come in that's not too bad."

"Hungry Charley's? That's still there?"

"Yeah." Dupree looked over at him in surprise. "Mostly just us local working stiffs go there. It's pretty good, actually."

"Sounds great. Let's go."

"Just let me lock up." Elliot checked his watch. "It's almost lunch hour anyway. What the heck, it's a slow day."

They walked along Center Street, and out to the mouth of the harbor where the fishing boats brought in the daily catch. Lowell kept an eye out for the two Feds, or any other unduly interested parties. But there were only a few stray tourists and the usual deliveries and so forth for the shops on the quay.

The restaurant was perfect. Aside from the smoke. Elliot was allergic, of course, and Lowell didn't much care for it either. Luckily, they got an outside table right on the dock, ventilated by a marvelous bay breeze. Lowell began to relax a little for the first time in three days. Since that phone call had come two days ago. The thought of it sobered him up again, and Elliot noticed the change.

"You OK, Tony? You still haven't told me what brings you back to the old stomping grounds. Surely not your father?"

Elliot knew full well about the estrangement. It had been his family too, at least on his mother's side. "I felt real bad about him, Tony. And you. I'm glad you turned out OK. Better'n I can say for—most of us. And my mom, well I'm sure you know, she took everything real hard."

"I know. How is she?"

"She died. Back in '77. Breast cancer."

Lowell felt a twinge. Nobody had ever bothered to tell him. Or maybe they'd just been unable. "I'm sorry," he said.

"It's OK. She was in a lot of pain. It was just as well."

The waiter came over, and Lowell ordered a Molson's, a bucket of Ipswich clams—a longtime favorite—and a Gulf grouper sandwich. Elliot ordered orange roughy and a Perrier. Lowell turned to his cousin, deciding the time had come.

"Elliot, I gotta ask you something. Do you remember a woman named Maureen Fitzgerald?"

"Vaguely. I remember the name, anyway."

"She worked over at Breezewood. Does that ring a bell?"

Elliot knitted his brows. "I can't say it does. Why?"

The waiter arrived with the drinks. Lowell gave Elliot a warning look, which just served to confuse him. As the waiter left, Dupree followed him with his gaze, then turned back to Lowell. "Tony, what gives? Are you in trouble?"

He remembers me better than he knows, thought Lowell sardonically.

"I have to level with you, Elliot, you deserve that much. The answer is yes."

Elliot let out a quick breath, which turned into a sneeze. "Jeez!" He felt strangely honored, in a way, at being asked to share confidences with this one-time famous photographer/detective cousin.

"Getting back to the Fitzgerald woman," resumed Lowell, choosing his words carefully. "From what I can gather, and this is where I hope you can help, she got put away around the time of Lucretia Hartley's slander trial. I don't know why, exactly."

Dupree snapped his fingers. "Oh yeah! She kinda freaked out, didn't she? I mean, when Henry—when h-h-he-" Elliot stammered, then sneezed.

"She may have. I think she was there that night. Anyway, she came to see me out of the blue, three days ago. It had something to do with that case."

The waiter interrupted with the food, and Elliot waited solemnly. Lowell tasted the clams before continuing. They were wonderful— an increasingly rare treat. He sipped his Molson's and Elliot stared at his orange roughy impatiently.

"How'd she know where to find you? I wouldn't have known."

"I think she found out from Caitlin Schoenkopf. Remember her?"

Another touchy subject, thought Elliot. "Sure, I see her around town now and then."

82

Lowell fought the impulse to grill Elliot about Caitlin, her life and loves, and decided against it. "Anyway, she found me."

"Where *do* you live these days?"

"The Gulf Coast. Like I said, she showed up and wanted to talk to me."

"What about?"

"She said she saw somebody push Henry Hartley that night."

Elliot blanched. "Jesus. You mean what Lucretia always said—"

"Yeah. I think so."

"But why? I mean, why now?"

"I don't know. She never had a chance to tell me."

"W-what do you mean?"

Lowell ate some sandwich and took a swallow of Molson's before continuing. Elliot hadn't touched his food.

"Something happened that prevented her."

A huge private yacht was cruising into the harbor, The *Dixie Queen*—one of many such craft in these waters. It was a classic example of a corporate tax write-off, by means of which top executives party big at the stockholders' (and ultimately taxpayers') expense. The ship, all gleaming white steel and fiberglass, proudly flew four prominent flags from its double masthead: the blue and white striped flag of the Palm Coast Harbor Yacht Club—a nautical version of a medieval battle pennant, plus the Confederate flag on the port side; and to starboard an American flag, above a white banner with a red and gold corporate logo resembling a spoked wheel with a rocket through the middle.

The logo was the logo of the Southern Oil Company, the company whose jaundiced eye had been fixed on the drilling possibilities of Manatee Bay—literally Lowell's backyard—for the last ten years and more. But it meant a lot more than that, around Palm Coast Harbor. The Southern Oil Company had been founded by Henry Hartley I.

Lowell watched the sailors on deck in their crisp white uniforms. This was another harbinger, a double-barreled doppelganger to remind him yet again of why he was here. Elliot glanced at the yacht and picked up on Lowell's thoughts immediately.

"Tony," he urged, paler now than ever. "I gotta get back. What're you trying to tell me?"

Lowell tore his eyes from the yacht and leveled his gaze on Elliot. His cousin sneezed but held his ground. "Elliot, Maureen Fitzgerald was killed last Thursday."

"K-killed?"

"Murdered. Right in front of my eyes. She wanted to hire me to reopen the Hartley case. I think somebody got to her to shut her up."

"Oh my God."

Elliot shrank away from him visibly. There was a look of horror in his eyes. He pushed back from the table, knocking his chair over. "I gotta go."

"Wait!" Lowell caught his arm. "I'm going to need your help." The waiter hurried over and picked up Elliot's chair. Elliot sat down again, in a daze.

"Everything all right, sir?" asked the waiter.

"Fine," snapped Tony. "Bring another Molson's, OK?"

"Right away. How about you, sir?" Elliot just shook his head, eyes fixed on Lowell. The waiter left, sensing trouble.

Lowell chose his words carefully. "Look, I'm sorry to dump it on you like that. She said she saw Henry get pushed. And she had a photo somebody took of Julie making out with some guy. His face is partially obscured, but I have an idea of who it was. And if it's who I think it is, it raises some serious questions of propriety."

"Wh—who? Of what?"

"I can't tell you yet. I have to be sure first. It isn't a matter so much of who, as of when. Maureen told me she was supposed to testify but wasn't allowed to. So something happened, maybe she cracked up first, I don't know."

Elliot shook his head, incredulously.

"I've got to find out what really happened that night," Lowell went on. "She's still my client, and I owe her that much."

"You going to talk to Lucretia about it?"

"Yes. But not yet."

"Your father certainly had an opinion."

Lowell's thoughts had wandered. "What?"

"About what happened that night."

Tony's mind raced backwards. "He thought something was fishy. I remember."

"Yes, but we all know where that got him. Now, get this. I went to the *Sentinel* to see if they have any old photographs—I was on that story myself, you know—and I ran into a small problem. Seems the place burned down back in, what, seventy-eight. No records."

"I remember that. Wait a minute. You think there's a connection?"

"I don't know. But when I went to the courthouse to look up the trial transcript, it wasn't there."

"That's impossible, they keep everything under lock and key."

"So, you tell me. And then when I was leaving I got jumped by these goons claiming to be Federal agents."

Elliot gaped. Things like this didn't happen in Palm Coast Harbor.

"That where you got all those cuts and bruises?"

"Either that or I fell off a roller coaster and forgot."

Dupree glanced over his shoulder. "I wish you hadn't told me all this, Tony. It sounds way over my head. If I didn't know you—not that I really do anymore—I'd swear you'd gone off the deep end."

"You mean like Henry Hartley did?"

Elliot's jaw dropped. He hadn't meant it that way. "All right, I'll look through the files, but it's going to take some time."

"Let me look with you."

"Sorry, it's not allowed. Files are staff only."

Lowell shrugged. "OK. Well, I appreciate this, Elliot. I really do."

"What can I say, you're still family. Sorta."

Lowell grinned in spite of himself. He waved for the waiter to bring the check.

Elliot looked at him, eyes grave. "Come back around six, and I'll see what I can find."

They got up to go. Lowell turned to his cousin once more. "By the way. You ever hear anything about gems, jewels? Missing or otherwise? Relating to the Hartleys?"

"No. Why?"

"Just something Maureen said. Forget it." Her words had been so jumbled, he realized, she might have meant something entirely different, in any case.

They headed back along the quay.

When they reached the entrance to the museum, Elliot extended his hand and Lowell shook it. They both smiled. Lowell turned to go, then hesitated. "Elliot," he said. "Be careful."

"Sure," came the reply, perhaps a little too breezily. That's when Lowell noticed that Elliot had stopped sneezing. Pondering the meaning of that, he put on his sunglasses, pulled the tennis hat down over his eyes, and hurried away.

10

Lowell wanted desperately to see Caitlin again. But when he called, whoever answered had hung up on him. Instead he spent the rest of the afternoon in the library. He needed a place of refuge to make some plans. It was the perfect sanctuary. In this, the age of illiteracy, hardly anyone went to libraries. And it might provide some of the information he sought.

He buried himself in the reference section, poring over old newspapers and magazines. As he'd suspected, the *Sentinel* didn't go back even ten years on microfilm. It just wasn't important enough, even to local librarian Marlene Sculley, who was a Swarthmore graduate and nobody's rubber stamp.

The *Miami Herald* and *St. Petersburg Times* had both done extensive coverage of the trial, as well as the *New York Times*. There was also a piece in the *Wall Street Journal*. All the stories, however, were on the same theme: basically, Lucretia Hartley's folly. They loved to tear her down, and he could hardly blame them. She'd brought it on herself, of course.

There was no mention of who was on board the boat, no photographs other than stock portraits of Lucretia and several of her son and his new wife, Julie, the rising New York opera star—or so the stories went. It was interesting, the way they portrayed her.

Julie Barnett was the singer on the tape Maureen had insisted on playing for him, back in that tawdry motel room. Lowell hadn't known right away, but it had dawned on him later. Once billed as

87

a rising star, she had dropped from sight in 1965—some said dwarfed by the shadow of Beverly Sills and others at that level. In any case, the famous polo playboy Henry Hartley III had married her, for whatever reason, and defended her. Possibly to the death.

There was someone else who had defended her later. Someone becoming prominent in the news. Judge Michael Butler Folner of Tampa had recently been nominated to the Supreme Court of the United States, championed tirelessly by the canniest dealmaker in Washington: Florida's fourth-term Senator Robert Grimm. Lowell had not been surprised by the nomination, despite the judge's conservative bent. Senator Grimm, as Chairman of the Senate Judicial Committee, was relentless when he wanted something. And there were those who said he held sway over the President for debts that went back many years. If Judge Folner indeed was in fear of exposure of some kind—something from the past that might jeopardize his appointment—then his connection to the death of Henry Hartley was a strong possibility. It would certainly explain the involvement of Federal cowboys. They'd have to check any candidate's background pretty closely, after recent nomination debacles. But what connection?

As for Julie, she had not simply taken the money and run off to Vegas. She had established herself on the Florida political as well as social scene with remarkable success. She had made a considerable impact in recent years as a high-profile fundraiser and activist for unimpeachable causes: care for the homeless, muscular dystrophy, and the March of Dimes.

Nor was there any evidence of wrongdoing on the part of the judge. Back while he was a young lawyer still wet behind the briefcase, he had represented Henry's widow Julie in her slander suit against Mrs. Lucretia Hartley, who had accused Julie of murdering her husband. And that remarkable case had made his career. But what of it? Legally, Julie had been in the right. The drowning had been ruled an accident by a grand jury. No evidence had been brought forth to change that and she won hands down, although the damage award had been excessive.

She'd already gotten control of half the estate from her husband's will. Years earlier Henry Jr. (the late Henry's father) had transferred half of the Hartley estate directly to his son, possibly as an affront to his domineering wife, Lucretia. That half had gone to Henry III's widow automatically. Lucretia's indiscretion gave Julie most of the rest. The younger couple had no children.

Lowell wondered suddenly if Henry Hartley III had chosen his own form of rebellion against his family. Conceivably, Henry had married Julie to spite his mother. Also, the media bias against the wealthy defendant had been considerable. A good lawyer might have manipulated that quite effectively.

But still, as far as hanky-panky went? It didn't make sense. If there had been anything untoward on the part of Judge Folner, anything at all, it would have come out years ago. Politicians and judges were under constant scrutiny. Weren't they? The fact that Judge Folner had married his client—along with her money—two years later, well, that might smell a little (it certainly hadn't pleased the remainder of the Hartley family a whole hell of a lot) but it was certainly legal. And just the sort of cowboy-make-good kind of story the public always loved. If you don't win the lottery, you sure as hell cheer for somebody who does, in hopes you might be next. Ditto making it big, by whatever means. It was an American tradition.

In his darker, more cynical soul, Tony Lowell, private investigator, Vietnam veteran, part-time college instructor, and one-time press photographer, also knew that success by murder was another time-honored American tradition. And to be fair, Americans had hardly invented it. It had worked for kings and shoguns, shahs and czars, tribal chiefs and military generals, since time immemorial.

Murder. Lucretia Hartley had dared to say it and had paid the price. And now Maureen Fitzgerald had done the same. Which gave Lowell an idea. He might yet be able to earn his fee. . . .

Quickly photocopying all the photographs and clippings he could find, he stowed them in his duffel and left the library.

Lowell had been watching for followers every moment. But all the same, he failed to notice that someone else had been in the library with him, the whole time, in a study cubicle just across the stacks.

It was nearly five by the time Lowell got back to the boathouse, stashed his gear, and took a shower. Stepping outside once again, the transition from the dark spaces of the loft into the bright light and heat of a Florida Indian summer afternoon sent a stabbing pain through his head, compounded by his thoughts and a gnawing thirst. He had an hour to kill yet and decided on the pubs. They would be crowded now, which would be to his advantage.

Checking to be sure the coast was clear, he trudged up the hill, ducked across the park, and strolled along Harbor Street. This was now the main drag of the new Palm Coast Harbor, fronting the boardwalk, where most of the tourists hung out. The locals, of course, usually never went out at all, in the common sense. They preferred to stay behind their guarded gates, throwing or attending lavish catered parties such as those who frequented Harbor Street could only dream of.

Two blocks away, on Ocean Avenue opposite the park, Elliot Dupree was out in the storage shed behind the museum in what used to be the garage. The shed was a simple frame structure with double sliding wooden doors, one of which Elliot had left ajar to allow the waning daylight in. His eyes weren't good, and the single overhead hundred-watt bulb was inadequate to the task at hand—going through box after box of old files and clippings.

Dupree felt a certain sense of urgency, enhanced by the retreating light. It was approaching dusk outside when he came across the folder marked "Hartley." He'd almost missed it entirely because it was in a box marked "Miscellaneous." The file had been put together by Ursula, the last of the Hartley relatives to stick around, aside from Lucretia herself and her useless niece, Edna.

It had been Ursula who had taken care of Lucretia's basic needs when the community had turned away. She'd kept the clippings and records more as a memento than for any potential legal purpose. They'd been languishing here for two decades and more: since well before Elliot had taken over management of the museum. That had been at a time when donations were nearly nonexistent and the building and grounds were in ruins.

Dupree opened the folder and pored through it—Hartley family snapshots from happier times, before Henry Junior succumbed to alcohol abuse and the icy condemnation of Lucretia, his wife, who despised all living things. This pattern of self-deprecation and destructiveness had appeared early on in the Hartley's only child. As heir apparent, Henry Hartley III had taken the brunt of his parents' expectations and disappointments, and had been unequal to the task.

Sorting onward, through various Hartley holiday gatherings—Dupree recognized his own mother and himself in one picture. It had even possibly been taken by Cousin Anthony, on one of those occasions when Santa came to Breezewood and all the children from the service-class families on the mainland were invited, as well as poorer relations (such as his own). He noted with a pang of sadness how the family gatherings were smaller and less jolly with each passing year. Even before the drowning.

Then he came across a thick brown envelope, tucked into the file, marked "The Accident." Inside were copies of the Coast Guard, police, and coroner's reports. Henry James Hartley III had died of "acute asphyxia and hypothermia" caused by extreme exposure and immersion. Also (a not publicly revealed sidebar) poor Henry had been somewhat chewed by sharks, prior to recovery of the body. There was nothing beyond the routine in either the police or Coast Guard reports. Mr. Hartley had been drinking on a party cruise on the family yacht, the *Southern Star*. He'd been on the aft deck in poor weather and had fallen overboard. Witnesses included both Mrs. Hartleys—the deceased man's wife and his mother. There was nothing that hadn't already been public knowledge long before the trial, and afterward.

The brown envelope also contained some photographs and negatives. The prints were old and yellowed, cracking around the edges. Some of the photographs appeared to have been taken at the infamous party in question, that night aboard the yacht. Revelers, couples, some familiar faces, most indistinct. The usual society shots, but Tony had indicated that something there might be important. The negatives were in a white business-size envelope, embossed with the logo and old address of the *Harbor Sentinel*. He put them with the accident photos and set them aside. There were other photographs too—8 × 10's with a *Sentinel* stamp in the lower corner. Photographs of the family members around the time of the trial—how gaunt and haggard they looked!

There were also copies of U.P.I. photos from the *Miami Herald*, including several taken of the trial aftermath. One was particularly striking. It showed a young woman in a simple, expensive business suit coming out of a courthouse building surrounded by reporters with microphones and flash cameras. Another showed the same young woman getting into a Lincoln convertible, the door held by a well-dressed young man in a dark suit and overcoat. Another, older man watched from the top of the courthouse steps. He looked familiar, somehow.

He found an article from the *Sentinel* he'd never seen before. About how attorney Mike Folner's law firm (based in Miami) had used a social psychologist to screen jurors for favorable anti–big-money bias; together with a pioneering use of representative mock juries, heretofore used only in law schools. Interesting. It wouldn't be hard to find a jury with a hidden bias against a wealthy dowager with a superior attitude. Which Lucretia had most certainly had. Very interesting.

Dupree almost overlooked the third group of photographs. They were taken the morning after the drowning incident, when the *Southern Star* had made port for the last time as the Hartley family yacht. They showed the various guests hurrying away in their waiting limousines, reporters swarming around, and a rather bedraggled Lucretia fending off questions. The new widow could be seen coming off the boat with the same man who was with her in the courthouse photos two years later. Interesting.

One still from this group particularly arrested his attention. It showed a middle-aged woman being ushered into a car, unnoticed by the crowd of onlookers. She appeared to be under duress. A man almost appeared to be forcing her into the car. He was holding her arm behind her. He looked like the same man as the one with the widow in the previous picture. A second man could just be seen, waiting in the car. The man in the car also looked familiar. The man on top of the courthouse steps! And then the resemblence to somebody utterly unexpected, in this setting and situation, was so startling that Elliot went back to the office for a flashlight and magnifying glass. This warranted a closer look. If only there was a better light in here. He'd have to see about that next week.

It was almost dark outside as Dupree returned to the shed, heart pounding. The bushes rustled in the evening breeze. A twig snapped, not far away. He didn't notice. Inside, he squatted on the floor by the box. Picking up the photo, he studied the man in the car, carefully. True, he looked much younger here, and had a mustache. But there was no mistaking it.

Excited, Dupree gathered up the white envelope and 8 × 10's and started to close up the shed. Then he noticed the poster, rolled up in a cardboard tube in the corner. He remembered it as being one Tony had once admired—a watercolor print of the village as it used to be, used to advertise a folk music festival the town fathers had allowed (much to their chagrin) back in the mid-sixties. He decided Cousin Anthony would be very pleased to have it. As a welcome home gift, of sorts. He placed the photos, articles, and negatives inside the poster before rolling it up again. Lowell was obviously traveling light, and this would make for a single relatively secure package, in the cardboard with the aluminum cap in place.

Satisfied that he had done as he'd promised and excited about his discovery, the feeling of dread that had come over him early in the day was almost gone. Carrying the poster tube and manila file, Dupree headed back to the main building.

Cousin Anthony would be along soon. And maybe this small contribution might cast some light on that terrible tragedy thăt had somehow refused to go away, so that they might all be able to rest easy. He for one was looking forward to it. It was awful, what had happened to poor Maureen, but it might have been anything—a random crime, a maniac, a bungled robbery. Anthony hadn't gone into detail. He might simply have reached a conclusion that was entirely inappropriate. Just as Mrs. Hartley had done. Or had she been right?

With those thoughts churning in his mind, Elliot entered the kitchen door of the museum, leaned the cardboard tube just inside the door, and tossed the file on the counter. After all that, he could use something to drink. He still had some Perrier left in the little refrigerator he used for his lunches. A Perrier would be just the thing, right about now.

The intruder entered the kitchen, silent as a cat, creeping closer as Elliot opened the refrigerator, back to the door. The small black gun barrel shone in silent menace.

Elliot sensed something. Half-turning, his mouth fell open to scream, but it was too late. The barrel flashed. He never even heard the little popping sound.

Two blocks away, in a crowded tavern called The Gold Coast Cafe on Harbor Street—built as part of the tourist boom since his last visit—Tony Lowell felt a chill come over him. As though someone had stepped on his shadow. He still had on his dark glasses and hat, but felt very exposed all of a sudden.

He finished his beer and stared out the window with a strange sense of foreboding. The last glow of sunset colored the sky, painting the mouth of the harbor with brilliant splashes of red, orange, pink, and violet. It reminded him of something, from long ago. Good old Elliot. He really had turned out well, aside from those allergies. I wonder if he ever tried hypnosis? I'll have to suggest it to him. I shouldn't have been so hard on him as a kid. But then, kids can be such cretins. I certainly was. As soon as I get this mess cleared up, I'll do something for him. Find him a nice girl, maybe. I bet he's still a virgin, poor guy. Lowell thought of the girl at the newspaper office and smiled to himself. Now there would be a promising match! He checked his watch. Five-thirty. Half an hour until closing time over at the museum.

A college football game was playing on the TV sets hanging from the ceiling at either end of the bar. Perennial powerhouse and local favorite Miami against some hapless victim or other. The crowd was animated, loving it as their latest local hero—some black-skinned young man from Overton who probably would not be permitted within a mile of this particular location without submitting to a body search—scored a touchdown. He then did a dance in the end zone that would probably get him arrested on the spot in Palm County.

Halftime came, and the station cut to a news break. Lowell's attention wandered back to the Courthouse, and what had occurred yesterday. Then the news seized his attention. A local reporter from Miami—one of those ubiquitous earnest young blondes in current favor—was standing on the steps of the Palm County Courthouse. She spoke, as though directly to him:

"I'm here where it all began for Judge Folner some twenty-five years ago. It was here that he made a name for himself. It was these very steps that served as the launching pad that is expected to carry him to the seat of the highest court in the land, two days from now . . ."

Lowell felt as though he was alone in the room. The football fans had turned their attention elsewhere: to their beers, or their dates, or their ferry schedules, since lodging was at a premium in the Harbor and most of them would have to be leaving before long.

The station cut back to the studio, where the anchorperson (another blonde, this one a little older) picked up the story:

"Meanwhile, in Washington, the Senate Judiciary Committee voted today to approve the President's nomination of Judge Folner to the Supreme Court, despite continuing questions regarding his personal wealth, estimated to be several billion dollars . . ."

"You mean his wife's wealth," muttered a voice, close by. Lowell looked around, startled. It was the bartender, removing his Kirin bottle. "Another?" he asked.

Lowell shook his head, and turned back to the TV.

". . . In hopes of clearing the way for a Senate floor vote as early as this weekend, the judge's principal sponsor, Senator Bob Grimm, is due in Tampa tomorrow for a rally in support of his old friend and colleague . . ."

The bartender switched channels in disgust, winning applause from the patrons. They knew nothing of Judge Folner's long-ago personal history. Or his relationship to this town. And couldn't care less. They wanted football.

As the bands left the field and the teams returned to resume the slaughter, Lowell checked his watch again. Six-oh-five. Time to go see Elliot Dupree and learn what he'd found.

As he left the bar, someone at the far end—obscured by the smoky haze and churning crowd—got off another barstool, brushed the pretzel crumbs and wrinkles from her Van Cleef & Arpels jacket and slacks, dismissed a leering patron on her left, finished her iced coffee, and sauntered out in casual pursuit. Police Detective Lena Bedrosian had arrived in town right behind Anthony Lowell: unauthorized, and on her own. She, too, had been doing some homework. Lots of homework. She had traced the dead woman to this town through an expired I.D. and information provided by the motel manager. She had learned that Lowell came from the same place, and also that he had returned here just ahead of her—a fact that pleased her not at all. There was something about this case that had drawn her to cross the line. Something she sensed but didn't yet understand. Part of it was her antipathy to Lowell and what—to her—he represented. But there was more. A sense of time passing, a ticking clock, and something of unseen proportions at stake. Something that centered here in this toney little town she had detested with all her being, at first sight.

She was as much in the dark as ever, however, as to who had killed Maureen Fitzgerald, or why.

Bedrosian stepped out into the evening chill, pulled her wrap around her shoulders, and peered into the darkness. She knew—or thought she knew—where Lowell was headed. But she didn't want to get too close. She knew him to be smart and streetwise, and not inclined to see being trailed in a favorable light. But he was her guide, just now, and she needed him to lead for the time being, until she got more of a handle on what was happening here. He'd come here for a purpose, she knew. And she felt certain that when she discovered that purpose, she'd be that much closer to solving the Fitzgerald murder. Meanwhile, she'd just have to bide her time.

Lowell hurried across the park to the Historical Society, strangely dark in the twilight. Odd, he thought. Elliot closes at six and promised he'd wait. He crossed the lawn and climbed the steps onto the veranda. The windows stared back at him, black mirrors in the darkness. He went around to the back.

"Yo, Elliot!" he called, feeling increasingly uneasy. He was sure it was his imagination, but he felt eyes on him again.

The garage door was half open, and he remembered Elliot saying that's where most of the materials were stored. So he'd probably been there. Damn. He wished he had a flashlight just now. Can't see a thing. There was a kitchen stoop and porch, similar to his own. No wonder he felt déjà vu as he climbed the steps. The kitchen door stood ajar. No lights inside. This did not bode well. If Elliot had gone for the day, he surely would have locked up. Or at least shut the doors.

"Elliot?" he called, once again.

No answer.

"Anybody here?"

Lowell considered the possibilities. His gut instinct was to get the hell out. But that meant leaving whatever evidence might be here—assuming Elliot had found anything—behind. And he had to get that evidence. He pushed the door open and went inside.

"Hello?" he called, once again, as he groped inside the door for a light switch. He found one and flicked it on. The sudden flood of light revealed rampant destruction. The telephone was torn from its jack and lying on the floor. Next to it lay a very dead Elliot Dupree.

97

Elliot's blank eyes stared wide at the ceiling as he lay, his face fixed forever in a look of surprise. After checking his pulse, Lowell saw the small, seeping hole in his chest and backed away, almost forgetting the evidence he had come to find.

"Sorry, Elliot. I really am," he murmured. It was a small prayer of penance. He almost stumbled over the cardboard tube propped behind the open door. Something made him stop, knowing it for what it was. Sure enough, his cousin, ever orderly, had written his name on the label.

Snatching the tube, he considered dialing 911 and decided against it. He'd have to find a working phone, and it was too late to help Elliot in any case. He left, that feeling of being watched stronger than ever. It was all around him, a malevolent presence.

As he stepped out the door, he heard footsteps coming through the trees toward him. He froze, gauging the rate of approach. He had only moments to retreat or make a stand. Not knowing what—or who—he was up against, discretion won out over valor. He took off, cutting across the park and adjacent gardens, heading in the direction of Pelican Street.

Detective Bedrosian had followed Lowell to the scene. About to reveal her presence and get some answers, she froze where she stood—on the front lawn—as Lowell ran by. Something was very wrong. She had to make a quick decision. Go after him? Or see what had spooked him.

Bedrosian deduced that Lowell would be headed for the boathouse. She could catch up to him there. Meanwhile, she'd better take a look inside. She headed for the back door, through which Lowell had just departed so quickly. As she mounted the steps, she heard a branch snap in the woods behind the garage. She switched on her flashlight and shined it into the trees.

"Who's there?" She called out, feeling suddenly exposed. It was against regulations for detectives to work alone on a murder case, particularly outside Manatee County. While for the most part she was a stickler and went by the book, some regulations she chose to ignore. (Particularly those she considered sexist.) She wondered, just now, at the wisdom of her stubborn, independent streak.

A twig cracked, then silence.

"This is the police! Come on out of there."

Footsteps moved away—not heavy, from the sound of them. She gave chase, but her attire was hopelessly inappropriate for hot pursuit. She quickly became entangled in the mangrove thicket, which extended to the dunes and the ocean beyond, and lost her quarry.

Annoyed, she headed back to the museum. Maybe it was time to make contact with the local authorities, she decided. They were going to be involved soon enough anyway. She didn't look forward to it, with all the questions, innuendo, leering, and patronizing comments that would inevitably result. But it came with the territory. She just wished that, for once, it would get a little easier. . . .

11

Lowell had no time to examine the contents of Elliot's findings. It would have to wait.

Clutching the mailing tube like an Olympic relay-race baton, he raced for the boatyard, and flagged down Ernie Larson's battered Chevy pickup just as it came lurching up the road, heading home for the night. Larson stared at him in surprise. He'd almost hit his friend before he even saw him. "Jesus, boy! You almost gave me a heart attack! What you doin' like that?"

Lowell looked around cautiously. "Ernie, I need a favor. I need you to drop me off at Breezewood, on your way."

"What you wanna go there for? Place got ghosts, what I hear."

"May be. There's a lot of that goin' around." Lowell's jocular tone rang hollow, but he didn't want to go into any more explanation than necessary. Not even with Ernie.

"It's your funeral," sighed Ernie. He threw the old truck in gear and lurched ahead over the sandy berm. He swung left onto Ocean Avenue without bothering to stop. "But they been askin' about you, Tony. The police come by this afternoon, and some other gentlemen who looked like trouble."

Lowell cursed to himself. There was no way he could tell Ernie about Elliot. Not now. "They been through my things yet?"

"Not yet. I told them they wanted to search my premises, they better come back with a warrant." Ernie laughed, gleefully.

"You're a good man, Ernie."

"Don't need no flattery. Maybe a new set o' tires, one of these days. Soon's your ship comes in."

Lowell laughed, in spite of himself. That had been an old joke between them. It fell kind of flat just now. He watched the dark profiles of the tall palms flip past as they headed north. Ernie squinted, trying to see the road.

The avenue was almost empty at night. The ferries were gone and the bridge gate was closed except to resident keyholders. The pickup's headlights pierced the darkness with probing cones of white light. The great beach houses were mostly hidden among the dunes and behind walls to the right. Mangrove swamps and bayous hung dark and threatening to the left.

Ernie slowed to a stop beside the dark, ivy-covered brick wall of the once-regal gatehouse. Lowell got out, still clutching the cardboard tube.

"You sure you wanna go in there?" Ernie called, eyeing the old place apprehensively.

" 'Fraid so. You better go on."

"You sure? I can wait, you need a ride back."

"It's all right. I'll manage."

Ernie frowned. "Well, my house is just over the bridge on the mainland. You still stayin' at the boatyard?"

"I'm not sure. I'll call you, all right?"

"Whatever you say."

"Thanks, Ernie. I owe you one."

"Yeah, yeah. You just take care o' yourself, hear?"

Lowell forced a halfhearted grin. Ernie hesitated a moment longer, and drove off into the night. Lowell stood a moment longer in the dark, then turned to face the great crumbling homestead beyond the wall. Maureen Fitzgerald had worked here once, and directly or indirectly, it had led to her demise.

Breezewood. Once the grandest of the grand. The largest, most magnificent, most costly to build, costly to operate, and costly to maintain single-family residence in all of Florida. The prime residence of the leader of the Newport and Palm Beach exodus, and seat

101

of the once fourth-wealthiest family in America. Built by the founding father of Palm Coast Harbor, and founder of the Southern Oil Company: Henry James Hartley the First.

The towering iron gates were coated with rust. The ivy was overgrown, untended. Years of neglect had taken their toll, even on the entrance to the place.

Once a gatekeeper had lived in the narrow, three-story brick structure that adjoined the gate. It was abandoned now, and Lowell reflected with a note of irony that most of today's yuppies would kill for just such a place to call home. As for the main house, to call such a monstrosity home was a joke. An insane asylum, more likely. Which it may well have become, he realized. Lucretia must be near death by now. So many years alone, uncared for (for all he knew), unloving and unloved.

There was a smaller gate within the main gate, intended for pedestrian access, so that the gatekeeper would not have to swing those massive iron appendages unnecessarily. It creaked in protest as he pushed it open and stepped inside, carefully guarding the cardboard tube. He was a trespasser, and felt like one.

The grass was high, the lawns fields of broken dreams. Spanish moss hung from the canopy of magnolias that lined the drive, reaching almost to the ground. The drive itself, once one of the wonders of the Gold Coast, was of white asphalt. It had been made with pure-white, crushed quartz gravel imported from New Hampshire, and sealed with a special clear oil that Henry Hartley's own chemists had developed. There was a quarter moon rising, and the drive sparkled in its dim light.

The great house's Georgian profile, all brick with four towers at the corners and a pitched white-tile roof—badly stained now with soot and mildew—loomed black against the night sky. The only sign of life was in the southeast tower, which was ablaze with light. A single light burned on the ground floor. Lowell headed for what he thought would be the service entrance, since the front door with its circular drive and portico was dark, choked with weeds.

Did she live alone now, in this vast tomb of memories? He didn't even know. Until now he wouldn't have cared. Lucretia Hartley was, or had been, a lot of things. Most of them unpleasant. But she was his best chance now for finding some answers to what happened long ago to her son, and more recently to his client. Also maybe for getting paid. Of course, judging by what he knew—combined with the looks of this place—that ten thousand was a fleeting dream. But a fee of some kind might still be possible, from Lucretia Hartley. If she had two nickels left, that is. Which she might not.

Tony Lowell had despised the Hartleys and all they stood for most of his life. Now, at the crumbling doorstep of the last of their prideful clan, all he could feel was pity. True, she had been cold and distant, often harsh, even cruel at times, to all around her including her own child. Lucretia Hartley had once had a reputation of never doing anything that didn't reek with self-interest. Rightly or wrongly deserved, this had been public knowledge that Julie's lawyers had exploited with great success. But what of that now? She had paid for her sins. With interest.

Lowell jimmied open the service entrance door and entered the house, ready for anything. He was hardly surprised by what he saw before him. Of course he knew the outcome of the slander suit had left Julie with all the Hartley fortune and Lucretia with nothing but the house and a small trust fund—he didn't know how much. Still, he hadn't expected anything quite like this.

"Hello!" he called, muscles tensing. The sound echoed into the distance and came back with no response. He had entered an empty room, if not an empty house. The kitchen was devoid of all accouterments of occupancy. He checked the cupboards to make sure. There wasn't a dish, a pan, a pot, a glass, a single morsel of food. Nothing. The only objects of any kind in sight were a wall telephone and an empty carton from a Big Mac lying on the counter.

"Mrs. Hartley?" he shouted. Again there was no reply, but that didn't necessarily mean there was no one home. He was virtually certain she still lived here. No one in town had suggested any different, and there was nowhere else for her to go. Other than an institution. Like Maureen.

103

"Anybody home?" Still no answer.

There was still electricity. Turning lights on as he went, Lowell moved through the kitchen and pantry to the breakfast room, and then the great dining room with the marble wall boasting an absurdly excessive row of three fireplaces, to the central parlor with its vast circular staircase that rose three stories. The great house appeared—in a word—vacant. Not a single piece of furniture. Not a single painting on the walls, scarred with large rectangular fade marks.

Lowell remembered reading that the first Henry Hartley had prided himself in having a fine collection of paintings—American art in particular—and had acquired a considerable number of Thomas Bentons. His son had added the works of some of the lesser known "New Frontier" artists of the 1940s, such as Yasuo Kunioshi. All were gone now. Not a single Oriental porcelain or Rodin bronze remained in the countless nooks and crannies; not a single Swedish crystal lamp, or Chippendale chair, or Louis the XVI table, or Sheraton sofa, no Steinway grand piano in the foyer, no tropical plants in the corners or hanging in the high windows to give Maureen's staff fits trying to water them; nothing.

He arrived at the foot of the stairs and started to climb. The entire house smelled of decay. Lowell wondered if it was possible that those who were doomed sensed it long before. Even brought their destruction upon themselves, drew it to themselves, somehow. Reaching the second floor, he moved along the hallway: actually a rectangular balcony running the entire circumference of the huge foyer below. Constructed to rival the Vanderbilts' "Breakers" in Newport, except more in the Colonial rather than Italian style, Breezewood was never meant for the raising and nurturing of a family. It was intended simply to house fashion, display wealth, and proclaim power, much as an Egyptian pyramid or Vatican mausoleum might have done. Small wonder life had been impossible to sustain here and had ultimately failed.

As Lowell made his way along the hallway, past chamber after empty chamber, he noticed a room that stopped him in his tracks.

It had to have belonged to the son—the drowning victim and would-be heir. The only furnished room he had yet seen, it looked as though it had been untouched for decades. It had a young man's single bed, simple cherrywood dresser, personal belongings, clothes in the closet. Lowell would have bet his own fortune, if he'd had one, that this room had been kept exactly as it was when Henry Hartley III left home. When in his mother's eyes he was still the innocent prince. Lucretia Hartley had stripped the house and her soul of all she had. Except for the remains of her son and the life he had lived here.

Everyone in the Harbor knew, of course, that Henry had moved away from home as soon as he'd been able—the moment he'd graduated from boarding school. Lowell seemed to recall something about him going to New York, to a university, to study drama or something artsy and inappropriate for an oil baron's son. That had been interesting and cause for considerable local gossip at the time. He and the other "locals" had often joked about it. Even as a youth Henry had been known to slum in the village, never revealing who he was. But of course everyone knew. He saw himself as a Shakespearean Prince Hal of sorts, and had made friends and relationships with Falstaffs wherever he could find them.

Lowell shrugged off the cloud of musty memories and unanswered questions, and left the room quickly. He decided that it was the only room in this vast mausoleum of money that had ever held evidence of life. No wonder it had been preserved. Even Lucretia must have sensed that, perhaps even fed off it all these years.

Climbing the stairs to the third floor, he turned toward the southeast tower, the one that had been lit. The ceiling mouldings were obscured by curtains of cobwebs. There was a door at the end of the passageway. It was quite narrow up here and dim despite numerous wall lamps, which he lit as he went.

There was a crack of light beneath the door. He had arrived. He knocked.

"Mrs. Hartley, are you there?" he called, once again.

He heard an ancient, crackling gasp within. And a long silence.

105

Finally there was the shuffling sound of footsteps approaching. The door opened, and there she stood. Still able to stand tall and straight, after so much hardship and defeat. She still had her pride, and defiance, he realized. She was still the grand dame, after all. She glared at him with tired, uncomprehending eyes.

"Who are you?" she demanded. He looked past her into the room. Lucretia Hartley had apparently consolidated all that remained of her life and her possessions into this one room. It was literally jammed with furniture of all sorts: dozens of tables and chairs, couches, antiques, love seats, desks, writing tables, and lamps. Not a houseful, certainly. But enough to open a large-scale antique shop on Rodeo Drive or Worth Avenue. Lowell saw why she had chosen this room to make her last stand. It was clearly the best room in the house, probably with a 360-degree overview of what remained of her husband's estate.

"Sorry to disturb you, ma'am. I'm a private investigator. I need to talk to you." Lowell handed her a dog-eared business card, stained with a nameless spill from some forgotten gulped drink, and watched her scrutinize it without comment.

Lucretia Hartley had aged. But she had not changed. In her own mind she was still prime minister and chief custodian of the great name of Hartley and all it entailed. Not even grasping the knowledge that history, and a legal-edged avarice far more modern and sweeping than her own, had rendered her impotent.

"What do you want?" she demanded, still holding on to the card. "You're trespassing." Her voice was as deep and regal as Lowell had imagined. Or perhaps even remembered. She was wearing a long black dress and a veil covered her eyes. One hand clutched a silver cross that hung around her neck on a silver chain. This surprised him. He'd never suspected her of being religious.

"I know. Sorry, ma'am. Just a few questions, if you don't mind. Then I'll go."

She lifted the veil and scrutinized him doubtfully. Her hair was white now, and face deeply lined from care and aging. She looked away, gazing out the east window into the night. The moon—in its

106

third quarter now—peered from behind the ubiquitous cumulus clouds that raced across the Florida night sky.

"What about?"

"It's about what happened to your son."

"I had a son," she finally said, nodding to herself. "But he's gone. Gone, into the deep blue sea."

Lowell was caught off guard. It had never even dawned on him that this woman might actually mourn the loss of her progeny. But then she had concealed so much of her true thoughts and feelings from the world.

"How did you get into my house?" she demanded. Still sharp and alert, at least in spurts and flashes.

"The door was open, and there was no answer," he replied, simply.

She sat down in the nearest chair, a prim Shaker rocker, oddly out of place among all the French and English rococo. It looked well used. "There's a maid who comes, sometimes," she muttered, almost defensively. "And the pastor comes, from the church. He brings me Big Macs. I like Big Macs." She turned to look at him. "Do you like Big Macs?"

Lowell looked around and selected a chair for himself. She glanced at him, as though surprised he was still there.

"I've seen you somewhere."

"It's possible. I used to live in town. Listen, Mrs. Hartley, I was asked to see you by your old housekeeper, Maureen Fitzgerald. Do you remember her?"

There was a long moment of silence. Then she almost spit out the name.

"Maureen! Left me at the mercy of those carrion-eating vultures. I always thought she'd come crawling back like a worm."

"Back from where?"

"Where they put her. To rot. They tried to put me there too," she went on, "but I fought them, and I won! I won."

No, ma'am, he thought. You lost. "Where did they put her, do you know? Was it a sanitorium? Is that where she was?"

She thought for a while, trying to sort out her recollections, then slowly nodded.

"Can you tell me what sanitorium? And where?"

She answered immediately. "Endicott. The one my own grandfather founded."

"Endicott Sanitorium?" That made sense.

She looked at him again, as though seeing him for the first time. "And Maureen sent you?"

"In a manner of speaking. She came to hire me. About what happened to Henry."

She seemed to physically withdraw, pulling into herself, as though closing her drawbridges.

Lowell searched for an opening through her tightly protected veil of memories. "When Maureen came to see me she said she saw someone push your son overboard the night that—the night he drowned. Unfortunately, she didn't say who, and she's no longer with us. So I am no longer gainfully employed. But I thought I'd come see you anyway."

Her eyes were reddened and mournful. "I've lost everything, you know."

"I know." He had a sudden thought. "Did you ever lose any jewelry, or anything like that?"

"No. I sold most of mine years ago. What little I had left." The old spark and anger returned again, for just a moment. "If I'd been stronger, I would have stopped them. My husband would have stopped them in a minute."

"Stopped whom?"

"Those filthy politicians!"

Something clicked in the back of Lowell's mind. Maureen had said something about politicians as well.

"Politicians, ma'am?"

She reached out with a long, bony hand—racked with arthritis and with blue veins bulging—and touched his face, gently. "You're hurt. Did you have an accident?"

He pulled back, involuntarily. Her touch was dry and rough, like an emery board.

"I'm all right, thank you. What politicians?"

"The ones who took Maureen. And all my money! Where is she now? Did they let her go at last?"

"In a way. She's dead. Murdered."

She gasped. "My Maureen? Murdered?"

"Afraid so. Someone wanted to shut her up. Presumably for what she saw that night, even twenty-five years after the fact."

She thought for a moment, then slowly got to her feet. Brushing off his offer of assistance, she made her way among the clutter of furniture to a large, gold-edged Louis XIV desk. Fumbling among a ridiculously massive set of keys, she found a small one, inserted it into a tiny drawer lock, and withdrew a tattered old checkbook. She turned back to him.

"I want to hire you. What did you say your name was?"

"Lowell. Anthony Lowell. Tony for short."

"And how much was my former housekeeper going to pay you?"

He hesitated. "That's not important. What's important is what she was going to pay me to do. What do you want me to do?"

She straightened up, noticeably. "I want you to find Maureen Fitzgerald's murderer. I want him brought to justice."

Things were definitely looking up.

"Would a hundred dollars do?" She asked, hand quivering over a faded blue check.

"Fine," he said, brightly. "Whatever you can manage."

She handed him the check. He accepted it gracefully and tucked it away with great care, as though it was the deed to Monte Carlo. It was probably worthless, he knew, judging from the way she was living. But he would do his job regardless. He was a professional. There was a matter of honor at stake. He'd worry about how to pay the bills later.

"I know it's a sensitive subject, ma'am. But I need to ask you something. About the trial."

She replied, almost to herself. "The one that was? Or the one that should have been?"

That caught his attention. "What do you mean?"

She spoke, as though in a dream. "She was screaming bloody murder after the drowning. We had to put her under sedation. But she saw what happened. And she should have reported it to the police. She should have testified at my trial. But she didn't come."

So, Maureen had spoken the truth. "Yes. She started to tell me about it and didn't finish. Why didn't she testify?" His pulse quickened.

Suddenly Lucretia laughed, an odd note in her voice. "She disappeared."

"You mean they sent her away before she could talk to anyone?"

"I never saw her after we reached shore the next day. They took her, and then it was only my word against that woman's."

"Meaning your daughter-in-law."

The old woman shuddered, even at the sound of the name.

"They sent Maureen away," she continued. "Later on they tried to send me away too. But I had a few things to say about that. I'm not without influence, you know. My husband was President of Southern Oil. Did you know that?"

"Yes, I know." He tried to get back on the subject. "Mrs. Hartley, you yourself claimed at the time that your son was pushed overboard. Did you see anything yourself? Do you have any knowledge of who may have done it?"

The light in her eyes flickered out. He had entered an area of memory too painful for her to contemplate, and she had shut down. "One if by land, and two if by sea," she murmured, in almost a singsong. "My son Henry went by sea, you know. Did you know him?"

"Sort of." Lowell actually had known him; he was one of the gang of various local Bardolfs and Pistols who ran with Henry, for a time. But did I really know him? he wondered. Not bloody likely.

She began to rock back and forth, clutching her silver cross. "We all expected him to marry Sissy Vanderveer. I remember her birthday party. She was such a spoiled child, but so beautiful." Lowell vaguely remembered Sissy. A rotten little rich bitch, she'd married a minor movie star who'd dumped all over her. Served her right. Lucretia continued her recollection: "She had a birthday cake that reached up to the mezzanine, with eighteen hundred candles. A hundred for each year. That was the day my son Henry left. He didn't like women very much," she added, shaking her head sadly. "I can't imagine why."

Lucretia reached out and rang a tiny silver bell on a tray stand next to her rocker. "Maureen?" she called. "Maureen, are you there?"

"She's gone, ma'am. Can I get you something? A cup of tea? A Big Mac?"

She shook her head. "The pastor will bring it. He's the only one who comes anymore. What happened to Maureen?"

He didn't have the heart to tell her again. She rocked herself gently, beyond noticing him now.

"So long, Mrs. Hartley." He rose softly, and left.

12

Detective Bedrosian had undergone a crisis in confidence shortly after her arrival at Palm Coast Harbor the day before. If she wasn't exactly trailing Lowell, at least she was on a parallel track. But where it was leading her, she was no longer sure.

The fact that Lowell had talked his way into an exclusive private colony had not necessarily surprised her. P.I.'s were good at that sort of thing. The gate guard had confirmed Lowell's recent arrival. The fact that a cop was after him served perfectly to confirm Harry Martin's suspicions. Especially a female cop. Now that was *really* suspicious.

"I knew that fella was no good," confided Harry. "What's he done? Some kinda drug scam?"

Bedrosian shook her head. "Just want to ask him some questions."

Disappointed, Harry told her where Lowell was headed, gave her directions, and let her through.

Bedrosian did some checking around, and what she learned about Lowell's family connections and background threw her into a state of utter confusion. Instead of a lowlife pseudo-private eye, as she'd thought, she was dealing with a decorated war veteran and the son of a cop—a police chief to boot! She simply couldn't fathom it. And because Anthony Lowell no longer fit her expected profile, Detective Lena Bedrosian, for the first time in her career, was at a loss.

A little more investigation at police H.Q. and city hall confirmed the identity of the dead woman, Maureen Fitzgerald. She'd been a local housekeeper for one of the old blue-blood families. The Henry Hartley family, a famous name, even to blue-collar types like Lena.

Then the call came in from headquarters, relayed through the Palm Coast Harbor Police Department. Apparently the Feds had gotten in on the case. Her superior, Lieutenant Jeffries, who was usually as straightforward as a country cousin, wouldn't say any more, preferring instead to emphasize his displeasure at her breach of regulations. She did get him to admit, however, that it had something to do with protecting the judge. That had to be Judge Folner, of course. The local hero back on the Gulf Coast.

With the possible exception of his charity-queen wife, Judge Michael Folner had done more for that part of Florida—from Tarpon Springs to Sarasota—than anybody since John Ringling. The Folners had built half the buildings at Sun Coast College, donated the entire Performing Arts Center, and financed more public projects than she could count back home. Small wonder he was headed for the Supreme Court, he deserved it. The appointment was supposed to be a shoo-in. So what were they worried about? And what did it have to do with some dead old lady—bless her soul and may she rest in peace, of course—and this Lowell guy? Unless there was something else, something entirely different at stake.

Nobody was saying. But one thing for sure—there was nothing to connect Judge Folner to the woman, or to this place for that matter. Until now. And that black guy, the boat guy, had been no help. He obviously was covering for Lowell. The deadbeat P.I. probably owed him money.

And what was with that admiral? She'd have to do some checking there. Something about the daughter, maybe an old love interest. She'd followed Lowell to the club, and observed for herself that there was no love lost between Lowell and the woman's father, that was for sure. Maybe the old admiral just felt the same as she did about hippy types, was all.

Then she'd followed Lowell to the library and stumbled across a bombshell. At the library, whoda thought of it? Her quarry had led her straight to it. Right in the reference section, no less!

She'd been careful not to be spotted. She'd kept her head low in a study carrel, and simply waited for Lowell to check out whatever he was looking for. He always wrote down the reference numbers, which made it easy. She simply slipped in and picked up the discarded slips of paper when he was finished. Then she checked them out herself.

That's how she'd learned that the judge's high-society wife also happened to be the former daughter-in-law of Lucretia Hartley, the employer of the dead woman. Interesting. She'd read up on the drowning, the mother's accusations, the contested will, Lucretia's slander trial, and the judgment against her in favor of Julie. And whaddya know? The attorney representing the plaintiff had been Michael B. Folner. The judge. So that was the connection. Well, there was no law against representing rich people or marrying money, which, while not exactly earning it, was certainly no worse than inheriting it. So what was the beef? At least the Folners had made some positive contributions to society. Plus it was well known back home that they'd been heavy backers not only of all four campaigns for the judge's political sponsor, Senator Robert Grimm, but also of the last two winning presidential campaigns. Again, small wonder the nomination had come Folner's way.

It had all begun to make her wonder once more about Anthony Lowell's own motives in this thing. It seemed unlikely he'd still be on a case when his client was dead. Maybe he had some angle with these Hartley people. The Feds seemed to consider him some kind of threat. Why? And what about the housekeeper, what had she done? Or wanted?

Then Lena had found the body of Elliot Dupree. What in hell was going on here?

It was time for this guy Lowell to start talking. And so she waited, trying to stay warm in the late-autumn nighttime chill, outside that huge monument to money where the old lady lived like a recluse. Lucretia Hartley was another person, she realized, who had a beef.

Bedrosian was going to have to talk to her. And that wouldn't be easy, because the local cops seemed to be pretty protective of their own.

At half past ten, Bedrosian heard a distant door slam and felt, more than saw, someone coming toward her through the night mist. She tensed, waiting to make her move.

Lowell reached the gate and stepped out into the roadway just as a car came around the bend, shining its lights onto the gates. He stepped back, hoping it was Larson, whom he'd called from Lucretia's kitchen phone. At the last moment he spotted the roof dome profiled in the moonlight, and ducked out of sight. The patrol car passed by, heading toward the bridge gate.

Lowell stood up, turned back to watch the road to the south, and a shadow loomed before him out of the gloom. Startled, he backed away. A flashlight shone on his face.

"Stop right there."

It was the unmistakable voice of Police Detective Lena Bedrosian. The woman had obviously followed him all this way. Pretty gutsy. She held a gun, pointed straight at him. It was an old Colt .38 Police Special. He noticed her hand was steady.

"Would you mind getting that light out of my eyes?"

She lowered the beam and trained it on his hands, noting the cardboard tube he was still carrying. "I thought I told you not to leave town," she said. "What's that in your hand?"

"I'll have to know you better. Look, I apologize for taking off like that, it's an old habit of mine when it comes to cops and women."

Bedrosian pulled her Anne Klein jacket closer against the night chill. "Why'd you lie about Maureen Fitzgerald?"

"I lied? Sorry if I did. Another bad habit."

"You said you didn't know her."

"Then I didn't lie. You asked me if I knew her. I said no. You didn't ask if we had any mutual acquaintances, or came from the same town, or whether I'd ever heard of her."

"What mutual acquaintances?"

Lowell shrugged. "I'm just being theoretical. Listen, I really love

115

standing around in the middle of the road in the middle of the night discoursing but I really have to go, so if you wouldn't mind too much . . ."

Bedrosian bristled. "I do mind. Maybe you should start by telling me about your little visit with the Hartley woman. My car's across the road in the trees. I'll give you a lift to wherever you're staying. Or is it still gonna be the boatyard?"

Lowell looked. She was parked about a foot from the edge of an alligator swamp. He wondered, with grim amusement, whether to tell her or not.

"Could you put away the gun first? Or do you consider me dangerous?"

Bedrosian studied him a moment, then lowered the gun, reluctantly. "Don't do anything we'll both regret, Lowell."

They crossed the road, Lowell in front, and got into the unmarked car, probably her own, he figured. She was a maverick, like him. Lights approached from the direction of the causeway. Again Lowell hoped it was Ernie. But there was no point in taking chances. Bedrosian seemed to share his concern, which was interesting. They both slumped down as the car passed by, slowly. A Ford sedan. It kept going and disappeared around the bend.

A thought crossed Lowell's mind. "Tell me something, Detective—Bedrosian. I remember names. And this name keeps popping up lately. Folner. That mean anything to you?"

She frowned. "What about him?"

"He send you down here by any chance?"

"Why would he? He's a judge, I'm a cop."

"And those two Feds who just drove by. Friends of yours?"

"What makes you think they're Feds?"

"Old acquaintances. They paid me a visit the day of the murder. Yesterday, was it? Or last month. I can't remember. Anyway, they made a point of trying to get me off the case."

"What's your point, Lowell?"

"My point is, I'm wondering why two alleged Federal agents would be hassling me for no apparent reason. And the only reason

116

I can come up with is that Judge Folner, whose nomination gets voted on in what, two, three days?, has something to hide."

"You're delirious."

"Suit yourself. What do you want from me anyway?"

"The truth, for starters. Like, are you gonna tell me what Maureen Fitzgerald came to see you about?" Her eyes fell on the poster tube again, questioning.

Lowell hesitated, wondering how safe it was. Did this policewoman have a hidden agenda of her own? Or was she as she seemed—just a cop trying to solve a murder. If that was all, she might be an ally. If she could stifle her typical cop attitude problems, that is.

"OK. But I don't think you're going to like it."

"Let me be the judge of that. Or did I use the wrong word?"

Smart woman, thought Lowell. That's good. Attractive too, in an uptight, overdone sort of way. That's bad. "I'm not about to point fingers," he began. "And she never got the chance. But she started to tell me about what happened on board the Hartley yacht the night Henry drowned. You know about that, I assume?"

"Yeah. I've been brushin' up on it. Go on."

"She told me she saw someone push Henry Hartley overboard that night. She claimed it was murder."

"So why didn't she come forward about this at the time?"

"I think they put her on ice, to shut her up. Then for some reason she got loose, years later. So they snuffed her."

"I see. And you decided not to tell me about this until now." She eyed the tube again.

"Maureen Fitzgerald was my client. I consider what she told me in confidence to be privileged. Even after she's dead."

Bedrosian controlled her annoyance. "I see. What other information or evidence you got there in your bag of tricks you been holding out on? You by any chance got a suspect in mind, for either of these two murders?"

Lowell hedged. He wasn't about to give up Elliot's materials without a fight. "I'm not the one withholding evidence. Maybe you

117

already know that the entire trial transcript is missing? Like it never occurred. How can something like that happen?"

"What are you talkin' about?"

"And the newspaper records burned. There are no photo records of that period. Maybe you can check the national papers. But I'm the one who provided most of them. I was the local stringer for U.P.I., too, back then."

At that moment Ernie Larson's pickup came around the bend, moving slow, lights off. Larson had seen police lights from across the water and had heard sirens earlier. He knew Lowell was in trouble. Bedrosian's back was to the truck, her attention focused on Lowell. Larson crept closer. Lowell kept his eyes fixed on the detective, revealing nothing. There was a breeze off the ocean, rustling through the palmettos and mangroves, and what little noise the pickup made was inaudible.

"What about the guy in the museum?" Bedrosian was saying. "You got an explanation for that? You left the scene of a crime. I'm the one had to call it in."

"Sorry about that. He was my cousin, and I was in a rush. Why, you think I killed him?"

"How should I know? I don't know what to think about you, mister. Except you're one weird son of a bitch who calls himself a P.I. and every time you talk to somebody they wind up whacked!"

The pickup glided up next to them, and Bedrosian almost jumped out of her pumps. In a flash the gun was out, leveled at Ernie. Her hand was steady. To his immense credit, Larson ignored it, leaned over and opened the passenger side door. "Need a ride, buddy?"

"Don't mind if I do," said Lowell, getting out of the car, challenging Bedrosian to stop him. "See you around, Detective."

She glared, knowing she was powerless to stop him. Anyway, there were too many pieces lying around out here to pick up. And if she didn't pick them up, nobody would. Certainly not those Feds. What if Lowell was right about them? What were they doing here, and why weren't they talking to her? Jeffries was holding back, and she didn't like that one bit. It was more than just a male, leave-it-to-the-boys thing. Something smelled.

But she wasn't through talking to this witness—or whatever he was—yet either. Lowell got on the running board, and the pickup began moving. "Lowell!" shouted Bedrosian, as the truck pulled away. "You need me! You need me to have what you know! What good's it gonna do you?"

Lowell knew she might be right. But he wasn't ready to come in out of the cold. Not yet. Not until he had proof. Solid proof that even the Feds couldn't cover up. And Bedrosian would have to be trusted, and he wasn't ready to trust a cop. Not even a woman cop. Or maybe, especially not a woman cop. Not yet anyway.

As the truck gathered speed, Ernie switched on the headlights and glanced over at his friend, worried.

"Jesus, the cops are havin' a cow, Tony. I heard on the radio somebody killed your cousin Elliot, over at the history house. They say some kinda voodoo shit went down."

Lowell buckled himself in. "I know, I was there."

"Jesus mercy! You was there? You didn't mention that before."

"I know. I'm sorry, Ernie, but I didn't do it, if that's what you're worried about. He was my cousin and a nice kid."

Ernie looked hurt. "I ain't worried about that. What you take me for?" He shook his head in dismay. "I just don't know about you white folk. This is some bad shit comin' down here, and now you up and got me involved."

"I'm sorry, Ernie. I sure as hell didn't plan on it."

"So, what'm I gonna do with you now?"

Lowell thought a moment. The Ford sedan was coming back the other way. He ducked below the dashboard. Ernie shook his head, his dismay deepening by the moment.

"Ernie, I need another favor."

"Another favor? You already owes me one."

"I know, I know. But I need to run down to Boca. I'll drive. I'll tell you the whole thing over breakfast. My treat."

"Yeah, yeah. But my truck don't allow nobody but me drivin', and you're still gonna owe me one!"

Ernie was pissed, and Lowell couldn't blame him. But there was nothing he could do about it just now. He needed him, more than he could admit right now. Maybe he could make it up somehow. To Estelle too—left home all alone like this. Right, he thought to himself. Like I was going to make it up to Elliot. Jesus Christ, what is happening here?

Lowell looked at the cardboard tube wedged between his knees. He'd been on the run ever since picking up Elliot's findings. It was time to take a look at what they were.

13

The Endicott Sanitorium was set in a former orange grove on the outskirts of Boca Raton. As manicured as a country club, it had much the same ambiance: guarded gates, trim Bermuda grass, and a curving drive edged with towering coconut palms planted by founder Jeremy Endicott, Lucretia Hartley's maternal grandfather. The main building was a spanking-clean, gray-painted Victorian resembling, for all intents and purposes, a resort hotel.

Its true intent, however, was to incarcerate the well-to-do no longer welcome in their family habitats or social circles (for whatever reason). This became more evident that Friday morning just after breakfast, when Ernie Larson pulled up at the gate in his battered GM pickup, stacked with lobster cages in the back.

Ernie and Estelle had graciously put Lowell up at their trailer for the night. Both had agreed (to Estelle's relief) that there was no point going down to Boca in the middle of the night. Ernie had sensed a change in Lowell from the time Tony had opened the mailing tube and read its contents during the drive home, but he had tried without success to pry any further information from him. To Tony's relief, he'd finally given up and gone to bed. They'd freshened up and taken off first thing in the morning, Lowell's only regret being that he didn't have any clothes to change into. At least he'd been able to shave and shower.

They followed the long, curving drive up to the main building, past several groups of residents out walking with nurses. As they

121

drove by, Lowell and Ernie were met with blank stares. Poor Maureen, thought Lowell. At least she got out for a little while, at the end.

The main entrance was watched over by a black armed guard. His job was to serve as general enforcer in case of any disturbances while otherwise masquerading as a uniformed doorman. The portal itself consisted of two huge solid bronze doors, with beveled diamond-paned sidelights. As they approached the building, the doorman didn't look at all pleased by the appearance of Ernie's pickup. He gestured for them to park around the side, at the service entrance.

That was fine with Ernie, who showed increasing signs of nervousness as they neared the place.

"This whole sanitorium thing is evil, if you ask me," he complained, in low, urgent tones. "Families 'sposed to take care of their sick ones, including the crazy ones. They don't just ship them off like they was outgrown shoes."

Lowell hopped out and strode toward the entrance, leaving Ernie muttering dire warnings.

" 'Morning," he said cheerfully to the doorman. "Which way is Registration?"

The doorman studied him a moment thoughtfully. Lowell's jeans and jacket were definitely not what was called for. But white folks did have odd ways about them. Seems like the richer they was, the older their clothes, some of them. He decided this one was rich. Probably had a mother or auntie or somebody to unload in this hellhole so's he could get at the money.

"Inside and to the left, sir."

"Thanks." Lowell was in.

The lobby had towering, bronze-plated Doric columns reaching to a gold-leaf frescoed ceiling, depicting the gods at the gates of Olympus. Nice and cozy, thought Lowell sarcastically, gazing around. Assuming an attitude of ease he didn't feel, he sauntered over to the white marble counter. A very pretty, dark-haired nurse looked up at him with a wary eye.

"May I help you, sir?"

"Yes. I'd like to get some medical information on a relative who was recently discharged."

"You'd have to talk to the doctor, sir. What was the name?"

"Fitzgerald. Maureen Fitzgerald."

The eyes narrowed, just a tiny bit. "One moment, sir, I'll have to check the records."

She got up and went into the office behind her. A different, more masculine face peered out at him for a moment through the crack in the half-opened door. There was the sound of voices, murmuring.

The girl returned, lips pursed tightly.

"Sorry, sir. I'm afraid I can't help you."

"May I see the Medical Director, please?"

"I'm sorry, he's in Miami, sir."

"But she was a patient here, wasn't she?"

"I'm sorry, sir. Our patient records are confidential. You'd have to speak to the patient's doctor. Even after discharge."

OK, have it your way. "Fine. So could you tell me who her doctor is? Or was?"

She hesitated, then reached for a Rolodex on the desk beneath the counter. Score one, thought Lowell. She's admitted Maureen was here. That's a start.

"That would be—oh." Whatever she saw gave her significant pause. Lowell took matters into his own hands. He reached over the counter and flipped the card back over in his direction.

"Dr. Morton," he read, quickly memorizing the address and phone number.

"Sir," admonished the nurse, pulling the Rolodex away. "That's confidential! And besides," she added, a touch of fear in her voice, "he's no longer here."

"What do you mean?"

"I mean, he's no longer with the hospital. He left."

"How long ago?"

"I really couldn't say."

But the red stamp across the file card had told him already. It was

123

stamped, "TERMINATED." With a date, "Sept. 19" of this year. Just over a month ago.

Suddenly Lowell had a strong desire to get the hell out of there. He forced a smile at the nurse, who was glaring at him now, hand poised over the telephone.

"Well, that's all right," he said, trying to relax her guard. "I'll just find a new doctor, I guess. You know how it is with these old fogies, they get set in their ways. She was taking Ritalin, see. And I wanted to know if we could ease her off it."

He didn't think she'd buy the lie, but she seemed to waver a bit. "I'm sorry we can't help you, sir. I'm sure you'll find a good doctor in her new town. Is she staying with you?"

"No, actually. But thanks anyway." He turned to go, cautioning himself to keep his cool.

"Where can we reach you?" she called after him. "In case I can get hold of the doctor?"

"That won't be necessary. Thanks very much."

He walked past the door guard, sensing a tension that was tangible.

He made it back to the pickup and jumped quickly on board. Ernie looked like he'd never been so glad to see anyone in his life.

"Go!" said Lowell. Ernie didn't need further encouragement. He already had the motor started and spun gravel as he turned onto the drive and raced for the exit. Lowell watched the sideview mirror as they drove, but there was no pursuit. Breathing a bit easier as they entered the boulevard, Lowell dug through his pockets and fished out a cap-less old Bic and a crumpled white envelope from an unpaid bill. He wrote down on the back: "Dr. Eric Morton, 2554 Country Club Road, Bal Harbor Florida. Tel 299-8789."

"You memorized all that?" remarked Ernie admiringly, as he sped westward on the highway with an audible sigh of relief.

"Just part of my job."

Ernie shook his head and drove on.

* * *

After a couple more cups of coffee and Danish at a Denny's as further bribery, Lowell informed his friend his services might be needed for a "quick run" down to Bal Harbor. Ernie glowered and muttered more prophesies of doom. Only when Lowell finally gave in and promised full disclosure, did he agree to go. And then only after insisting that Lowell call ahead first.

Lowell was pretty sure no doctor would give out patient information over the phone. On the other hand, he owed Ernie the chance to avoid another trip, if possible. It was a moot point. The line was busy.

They headed back to I-95 and south. "Now you gonna owe me *two*!" grumbled Ernie.

During the drive down to Bal Harbor, Lowell maintained a watchful eye on the road behind them. For the past twenty minutes a helicopter had been traveling in the same direction a half mile or so ahead, to the right. When they exited at Route 826, it vanished from sight.

They stopped off at a Village Inn for a bite, just off the exit, and Lowell tried the doctor's number once more. Again it was busy. Ernie argued for a while about the merits of going out to the house, but Lowell insisted.

"We've come this far. Let's check him out."

It was nearly nightfall by the time they found Country Club Road: part of a new upscale waterfront housing tract along the Intracoastal Waterway. In keeping with Florida's laissez-faire traditions, the developers hadn't bothered to put numbers on the walls or curbs or install street lighting of any kind. The neighborhood was uncannily dark, enhanced by the prevalence of masonry walls in front and fortresslike facades on many of the houses. They had a hard time reading the house numbers, many of which were not even posted.

"Man, I'd hate to be a mailman 'round here," growled Ernie.

"I'd hate to be anything around here."

They finally resorted to shining Lowell's flashlight on front doors and mailboxes, to read the few legible numbers. That was how they eventually found the house.

"You gonna be all right?" asked Lowell, feeling increasingly guilty for dragging his friend into this mess. Ernie had gone well beyond the call of duty already. "This shouldn't take too long, you're welcome to come with me if you want."

"No thanks. Folks around here see a black face turn up at their door after dark, they liable to either have a heart attack or reach for a shotgun. Don't need the aggravation."

"Right," said Lowell, not knowing what else to say. "I ﹍ be right back."

He crossed the wide lawn, noting that the grass crunched under his feet. It hadn't been watered in some time. A shiny black BMW 630i was parked in the driveway. The garage door stood wide open, which suggested the doctor was in. Entering the wide portico over-hanging the entrance, he rang the bell—one of those irritating electronic contraptions that emitted an allegedly musical melody. He could hear sounds inside, probably a TV. Either someone was there, or the good doctor was one of those ultraparanoid types who left all sorts of appliances on and other subterfuges (such as cars in driveways) when they were out of town.

He rang again. Unlike the rest of the neighborhood, the house was practically ablaze with light. There were two wide, colonial-style multipaned windows to the right of the front door. Both were brightly lit and only partially curtained. After a moment, Lowell glanced back at the pickup and walked over to the nearest window. The curtain was open a careless six inches or so, enough to see inside with no trouble. In what appeared to be the living room, the television was on—a new, wide-screen projection model—facing the win-dow from the far side of the room. A cartoon show was playing. An odd choice, he thought, for a doctor, unless there were kids in the house. But there weren't, he was pretty sure. He would have seen or heard some signs of them by now. There was only a single leather reclining lounge chair, in the center of the room. The chair was tilted back partway. He could see an arm on the armrest, and the top of a head. Bald, with a wisp of brown hair around the sides. The telephone lay on the table top nearby, off the hook.

He rapped on the window. There was no response. Then he noticed the smell. Pulse quickening, he ran back to the pickup.

"Something's wrong."

"I don't even wanna know."

"I'm going around back to get a better look. Honk if you see anyone coming."

Lowell hurried back across the lawn, heading around the garage side of the house. The fact that the garage door was open indicated that the doctor had probably intended to go out again soon. Hence the car still in the driveway. There was a brand-new Yamaha 650 motorcycle parked against the inside wall of the garage, and about a thousand dollars' worth of Rossignol and Nordica ski equipment. So he is the trusting sort, thought Lowell, moving cautiously around to the back.

As with most new developments, there were few trees and a lot of open spaces dotted with token shrubs. The waterway was visible now, water dancing in the darkness, reflections of distant lights glittering. There was a private sea wall with its own dock and davits at the rear of the property, and a thirty-foot cigarette boat. The doctor had the so-called good life down pat. Lowell moved around the unfenced forty-foot swimming pool—unused, untended, and green with algae—toward the high sliding glass doors at the back of the house. He'd seen those windows from the front. They were uncurtained, and he knew he'd have a good view inside.

Keeping low and close to the wall, he approached the window. Slowly, cautiously, he moved to the glass and peered around the edge. The smell was much worse now. Almost overwhelming.

The doctor stared straight at him, a look of shock on his face. He didn't see Lowell standing there. Or anything else either. For the third time in three days, Lowell found himself looking into dead, accusing eyes. Like the others, Dr. Morton had been caught by surprise, a small-caliber bullet in the chest.

Lowell walked back to the pickup, trying to collect his thoughts.

Ernie needed no coaching. They were moving before the door had even shut.

"What happened, he pull a gun on you or somethin'?"

Lowell remained silent for a moment. Ernie rounded the next corner, tires squealing, and gave him a look. And then the fear crept over him.

"Jesus Christ, boy. What'd you see back there?"

"You don't want to know."

"It's a little late for that, ain't it? What's goin' on, Tony? You better start levelin' with me, or you can goddammotherfuckin' walk!"

Lowell knew he was right. Ernie was involved, had trusted him, and deserved to know. He told him about the visit from Maureen Fitzgerald, and the killings.

Ernie figured it out right away. "Shit, boy. You got a maniac on the loose."

Lowell had to disagree. There was a pattern, all right. But not the kind maniacs tended to create. Maureen had gotten it just when she'd been about to reveal some key information about a long-ago drowning she'd claimed to have witnessed. Elliot, who like Maureen had never harmed a soul in his life, had been on the telephone—it had been lying on the kitchen floor, Lowell remembered. He, too, may have been about to reveal something crucial, and awful. And now this. A psychiatrist had to be a listener, it was his job. So he'd surely have heard Maureen's story at one time or another. And whether or not he'd given it any credence hadn't mattered in the end. The killer was obviously taking no chances.

On the other hand, Ernie could be right. He might indeed be dealing with a lunatic. The destruction of the museum was not the work of a sane or stable person.

Ernie tore through a traffic light, watching the rear-view mirror now with a paranoia that echoed the watchfulness Lowell had shown on the trip down.

"Maybe you better get with that cop again," he told Lowell. "You cain't deal with something like this alone."

128

"Maybe. Sorry I dragged you into it."

"Well, you shoulda thought about it. Now Estelle, she's gonna kill me. Runnin' around all over hell with you, all hours day an' night, dead bodies right an' left. How'm I s'posed to explain all that?"

"Just tell her it's my fault. That she'll understand."

"Shit, boy. She knows that already!"

They drove back to Palm Coast Harbor: Ernie straining to see, too stubborn to let Lowell drive, too angry to talk. Lowell remained silent in his thoughts, staring into the darkness.

A helicopter crossed the freeway, low, just behind them, as they reached their turnoff. Lowell saw the lights in the side mirror but said nothing. Ernie had enough to worry about. Besides, helicopters in the sky weren't that unusual.

It was nearly ten by the time they crossed the causeway to the island. The gate was on key lock, the guard long gone for the night. The town had installed this new system after much discussion. It seemed a waste, in the minds of some residents, to have a round-the-clock gatekeeper in the off hours. This island was truly a refuge, and islanders did little coming and going, other than by yacht or to the West Palm Beach Airport by limousine. The gate's primary function—controlling service access and keeping strangers at bay—was served even better, in a way, with the automatic lock. No one could talk their way in past a machine the way Lowell had done with Harry Martin.

Ernie Larson, an authorized merchant, inserted his card into the slot, and the gate opened obediently. Sullenly, he drove along Ocean Avenue and slowed for the turn at Pelican Street.

A blue Ford sedan was pulled across the road fifty yards in front of them, blocking their way.

Larson braked to a stop, with an accusing look at Lowell. "Now what's this shit? Looks like a roadblock!"

"Better turn around." Lowell calculated his chances of making a run for it. But he couldn't just ditch Ernie.

Up ahead, Special Agents Lefcourt and Werner got out of the car and walked toward them. Larson squinted at them, trying to see. "Who they?" he demanded.

"I think they're Feds," replied Lowell, apologetically.

"Oh, that's great, Feds. What in hell they want?" Lowell, in his abbreviated account, hadn't mentioned the Feds.

"Ernie, I'm gonna draw them off. Soon as I do, I need one last favor."

"I can't count that many, boy!"

The two men didn't seem hurried. They must be pretty confident, thought Lowell.

"You remember the admiral's place?" he asked, quickly.

Ernie gave him an exasperated look. "Your girlfriend's daddy's place? You ain't gonna go there!"

"I have to." He handed Ernie the cardboard poster tube. "As soon as you can, bring this there, along with my stuff at the loft, and give it to Caitlin. Nobody but Caitlin. Can you do that?"

"I got a choice?"

Lowell laughed, in spite of their predicament, and opened the door. "I don't make it back, it's yours. How's that?"

"I wouldn't want it. Go on, get outta here, damn crazy honky fool!"

Lowell jumped and ran. Ernie shook his head in exasperation, turned sharply, and cut across the corner of the park onto Harbor Street, burning rubber.

Werner and Lefcourt didn't even hesitate. As Lowell sprinted across Ocean Avenue toward the beach, they went after him. The accomplice could be dealt with later.

14

Two hundred miles across the state, in a plush office atop the First Florida Tower in Tampa, Judge Michael Butler Folner stared out the window at the city lights winking below. Tampa was his city in so many ways. His public life had been exemplary, presiding over the Hillsborough County Superior Court during times of unprecedented challenges to South Florida's long-cherished traditions and its legal system. It had been his timely opinions that had protected developers—the lifeblood of Florida's nonagrarian economy—from relentless assaults by environmental groups and other ill-advised crazies determined to stop growth and development at all cost. He had successfully ruled to reverse the lower court decision of "Gormley vs. Brampton," which had given that city the right to impound privately held tracts for public services and impose stiff fees on developers for schools, water and sewage treatment facilities (he'd been advised the current ones were already more than adequate), libraries, and other unwanted so-called improvements.

He'd led the fight against city and county taxes and tax overrides—efforts by certain local politicians to soak productive sectors of the public in order to feed the demands of other, usually totally nonproductive ones.

Most recently, he'd led the battle to fight the imposition of quotas on the city and county's social and economic institutions—utterly misguided attempts by armchair liberals to deprive Americans of their most basic freedoms. Such as whom to associate with, live with, work with and for, and socialize with. They had already scuttled the Gasparilla Parade—his own personal favorite—and he'd vowed it would not happen again.

Judge Folner's real contributions, however—the ones that had finally earned him this much deserved, about-to-be-received reward (how incredible it would have seemed twenty years ago: a seat on the Supreme Court!)—had been much less flamboyant, public, or judicial. A phone call to a colleague in Miami to deter bank regulators from interfering with perfectly legitimate business activities; a check to a senator in North Carolina for a favored project in danger of budget cuts; a line of credit at one of his holding company's banks in Houston, or funds for a congressman in peril of losing his seat (and a critical Finance Committee chairmanship). Next to God he had only one authority to answer to, in his view. And even that obligation was carefully balanced. That man had done much to make him what he was today and what he was about to become; but he was also the man Folner had helped to become Florida's senior senator, and now ranking member of the Judiciary Committee.

It was the senator who was the real power behind his nomination. Folner cared nothing for the policies of the current President and owed him nothing. The debt at that end was all in his favor, and a very great debt it was indeed. Judge Folner and his wife, together with the senator, had been the architects of the President's entire Southern coalition, bringing in the key votes from Texas to Florida that swayed the election. It had all been done with a tremendous media blitz, and all it took was money. Lots and lots of money. The President owed Mike Folner, and this was to be his reward. And it was all coming together this weekend. The senator was going to be in town to celebrate his certain confirmation, with the President's "warmest blessings." There was going to be a black-tie affair such as the Gulf Coast had never seen, at the Belleview Mido across the bay. And he, Michael B. Folner, would finally attain the third cog in the wheel of destiny, the one that most men would never dare even dream of and few besides himself would achieve: fortune (that part had been easy); fame—that had been of the least interest, but he had accepted it as a necessary appendage to public life (about which he cared far more); and now at last: power. True nation-shaping, destiny-shaping power. He would hold in his hands the fundamental course of judiciary progress for the next quarter century and beyond. And he could hardly wait.

There was just one problem that was nagging him, like an old war wound that had festered of late. Nothing too serious, nothing a quick bit of outpatient surgery couldn't take care of. Julie had recently begun having nightmares. She couldn't tell him much—or wouldn't. But she had admitted that she was troubled about her Hartley past. He'd hoped that chapter had been closed forever. Had something happened to reopen it? He read the papers selectively, supplementing that with briefings from his aides on matters strictly relevant to business at hand. And that business was the Supreme Court. Funny, though, that yesterday the President himself had called to ask if things were all right.

Had something gone wrong? He knew that despite his position, despite his potent support, he was vulnerable. Hell, everyone is vulnerable. We all have an Achilles' heel somewhere. But he could hardly ask the Chief for a reason for his question. Of course things were all right. Why shouldn't they be? His record was utterly immaculate. He had made sure of that from the very beginning. His personal moral behavior; his and his wife's exemplary charity work; his religious pursuits (Baptist, like all good Southerners, which is what had finally convinced the President); his financial responsibility; his care to place his control of Southern Oil in a blind trust from the time he had entered public office fifteen years before; all had been conducted with the greatest discretion. He had never slipped up. Not once.

Yes, he had represented Julie Barnett Hartley and won her that unprecedented award from that old fool of a judge; and yes, he had married her two years later and thereby shared the rewards he had won for her. What of it? His early opponents had raked him through the coals for that to their own undoing, because he had known all along that his success perfectly mirrored the aspirations of virtually all Americans. He had done and had continued to do what most of them could only dream about. Or vicariously read about in pulp novels, or enjoy in fantasy films. In the most basic terms, he had made it big. Would the people condemn him for this? Never. And of course they hadn't. Even the rising red tide of liberalism (how he had hoped it had been banished for good) had failed to sweep him aside in more recent upheavals. He was a survivor. And with each passing crisis, his power was solidified all the more.

He checked his watch. It was time to call Rolfe for the car, time to go home. There was much to do before tomorrow, and most of his cases still pending could wait. He wanted to clear his desk before heading for Washington. It wouldn't be fair to burden his successor unduly—but still. The senator didn't come to town very often, and he wanted to be ready.

As he gave Rolfe the word and hung up again, he decided to call Julie. She had been such a tireless, dedicated supporter all these years—not just of his career but of so many worthy causes. They had grown apart, despite the commitment they had made to each other. It would be a good idea to give her some attention for a change. Lord knows, she deserved it.

Dormond, his personal secretary, answered. "Folner residence."

"Dormond? Is Mrs. Folner there?"

"No, sir. She's not back from the luncheon in Sarasota. Is there any message?"

"No, just tell her I'll be home early, and I hope she'll be able to join me for dinner."

"Very good, sir."

He hung up. As usual, she was off helping the disabled or destitute or something. Good old Julie, he thought, picking up his raincoat. She was so loyal and dedicated and had gotten so little from him in return, in the way of simple love and attention over the years. But that had been part of the bargain. She knew who and what he was, they had always understood and supported each other, and that would never change. He realized, though, as he went into the now-empty hallway, she must be lonely. It was a hard lot, being the

134

wife of a politician (which, more than a judge, is what he truly considered himself). And she had borne it with astonishing patience and dignity over the years.

A glance through the floor-to-ceiling windows as he left his office suite had told him it was starting to rain. Rolfe hated negotiating these roads—too damn many people!—in the rain.

He entered the elevator, pressed the button to P-5—the executive garage—and rocketed downward. Rolfe would be waiting with the Rolls. Just as he'd done for seventeen years. Some things, he vowed, would not change. Must not change. No matter what.

Across the state, Tony Lowell was bitterly regretting that he'd neglected himself physically. He hadn't slept since yesterday, had been through a series of severe shocks, and now this: two trained commandos (and he recognized the skills because he'd had them himself at one time) on his trail.

He did have certain advantages. He knew the island. Even after all these years. He'd run from the wrath of his drunken father often enough in his childhood to have worked out an intricate network of escape routes through neighboring estates, the open dunes, and the myriad woods and swamps of mangroves.

Already, he'd led his unsuspecting pursuers into two bogs— hazardous enough even when you knew the way, and inhabited by at least two known alligators, not to mention several other possibly unpleasant species of flora and fauna. Then he'd taken them into a thicket of mangrove so dense even a muskrat would think twice. Yet they were still right behind him. He could hear them crashing and cursing, relentlessly closing in on him.

He, himself, couldn't take much more of this cross-country trail-blazing. He decided to try a different tack. Choosing his moment, he broke from the bushes and cut across the road. Admiral Schoenkopf lived at the very southern tip of the island, on the bay side. Lowell had originally intended to work his way along the beach, but the dunes were heavy going, and the likelihood of being overtaken was increasing with every passing minute.

His plan was simple and dangerous. If he could get around the Feebies' car—in effect doubling back—and down past Ernie's boatyard to the end of Pelican Street, there was an old dock where he'd fished when he was small. Once there—if the damn dock still existed—he'd swim for it. He was a strong swimmer, and while the water was cold now, it wasn't overly so—around 70 degrees. There used to be a small beach across the harbor, not more than two hundred yards away. If he could reach the other side, bearing in mind strong riptides when the tides were going out—shit, what was the tide now? He had no idea—anyway, if he could make it, they would have a hell of a time picking him up. Hopefully two decades of storms and shifting sands hadn't obliterated the beach. Otherwise he'd be trying to come ashore into an impenetrable barrier of mangrove: impossible by day, let alone in the dark. He'd have to take that chance.

Once he gained shore on the other side, he would be home free. Lowell happened to know a narrow path, along the bay front, that led the entire length of the island. Directly to the Schoenkopf place. At least it used to be there. Again, he'd have to take that chance. He'd used it many a time avoiding the admiral's spies, or his father's, in order to see Caitlin.

He'd use that path again now. And if it was overgrown, he'd just have to clear a new one somehow. Or fight his way through it.

Cecil Lefcourt spotted him right away, crossing the road. He shouted to Werner and broke into his kickoff-return charge. The distance was about the same, and he'd covered it in 4.5 seconds in his days with the Redskins taxi squad. Before the career-ending shoulder separation. But as he crashed across the corner of park that lay between Harbor Street and Ocean Avenue where they intersected Pelican, Lowell was nowhere in sight. Lefcourt swore, mostly to himself. Werner caught up to him in a moment.

"Sly son of a bitch," growled Werner. "He doubled back."

"He probably cut through the woods to the boatyard. That's where he's been staying, his stuff's all down there."

"He's looking for something, same as us. Let's just hope we find it first."

"Maybe he already found it."

"We'll know soon enough. That's a dead-end street, down there. He just boxed himself in."

Lefcourt laughed. They climbed into the Ford, Werner driving, pulled it around, and headed down to Larson's Boatyard. They didn't anticipate any further trouble. The stag had been run down, and was about to be cornered.

Lowell's bags and papers were safe at Caitlin's by now. Ernie had watched the two men chase his friend into the bushes, and had immediately put his money on Lowell. In the Civil War, the South had won many a battle by fighting on their own turf—just like they'd finally lost when they ventured out of it. Lowell, while not in the best of shape, was no pushover. He'd had commando training himself. And he was on his own turf.

Ernie had calmly turned around in the post office parking lot, driven straight back to Pelican Street, gone around the Ford still blocking the road, and gotten Lowell's things from the loft. He'd even driven right by the two suits, on their way back to the car.

There'd been no problem dropping Tony's things off, except the Schoenkopf butler or whoever the racist bastard was who answered the door wouldn't let him see Caitlin. So he'd had to leave the stuff. Well, he'd done his best. It was Lowell's worry now. He for one was ready, finally, for a good night's sleep. Ernie turned north once more on Ocean Avenue and headed for the bridge.

Lowell saw the Ford's lights pulling into the abandoned boatyard from the end of Pelican, just as he reached the old dock. Even if they figure it out, he knew, there isn't much they'll be able to do.

There was no way, in his mind, that they could know about Caitlin. She was his own private memory, unconnected in the public's knowledge to the Hartley scandal in any way.

The water was pitch black when he got to the end of the dock, flowing in, a gentle current. Good news, because that meant high water and no rip tides. All he needed to worry about was drowning. Small worry, right about now. He stripped down to his shorts, rolled his clothes in a bundle, took a breath, and slipped into the water, gasping at the night chill.

Using the lifesaver's inverted breast stroke, he worked his way out into the channel. All the boats were in for the night, another advantage. But with the harbor shops and restaurants closed, he was on his own. If he were to slip under now, no one would ever know. He'd probably wash ashore somewhere near Ft. Lauderdale. Not a pleasant thought. And he was beginning to tire.

Checking his watch—a waterproof diver's Rolex Oyster with a luminous dial and probably his only material possession of value— he noted the time. Eleven-fifteen. He was about halfway now, holding the clothes as high as possible away from the chop. Then he felt something. A warm current, eddying slowly past. He froze. A shark? They were known to enter the estuaries. My God, if so, it's huge. He decided that if it attacked he'd try to hit it in the nose as hard as he could. He might scare it away, if he was lucky. If not, could he yell for help? He looked toward shore. The only chance was the two Feds—the very people he was running from. Whatever they had in store for him had to be better than becoming shark food. But they were out of hearing. A hundred yards away, the lights from the Ford sedan were moving out on Pelican Street again, toward the dock. Those guys were smarter than he'd anticipated. All the mistakes he'd ever made came swarming over his mind, like pirhana. At that moment he knew that this return to his home town, his past, this total immersion in the bloody business of others, this questionable determination to set things right—all could be rendered meaningless in a moment. Perhaps they never did have meaning: a chilling thought.

Then he heard the water rushing, swirling closer. His mouth fell open in an involuntary scream, and he stifled it at the last second as a huge, slippery head rose from the water, snorted out a stream of water, and nuzzled him with a whiskery kiss. Lowell almost laughed out loud in relief—and wonder. A manatee! A manatee in the harbor, alive, well, and wanting to play. It was like a celestial omen, a revisitation of his childhood. He had a guardian angel.

"Hey, friend!" he gasped, choking as a wave hit him in the mouth. "Thanks. I'm OK. Thanks!" He had forgotten all about his clothes, which were now floating away in a bundle. He swam after them, gasping, and the manatee followed. He exulted as the great, gentle beast nudged the bundle back toward him. Lowell grabbed the wet clothes, about to sink, and with his other hand reached out and grasped the animal's back as it swam beside him. He could feel the propeller scars, deep furrows. He wondered how much pain these gentle, nearly extinct creatures felt when struck by a speeding runabout. Anything larger usually would kill them. The creature couldn't answer. It snorted another snootful of water at him, nudged him once more in the direction of safety. With one last gaze of its huge, soulful eyes—just visible in the moonlight—it was gone.

Lowell didn't remember how he made it the rest of the way, except that he did. The beach was long gone. But he swam on, eventually reaching a crumbling boathouse belonging to a snowbird lawyer from Boston. The shack was empty now, a hundred yards or so south of the harbor, on the Intracoastal Waterway. He found a ladder up to it and stumbled in around one A.M. There was an old air mattress, a tarp in a corner, a couple of ratty towels. He was asleep before realizing how close to hypothermia he'd come.

He awoke shortly after dawn, aroused by the sound of a shrimp boat motoring past close to shore, heading toward the trawling grounds off the south inlet. The weather was summery, the temperature rising fast. He sat up and shook off the damp and chill. Cumulus clouds were billowing to the south. Unusual for this time of year, was his first thought of the day. His second thought was to get to Caitlin's, find her, and make her listen.

The chill subsided as he began to move, walking along the water's edge. The old path was still there, probably the carefully guarded secret of a whole new generation of kids. Were it not for the danger of the situation, he might have enjoyed himself. It was a gorgeous day, the skies as only Florida skies can be: blue and white, and pink and blue again, everywhere changing and colorful. The scent of sea spray and winter citrus filled the air. A flock of great blue herons flapped by, skimming the water with their long, dangling legs, in pursuit of a school of herring. The water was calm and clear—he could see the white, sandy bottom and the schools of greenback minnows and pinfish—much clearer in the late autumn when most of the power boaters were gone. Then he remembered the manatee. Had that been some sort of delirious dream, or had it been real? He searched the bay, but the chances of seeing it or another one were slim to none.

The admiral's pier was a hundred feet long, jutting into the waterway where it opened into the wider bay and the Atlantic inlet beyond. There were two sailing yachts moored to the leeward side: a white, thirty-five-foot Catalina ketch, and a glossy black twelve-meter yacht Lowell knew as though he had seen it yesterday. He's still got it, he exulted, feeling almost as if it was his own. The *Wellington*! He and Caitlin had crewed on her together in the America's Cup trials back in the early sixties, before Vietnam, before Martin Luther King, before acid rock and LSD and agitprop and civil rights and no more war and college and—my God! Was it *that* long ago?

The house was a long, white two-story colonial, redolent of shiny new money. The admiral was the only so-called self-made millionaire in the Harbor community, a fact of great significance to some people.

Lowell, who had never given a damn about such things, studied the grounds and rear of the house. He wanted to determine who might be up and about, and where they were on the property. The gardener was out front, just firing up the Lawn Boy. He wouldn't be a problem.

140

Someone was in the kitchen, cooking breakfast. The aroma of frying bacon and percolating coffee was enough to drive Lowell into a paroxysm of salivation. He hadn't eaten since the Village Inn, over twelve hours and one hell of a lot of energy output earlier.

He couldn't risk being seen by anyone other than Caitlin. Anyone else would alert the admiral, who would probably send at once for the Army, Navy, Air Force, and Marines. In no particular order. Not to mention the police. Lowell was in no mood to talk to the police, yet. Not until he'd seen Caitlin again. And gotten some answers which he felt increasingly certain she could provide.

Moving carefully along the wooded edge of the property, he skirted the rose garden and the Japanese garden—the admiral's pride and joy—and reached the large hedge of rhododendrons at the back of the house. The kitchen door was just off to the right. Caitlin's room, as he well remembered, was directly above where he was standing. Maybe the old pebble on the window trick? Except the only time he'd ever actually tried that, he'd broken the pane and gotten chased away by a now-deceased ridgeback.

A telephone rang inside. A voice answered, agitated. He crouched low, waiting. The deep voice was unmistakable: the admiral. He heard the phone put down. Footsteps, more voices, and the side door leading to the garage opened and slammed shut. A car started in the garage. The automatic door rumbled open, then the engine sound revved and receded. Lowell's spirits soared. The admiral, his lifelong enemy, had left!

Wasting no more time, he took the frontal approach, marched up to the back door, and knocked. Caitlin herself answered, looking utterly ravishing in white sailing attire: shorts and tank top. It had been Caitlin the whole time in the kitchen, ten feet away. Cooking breakfast. As she stared at him in astonishment, Lowell was immediately conscious of the fact that he, unlike her, looked anything but ravishing. In fact, he was beginning to feel like his "old" self—that of the scruffy, intellectual college bum—by default. He hadn't bathed since he'd showered at Ernie's the day before, other than in

141

the drink. His wet clothes looked like hell, and for the first time in two decades he felt self-conscious about his appearance.

"Tony, my God, what are you doing here?" she gasped.

"We've got to talk."

She looked over her shoulder, as though expecting someone. Her father had just left, he knew, and her mother had moved away years ago. Even before he had. So who was she watching for? The help? He couldn't worry about that just now. He sniffed the aroma wafting through the kitchen. She looked past him into the yard. "Look, come in, just—I don't know. I was just having breakfast, are you hungry?"

"Does a shark have fins? I'm famished, to tell you the truth. I was minding my own business down by the harbor when this little thin stream of bacon smoke came along, grabbed me by the nose, and dragged me over here. It's not my fault at all."

She didn't laugh but held the door for him grudgingly. He entered the kitchen. It had been brand-new, the latest in everything, last time he'd been here. It hadn't changed a bit. Oddly comforting, he thought, taking a seat at the large breakfast bar set up on three sides of the center range. The rasher of bacon smelled delicious. Caitlin carelessly tossed a half-dozen eggs on the Jenn-air griddle, not bothering to ask how he liked them. He didn't care. Fried cardboard would be just fine about now. She poured him a cup of fresh-brewed coffee. Finally, as she set it before him, she stifled a giggle.

"God, look at you. You look like Charley Tuna!"

Lowell laughed, the ice broken. "Thanks. Except it's me they're fishing for. There're nets out all over town. Or haven't you heard?"

She frowned and looked at him sideways, as she turned the bacon. She remembered his changing eyes with a sudden pang. They were somber brown now, reflecting his mood probably, as well as her own. "How did you know I'd be here? I know you saw me at the club but—"

"I just took a chance." He glanced nervously towards the driveway. "Is your father—?"

142

"Gone to town. He got a call this morning."

She turned and faced him, solemnly. "There's been another murder. Your cousin. And the police are looking for you. If I thought you had anything to do with it I wouldn't have let you in but still—first Maureen, now Elliot."

"That's what we need to talk about."

She studied him, questioning, seeking reassurance.

"Caitlin, did Ernie Larson bring my stuff over last night?"

"Somebody dropped something off, but I was in bed."

"Oh. So that's why you weren't expecting me."

"Wait here a minute, I'll be right back." She went to the door, checked the hallway, and disappeared. Lowell watched her go, feeling the loss anew. This was one hell of a woman he'd walked out on twenty-five years ago.

He sneaked a slice of bacon, then she was back, with his two bags and the cardboard tube.

"These yours?"

He silently praised Ernie to the gods. "Yes. Thanks."

She didn't press him further until he had eaten, packing in a rasher of bacon, six eggs, and a quart of fresh-squeezed Florida orange juice. He insisted on clearing up the dishes while she watched, arms folded. Waiting.

"OK. Are you ready to talk?"

His stomach was appeased, but now he felt unclean again. "Any chance I could borrow a shower first? I'd feel a lot more human."

She didn't argue. "Follow me."

She led him through another doorway and down a long Berber-carpeted hallway with bright modern paintings on one side—all slashes and splashes of color. Lowell recognized a Pollock and a Rauschenberg. Wide French windows dominated the opposite wall, with drip-irrigated planter boxes along the baseboards. Blooms flourished in a myriad of colors: pinks, whites and purples, reds, yellows and violets—petunias, begonias, geraniums, gardenias, portulacas, purslane, and white birds of paradise (which Lowell had always considered gross). At the far end, he remembered, was the solarium. They had spent many a dreamy afternoon there on those wonderful days and weekends when the admiral had been on sea duty. A lifetime ago.

In lesser homes in this part of the country it would have been called the "Florida Room," but this was a true solarium, with French doors and windows all around on three sides and curved skylights above. Lush with tropical plants, and tastefully furnished with peach and pale blue upholstered rattan furniture (the furniture was new since his last visit), it was truly a beautiful space.

With a curt toss of her head, Caitlin pointed at a door adjacent to the one they'd just entered through.

"In there. Help yourself to towels and whatever. Do you want a change of clothes?"

He hesitated. "Well, I do have my Navy uniform but—"

She rolled her eyes. "I'll see what I can find." Looking him up and down, she left the room. Leaving him feeling foolish and exposed.

The bathroom was tiled with hand-painted Portuguese ceramics, white with discreet patterns of peach and rose blossoms. The fixtures were brass—suitably naval, he thought—and there was a shower with an etched art-deco pattern engraved on the opaque glass door. It was a profile of a nude woman: knees bent, back arched, arms outstretched as though celebrating the firmament—and one of the most sensuous depictions he had ever seen. All this was new, he realized. Previously, this had been little more than a lavatory and changing room for the pool, which was visible through the French exterior door beyond the shower and double-sink vanity.

Lowell made sure both doors were locked before entering the shower. He didn't want any more surprises just now.

15

Twenty minutes later, Caitlin Schoenkopf and Tony Lowell sat across from each other on upholstered rattan armchairs, a white onyx coffee table between them, sipping cappuccino and nibbling on bagels and cream cheese. Caitlin stared at the floor, at the wall, not looking at Tony. Waiting. He studied her fiery green eyes in wonder. She was half-Jewish—her mother was Irish—like mixing nitrogen and glycerin—and with a temperament to match. Finally, she looked at him and forced a puckish smile.

"Father's clothes suit you."

Lowell was dressed up like a kewpie doll, in his own opinion: a spanking new, bright white nautical outfit of matching shirt and slacks (an inch short) complete with blue anchors on the pocket flaps. He wasn't impressed. His eyes had turned gray, she noted. Matching the gathering storm clouds visible across the bay.

"Well, that's as far as it goes," he growled.

"All right. So why did you come here, Tony? You know how father feels about you."

He struggled for the right words and, as usual, with her, came up with the wrong ones. "And how do you feel about me?"

"Stop it!" she cried. "Tony, what happened to Elliot? And Maureen?"

"Hey," he said, recognizing her look and hating it. "Come on."

"I'm sorry. It's just that—"

"Dammit!" he threw down his bagel angrily. "I came to see you,

145

as the one person who would know better! Do you really think I'm going around killing people? Is that what you really think?"

"No! I don't! I just—I'm afraid. These things that are happening. And there's been nothing in the papers. Why is there nothing in the papers?"

"I don't know." He hadn't had the time or opportunity to read the papers. But he wasn't surprised. If someone would go to such lengths to delete the past, they wouldn't stop with the present. "I'm trying to find out. Listen, I need to get my bearings here. What happened to Elliot was my fault, I got him involved in this thing—"

"What thing?"

"I swear I don't know yet but it has something to do with power and money, and people you and your father are a lot closer to than I am. Caitlin, I need your help."

She stared at him a moment, wanting to believe. She let out a sigh, almost of relief. "Thank you for being honest with me at least. Father does not hate you by the way. He's just very angry with you."

"He and everybody else." He tried to laugh it off. "Anyway, fathers always hate their daughters' boyfriends. Don't they?"

"There was more to it than that, and you know it. Why do you hate your father? That's a lot worse, if you ask me."

She had him there. He wasn't even sure why, or whether he did anymore. He'd meant to find out who was handling his father's affairs. God knows he'd been negligent long enough. He wondered if Caitlin knew.

"He never saw me as a person. He was never there for me—he never spoke two words to me I can recall other than 'where the hell you been,' or 'shut your mouth!' And he treated my mother like shit. I can still remember him locking her out of the house at night, then passing out, drunk as a skunk."

"I know. I'm sorry."

"Well," he said, brusquely. "Enough about fathers. Let's get back to the present, unpleasant as it may be."

"Tony," she sighed after a moment, not taking the hint. "It isn't like you think."

146

He looked up at her, sharply. "What do you mean?"

"Father had some kind of a problem with your—with Chief Lowell. The chief was interfering with him in some way, something to do with business. I don't know what."

Lowell raised his eyebrows speculatively. This opened up some very interesting questions. But they were questions he didn't care to explore just now.

"Forget it. I've got more important things to worry about at the moment."

She wasn't finished yet. "It wasn't my father that broke us up."

"I know. It was me. I took off, and even after all these years I still can't explain that to myself. Let alone to you. All I can say is it was the stupidest thing I ever did, bar none."

"Stop it. The die was already cast by then. You'd already been banned from seeing me, remember?"

He smiled, in spite of it all. "That didn't stop us."

She looked away, blushing. "No. No, it didn't. But it sure slowed us down, as I recall."

His smile vanished. "Wait a minute. Your father—and mine—? You're saying that they—"

"The chief came to see Father. Actually, they wouldn't even speak to each other personally. He sent some sort of emissary. A cop, I think. Ordering him to keep me away from you. I think Dad was terribly insulted, I remember him screaming at Mom—it wasn't long after that that she left."

"But why? Just because of some business arrangement?"

"Partly. But there was more to it than that. Father always felt that it was because he was Jewish."

Tony was silent. He knew it was true. His father had been a bigot. A low-class, redneck bigot, who thought he was better than a top military officer with one of the finest homes and daughters in Florida. All because they were Jewish. Half-Jewish, actually. He had known this all along and somehow repressed it.

"You know who takes care of him now?"

Caitlin flushed slightly. "Do you really care?"

147

"No. But he is my father."

"Well, your cousins in Jupiter have power of attorney and charge of the pension and so forth. He's in a nursing home across the bay. They make sure he gets fed and sees a doctor once in a while. That sort of thing."

He stared at the floor, ashamed. "Jesus," was all he could manage to say.

"Anyway, it's no big deal. The place is clean and legit. And the pastor from the church pays him a call now and then. His needs are simple, apparently."

Tony thought of Lucretia Hartley and her Big Macs. He rose and walked to the window wall, staring out at the rose garden and bay beyond. Steam was rising from the lawns, where the sprinklers were still running.

"It's gonna be hot," he murmured.

She came over beside him, tentatively. "I know. Unusual for this time of year. Look at those clouds!"

He looked, then turned to her. "Your father's gripe was with my old man, not with me at all. Why couldn't he see that?"

She sighed. How complicated life was, and how simple it should be. "That's just it. Father had these great ambitions, don't you see? He was a regular Jay Gatsby. He came from a family of Navy brats, worked his way through Annapolis and up through the ranks, then went out and made—money. He wanted to be like—like Mr. Hartley. He wanted to be accepted as part of the upper crust of society. But they would never let him in. He was new money, don't you see? Not old. He wasn't good enough. That was aside from the Jewish thing."

"I still don't get what—"

"No, you see, what *really* got him was that you didn't respect that. You wanted to drop out, be a hippy or whatever, wear dirty jeans and long hair. The whole sixties thing, and he despised that more than anything. You have no idea how he despised that."

"Actually, that part I was able to deduce."

The corners of her mouth curled up, just slightly. God, I still love this woman, he found himself thinking. "So now you understand. Father is angry with you because your dad rejected him despite his values; and then you rejected him because of them."

He whirled on her. "Hey, I never rejected him."

She put her hand out and touched his arm gently. His entire body caught fire.

"You did. Of course you did. He was the establishment. The military establishment that you always railed against. Of course you rejected him."

"I went to fight the war, didn't I? And I got the scars to prove it!" He started to pull on his buttons. She stopped him, fingers lingering a moment.

"Yes, but not because you approved of it. And certainly not to please him."

He pulled away, unable to trust his feelings just now. "What your father never understood was that I had to be more than just another blue-collar yo-yo from Main Street. More than anything else, I wanted to be recognized, acknowledged, accepted for my accomplishments. Basically, I wanted to be somebody."

"So you and he were two peas in a pod, don't you see? Besides, you did it! You became the best photographer in the business back then. We had copies of all your magazines, all over the house."

He shook his head, furious with himself. Hating the way he'd squandered a love, a career, two decades of his life, and for what? Only to wind up solving seedy crimes and seamy divorces. It made him sick to think of it.

She seemed to read his thoughts. "What happened to you, Tony?"

He tried to laugh it off. "Same thing that happened to my whole generation. Too much drugs, and rock and roll."

She turned away from him angrily. "Can't you take *anything* seriously anymore? What *happened* to you?"

"A lot of people have been asking me that lately," he muttered, staring out across the broad lawns and gardens, toward the water. He

149

was thinking about the manatee, and his swim across the harbor last night. "I get by."

Caitlin sighed and sat down on the nearest rattan love seat, crumpling a corner of her sleeve in her fingers, like worry beads.

"Maybe it's I who missed the boat then."

He sat down, next to her. Careful to keep a discreet distance between them. She looked almost frightened.

"Why *didn't* you ever get married, get out? I mean, you're so attractive, you've got everything. Why *are* you still here?"

She smiled bitterly. If he only knew, she thought. But I'm not about to tell him. Not now. He's already forgotten about Maureen's message. The one I sent her with. I'm not going to remind him.

"Maybe that was my own kind of rebellion, Tony."

He moved closer, unable to help himself. She watched him coming, half-excited, half-afraid. She knew she wouldn't be able to stop herself. Or him.

"Some rebels, you and me," he said, shaking his head.

"Don't," she murmured. He seemed to tilt toward her, and her whole world turned upside down. This was going to be her downfall, she knew. But she couldn't help herself. She leaned forward, toward the cause of twenty years of torment and wasted youth.

"I never got over you, Tony Lowell. You ruined me for life."

"I'm sorry. Caitlin. Sorry, sorry, sorry."

"You're not forgiven," she murmured and they kissed. And the old passion, twenty years suppressed in both of them, finally rose to the surface and exploded forth like steam from a geyser.

"Wait!" she cried, breathless, breaking away. She rose and half-walked, half-ran to the door. He followed her, afraid she was going to leave. But she locked the deadbolt and turned back to face him, breathing hard. And then they flew into each other's arms, buttons and zippers popping right and left, fingers groping, clothes torn away and left where they fell, skin on skin.

They made love on a chaise lounge, mouths exploring each other like two starved children, tasting each other's sweetness and salt, hands caressing each once-familiar orifice and surface and fold,

150

remembering, renewing, rediscovering. Finding new wrinkles: a crease here at the corner of her eye; a little padding above his hip, a tuft of hair in his ears; a streak of gray just above, so distinguished, and sexy! A tiny band of fuzz above her lip. Not there twenty-five years ago. Or that blue vein on the inside of her thigh—the skin almost transparent, yet still so firm and perfect.

The passion of their reunion was total and without regret or recrimination. And so they made up as best they could for two decades of lost love, and they both came together as lovers so rarely do. Afterward they lay together, side by side, legs intertwined, sweat and saliva, body fluids mingling; he still inside her and firm enough for more; she content to rest, nipples and vagina sore from his lips and tongue and teeth and the size of him! She'd forgotten that part; his cock sore for the same reasons; both unaccustomed to such attention; she staring at the ceiling fan going round and round, her own head spinning, his eyes closed; numb. Both wondering what was to happen next.

Finally, he pulled away, sat up and started to dress. She watched him, a sudden terror gripping her, feeling it all trickling away once more.

"What do we do now, Tony?"

He looked at her, understood her fear, misconstrued. He didn't want to leave her. Not now. Not ever again. But there were events unfolding beyond his control, and he had no choice. He had wanted her help. But could he do that to her now?

He leaned over and kissed her furrowed brow, trying to remove the wrinkle of concern. Knowing that it was justified.

"Caitlin," he began, searching for the right words, "do you think it's possible to make things right again?"

She sat up, covering herself instinctively. Watching him dress, wanting to hate him for it.

"Like what?"

"I'd better show you." He cinched the admiral's too long belt, and went over to the coffee table where he'd left his belongings.

Picking up the poster tube, he removed the cap and carefully took out the poster.

Pulling on her panties and shorts, she picked up her blouse and came over to him. He wanted to make love to her again but restrained himself. Hoping upon hope that somehow they could be free at last to be together, when this was all over. He unrolled the poster, set aside the clippings, and showed it to her.

"Remember this?"

She let out a breath of girlish surprise. "The Folk Festival! You took me there to see the Lovin' Spoonful! We were what, eighteen? Where did you get this?"

"Elliot."

Her face fell, and she put her blouse over her still-inflamed breasts, protectively.

He unfolded the clippings and photos Elliot had so carefully saved for him and laid them out on the table, pushing the cups and dishes to one side. Pulling on her blouse, she came closer, curiosity getting the best of her.

"Someone killed Maureen Fitzgerald for something she knew and kept quiet about for two and a half decades."

"But why? I don't understand."

"I think she had knowledge that could implicate Judge Michael B. Folner, our about-to-be new Supreme Court Justice, in some kind of conspiracy. A conspiracy that may have led to the death of Henry Hartley and the financial ruin of his mother."

She stared at him, shocked. "Do you know what you're saying?"

"I know. It sounds incredible. But she told me she saw someone push Henry Hartley overboard. And she used the word 'murder.' She was very explicit about it."

Caitlin shook her head, trying to absorb this.

"There's more," he went on. "She brought a photograph, I'm pretty certain it's of Julie, kissing some man, which I think Maureen believed might have changed the outcome of Lucretia Hartley's slander case."

She frowned. "Can I see it?"

He dug it out of his pack and handed it to her. She studied it while he sorted through the other materials. "They look like they're in love," she said, handing it back.

He nodded.

"But even if it's him, they're married."

"Yes. Now. But that's not all. There's another of Julie on the boat the night Henry drowned with a guy who isn't Henry."

"You can't draw conclusions from that either. She probably mingled with everybody."

"Maybe. But not everybody would be feeling her up, would they?"

She gasped and leaned closer to study the photo. The image was indistinct, but it was possible that a hand—blurry and in shadows—might be cupping the woman's breast. The man's face was barely visible.

"You can't tell from this. Assuming that's Julie, how do you know that's not Henry with her?"

"Because," said Lowell, tapping the left-hand corner of the picture, "I was there. This is Henry here. The one coming up the companionway." He pointed at a shadowy figure in the foreground, back to the camera, approaching the couple in the background. She shook her head. Julie she recognized right away. But the man with her, and the one moving toward them? It might be Folner and Henry. Or it might not.

She shook her head, unconvinced. "It could just be some masher, somebody with one drink too many hitting on her. You're going to need more than this, Tony."

"All right. But Maureen also implied she saw some hanky-panky going on. 'He was kissing her,' she said. That doesn't sound like she meant her husband."

"Maybe not. But—"

"Caitlin, somebody killed Elliot to keep him from uncovering these, I'm certain of it. I think what they are going to add up to is proof that Judge Folner was in fact involved in something that makes him, at the very least, unsuitable for the high court."

She caught her breath. "If that's true, then you are in terrible danger. You've got to get out of here, go to the authorities or—"

"What authorities? The ones who are after me now?"

"I—I don't know!" She touched his arm, as though afraid it would be for the last time.

"Take a look at this," he went on, showing her the photo in front of the courthouse. "This is young widow Julie after she's just won the slander trial. With Mike Folner again. That's him here."

"Yes, but he was her lawyer, wasn't he?"

"Exactly."

"And you think Folner's behind all this?"

"Let's put it this way. He's got the most at stake here. His entire future is riding on this nomination."

"You're saying this Hartley thing could ruin him? That he might go to any lengths necessary to cover himself, even murder?"

He shrugged. "I'm saying it's possible."

"That's quite a reach, Tony. I think you'd better get some proof first. These photos don't look like they'd prove a thing."

"I know. But there are other shots I haven't had a chance to look over yet. There's something in here that was damning enough to cost Elliot his life. And I don't know what it is yet, but I'm going to find it. If I can just get these back to my photo lab, and then access a computer somewhere, there are things that can be done. Image enhancement. Details that can be brought out. I've got to do it, Caitlin."

"Why you? Why does it have to be you? Can't you give it to the police and let them handle it?"

"I've thought about that. But there're two things. First of all, Maureen hired me. Or she was about to when she got whacked."

She turned away, hand over her mouth.

"Then, there's a cop who's been tailing me since Gulfbridge. She's only interested in who killed Maureen. I don't think there's a frog's chance in a pool of snapping turtles that she'd touch this thing. Who would? This guy Folner is Senator Grimm's pal, for chrissake! And you know how much weight that old bastard carries."

"Oh my God, Tony!"

"And that's not all. I saw Lucretia Hartley last night. She's crazier than a loon. But she told me that Maureen Fitzgerald was grabbed and taken away before she could go to the police. She was never allowed to testify at the trial either. Which confirms what Maureen was trying to tell me."

"You can't take that seriously. I mean, Lucretia was ranting that sort of stuff all along, wasn't she?"

"Right. Which is why nobody took her seriously after awhile. But what if she was right? Maureen herself said she'd seen a murder. And that she was taken against her will. Was she loony too?"

"They put her away, didn't they?"

"Yes, and didn't you ever wonder why?"

"No. We all assumed she just flipped out. They sent her to Endicott, right?"

"Yes. And there they kept her until a doctor let her out a few weeks ago. Did you know about that?"

She faltered and looked away. "Y-yes. But—"

"Then maybe you should know that doctor was also murdered."

Caitlin looked stunned. He touched her arm gently.

"I'm sorry, Caitlin. To dump all this on you like that. But I think Maureen was deliberately prevented from talking, was deliberately put away to discredit her—forever! And her getting out when she did was a mistake by a conscientious doctor who violated orders—from somewhere—and paid for it. First with his job. Then with his life."

She began to tremble and spoke as though in a trance, her voice a monotone. "She came here after the doctor let her out. She used to take care of me when Father was away, remember?"

Of course. How could he have forgotten? That was when they met. As two kids in adolescence, just discovering their independence. And their sexuality. It had been a powerful mix. All those memories of adolescent discovery and infatuation must have blotted out any

155

recollection of the woman who had allowed it to happen. Now he owed Maureen more than ever.

"She was like a ghost come to life," Caitlin went on. "I was so shocked. I think she wanted to see Lucretia, but she was afraid. I think she wanted to make amends for what happened."

"Did she indicate anything about some kind of jewel? Like something she might have taken, maybe wanted to return? Anything like that?"

"No. Why?"

"Forget it." He decided to drop the jewel angle. He'd probably misheard Maureen's gasping final words. In any case it was pretty much a dead end. Nothing relating to any missing gems or jewels had turned up. "Go on," he said.

"Well," she continued, "she was looking at the paper that morning when all of a sudden for no reason she suddenly had to see you! Tony, I didn't know what would happen!" Caitlin was in tears now, sobbing. And he couldn't help her. He was too numb. "I-I knew you were a private investigator. And I wanted her to—to bring you a message!"

Tony's mind was racing. "You knew where I was all these years?"

"Yes, father's attorneys had you traced. He— I wanted to call a million times. You have no idea."

He looked away. He had a pretty good idea actually.

"What message?" he finally said, his voice barely audible. "I never got it."

That explains a lot, she thought. I didn't think he could be *that* uncaring.

"Tony," she began, "when I said some things never change— that wasn't quite true. There was something that happened between us that did change things, in spite of the war, in spite of our parents, in spite of everything. But it was too late."

"You're talking in riddles," he said, turning to the window. "Get to the point."

Outside, he could see the driveway snaking through the pine woods that dominated the southern section of the island, on out to

156

the dead end of Ocean Avenue. Off to the right, a blue Ford sedan appeared like a specter, gliding slowly down the service road toward the house. Behind it was a black Mercedes—The admiral's car! was his instant thought—and behind that two Palm Coast Harbor police cars.

He pulled back quickly from the window, and Caitlin looked at him in alarm.

"Is it my father?" She looked past him and caught her breath. "Oh my God, he's brought the police. How did he know to—"

"Never mind that now. I have to get off the island. They've been looking for me since last night, and they'll be watching the ferries and the bridge." He looked at the dock, then at her.

She gasped. "The *Wellington!* But you'll need help with that. I'm going with you. We were going to go out sailing this afternoon. The gear is on board but—you can't sail it alone."

He felt torn. There was nothing in the world he'd love more than to go out with her again on that boat. But not now, for God's sake, not like this.

"I can't let you risk that. I can solo it, I have to. Caitlin, please."

The cars had reached the turnout now and slowed to a stop. She could see the two agents get out, and her father come over to join them, followed by four local cops—almost the entire force. Apparently departmental loyalties ended with the next generation. Her heart pounded, trying to decide what to do.

There was a loud knock at the door, making them both jump. The knob rattled. My God, she thought. Please, don't let it be—

"Mom!" came a clear, strong young female voice through the door. "Are you in there?"

Tony realized, with a shock, that he'd heard that voice before. "Mom?"

"J-just a minute!" Caitlin didn't dare meet Tony's eyes, now wide with wonder.

Caitlin hurried to the door, events now careening out of any hope of control. She unlocked it. A stunning young woman entered, blond, around twenty, wearing short-shorts and a baggy sweatshirt.

157

The same young woman with whom Caitlin had been playing tennis.

"Mom, the police are here! What's—" She caught sight of Tony and stopped, flustered. She looked back at her mother. Questioning. Caitlin held her breath a moment, trying to hide her utter, complete panic.

"Ariel, this is—an old friend, Mr. Lowell. Tony, this is my daughter, Ariel. Honey, no questions now. I want you to go to your room and stay there, please. Hurry!"

The young woman hesitated, gave Tony a sharp, inquisitive look, and shrugged. She trusted her mother implicitly. She'd find out later what this was all about.

"Yes, Mother."

The young woman hurried away with one shrewd, quick backward glance. Tony stared after her. He should have known. How could he have been so blind? She had his changing eyes and patrician nose. But, he thought with his irrepressible sense of humor— she's beautiful all the same.

His daughter!

He turned back to Caitlin, knowing there was no time. For anything. "Why didn't you tell me?"

"I tried to." Her terror had turned now to hopelessness. She looked at him, pleading. "Please go, now. If you have to go, go!"

He was frozen to the spot, unable to move. They could hear footsteps running across the drive. She literally had to push him out the French door to the rose garden, shoving his things into his hands. He ran. Dog-tired, but now motivated by a new sense of purpose. He had a daughter. And somehow, some way, he was going to see her again.

16

The twelve-meter sloop *Wellington* had been built in 1961, at a cost of over $200,000. It would cost ten times that today. The admiral loved it as his most prized possession, and kept it spic and span and as shipshape and seaworthy as the day it was launched. His dream was to race it again one day. Today was to have been a practice run for that unscheduled eventuality. The weather was perfect—unseasonably warm, winds steady from the southeast, at 12 to 18 knots, only a slight chance of thundershowers. Thundershowers, in October!

Unfortunately for the admiral, his longtime adversary and archrival for the love and devotion of his little girl was going to be needing the boat today. So sorry, Admiral, but you know how it is. And thanks for having it rigged and ready.

Lowell cut through the gardens and sprinted the remaining hundred yards across the open lawns before being spotted. It was the admiral himself who saw him. Yelling for the police, he knew at once what Lowell was up to.

"Sergeant!" he shouted. He'd had a bypass three years ago and could no longer run. The others would have to take the baton, and godspeed to them. If he had his way, that young man, once apprehended, would spend the rest of his days doing hard time at Leavenworth. Or Tallahassee. Or wherever they put people for capital crimes.

Lowell made it to the *Wellington* without looking back. He could hear the admiral's shouts and curses behind him. There was no hope of slipping away now. He could only hope they didn't have a power launch too handy. The cops had one, down at the Harbor. But the Harbor Patrol usually used it at the north end of the island to monitor marine traffic at the drawbridge. On a day like today there'd be a lot. Which would give him some time. Maybe twenty, thirty minutes.

He threw his gear into the cockpit, freed the stern line, leapt on board, and froze.

Someone had gotten there ahead of him. Someone waiting calmly, arms folded. Wearing an expensive, blue worsted business suit with ruffled white blouse. Neatly pressed as always. Detective Lena Bedrosian seemed in no hurry.

"How the hell—?"

She shrugged, smugly. "I've been watchin' you. I know about you and her. I know about you and boats. And I know about you and cops. I knew they'd come for you, added it all up, and figured you'd have to come this way."

He had to hand it to her.

"From what I hear about you," she continued, "this isn't the first time you've done this."

Lowell's hopes plunged. "Done what?"

The detective nodded back at the house, where two blond women had just appeared on a second-floor balcony, watching their departure like ancient mariners' wives on a widow's walk. "Left them two. She really does look like you. I saw her in town. She is your daughter, right?"

Lowell glanced back again, helplessly. He had maybe half a minute, and this policewoman was going to toss it away like a stale cigarette.

"I never knew until now. What did you expect me to do, bring them along?"

Bedrosian shrugged. "Guess not. Guess you got a problem, don't you?"

Responding to the admiral's shouts, Werner and Lefcourt came around the side of the house, looked where he was pointing, and stopped in confusion. Lowell they expected to see. But who was this well-dressed woman who seemed to have appeared out of nowhere? They broke into a run, the admiral panting behind. The local cops were still stationed out front, there was no time to get them.

Lowell watched them coming. "Look, Detective, I'm kinda in a hurry. Are you on the boat or off?"

He brushed past her and hit the auxiliary diesel starter button. The admiral had put in a diesel after the trials to facilitate recreational sailing. It cranked over but wouldn't start.

"Come on!" he tried it again. In frustration, he turned on Bedrosian, still leaning against the gunwale. "You wanna make yourself useful, untie the goddamn bow line. I'm shoving off!"

The Feds were halfway across the lawn now, former Washington Redskin Cecil Lefcourt leading the charge.

Bedrosian glanced at them, icily calm. "That mean you're ready to talk?"

"Only if you help me get outta here!"

The detective considered quickly. She wanted to talk to Lowell urgently, and knew the Feds would have other, very different priorities. This would be her last chance.

"OK," she decided. "We take a little sail, have a little talk. But you're still gonna have to deal with them, you know."

"I'll worry about that later. Let's go!"

Bedrosian moved. But her leather soles were slipping on the deck. Lowell cursed, trying the starter again.

"C'mon! C'mon!"

The detective made it up onto the bow deck and managed to free the line from the jam cleat, just as the engine caught. Sputtering in loud protest, the diesel kicked up a cloud of black smoke as Lowell thrust the drive forward into gear. No time to warm it up.

They were clear of the dock by six feet—the smoke actually to their advantage—when Lefcourt arrived, swearing, at the spot they'd just vacated. Lefcourt on the dock and Bedrosian on board

161

the boat took measure of one another, as the distance between them grew wider. Werner joined his partner and shouted:

"Lowell! What the hell are you doing? Bring it about!"

Lowell chose to ignore the command and headed for open water as fast as possible.

The admiral came lumbering across the lawn toward them, waving his arms. The local cops converged around him, gesturing apologetically.

"Lowell!" Breathless with rage and exertion, the admiral shouted at the agents. "Stop him. He's stealing my boat! That's grand larceny, by God!"

One of the cops reached for his gun. Werner put a hand on his arm, with a shake of his head. "That's a woman on board. Better let us handle this." He cupped his hands and shouted: "Lowell, we just want to talk!"

The cops conferred with the Feds in urgent tones. Werner nodded, whispered to his partner, and shouted out to Bedrosian. "Lady! Are you Detective Lena Bedrosian, from Manatee City?"

"That's right," she called back.

"Your captain is working with us. Bring the suspect back, now!"

"He's not a suspect! Anyway, I'd have to hear that from the captain!" She replied.

"You'll be briefed. Bring him in!"

"I *am* bringing him in!"

She ignored Lowell's glare at that.

"Lowell! This is your last warning! Come about or the admiral presses charges!"

"Can't hear you," responded Lowell. "Too much engine noise!"

Werner and Lefcourt exchanged looks, nonplussed. The yacht was pulling away steadily. Bedrosian grinned. She had a police officer's natural resentment and suspicion of Federal agents. Especially the way they assumed priority over local jurisdictions. Besides, from her limited experience, most of them were even worse chauvinists than the local cops.

"Detective Bedrosian! For the last time. We are Federal agents,

162

with orders to detain this man. You're interfering with a federal investigation. Bring the goddamn boat back to dock!"

"I can't!" She spread her palms in regret. Suddenly the helpless female. "I don't know how to sail!"

"Do something, for God's sake!" shouted the admiral.

Werner swore, looking around. His eyes fell on the Catalina. So be it. "You're the admiral, Admiral." He gestured to his partner. "Come on," he said. "We're going after them."

"Wait a minute," protested the admiral. "In my boat?"

"You have a better idea?" demanded Werner. "By the time we get harbor patrol or a chopper out here, they'll be across the channel."

While the admiral blustered some more, Lefcourt surveyed the situation. This was something new to him. Closest he'd ever come to a sailboat was the Staten Island Ferry. He wasn't fond of open water. Still, he'd had scuba and water-safety training, and was a competent swimmer. He wasn't worried about handling it. But a glance south told him they might be in for a rough time. There were storm clouds gathering.

"I'm holding you and your agency responsible for both those craft, you don't bring them in as is!" threatened the admiral.

Werner ignored him. He didn't want to have to deal with the old fart just now. Let alone those local yahoos. He'd been raised on Long Island, and knew boats the way teenage boys knew cars. If they wanted to make a chase of it, that was a contest he would most certainly win. He ran back down to the Catalina and jumped on board, Lefcourt right behind him. The Catalina was a good boat, fast (by motor-sailer standards) and easy to sail. Its one weakness was a lack of structural durability; they weren't designed for heavy weather. Even so, no way that huge black dinosaur up ahead would escape, twelve meters or not. It depended on sail power: massive square footage of canvas, which needed a crew of at least eight to run. No way Lowell and a lady cop in a three-piece suit could do it. No way in the world.

With an apologetic wave to the admiral—now livid at the sight of both his prized boats being commandeered—he shoved off, jimmying the ignition. The engine started immediately. Lefcourt didn't have to be told what to do. He cast off both bow and stern lines like a veteran sailor, and they surged out onto the bay in full pursuit.

While Werner manned the helm, Lefcourt checked his weapons. He had the 9-millimeter Baretta, of course. And a collapsible, high-powered Remington 700 BDL .308 sniper gun. Bolt action, single shot with immense accuracy and stopping power, popular with the C.I.A. It might be necessary, this time out. Woman cop or no. But he'd make that decision himself. Not this hothead Werner he was beginning to get tired of.

The Catalina was moving smartly now. Werner expertly pointed up at an angle that would intersect with the twelve-meter's still-erratic course in a matter of minutes.

Badly winded, the admiral finally reached the pier and threw down his hat, furious. He whirled on the hapless policemen, who withered before him. Someone would have to bear the blame for this, and they were all too handy.

On board the *Wellington*, Lowell struggled to cope with the crosswinds, now from due east. The woman detective was no help at all, and he was going to need some. Seeing the two Feds launching the Catalina, it didn't surprise him. The small guy had shown some knowledge of boats, and the big guy could probably raise a Genoa with his left hand while reading the directions with his right. These guys would be hard to shake. Jesus, just what he needed, on top of everything. He checked the wind and the markers, and nudged the power on full. They were clear of the Schoenkopf's private inlet, heading toward the open bay.

Bedrosian ignored the chase, preoccupied with her shoes. She tried to wipe them off with a corner of the hatch cover. Lowell stifled a snarl. "Better get rid of those, or you'll fall on your ass. You need rubber soles on a boat."

The detective hesitated, then complied sullenly. "So," she intoned, "you gonna tell me yet? How come two people are worm food and you got the whole United States of America after you?"

"Three people," corrected Lowell, adjusting the course slightly. "I found another one last night."

She tried to cover her surprise. "What!? Who?"

"Maureen's doctor. I went down to see him about her, and somebody else got there first."

She stared at him. "Jesus Christ. I don't believe this. What are you, the Grim Reaper? Did you call the police?"

"No time." Lowell opened a locker beneath the wheel box and took out a pair of binoculars, which he trained back on the Catalina.

"Incredible. You got charges piling up right and left: stealing a boat, leaving the scene of a crime, what else you got up your sleeve?"

"I got his daughter's permission." He nodded aft. "You know for a fact those guys are what they say they are?"

Bedrosian spread her palms. "Hey, I only know as much as you, mister. You're the one who checked their credentials."

Lowell handed the binocs to Bedrosian, who almost slipped and fell trying to adjust them. "Better remove the stockings, too."

She glared and handed back the binocs. She couldn't tell anything by looking anyway. Except they meant business.

"You know boats at all?" Lowell wanted to know.

"My father was a sponge diver. Went down in a squall off Crystal River when I was ten. I swore then I would never go near another boat again. Up until now I was doin' just fine."

"Sorry about your father. But maybe since you're along for the ride, you might lend a hand. With this wind we can beat any auxiliary inboard, if we can get some sails up."

"You're the captain," she snapped sarcastically.

Lowell took that for what it was worth. "Fine. Then see if you can untie that tarp and loose the main."

"Who the what?"

Lowell pointed at the boom, braced above Bedrosian's head—suppressing his annoyance. "That canvas there. Unwrap it."

With a scowl, Bedrosian sat on the gunwale, pulled off her stockings, and went to work on the tarp. She had no intention of losing

165

sight of her reason for being on board, however. "Lowell," she shouted, into the rising wind, "who're you workin' for now?"

"Lucretia Hartley." Ignoring her outraged stare, he kept his eyes fixed on the horizon. Huge cumulus clouds were billowing skyward, to the south. Very unusual for this time of year, but it was an unseasonably warm day, so you never knew.

"Another old lady. Maybe you should consider retirement."

"Maybe you're right."

Lost in thought, Bedrosian forgot the tarp, which suddenly came flying loose. She dived after it, feeling ridiculous, her jacket sleeves rolled up, feet bare and cold, lace collar flapping in the wind. Struggling with all her might, she managed to get hold of the sheet. Furiously, she tore at the sailor's hitch until it surrendered, and the line was free. The canvas came tumbling loose, caught the breeze and billowed out, heeling the boat sharply over to starboard.

Lowell yelled, turning up into the wind. "Watch it! Can you reach that halyard? The rope tied off on that cleat!"

"What the hell's a cleat?"

"Jesus." Lowell knew at this point that they were in deep trouble. By contrast, a hundred yards behind him Bud Werner on the Catalina had a novice but highly competent mate—strong, determined, and a quick learner. If Lowell didn't do something, they were going to overtake him very quickly. And for starters, he was going to have to handle the rigging himself.

"Take the helm!" he shouted, indicating the wheel. "Just steer dead ahead. I gotta get the sails up. This was never intended to be a motor boat!"

They switched places, and Lowell managed to get the main halyard power winch operating. Bedrosian watched in awe as the enormous mainsail rose up to the sky, eight hundred square feet flapping like great pterodactyl wings, to the top of the sixty-five-foot mast. Now to winch down the boom vang, then, block and tackle clear and set, easy, easy, ease the main sheet through the winch, pull fast, and—

"OK, here we go!" Lowell kicked out the boom cradle, let loose the main sheet, and watched the sail fill out, luffing wildly. "Hold your course, I'll take over."

He scrambled back, grabbed the helm, and headed up into a starboard tack. The boom swung sharply to the right, almost decapitating the startled cop, who had to scramble for a handhold as the boat heeled way over, water pouring over the rail. Lowell loved the feel of wind and water rushing past, the tug of the sail, the power of nature held in his hands (with the assist of two ninety-pound power winches). This would have been Lowell's idea of heaven but for the fact that he had a woefully inexperienced mate, and they were in dire straits.

He glanced back. They were pulling steadily away from the Cat. But Werner was scrambling out onto the foredeck to hoist his own sails. So, thought Lowell. It's going to be a race. But this time, I intend to win.

Something skittered across the cockpit floor with a hollow, rattling sound. Bedrosian saw it first, reached down, and snatched it up. Shit, thought Lowell. Elliot's papers.

There was a rumble of distant thunder. Lowell studied the sky ahead, darkening rapidly. Thunderheads! Bedrosian seemed to sense that there was a problem. She followed his gaze. Lowell had to make a decision. Head into the storm, or run before it? Either way would mean strong winds and rough seas. But running was always dangerous, especially when grossly undermanned, and the only way to go was up the bay toward the bridge. The other option was better—if they could make it. The inlet was less than a mile away, and the open sea lay beyond. He'd take his chances on the open sea.

Bedrosian seemed to read his thoughts. "Lowell, there's a storm coming! What the hell are you gonna do?"

"We need another sail. I'm going to shorthaul the main and fly the jenny. Can you take the helm again?"

She felt sick. All in all, she'd as soon be walking on coals. Enough already, she decided. Enough of this constant struggle to prove herself. It was time to throw in the towel. Head for shore and safety. She could take her lumps with the Feds. As for this guy—

"Maybe we better turn back," she shouted, as Lowell fastened the main sheet and turned the wheel over to her once again.

"Just hold the course steady."

She started to object. Lowell ignored her, scrambling along the gunwale to the foredeck. The seas were getting choppier now, and the footing tricky. He had kept on his own old sneakers; the admiral's Docksiders that Caitlin had offered were too tight. But sneakers weren't the greatest boat shoes either. Hanging on to a forestay, he managed to pull the hatch cover to the sail loft below. Now to get the Genoa rigged and hoisted. Normally, there would be three men just to do this one job. But he'd manage it. If that cop didn't capsize them first. Bedrosian was trying to hold course, but it was difficult even for a seasoned sailor, and getting more so by the minute. Lowell knew he would have to hurry.

Thunder again. Closer, more insistent. With a gargantuan effort, he heaved the huge sailcloth up onto the deck, scrambled after it, and located the clew. Clamping on the halyard, he slipped the hoist into its notch and reached for the power winch, hoping the power assist was still working. Otherwise, the race was over.

The winch worked, and the sail rose majestically into the bright sunlit sky, almost heaving Bedrosian overboard as it caught the wind. Lowell cursed himself for not remembering the sheets, but managed to catch one end as it whipped back and forth and loop it around the hand winch on the starboard side. Now for the other, then he'd have control—or would once he regained the helm.

Bedrosian was more than ready to oblige, staring in wide-eyed wonder at the huge canvases billowing above.

"How in hell did you get those up there?"

"Kinda wonder myself." Lowell trimmed the sails, the wind took hold, and they were flying. "Better hang on, we're in for a ride," he warned. Bedrosian didn't need to be told twice.

Lowell watched the skyline and the approaching squall. Florida thunderstorms were legendary. The sheer suddenness of their appearance, the violence of their passing, the intensity of the thunder and brilliance and voltage of the lightning—it was often as not as horizontal as vertical, as explosive as piercing, making for a phenomenon unparalleled anywhere on Earth.

Lowell was about to come about when a helicopter, a Bell Jet Ranger, loomed out of nowhere, coming on fast. It was on top of them in an instant, hovering above the stern, flattening the chop before he'd even seen it. The sound of its approach had been muffled by the rumbling thunder. But Bedrosian had spotted it and was ready; she stood waiting. Already the detective is getting her sea legs, was Lowell's oddly admiring thought.

A sandy-haired man in sunglasses and a short-sleeved white shirt leaned out of the side door with a bullhorn and shouted above the din: "This is the F.B.I. You are under arrest. Turn back to shore. You are under arrest."

Bedrosian flipped her wallet open and flashed her police badge up at them. "I'm a police officer!" she shouted. "This man is in my custody!"

Up in the Jet Ranger, the two men strained to see what it was she was waving at them. Keller, the pilot said, "Who the hell is the dame?"

"Looks like she's flashing a badge. May be a cop," came the puzzled reply.

"Fuck it," growled his partner, Durkin. "They said take out the guy. They didn't say anything about a woman or a cop."

The *Wellington*'s towering mast was whipping back and forth, dangerously close to the rotor blades. Keller pulled back a little.

"Better tell them again. We don't know who the woman is, and if she's law enforcement that changes the whole ball game."

Durkin raised the bullhorn once more: "This is your last warning. Heave to! You are under arrest!"

Lowell chose to ignore them. He was watching the squall line now, calculating the distance. He estimated it at a quarter mile. Pointing up into the wind and close-hauling as much as he dared, he headed straight for it. The Catalina was hanging back now, presumably allowing the Jet Ranger room to operate.

Bedrosian didn't notice what Lowell was up to yet. Neither did the two men in the chopper.

Keller ran out of patience. "Better give 'em a warning shot. He doesn't look like he's slowing down any."

"You gonna take the heat for this? We shoot a cop all hell's gonna break loose. Especially a woman cop!"

"Just do it!"

Durkin shrugged, and reached for the gun rack behind him. He pulled down an M-16 A-1 .223-caliber automatic assault rifle, and snapped a fifty-round cartridge into the chamber. He'd aim for the instrument panel and give them one quick burst. It usually did the trick, lots of flying glass and wood chips. Usually scared the shit out of any sane person. And if they did show any resistance, he'd knock the guy to the deck with a burst to the legs or shoulder, and let him crawl. The woman would get the message, badge or no badge. He'd seen that ploy enough times not to give it a second thought.

"Watch the boat, Durkin," warned Keller. "Word is, it's some retired admiral's, and he doesn't want it chewed up any."

"Fuck him. He wants our help, he takes his chances," growled Durkin. He raised his aim and carefully fired a quick burst into the water. Just to get their attention.

"Son of a bitch!" Bedrosian dove for cover behind the bulkhead door, scraping her knee. She looked out, shaking her fist angrily. "You assholes! I'm a cop, godammit!"

"They don't seem impressed." Lowell's eyes were fixed on the squall line: an almost solid wall of rain, with eddies churning at its front edge. It was going to be one hell of a blow.

The helicopter moved around to the bow of the twelve-meter, trying to get directly in front of them. Lowell wondered if they'd even noticed the weather front yet. They were about to get an ugly surprise if they haven't, he thought.

Both men in the chopper had their eyes riveted on their quarry. Keller was trying for radio confirmation as to the next move, but the static was getting heavy. Durkin stared down at Lowell balefully. He moved his hand along the stock, seeking a good firm grip in the lurching air. Sighting carefully, he tried to compensate for the movement.

Suddenly there was a tremendous clap of thunder simultaneous to the flash, almost directly overhead. Bedrosian whirled as though struck, and her jaw dropped. "Holy mother—!" she muttered, as the squall hit.

The Jet Ranger was knocked almost ninety degrees horizontal by the frontal assault. Keller, the pilot, had to fight for his life, literally, to right the machine and pull out. Winds howled, and rain poured into the open cockpit in buckets amid an almost constant barrage of thunder and lightning. Keller managed to get the Ranger out of there. Barely.

As the pilot fled for the far shore and safety, he glanced at his partner. Durkin was frozen to his seat, gripping the sides with both hands, knuckles white. The gun lay on the floor, forgotten. The front of Durkin's pants were soaking wet, the stain spreading outward. He didn't notice yet. He wouldn't. Not until they had safely landed.

Down on the boat deck, Bedrosian managed to hang on. Lowell crawled over and handed her a life preserver, with a length of rope.

"Put that on," he shouted, above the howling wind, "and tie yourself to that cleat over there!" Bedrosian nodded.

Waves were breaking over the gunwale, as Lowell fought to keep the boat from capsizing. There was much too much sail now. He should have known better. It had been too long.

"Bedrosian!" he shouted, into the wind. "You're going to have to steer!" She shook her head. No way. She could hardly stand, let alone navigate.

"I have to bring in the sails or we'll go over!" That possibility worried Lowell above all others. But it wasn't the only worry. Lightning was crashing all around, and he'd seen it light up the spars of a full-fledged barkentine like a Christmas tree.

Another wave crashed over them, and it took all Lowell's strength to turn into the wind enough to luff the sails. But that left them at the mercy of the seas, and Bedrosian saw the danger.

171

"I'll take it!" she scrambled to the wheel post. Lowell gave it to her, and crawled up to the bulkhead and foredeck ladder. Bedrosian pressed the starter, and the diesel sputtered, then started. A few memories came back from her father's day. Lowell nodded, approving. The engine power would give them some control at least.

Lowell climbed out onto the top deck, fully exposed to the elements, knowing he would have to handle stainless-steel winches and sails that were waving, beckoning to the electrical storm like Ben Franklin's kite. But he had no choice. Since he had already loosed the main and Genoa stays, the sails were whipping back and forth like the tail of a giant stingray. And the boom—no time to get that brace in place, until the sails were down. All he could do was tie the downhaul tight, aft of the cockpit, and hope for the best.

Now for the halyards. If he could just release the winch lock—there! The Genoa came flying down, the gale trying to tear it free. He knew he would never be able to bring it in against such winds. With an odd pang of regret, he dug his Swiss Army knife from his pocket and cut the great sail loose. The wind immediately seized it like a prize, and bore it away into the stormy mist like a huge white bird. Somebody over on the mainland was going to be in for a hell of a surprise not long from now.

Immediately, the boat began to right itself, the heavy keel giving it ballast and stability. Next came the mainsail. Maybe he could short-haul it, as he'd planned to do earlier. That meant wrapping and folding half its yardage, then tying it off to make a half-sail. This was a sailor's foul weather improvisation, when there was no time to change to a smaller sail, or no such sail was available. A bear of a job to be doing in a storm while the boat tossed and heaved, at the mercy of waves and lightning. Meanwhile that landlubber cop was at the helm doing God knows what, and he'd be lucky to stay on board long enough to find out.

Bedrosian held course and watched Lowell's ordeal, unable to assist, not fully comprehending. It seemed like a slow-motion dream, as Lowell pulled himself, foot by foot, along the entire length of the boom, gathering sail, folding, wrapping, and tying it off.

The squall had already lessened by the time Lowell collapsed onto a flotation cushion in the corner of the cockpit, exhausted. Bedrosian regarded him a few moments, then heaved over the side. They had come through the worst of it.

The Catalina had vanished, lost in the storm.

17

The storm departed as quickly as it had come, disappearing across the water like a curtain opening up to reveal a once-again dazzling afternoon. The clouds were unmatched in beauty: huge, towering white formations of enormous stored power. Like giant stacked scoops of melting vanilla ice cream, flowing and churning. The thunder receded, and the waters of the bay flattened out once again, as though nothing had happened.

Lowell inspected the yacht for damage and noted with satisfaction that there was none, other than a small rip on the outseam of the mainsail. Easy to repair.

Bedrosian had the look of someone who's just come out of a triple bypass, surprised to be alive. She shook it off and glanced down at her drenched, ruined clothes—scuffed and ripped from the chafing and tumbling struggle to stay afloat and on board.

"Well, there goes a five hundred dollar suit."

Lowell wasn't sure if she was serious or not. "Lucky you're not out a lot more than that."

Bedrosian scowled. "To hell with that." She decided to change the subject. "Where does a government employee get the bucks for a boat like this anyway?"

Lowell shrugged, remembering Caitlin's vague comparisons of her father to Fitzgerald's Jay Gatsby. "This is the land of opportunity."

"Right. Like that opera singer who married what's-his-name,

Hartley. Looks like she lucked into a nice little opportunity, didn't she? That Folner musta been one hell of a lawyer."

"Yeah. Is this a great country or what?"

She gave him a sharp look and turned her gaze to the shoreline, while Lowell repaired the rigging. If he wasn't so exhausted from the storm ordeal, he'd loose the main and haul it up full again. Instead, he let the boat drift, moving softly, for the moment. He shut down the engine, tired of the noise and fumes, wanting to conserve fuel.

"I just figured out what it is about this place," remarked the cop, as mansion after mansion floated past. They'd actually been blown north almost to the causeway. "Everybody around here is either a millionaire, or sleeps with one."

Lowell laughed. The detective was closer to the truth than she knew. He indicated the poster canister, wedged under a bilge pump handle on the floor of the cockpit—forgotten until now. "Go ahead and take a look at what's in there."

Bedrosian glanced at him, picked up the wet but still intact tube, and ducked down below into the galley. Lowell watched the sky, for any more surprises. A glance aft, in the direction they'd just come, produced one right away. The Catalina. Still on their course, running a single jib on each mast.

"Jesus!" he exclaimed to no one. "The guy can sail!"

Down below, Bedrosian studied the articles and clippings with marked skepticism, at first. Most duplicated what she'd already seen. There was nothing particularly new or revelatory. The girl kissing the guy looked like Julie, but he looked like her husband, so what of it? The man by the car after the trial was probably Folner all right. But again, so what? He was supposed to be there. She couldn't make much of the negatives—mostly society balls and such. But there was one photo—of a man on a boat. He was in the shadows, near the stern it looked like. With some woman. She looked closer. The woman looked like Julie again, and the other man she guessed would be Henry. They appeared to be in some kind of intimate embrace. But who was the third man walking toward them? She'd have to run that by this Lowell guy, she guessed. Since he was

175

into photography. Maybe he could blow this one up, too. There were some negatives. She checked, and found one that matched the photo in question.

Then she noticed a clipping that was very interesting indeed. "Hey, Lowell!" she called, up through the hatchway.

"Better come up here," came the reply, in even tones.

Holding the papers, Bedrosian climbed the ladder and followed Lowell's gaze aft. To the Catalina. A good half-mile back, but still coming. Lowell had the binoculars out and handed them over. Bedrosian focused and could just make out the small man—the one in charge, she figured, him being the white guy—hoisting a sail. So, it was going to be a race, once again.

"What I'd like to know is why those guys don't radio for another chopper or a police launch, they want you so bad. We're sitting ducks on this floating dry goods store."

"Good question. Maybe they're hoods. Or freelancers. Maybe the storm took out their radio. Maybe their whole operation is bogus. There's a lot of possibilities."

"Maybe." Bedrosian brandished the second article at Lowell. "I was goin' over these papers. There's a little item here that—"

"Take the wheel a sec, wouldja? I gotta get some sails up again. Those clowns are too close for comfort."

Bedrosian stuffed the papers under a hatch cover and held the wheel, irritated, as she watched Lowell climb onto the foredeck to winch the halyards aloft again. He was good-looking, she had to admit. Fascinating eyes. She suppressed the thought immediately, annoyed with herself. Impatiently, she shouted over at him.

"What the hell is all this about a missing witness?"

"Not missing, just indisposed," replied Lowell. Shit. What else does she know by now?

"Oh, yeah? You knew about this, didn't you!" Forgetting the wheel, Bedrosian took out the article and began to read, voice barely carrying in the steady breeze. " 'Lucretia Hartley, defendant in the celebrated Hartley versus Hartley slander suit, has demanded throughout the trial that she be allowed to subpoena a key witness.

However, Judge William Davies has ruled that the witness in question, having been found by a court-licensed psychologist to be mentally incompetent, cannot testify.' That was your client, wasn't it, Lowell? That was Maureen Fitzgerald! And you knew it!"

"OK, I knew it. But the fact is, whatever she was going to testify would've been disallowed in any case. Besides, there's no proof it was her."

"What do you mean?"

"I mean, the transcript is missing, and there's no other records."

"The missing transcript? Come on, somebody must have a copy."

"Yeah. Mike Folner's law firm maybe. Who else? The Hartley lawyer was a one-man operation. A geriatric basketcase the old woman hired because of his alleged blue blood. Which had probably crystallized by then. He died ten years ago, with no children. You can forget him. Ditto the judge. He died the same year. I looked it up."

"You keep dragging Judge Folner's name into this. That sounds an awful lot like slander again. Especially with no proof."

"Have it your way. Meanwhile, let me know when you come up with a good explanation for an unmarked chopper that shoots first and asks questions later. Not to mention a sailboat that won't quit."

Lowell cleated the sails and jumped back down into the cockpit. "And regarding Ms. Fitzgerald. You wanna know what I *don't* think? I don't think she was incompetent at all. I think she saw something that night. She told me as much before she died. She said she saw somebody push Henry overboard. She was very clear about it."

She glared. "Another minor detail you neglected to mention before."

"I needed proof. She's dead, so there's no more witness. The rest is all circumstantial."

"Yeah, too bad. 'Cause whatever she saw, it sure as hell isn't in any of them pictures you got."

"I'm not so sure about that," said Lowell. "In any case," he added, "with Maureen out of the way, Julie won. And Mike helped her."

"That was all legal, fair and square."

"Legal and fair are two different things, aren't they? Especially when Maureen Fitzgerald didn't get to testify. They also overlooked one small little thing that isn't in any of those stories, which I haven't gotten around to mentioning."

Bedrosian glared. "Yeah? What was that?"

"She had a boyfriend."

Bedrosian looked confused. "Who had a boyfriend?"

"Julie."

Glancing back at the Catalina again, Lowell put the helm on automatic pilot and faced her. "Let me spell it out for you. Henry Hartley the Third was gay. It was the worst kept secret in town. He married Julie for show. She married him for money. And she had a boyfriend."

"How do you know all this?"

"I knew him. And I was there that night."

"You—?"

"Staff photographer, *Harbor Sentinel*. First day on the job. I blocked most of it out, to be honest. Until now."

He gestured for her to follow and led the way down the hatch. Spreading out the photos and documents, he fished out the shot taken on the boat. "I have reason to think this was taken the night of the drowning. And I think I was the one who took it. And I think this guy here"—he tapped the man with Julie—"is our pal Mike Folner again. Being a lot more than just friendly."

She stared. "Come on. That's Hartley. It's gotta be."

"No." He tapped the man moving toward the couple on the stern. "*This* is Henry Hartley. I knew him. Folner was on the boat that night. I saw him. I'm certain of it."

She wouldn't believe it. "You really have it in for this judge, don't you? One foggy photo that could be anybody and you're ready to hang the man. You got any better proof than that?"

178

"Not yet. But now take a look at this." He handed her the one of the kissing couple in New York.

"What about it?"

She glanced at it and dismissed it at once. "That doesn't prove jack shit, pal. So it's Julie. So she's kissing some guy."

"It's Folner again."

She shook her head. "So she kissed Folner a few times, so what? They were friends. It's allowed."

"Maybe. But she was mighty cozy with our man Folner, not only after the marriage but during it. Not to mention the fact that they got married after Henry got pushed. I think this is evidence that Mike Folner was her boyfriend the whole time."

She frowned and dismissed the second photo out of hand. "This could have been after the trial. It could have been some big festival, when everybody kisses everybody. You don't even know for sure this guy is Folner."

"I know it is. He was with her that night on the boat when Henry went over. And he was with her when she took Lucretia for all she had. What does that sound like to you?"

"It sounds like bullshit. It wouldn't hold up in court for three seconds, and you damn well know it!"

He knew the detective was right. But for the first time in decades, Lowell remembered the night clearly, forcing aside an emotional curtain that had been drawn tight ever since . . .

It was New Year's Eve, January 1, 1966. They had been en route to Grand Bahama Island on an all-night cruise: a hundred celebrants on board, plus a twenty-piece band—the core remnant of the Count Basie Orchestra. About sixty miles out, in international waters, the weather had turned foul, and the skipper (Lowell could no longer remember his name) had ordered everyone on board to stay inside. Defiant by nature, Lowell had been up on the top deck, drinking stolen champagne and feeling like Che Guevara at a country club. He knew he'd screwed up. He was supposed to be on duty, having taken the job that very week as the alleged society photographer. They'd reluctantly agreed to take him on, despite his blue-collar background. Or perhaps because of it. Or because of his connections at police H.Q. And he'd been thrilled to be a participant in what he romantically imagined to be the Fourth Estate. He saw himself as a spy of sorts, a closet peasant among the Romanoffs.

He hadn't thought about it in years, that night on the yacht. Mrs. Hartley had gotten rid of the vessel immediately after the "accident." But it had been one hell of a boat: a hundred and sixty-two–foot Trumpy, all solid mahogany and teak, brass, spit, and polish, with twin Daimler diesels and twenty luxury staterooms: enough to sleep forty in sybaritic comfort and bunk dozens more. Plus a crew of ten. Apparently Henry Junior had commissioned that yacht during everyone else's Great Depression, when he'd been young and feeling his oats, before his grandfather had even been in the ground a month. Of course, later tycoons such as Onassis had bought bigger boats, with swimming pools and spas and floating crap games and what have you. Yachts tended to be bought and sold like cars among the rich and famous. But Henry Junior and Lucretia had hung on to the *Southern Star*, their beloved "steamer," as they called it, in the firm belief that it was—in terms of workmanship, materials, and innate quality—the finest motor yacht ever built. And they were probably right.

That night, while Lucretia held court in the main salon, surrounded by her usual sycophants and well-wishers, the social climbers and fellow elite, there had been an atmosphere of—what was it? Not condescension exactly. Not derision, no one would have dared. But people were watching her with X-ray vision. Gauging her reactions. Measuring the stiffness, as it were, of her upper lip. Julie, of course, was the cause of it all. This had been Julie's official welcome to Society. Her coming out. Regardless of how she had done it, regardless of her previous status—low, certainly, in Lucretia's eyes—she was now Mrs. Henry Hartley III. Wife of the heir to the Hartley fortune, a known talent in her own right, and a dazzling beauty that nobody could deny, she wore the mantle with astonishing aplomb, considering her roots. Oh yes, Lucretia had dug up those Appalachian roots quickly enough. If only to rub her son's face in them.

But, as Lowell had sensed, it had been Henry doing all the rubbing. Lucretia never caught on to his bohemian lifestyle in New York or even that he was gay. And he took delight in her ignorance. Julie, to Henry, was the perfect front, the perfect trophy wife in every respect. She had looks, talent, social graces, and his mother hated her.

It had been Michael Folner, actually, who had introduced them.

Lowell had known about it from the first because Henry had confided in him, one drunken night at Charley's. For some reason, Henry III had seized upon the police chief's son as someone he felt he could confide in. Henry secretly admired Lowell's rebelliousness and devil-may-care attitude toward the whole society thing. He'd always feared censure too much—particularly that of his mother— to pretend anything other than absolute conventionality. And yet, his true life, his secret life, was anything but conventional.

Henry had gone to New York, on the pretense of taking courses in business at New York University while assuming an apprenticeship of sorts with Salomon Brothers down on Wall Street. Lucretia owned a townhouse on East 63rd Street and had expected Henry to stay there. But instead, he'd taken a loft in Soho and begun associating with the art crowd and bohemian types. During a booze and pot spree at The Harbor over Christmas that year when he was home for the holidays, he'd told Lowell about the New York scene, and being gay, and how wonderfully liberating it was. He also told him about a friend he'd met at the university. A law student, but still very "creative." And gorgeous.

Not long after that, Henry had revealed that he was in love. But he knew he could never allow such knowledge to reach the ears of his family and had kept it his own dark secret. Over a subsequent bottle of champagne, during the following spring break, Henry told Tony of his infatuation with his New York friend. Lowell could sense that he was particularly troubled, in that his love was unrequited. The friend, it seemed, was straight. But they had worked out a plan together. Henry needed a "front." And the friend had introduced him to a beautiful, talented opera "star," loads of fun, and a good companion (and cover) for a dashing gay prince.

The wedding had taken place that fall of 1965, in a private civil ceremony on Barbados. Just Henry, the girl Julie, and the mutual friend who'd brought them together: Michael Folner.

Three months later, on New Year's Eve, Henry Hartley the Third had fallen overboard from his mother's yacht, over the stern rail, and drowned. Tony had been too drunk to remember it well, and had nearly been fired for failing to document the incident. The only thing that had saved him had been that he'd been hired as a society photographer, not a news stringer. He'd done his job. The society shots were fine. Only his mind had gone out of focus . . .

"So." Bedrosian broke into Lowell's reminiscences. "You're telling me that Judge Folner arranged the marriage of Julie Barnett to Henry Hartley, then conspired with her to waste him and take the money? Is that it?"

Lowell didn't say anything, knowing how it sounded.

"This gets better and better," she snapped, sarcastically. "I suppose you also have tons of evidence and lots of witnesses to corroborate that bucket of worm shit, too."

"You seemed interested enough to follow me around the last three days. I'm just telling you how it was. You're the cop, for chrissake. Do your job."

"I'm trying to. You're not making it easy, though. First you hold out on me, then dump crap like that in my lap—"

"Look, somebody killed Maureen Fitzgerald because she saw something she shouldn't have. She was a witness!"

"Yeah, well, unfortunately, she's dead."

"Yeah. Murdered. Right after telling me she had witnessed foul play."

"She told you that?"

"Yeah. What was that, a coincidence? Then my cousin Elliot

comes across these clippings. Maybe he tried to call someone. The phone was on the floor, in case you didn't notice. So they shut him up, too. Then Maureen's doctor gets snuffed because he's her therapist, and you can figure she probably told him everything she knew."

"See no evil, speak no evil, hear no evil," muttered Bedrosian. "That what this is supposed to be?"

Lowell shrugged. "You tell me."

She resisted a growing urge to slap him one. "You said it yourself. You got no evidence these killings are even connected, other than circumstantial."

"I think I do have evidence." He pointed at the stack of documents. "I think Elliot found something, and those guys back there know it. I just haven't put my finger on it yet."

"Yeah, well, I ain't holdin' my breath," she snapped.

"Suit yourself," said Lowell. "But you know what I'm going to do, first thing I shake those clowns?"

"*If* you shake them, you mean."

"First thing I'm gonna do," he continued, "is pay a little visit to your idol, Judge Folner, and find out—"

Bedrosian was already in a foul mood after her unwanted boat ride. This was too much.

"Go to hell, Lowell!" she shouted. "You mention the judge's name one more time, or go near him, I'm gonna put you in cuffs and leg irons and personally hand you over to that goddamn Junior Edgar Hoover and—Eddie Murphy back there!"

Lowell stifled a wry grin. "Suit yourself, but I think—"

"You think too much. You wanna know what *I* think? I think you're one crazy son of a bitch who calls himself a private eye while he runs around getting innocent women knocked up, in between knocking their relatives off for reasons that are gonna get you a first-class seat on the next charter jet to death row, if I got anything to—"

A shot rang out, and Lowell could feel the shock wave of a bullet inches from his ear. He spun around, and the two of them hit the deck.

While Lowell and Bedrosian were arguing, Werner had brought the Catalina within a couple hundred yards, quietly adding twin mainsails, jennies, and full auxiliary power. Lefcourt, now well within rifle range, was tired of playing games. Cop or no cop, he was going to finish the chase, now. Taking careful aim, he squeezed off what under normal circumstances would have been the deciding round.

Unfortunately for him, the wind shifted, and the shot missed badly. Lefcourt didn't want to just blast away. Too much chance of killing the cop by mistake. And there'd been enough killing already on this thing. Taking aim once again, he flicked the safety and fired. Shit. The boat shifted again. Now his mark was down below the whadda-ya-call-it. Gunwale or something.

When the shot fired, Lowell ducked. Then, grabbing his duffel, he pulled the Nikon, checked the action, glanced over the rail, and snapped a couple of quick frames. He heard cursing from across the water. Good, he thought. They're vulnerable to exposure. Calculating the distance between the boats, he risked a look the other way, and his hopes soared. The inlet! Not more than five hundred yards ahead. An incident from his youth—one that had involved Elliot's borrowed boat—gave him an idea. Where was the tide? Last night it had been going out. Eighteen hours—in, out—it would be in now. Good! They'll be more likely to take the bait.

"Bedrosian!" he called, keeping his voice low. She had managed to remove herself to the galley down below, where she was frantically checking her own relatively useless service revolver. "You there?"

"Keep down. That was no warning shot."

"Lowell!" Werner shouted, voice echoing across the water. "Heave to! You can't escape! The Coast Guard is on its way, and we got people waiting for you anywhere you make land!"

Lowell considered and decided it was a lie. If they were legit, they could bring in as much backup as they needed, any time they wanted. So why hadn't they?

A bullet struck the mahogany panel just above his head. "Shit!" he exclaimed to himself. He was going to have to get another sail out and put some more distance between this boat and theirs. And with the big jenny gone, that meant the spinnaker. Jesus.

"Bedrosian!" he signaled. "I need you to navigate!"

"Like hell," came the reply. "I'm off the case, pal. You got too many enemies!" And too few friends, she might have added.

"I didn't figure you for a quitter."

She flared. "Watch it, Lowell. I'm only gonna take so much from you."

Lowell crawled up past her onto the foredeck. "You gonna help or not?"

"Last warning!" Werner shouted again.

Lowell slid his way around the mast to the sail loft hatch and pried it up, bracing it open. It would provide a small amount of shelter. But once he had to get up in that sling, he knew, he was a sitting, or rather flying, duck. Maybe he could bluff them. He stripped off the admiral's white shirt and waved it, like a flag.

"I have to strike the sails! I need three minutes! The rigging's jammed!"

Werner scowled. "I don't trust this guy," he growled. "He's too damn cool."

Lefcourt lowered his rifle. He could shoot now or later. It was obvious they were about to catch them shortly anyway. Werner cupped his hands. "All right," he yelled back once again. "You got three minutes!"

On the *Wellington*, Bedrosian was thoroughly mystified. "What the hell are you up to?"

"You'll see in a minute. Keep steering toward that green buoy up there. See it?"

The detective hadn't been steering at all actually. They'd been drifting. But with a truce on, she complied. "Yeah, got it."

Lowell quickly rigged the spinnaker halyard to the grommets, keeping the sheets and brilliant red furls out of sight. His plan required climbing the mast. Something he'd always hated, but he had no choice now. He wrapped the halyard around his waist. Rising, he pointed aloft for the benefit of his pursuers, grasped the tall wooden spar, and reached for the first handhold. He began to climb. It was a lot like the way Polynesian boys climbed coconut palms, he thought wryly. Except here there were toe and hand clips intended for the purpose, and other emergencies.

Twenty feet, fifty feet. Sixty feet. His hands were numb now, his muscles burning from the strain. Five more feet to the big pulley on the masthead.

"You're out of time, Lowell! Get down and drop anchor, now!"

"I can't, I'm stuck! Let me just free the goddamn cleat, OK? I'm almost there!"

Silence from the Catalina. Well, he thought. That beats shooting. Reaching up, he threaded the halyard through the pulley, yanked it down the other side, and refastened it around his waist.

"What the fuck's he doing?" demanded Lefcourt, watching through binoculars.

"Wait a sec," muttered Werner. Then it dawned on him. "No, he hasn't got the ba—"

Lowell dove. Like a bungee diver off the towering mast, the rope playing out behind him.

Bedrosian's eyes widened, disbelieving, her first thought that Lowell—cornered—had chosen this moment for a spectacular suicide.

The two men on the Catalina gaped, goggle-eyed.

Then the spinnaker, cleated to the other end of the halyard, rose majestically from its hiding place in the loft below (God, don't let it jam! was Lowell's one coherent prayer) and soared aloft. The weight countered his perfectly. His fall was slowed exactly like that of a parachutist, and he floated to the deck as the spinnaker—in so many ways a functional parachute—caught the wind and billowed out.

The great twelve-meter leapt forward through the water. The inlet was now only a hundred yards ahead, and Lowell could see the sky-blue waters, breakers foaming white beyond. And something else: a bank of heavy fog rolling in as the warm air and winds receded. It was more than he could have hoped for. Quickly untying the line from his waist, he scrambled aft and jumped down to the cockpit, keeping low. Bedrosian stared, speechless.

"OK. See that depth gauge. That one, there?" Lowell pointed at a brass instrument, showing the depth at 12 feet. "Keep an eye on that. It's going to rise sharply. When we reach three feet, kill the engine."

The cop shook her head, and glanced back apprehensively. Werner and Lefcourt were now recovered from their stupefaction. Meanwhile Lowell had gained fifty yards on them, and was no longer comfortably within range for an accurate disabling shot.

"Son of a bitch!" was all Werner could manage. Cursing Lowell. Cursing the busted radio. "Son of a bitch!"

Grimly, Werner trimmed his sails, wondering whether he could fly a spinnaker, too. He'd never done it alone, but there might be no way to catch them now otherwise. Then the wind shifted. From the north, almost due east. He could see the spinnaker pushed off to the starboard, no longer effective. He let out an exultant yell. With the jenny already in place, he now had more reaching power than Lowell, whose great grandstand play was for naught. The Cat began to regain lost distance rapidly.

Lowell couldn't worry about that now. He was down in the hold, and Bedrosian was virtually certain that he'd finally gone off the deep end.

She would play it out anyway, too far gone to turn back. Steering for the buoy, directly off the point of the next barrier island south, she pushed the engine—their main source of power now—as fast as it would go. Closer now, the point loomed. She started to fret. Weren't they in kind of close?

"Lowell, what the hell you doin'? We're gonna run aground!"

"How many feet?" came the muffled shout from below.

She had almost forgotten to watch. The gauge was steady at

twelve. Then, suddenly, it began to drop. Eleven. Ten, nine—she began counting down out loud. "Eight! Seven! Six! Five! Four!" This was it. "Three feet!"

Bedrosian hit the switch and the engine died. There was a vast silence on the water. Then a peculiar groaning noise, deep below. Lowell, using a power winch, was hoisting the single feature that was unique to the *Wellington*, among all America's Cup competitors of its time.

Up in the cockpit, Bedrosian was near panic. "Lowell, for God's sake, we're inside the buoy!" The sandy shoal was visible, not twenty yards away. She could see the bottom clearly now. They were going to run aground any second.

Back in the Catalina, Werner ignored the buoys, grimly focused on the stern of the *Wellington* directly ahead. Closer now. Lefcourt had the Remington ready once more. Calm and steady. No way he was going to miss this time. But where was the target?

"Lowell, are you crazy?" Bedrosian was shouting. She didn't have to be a master seaman to see what was happening. "We're going to hit bottom!" She held her breath as the shoal bottom rose up at an alarming rate, closer and closer. The boat began to shudder, and heel over sharply, skidding as it went.

"Lowell!"

Suddenly they were over the shoal—still moving! And beyond. Bedrosian could only stare dumbfounded as the depth gauge reading began to rise once more. "Five feet, now! Six. Seven. Ten!" They were clear!

Lowell's head popped up into view. "We only draw thirty inches with the centerboard up. We cleared with room to spare."

That had been the admiral's secret weapon: a movable keel. The admiral had insisted that his boat be usable in the shallow coastal waters he loved so much for pleasure sailing, after the races. The designers and builders had screamed. It did show a certain lack of commitment to the cause but a lot of good sense. Why waste twelve meters of marvelous craftsmanship on a single long-shot race? And so the designers had reluctantly built a ton of lead ballast into the sister keelsons on either side of the massive keel, plus another thousand pounds into the centerboard itself: enough to counter the top-heavy weight of the huge mast and rigging under most conditions. It had been this keel, and the necessary top-heaviness of the boat, that had worried Lowell the most during their run through the storm. He tipped his hat, silently, to Bertram Scott, the designer— wherever he might be. His boat had exceeded expectations.

They were through the inlet into the breakers, and the fog bank was dead ahead. Once in there, no spotter plane or Coast Guard cutter or whatever else was sent after them would be able to find them. They'd just be another blip on the radar screen—one of hundreds.

But what of the Catalina, now directly astern?

Lowell couldn't resist a look. Nikon focused on infinity, quick shutter speed for depth, he rose up and found himself staring straight into the barrel of Lefcourt's rifle, cross hairs trained squarely on him. The finger began to squeeze. Then he heard the sound—soft, sudden, and dreadful to a sailor. The Catalina struck the forgotten sandbar, shuddered to an immediate halt, and its two startled occupants were hurled into the bay.

The race was over.

As the twelve-meter sloop *Wellington* sailed majestically out into the Atlantic, its crew of two danced wildly around the deck in a moment of madness and celebration, forgetting themselves.

"We did it!" Bedrosian exulted. "We did it!" Then, with a look back at the grounded fiberglass ketch, she had to ask. "What happened?"

"Fixed keel," grinned Lowell. "They never had a chance."

At that moment Tony Lowell would have given anything in the world for a cold bottle of Kirin and a couple of hundred-watt speakers blasting Steppenwolf's "Born to Be Wild." But Lena Bedrosian, still proudly at the helm, simply stared in wonder at the ocean waves breaking ahead, the sheltering fog beyond. By now she'd forgotten all about her ruined blue suit.

18

Acutely aware of the cutter that had been dogging them some-where off the starboard beam for the past half-hour, Lowell made a decision. They had been concealed in the fog since losing the Cata-lina at the inlet sandbar. But both knew it was a matter of time before more serious, intensive pursuit would ensue. Their boat was highly distinctive and easily identified. Bedrosian was pretty sure a spotter plane had picked them up on radar an hour before, flying low over the water. Then the cutter had come. She remembered from her childhood the unmistakable throaty rumble of their heavy diesels—much heavier than any pleasure or commercial craft. They weren't making any overt moves just yet. Maybe they didn't feel any need to. Perhaps unlike the two Federal agents, they had other priorities. But they were out there, all the same.

Just before sunset, Lowell proposed a move. They should beach the twelve-meter at once—the moment it got dark. It would be dangerous and tricky in the rough Atlantic surf, but he saw no point remaining at sea through the night. They were bound to be caught come daylight when the fog rose, if not sooner. Their best chance lay in the first hour of darkness. Before the opposition, whoever it might be, would have a chance to regroup.

There was an empty stretch of beach on Huntington Island north of St. Lucie Inlet that Lowell knew about. He'd gone there with Caitlin on day cruises more than once. Not with the *Wellington*, of course. He'd been there again a few years back, and not that much had changed. The developers had not cast their dark shadow there yet. The area was still mostly empty dunes, sea oats, scrub pine, and mangrove. A small road led to a little-used drawbridge to the mainland. They might have a chance to pick up a ride, maybe even rent a car in one of the towns nearby. Both agreed it was too dangerous to return to Palm Coast Harbor for their cars until they had a clearer sense of where they stood. They wouldn't actually run the *Wellington* in, he explained. That would probably tear out the admiral's prized keel and break her up in the surf. They would drop anchor about a hundred yards out, and take the dinghy in.

Everything had gone fine. Until the last breaker had crested over the dinghy's stern and swamped them.

Lowell managed to preserve the poster tube, but his leather bag and navy duffel were soaked. Luckily the surf was calm. The water, however, was chilly, and they were having a hard time staying on their feet. Bedrosian was sullen and silent as they waded ashore, soaked and shivering.

Lowell studied the moonlit seascape, trying to get his bearings in the darkness. There was just enough moon to make out the beach. It was ghostly white, stretching for miles to the north, dotted with an occasional beach house or condominium. Heavy clouds were racing in from the ocean, with a threat of rain by morning. Bedrosian carried her pumps and gun. There was no further mention of her broken nails and ruined designer clothing. It was difficult going in the heavy sand.

"I'd build a fire, but we can't risk it," said Lowell, sitting down after ten minutes and small progress. He pointed. "The road is just beyond that dune. I just have to catch my breath."

Bedrosian, fifteen years younger and in a lot better shape, said nothing. She stayed on her feet, keeping watch. A hundred feet out the yacht danced in the waves. An old rocker and roller like me, Lowell thought. Black profile pitching and heaving, its spars and rigging groaned against the tug of the surf. The Coast Guard would tow it back at daybreak, he felt certain. Now to avoid being towed anywhere, himself. Walking behind her, he regarded the detective's slightly broad buttocks and muscular legs with idle curiosity, wondering what she'd be like in bed. Demanding, he decided. Impatient. Cold. But competent. The bottom line? She was a cop.

Two hours later, they reached the mainland, cold, wet, and exhausted.

"I still can't believe I let you hijack that goddamn boat," griped Bedrosian. Aside from that they'd spoken very little. Lowell, lugging his waterlogged gear and clinging stubbornly to his now-wet cardboard tube of evidence—of what?—was questioning his own judgment. He wondered what he was doing schlepping a heavy camera around. He always kept it sealed in a plastic bag against the wet, so it was presumably still functional. But he wasn't a photographer anymore. Hadn't been for two decades. What good were a few frames of some stiffs or shooters gonna do? Far more important were the shots he and some forgotten stringer had taken twenty-five years ago. More important maybe than he knew, even now.

Just over the drawbridge stood a gas station with a fishing dock and small diner. Eerie and isolated in the fog.

"Well," sighed Lowell, as they headed for the bright neon sign, beckoning like a glowing blurry finger. "Where do we go from here?"

"For starters," muttered the police detective, fishing into her pocket. "I'm placing you under arrest." She produced a pair of cuffs, seized a surprised Lowell's wrist—and snapped them on, commandeering the cardboard tube. The other cuff went onto her own wrist, now in possession of the evidence.

Lowell wasn't particularly surprised. It wasn't as though they'd become lovers or anything. He just wondered what had taken the woman so long.

"Mind if I ask what this is for?"

"Tell you in a minute. Damn, where's that Miranda card? Oh here it is." Bedrosian pulled out a limp, wet, wallet-sized card, and squinting under the parking lot light, read Lowell his rights. Finished, she explained: "I'm arresting you for leaving the scene of a crime. Make that two crimes. For obstruction of justice. For endangering a police officer. For refusal to submit to arrest—" She raised her hand at Lowell's protest—"let me continue—for grand theft and larceny, and for protective custody as a material witness. Did I leave anything out?"

"Well," said Lowell wryly. "At least you didn't mention murder."

"Not yet, anyway. C'mon, let's get inside, I'm freezing my buns off."

"Sounds good to me."

Inside the restaurant, the only customers were a truck farmer from Okeechobie and his son, getting ready to return from a produce delivery to their regular clientele on Huntington Island: six mom-and-pop stores and a fish restaurant. Except two customers had just switched on them, to one of the major distributors. They'd stopped to beer their blues away awhile back, and were now working on carbohydrates and coffee for the trip home.

The sight of this strange pair coming in out of the fog—both soaked, handcuffed to each other: a woman in a tattered business suit, a man looking like a water-logged ice cream vendor, was enough to make them choke on their coffee.

"Hot damn," muttered the son, Lester. "Lookie here. Wonder which one's the cop."

The father looked and shook his head. "Some damn fools can't find their way out of a paper bag, let along a fog," he muttered. Served them right. The woman approached Ned Charles, the proprietor, and flashed a badge.

"Sorry to bother you," she said. "I'm a police officer, and this man is my prisoner. We need a car."

"No cars here, ma'am," replied Ned. "Maybe up at Port St. Lucie, I think they got an Avis up there. How far you gotta go?"

"Gulf coast. We could use a couple of coffees, if you don't mind. And I'll take a burger platter. You want anything?" she asked Lowell.

Lowell felt as if he hadn't had a square meal since the Beatles

193

broke up. But he was too tired to eat. He shook his head. "Just coffee."

"Better eat something. We got a long way to go."

Lowell relented. "OK. I'll have steak and lobster tails, Caesar salad, baked potato with sour cream and chives, blueberry pie à la mode, and a nice Chardonnay, not too fruity."

Bedrosian glared. "Give him a burger and fries, with slaw."

The coffee tasted wonderful. Even though it had been boiling in the pot for most of the day probably. Lowell sweetened his with real milk and honey, and it was almost as good as a cappuccino, just now. Bedrosian took hers black and sipped absently, lost in dark thoughts, unaware of the men ogling her.

Ned served the food, and they ate quietly. Lowell wondered when the two farmers were going to leave. He was worried about who might come in next. Bedrosian had said she had no intention of turning her prisoner over to anybody without direct orders from her superiors relinquishing jurisdiction. There were too many questions she wanted answers to, first. This whole thing with the Hartley drowning, and now this Folner connection.

Lowell contemplated his sudden turnaround. On board the *Wellington*, he had been in total command. Funny how quickly things change. This new development stuck in his craw like bad food. At least this cop seemed to be surprisingly uncorrupted and dedicated. That might still be useful, if they could get back to the Gulf coast in one piece. All they needed to worry about were alligators, snakes, cops, shooters, choppers, fatigue, transportation, and now, rednecks.

Otto, the farmer, spoke. In slow, measured tones.

"How come you two walkin' around lookin' like you been dipped in cow piss? This some kinda weirdo sex thing?"

Bedrosian ignored him. Lowell couldn't, he was inches away.

"Took a bath. Try it sometime."

Lowell's sarcasm did not escape the farmer. It was just the sort of provocation he was looking for. But he let it simmer a bit and percolate. Tension mounted.

"Took a bath." Otto nudged Lester. "They took a bath." He looked back at them, scornfully. "What's-a-matter? Don't got enough sense to come in outa the wet?"

"We just did." That was Bedrosian now, with an easy smile.

"Yeah. I guess you did." The farmer nodded some more, grinned, and seemed to reach a momentous decision. He finished his coffee and turned to Bedrosian, with a wink. The danger had passed.

"We're headin' for Palmdale, ma'am. West of Okeechobie. You want, you can ride in back. Cost you twenny-five apiece."

Bedrosian raised her once-perfect eyebrows and considered. Lowell knew there were a lot of risks in trying to rent a car. Especially if there was any kind of dragnet out. Palmdale was mid-state, and they could pick up Route 27 up to 60 and on over to Tampa and the Gulf from there. Maybe they could catch another farm delivery. Maybe. The man seemed sincere. As though they'd passed some kind of test. He'd better be watchful, though, just in case.

The cop didn't look forward to a hundred miles in a farm truck, in the middle of a cold night, soaking wet, in close proximity to this strange, unkempt man. Make that three strange, unkempt men. But at least it was partway home.

"It's a deal," she decided, reaching for her wallet. She carried it in her jacket, like a man. It was soaking wet.

Lowell shrugged. He didn't look forward to the trip either. But at least it was better than jail.

19

Two hundred miles to the west, Police Headquarters at Manatee City was buzzing. Deputy Sheriff Pilchner, Sgt. Allenson, and Lt. Arlin Jeffries had all been summoned to Chief Sturbridge's office for a late-night briefing. Bob Sturbridge was a huge, melancholy man of great weight and indeterminate age. He had a master's in Criminal Justice from Georgia Tech and could, as he was quick to tell those who would listen, have been any damn thing he wanted to be. He had accepted the appointment as chief in a time of political upheaval. When Mayor Butch Hannah and his cronies were all caught with their hands in the developer's front pockets and their tongues up their anuses, the county supervisors had come in with a court order—from "Mr. Clean" himself, Judge Folner, no less—to clean house, or pack up and get out. The local press, particularly the big papers from Tampa and St. Pete, had been relentless, and there was no way to wipe out their dirty tracks. So they'd all gone: mayor, fire chief, police chief, highway chief, and chief of economic development.

In the aftermath, with everybody feeling snake-bitten, there had been precious few qualified candidates to run the city. So the offer had come down from Supervisor Engberg for Bob Sturbridge, the underachieving head of a small but immaculate Atlanta security firm—Sturbridge Security—to take the job.

Now five years later, Sturbridge was figuring, had come payback time. His men had gathered and were waiting—all except Captain

Carrera, who was on administrative leave because of the shooting of a young black kid while in detention two weeks ago.

He turned away from the window where he'd been gazing into the darkness to face his officers. "You all know about the Folner nomination and the senator's big bash this weekend. We've been asked to be on backup from the Pinellas sheriff. They sniff a fart on the wind concerning this Fitzgerald thing, and we're gonna have to give them that much. At least it isn't happening in Manatee City, and thank God for that."

The men waited for the other shoe to fall. Especially Pilchner, who had been scared shitless when the call came. He'd been in bed porking a waitress named Lorraine and thought somehow his wife— supposedly at Bingo—had gotten onto him and turned him in.

"The problem is this," fumed Sturbridge, wishing he hadn't had to give up smoking, knowing it would kill him quickly if he resumed and not even caring except that his wife would finish the job if the cheroots did not. "I don't know where we stand on this Fitzgerald thing, and whatever the hell is happening 'cross state. Where the hell is Bedrosian, Arlin? And why the hell hasn't she reported in?"

Jeffries winced. Bad enough, she broke regulations by going it alone. Then he'd sent word via the two federal agents who'd shown up for her to come in, and let them take over the Fitzgerald case. Those guys were strange ones, he'd had to admit. They'd been hanging around since the Fitzgerald shooting, and then when Lowell disappeared, they'd vanished right afterward. Then Bedrosian had hooked up with this P.I., who was also a suspect and had also vanished. Insubordination hardly sufficed to describe such actions. Blatant dereliction of duty, and possibly conspiracy in a capital crime, were charges being whispered around headquarters the last few hours. He didn't like it one bit. There were too many people more than ready to bring down a woman detective, given the chance. But Jeffries liked Lena Bedrosian and felt he knew her well. Everything about her was straight, narrow, and by the book. Why would she turn now? And for what? As for Lowell, what made him tick? He'd heard Lowell was a reasonably good P.I. by local rep. Unorthodox, as P.I.'s tended to be. But he wasn't the type to get involved in capital crimes without a damn good reason.

Lena Bedrosian had taken off like a lit skyrocket over this Maureen Fitzgerald thing. Her last report had linked the dead woman to the old Henry Hartley money, and something about Judge Folner. Jesus. Now what? Those two Feebies had hinted at some kind of conspiracy to stop the judge's nomination by damaging his reputation. Conspiracy by whom? This P.I. guy? That seemed unlikely.

"I talked to her yesterday morning, Chief," he ventured finally. "She called in from over in Palm County where she went after this witness, Anthony Lowell."

"And who's over there with her, Jeffries? She knows the regulations!"

"Yes, sir. She didn't—"

"Forget it. We'll talk about that later. OK, so this guy Lowell takes off, then we get word there's some kind of killing spree goin' on over there, Lowell's the only link between any of 'em, and now he's vanished. And our gal with him."

"What's all this got to do with the Fitzgerald case?" asked Pilchner, wondering what he was even doing at this meeting.

The chief gave him a tired look.

"That's what I want to know, and that's why we're here," snapped Sturbridge. If there was one thing he hated it was incompetence. That and having to wash other people's dirty laundry. And his gut instincts told him there was something about this case that smelled of very old, very dirty laundry.

"Anyway," he continued, "Lena is out there on the Fitzgerald case; Lowell, an eyewitness to her killing, claims she was his client, which gives him some sort of status, in his opinion. Meanwhile some nut's running around popping anybody who ever had anything to do with this situation. Now I don't know about you clowns, but this is starting to make me very nervous."

Jesus, Jeffries was thinking. I'd be more than nervous. What in hell is Lena into out there? God, I hope I can bring her in, before these ass-kissers have to feed her to the wolves.

"What do you want from the Sheriff's Department?" Pilchner demanded, more confused than ever.

"Just—stand by, that's all." Christ, thought Sturbridge. I got no patience for gravelheads just now.

Allenson had been mostly silent until now. "I don't get it at all. If Lowell was a suspect on the Fitzgerald thing, which I personally doubt because I was there, sir, on the scene—then why wasn't he arrested?"

Sturbridge smiled, in spite of himself. These are good men, he thought. Let's hope they survive this mess. "Well, Bill, you've hit the nail on the head, haven't you? Why indeed? Unless maybe there's no case worth jack shit against him."

"So, what about these hits?" persisted Allenson. "Where do they fit in?"

My God, thought Jeffries. And Lena is with him, isn't that what they said? The men stared at each other in worried speculation. Come on, Lena, he fretted. Where the hell are you?

At four A.M. the next morning, an old stake truck approached the outskirts of Brandon from the east. The truck was loaded with livestock for a Bradenton meat-packing cooperative, one that had bought the truck owner–rancher's high-grade hogs for the past ten years.

Oscar Salcedo, the driver, didn't know of such things. He knew of six mouths to feed, including two uncles recently released by that *chingalero* Castro, and that this was the best job he'd ever had. Six-fifty an hour, plus discounts on any surplus meat or produce the ranch might have after harvest and shipment. It was lousy hours, but that was OK by Oscar. He never could stand the family bickering in their little trailer most of the time anyway. And now he had an extra twenty that he'd charged the Anglo *policia* when he'd picked her and her prisoner up on Route 27 two hours before.

Having learned from hard experience, Oscar was watching out for drunks, who were rampant at this hour. They were usually the only cars on the road, in fact, aside from occasional newspaper carriers and traveling salesmen getting an early start. This was the hour of the stone-blind, dead-weary drunk—the most dangerous creature alive. The kind that had been at it since eight or nine last night, starting out with buddies after work or the game at the gin mill, moving on to the pickup attempts, usually failed, with the occasional score, more drinking, staggering to some *chingalera* motel or sleazy apartment, drunken attempts at seduction and inept love-making, and a staggering departure. Usually preceded by an unceremonious boot. The Highway of Amor Perdido, Oscar used to call this road. But that was before his own wife left for that stinking *drogado* cousin of hers from Little Havana.

The policia and her prisoner were asleep next to him. He hoped she was OK, it was pretty cold. The heater was basically worthless. As for the gringo, he was keeping watch on him. If he made a move on her, Oscar would pitch him in the ditch like so much *basura*. He'd agreed to take them to the coast. After that she was on her own.

At first daylight, Lowell and Bedrosian woke up, cursing their aches, pains, reeking clothes, and travel conditions.

"You mind if I look at those clippings again?" Lowell asked.

"I'll do the lookin'," snapped Bedrosian, with a glance at the driver. She looked at the cannister. Could Lowell be right? Could there be something in there to cause three murders? If so, she hadn't found it yet. She had to get these negatives printed up as soon as possible. If for no other reason than to put to rest Lowell's innuendos regarding the judge.

She slid the materials out of the tube—keeping them from the driver's line of vision—and squinted at them in the dim, early-morning light.

"From the look of it, your shot of this so-called mystery man is useless, Lowell," she said, keeping her voice low.

"Maybe. But somebody is sure as hell worried about something in that pile."

"OK, so what if this does turn out to be Folner? That still don't prove nothin'. According to you he was a friend of the family. So to speak. Nothing wrong with that, legally. Or defending a defamed friend; or marrying the widow later on. So why bother to conceal the fact that he was there—if he was there at all? It don't make sense. Unless . . ."

"Unless what?" Lowell glanced at Salcedo, who seemed oblivious.

"He doesn't speak English." Bedrosian turned to the stack of photos again. Lowell looked at the driver doubtfully, shrugged, and picked up a loose photo. The cop glanced at it, and then looked closer. "Who's this guy sittin' in the car?" She finally asked, showing it to him. "Looks familiar."

Lowell had not had much time to study that particular photograph earlier. But he'd noticed something and wondered the same thing himself. "You're asking me? I'm just a prisoner here."

"Come off it. The more cooperation I get out of you, the quicker you'll be back on the street."

Lowell thought that one over and nodded. "OK. I don't know him. I'd agree he looks familiar, though."

"He's not a reporter, that's for sure."

Lowell gave her a calculating glance. Salcedo looked over a moment. Bedrosian glared and he turned quickly away. "How do you figure that?"

"The clothes. Look at the clothes. Reporters are slobs. This guy's got style. I could swear I know him. Maybe it's the mustache or—"

"His face is in the shadows. But the woman is definitely Maureen. And I know you're not going to like this, but the man holding her arm is your friend. Folner."

She shook her head. "There you go again. Another foggy innuendo, based on some blurry, out-of-focus—"

He leaned forward excitedly. "Wait a minute. Look at this!"

She looked. "What about it?"

"What does this look like to you?"

"Like somebody being taken—"

"She told me!" he suddenly exclaimed. "She said she didn't want

201

to go, that they made her!" he finished for her. "This is proof! They're taking her by force. Look at her arm."

She frowned. "But she was wacko, wasn't that how the story went? That she went crazy?"

"Do you see any doctors? Do you see an ambulance? Or any cops for that matter? These men are civilians. Mike Folner is forcing her into that car, with that other man—" He stopped suddenly and reached for the pile, jerking her arm. She jerked back. "Wait a sec'," he said. "I think there was another shot in there. Of the same guy."

Giving him a look, Bedrosian grudgingly searched through the file, and found the second photograph. Taken at the courthouse. The man standing in the back while Mike Folner escorted his triumphant client, Julie.

"Yes!" he insisted. "Same guy. Still can't see his face too clearly. I've seen him a million times, I'm sure of it. But different, somehow."

She shrugged and put it aside. "So what?"

A thought struck Lowell. "Didn't Folner work for one of the big law firms in those days?"

"You askin' me? I was still on the Pep Squad back then."

"Yeah, sorry. Seems to me there was another lawyer, though. Somebody behind the scenes, who masterminded some of those legal maneuvers they used—"

Bedrosian's thoughts raced to the Miami article, and she dug for it. "You mean, like using mock juries? And hiring psychologists to survey public attitudes about money? That sort of thing?"

"I heard something like that a long time ago. I'd forgotten about that."

She dug out the article. "Doesn't name him." She looked at the picture again. "This might not even be him anyways. I wish we had a better picture. You don't recall who it was?"

"Nope. He was a shadow man in more ways than one."

"Maybe you're right. Maybe I'm the one who should ask Judge Folner about this."

202

"Good luck. He may not care to tell you."

The cop glared at him, then back at the photos a moment longer. The truck slowed down. The meat packing plant was just ahead. They were almost home.

"Estamos aqui," announced the driver.

"Maybe," suggested Lowell, offhandedly, "we should talk to the judge together."

"What?"

"I'm your new partner, Detective. You need me. Haven't you figured that out yet?"

"Maybe *you* haven't figured out that you are wearing handcuffs, and I'm the one with the badge."

Lowell shrugged. "Have it your way. But I'm the one he wants to talk to."

"Wants to?" Bedrosian glared, wondering herself. Somebody sure as hell wanted this guy bad. He might be right.

Oscar pulled over to the curb, at the packing plant gate, hopped out, and opened the door for them, careful to give them plenty of room.

"End of the line, *amigos*," he called cheerfully. "And don't worry, your secrets are safe with me!"

Let's hope so, was the immediate thought that came to the minds of both detectives, as they sheepishly gathered their belongings and climbed stiffly out of the truck—clothes still damp, reeking of sweat, mildew, and pig. A new day had begun. It was going to be a long one.

20

Lt. Arlin Jeffries of the Manatee City Police Department was up at five A.M. with a dull, throbbing headache. He'd put off his promise to help his twelve-year-old daughter Kimberly with the Halloween decorations for a second straight day, and she had not been gracious about it. She was planning a slumber party with six friends, and parental cooperation was a must for such things.

But Arlin had other worries just now. Major worries. His top detective, Lena Bedrosian, was still missing in action. Chief Sturbridge, usually a most saturnine man, was in a state of apoplexy.

Getting up and looking out into the predawn gray, Jeffries stumbled into the bathroom and contemplated his stubble in the mirror. Evelyn, his wife, was already downstairs in the kitchen, getting breakfast and coffee ready for himself and the kids. My God, what a trooper that woman was. More like her, and this world would be a peaceful, happy, productive place—or else! On the other hand, Kimmy and Devon were squabbling as usual over the bathroom. So much for world peace. Kim had actually demanded that he provide her with a bathroom of her very own. Sure, I got ten grand right here, honey. Kids! She'd been his little princess, a regular peach right up until puberty hit. Amazing how those hormones kick in and kill all the brain cells just like that.

He hadn't slept well either, which didn't improve his mood any. If only Lena would call in, let him know what was happening, explain herself. Last he'd heard she'd tangled with those two suits that were here last week. That P.I. Lowell was the one they seemed to want. But Lena Bedrosian was real big on rights, and duty. If she felt it was her duty and her right to protect her witness, and bring him in herself, then by God that's what she would do. And, he thought grimly, squirting a mound of shaving cream into his palm, if that's what she's doing, more power to her. I just don't know if I'm going to be able to cover for her, though, when the shit hits the fan . . .

The phone rang downstairs. Evelyn picked it up from the kitchen before he could get to it. He knew right away it was the call he was waiting for. Nobody would have the nerve to telephone at 5:30 A.M. unless it was damned serious. Which meant Bedrosian.

"Honey, are you up?" Evelyn called, at the foot of the stairs. "It's Lena."

" 'Bout time. Tell her I'll be right there!"

"Hurry! She's on a pay phone, says she's out of change."

Not even taking the time to shut off the water, Jeffries ran for the bedroom and grabbed the extension.

" 'Morning Arlin."

"Lena? Where the hell are you? I'll call you right back."

"I can't divulge that, sir. I don't know who might be listening on your line. Sorry to bother you so early."

"To hell with that. Why didn't you bother me a little earlier? A lot earlier. Like maybe sometime in the last two, three days?"

"It's a long story, Lieutenant. We've had kind of a bad night, but I got Anthony Lowell with me. I need to know if I can bring him in."

"What the hell you mean 'can you bring him in?' We been lookin' for you and him for two days!"

"Sorry. But it's gettin' a little complicated. We got people on our ass with choppers and snipers."

"Who? The Medellin Cartel, for Chrissake?"

"No, sir. I think it's the Feds."

What in hell—? Snipers? This was getting out of hand. "Lena? Just bring him in. The chief's having another cow. I'll deal with

205

him, but you just come on in on the double. I'll meet you at the station."

"I'm not sure that's a good idea. Considering what's been happening, I'm concerned about the safety of my witness. Not to mention my own butt."

"Your butt is in the rack already, Lena! We got complaints from Palm County about—" There was a loud click on the line, which meant time had run out. "Lena, can you hear me? Give me the number!"

"I don't think I'd better do that, sir. I'll be in, soon as I can."

"Wait a minute, goddammit, if you don't—!" Click. The line went dead. Jeffries launched into a long series of very loud expletives, slammed down the phone, and looked up to see someone standing in the doorway. His son Devon, age nine, looking at him with a mixture of fear and awe. Great. I've just taught my kid twenty new ways to swear. Nice going, Lieutenant Asshole.

"Dad, you OK?"

"Yes. Sorry, son. Just some bad news from the station. It'll be OK." He touseled his son's hair, feeling very much ashamed. Evelyn came up the stairs, with an accusing glare.

"Arlin Jeffries, I've a good mind to wash your mouth out with soap. Carryin' on like that in front of the children."

"I know, I'm a bad boy and I'm buying dinner for everybody, tonight at Chuck E. Cheese's. Right after we get those doggone decorations up."

"I heard that!" called Kimmy, poking her curler-infested head out the bathroom door. "You better, Dad."

"Will you hurry up, Kimmy?" shouted Devon. "I gotta go."

"C'mon, son," said Jeffries gently. "You can use mine. Just this once."

Evelyn shook her head and marched back downstairs muttering dire threats about rules and burned coffee. Knowing what a privilege it was that had just been bestowed on him, Devon was much appeased. Throwing a smug look back at his sister, he followed his father to the master bathroom and was very careful not to pee on the

206

top of the bowl. Like he usually did just to annoy his sister. He even put the seat down afterward. This was going to be a good day, he decided. And wait till the guys hear those cool new words my dad said!

Twenty miles north and across the Suncoast Skyway, Julie Barnett Folner was preparing herself for a breakfast meeting with the St. Petersburg Coastal Committee. They were a heavyweight organization of top Pinellas County civic leaders, financiers, and activists, in whose hands almost any key decision determining the fate of that bustling Gulf coastline lay. She was lobbying for county funds for a new beach restoration on Sand Key. She had become a tireless campaigner over the years. Her opera aspirations were long behind her, but a need to be in the limelight remained ever present. Her husband was a celebrity, of course. But she loathed the role of a celebrity wife, and he had always encouraged her to stake a claim of her own in the public eye. She had to admit to herself that she had mixed feelings about their impending ascent to Washington. She knew she would love the hurly-burly social life and constant need to be "on." She was always "on" anyway, so that was no problem.

The problem was getting over this last final hurdle. She and Mike had planned it all so well, so carefully, from the very beginning. How could this be happening now—this old woman with her accusations coming out of nowhere—and then these other meddlers and malcontents out to tear away the very fabric of her dreams?

The senator was getting nervous. She'd have to do something about that. And fast.

Ten miles away, outside Bradenton, Lena Bedrosian risked using her badge in order to commandeer a cab. She and Lowell climbed in the back, recharged by two hot coffees. A bag of refined sugar and bleached flour from Donut City served as a buffer between them.

"We going in?" Lowell wanted to know.

"Not yet."

Lowell could tell by the way Bedrosian had terminated the call that something had scared her off.

"Good thinking. If I were you I'd want to get my shit, not to mention evidence, together first. Into a nice, tight, safe package that can't just be swept under the table. Then I'd see about washing my face."

Bedrosian glared. "Speak for yourself. All I got now is a crazy man who claims to be a P.I. with a lot of wild innuendos about one of the most important people in West Florida. Make that Florida. Make that America."

"Look, I don't blame you for thinking twice," said Lowell. "We're talking about a man who beat a powerhouse family into oblivion when he was still a jerkweed. Pretty scary to think what he might do—might be able to do round about now."

For Bedrosian, the question came back, again and again, to murder. Three murders, maybe more. Did those Feds, did her own commanding officers, intend to sweep them under the table as well?

"You do know they're probably going to try and pin them on you, don't you? Let's face it, that would be a convenient solution. *The* convenient solution. That way, nobody important gets their nose bent out of joint, everybody's happy, and life goes on. Y'know what I mean?"

"Yeah, I get your drift. But pin them on me based on what, exactly? Or doesn't that matter to you and your Feebie friends?"

"Circumstantial evidence. You were first on the scene for all three murders. From two of them, you take off, don't even report. Very suspicious. Then you evade questioning, steal a yacht. Let's face it, if they can hold this guy forever for allegedly selling dope to Dan Quayle, they can sure as hell hold you!"

"Good point. That's what they did to Maureen Fitzgerald. So why don't you just hand me over? You still got time to be a hero."

"Heroine."

"Whatever."

"Look," snapped Bedrosian. "You are not one of my favorite

208

people. But I can't see you as no killer. A pain in the ass, yes, but that ain't a federal offense. It didn't add up from the beginning, much as I might prefer it otherwise."

"Thanks. I think. But the people after us don't seem to care too much about that. It seems pretty damn obvious that whoever had those three people hammered is either in collusion with, or working in competition with, alleged so-called Federal agents."

Bedrosian shook her head. "I can't believe that. You said yourself they might be phonies."

"But that doesn't make it safe to go in. There are ways of reaching people. Even cops."

Bedrosian thought about her conversation with the lieutenant. Had they gotten to him somehow? Which begged the final question. Was this strange, complicated, unkempt, sort-of good-looking rebel Lowell right about all this after all? She had no choice but to carry on with her job and find out.

"Yo. Where we headed?" the cab driver wanted to know.

"Hold your horses." Bedrosian studied Lowell, thinking fast. "I want to print these negatives," she decided. "And I don't wanna wait for Photomat or whatever."

"I wouldn't trust them anyway," said Lowell. "And it just so happens, I have a darkroom."

"That so?"

"It's my other profession, remember? Freelance photographer."

"Yeah, yeah, I just don't recall you mentioning a darkroom. But then there's a lot you probably haven't mentioned yet."

"That's true. Like, I haven't mentioned my favorite foods. Which don't include donuts."

Bedrosian ignored that and made a quick decision. One she hoped she wouldn't regret later.

"OK. We go to your place. Give the man the address."

Lowell complied, hoping the driver could be trusted. He was an independent, which was why they'd risked him. That meant there would be no central dispatch the cops or Feds could check on or commandeer, in case there really was a dragnet out. There'd been no sign of one, except for a larger than usual number of troopers on the road last night. But it was a Friday night, so that was inconclusive. There was a good chance this situation was so sensitive it was still being kept tightly under wraps. Which should help. Also, the driver was West Indian. Which meant probably a refugee, maybe even an illegal. Which meant that, like the last driver, he would prefer to avoid the cops as much as they would.

Bedrosian had flashed her badge and told the obviously frightened man this was police business, and he was not to discuss it or mention their passage to anyone. The driver seemed more than eager to comply. Lowell hoped he would.

The cab passed through the sleepy town of Gulfbridge without incident. The Oyster House was open for breakfast, the usual crowd, and there was little other activity.

As they turned onto Mangrove Road, Lowell felt the tension rising. Their plan was to lay low and continue past if there were any indications of surveillance. They would then have to return by the same route, however, because there was no other way off the key. Neither of them was in much of a mood for another late-October swim.

As they drew close to Lowell's property, the road seemed clear and empty. So did the grounds and driveway. The cab turned into the drive, both detectives in the back taut and watchful.

"All right," Bedrosian ordered, as the cab stopped in front of the shed, out of sight of the road. The unfinished schooner lay on its cradle before them, just as Lowell had left it. The house sat empty. As though watching them.

Bedrosian tipped the driver lavishly as a further incentive for silence, and he drove off, happy for the money and even happier to be rid of them.

"Listen, Bedrosian. How about removing these cuffs? You don't really think I'm going to bolt, do you?"

"Quiet!" she ordered, watching and listening. They approached the rear of the house, unobserved. Holding Lowell's sodden gear for him, she gestured for him to open the door. Lowell had to fish for

210

his keys, unaccustomed to locks, and find the right one. Bedrosian shuffled impatiently as a car drove past out on the road, the rushing sound of radial tires a loud contrast to the cries of birds and insects in the nearby woods and marsh.

Lowell struggled, hampered by the cuffs, but finally got the door open. They went in. The kitchen was its usual disorderly self. Dirty beer mugs and a few plates and dishes littered the sink. The old Frigidaire grumbled its sullen greeting. A faint wisp of gas seeped from the stove pilot.

Bedrosian followed Lowell into the living room—studio and stopped cold at the sight of wreaked havoc. Lowell just stood there a moment, numb. To say someone had trashed the place was putting it mildly. His boxes had been pulled apart, the contents scattered. Papers, photo materials, furniture, files, drawers, everything had been ransacked. Bedrosian caught her breath.

"Looks like you've had visitors," she observed.

Lowell knew he should have expected this.

Bedrosian looked at him a moment, thoughtfully. "Well, either somebody doesn't like you very much, which is easy to believe, or they think you've got somethin' here they want."

"No shit," he muttered, still taking it in.

She walked over to the gallery wall, which had been left undisturbed. She gazed at one particular blowup. The Beatles at Shea Stadium. She gestured at the wall. "You know, I was there."

Lowell stared. "Where?"

The detective tapped the poster. "Shea Stadium, 1964. You take this shot, too?"

He ignored the question. "You were *there?*" This was too much. She had to have been what, five or six?

"My mother took me. She was a big fan. We were staying in New York at the time, visiting relatives, and an aunt or someone had gotten hold of some tickets. Dad thought it was a stupid idea and missed out on history, I guess."

Lowell shook his head. "Christ almighty. A future right-wing yuppie cop in high heels and designer clothes, and *she* got to see the

211

Beatles. So much for justice in this world. Most everyone I knew would've killed for a ticket. I only got in on a bogus press pass and my friends wouldn't speak to me for a month." He frowned, remembering something. "Wait a sec—"

"They were overrated anyway. I'll take Elvis."

"Wait a sec. Do you remember any of it?"

"Not really. I was too young. It was noisy, I remember that much. The crowds were mind-boggling. But I don't—" she was stopped cold by his expression.

He turned and dragged her over to where he had dropped his bag and the cardboard tube, upon entering. Pulling out the contents, he found what he was looking for: the photo of the couple, kissing. He looked over at her. "This was there."

She blinked. "Say what?"

"Shea Stadium, 1964. She was there, too."

She joined him, dubious. "How can you tell?"

"Look at the button!" He tapped the photo in excitement. "She's wearing the button. It says 'Beatlemania.' You should remember, if you were there too."

She shook her head. "Anybody could buy one of those buttons. There was a show years later by the same title. It doesn't mean a thing."

He couldn't deny it. But staring at the photo once more, he began to pull together a jumble of scattered recollections. He had been in New York not as a news photographer but as a student, on a lark. He'd done a roll of Tri-X as a school project, and had managed to finagle his way into the press section with skills that would save his neck a thousand times afterward, and probably did as much as anything else to shape his destiny as a private eye.

He couldn't actually read the lettering on the button, but it didn't matter anymore. He knew what it said. It all came back to him. No wonder Maureen had brought it to him. She'd gotten hold of it somehow, possibly from Lucretia, or by some desperate means that belied her timid frailty. Hadn't Caitlin mentioned the old woman had come back to the island to see her? And so she'd taken the photo

212

to a detective who was also a photographer—and who had also been at the scene of the alleged crime. It was the natural thing to do. Cursing himself for his thick-headedness, he handed the print back to Bedrosian.

She looked at the two lovers again, still unconvinced. "This is what you've been gettin' at? You're saying this was Folner and Julie together, way back in '64?"

"That's what I'm saying. Which is two years before her marriage to Henry."

"Even if you can prove that's him, it still doesn't prove he committed a crime."

"Maybe not. But it's another piece of the puzzle."

"I think you have a better case with the one on the boat," she said. "It's definitely a no-no coppin' a feel with somebody else's bride. Although in those days that wasn't a crime either."

"It's not exactly a recommendation for the Supreme Court."

"Probably not. But that's not what we're after here, is it? Keepin' Folner off the bench?"

"No," he admitted. "But if I can bring this out a little, show it's him, show him we have proof he was in an adulterous relationship with Julie, he might break. It's worth a shot."

"Maybe. But is it worth gettin' shot at?"

He grinned at her observation, despite his predicament. He picked up the white envelope with the negatives. "Let me experiment with some of these. I can do some things that might make the images clearer, more legible. It'll take time, though."

She shook her head, finally. "So what if you nail him? So he knew her back then. She ditched him for the guy with bucks, who drowned. When she got in trouble, he stuck by her, helped her out, they fell in love, and got married. They're still married today. That makes them the perfect couple. Where's the beef?"

"It's too neat. It's way too neat."

Bedrosian stared at some of the news photos on the wall. She tapped one of Nixon, in front of the Watergate.

"Hey, I've seen this one." She checked the signature and looked back at Lowell, with a new dawning of respect. "You took this?"

"All of them. It used to be my job, remember?"

She contemplated him anew, with a look of mixed awe and more than a little renewed distaste. She'd never been a fan of the media. But still, this was big-time stuff. She examined some of the others.

"Look at all this. I remember that one too. You were some kinda hotshot photographer, weren't you!"

Lowell shrugged modestly. "Once upon a time." It had been something to do, for a while. It had given him a certain degree of self-respect and independence. For a while. But it hadn't lasted.

Bedrosian shook her head in genuine amazement. "You were good, Lowell. What happened? You O.D. on free love?"

"It was time for a change, that's all. Speaking of changes, I'd like to get out of this toy sailor suit and into something clean. And dry. I can probably scrounge something up for you too, if you want."

The police detective considered, then shook her head. "I'll wait," she said. However, much to his surprise, she unlocked his handcuffs.

"Go ahead. This is the second time I'm trusting you. Don't let me down or you're road kill. I'm stickin' my neck out enough on this thing. But I'm gonna let you work on those two photographs."

"Which two photographs?"

"The one that might be Folner groping Julie on the boat, and the one of the abduction on the dock." She fished the second photo out of the pile and scrutinized it once more, before handing it to him. "She definitely looks like she doesn't want to go. If you can positively identify that's Folner taking that woman by force, then you may have a case. It's called kidnapping. Then I'll supoena the medical records, court records, whatever I can find to determine how she got put away, by whom, and exactly when."

"Thanks," said Lowell, rubbing his wrists. "But don't hold your breath. I may or may not get an image we can identify."

"Hey, you gonna build me up for all this for nothing? No way, pal. You got your chance. You better deliver."

"I'll do my best. You coming?"

"Uh-uh. You're a big boy. You can dress yourself. Just make it fast."

Lowell hurried upstairs, washed up the best he could, scraped a razor across his face with minimum damage, put on some reasonably clean slacks and a button-down sport shirt, and headed back downstairs.

"The darkroom is over here," he indicated.

She shook her head. "No way I'm goin' with you into some darkroom."

"Too bad. You might learn something."

"Yeah, right. Where is it?"

"Over there," Lowell pointed. "Or it used to be."

He opened the darkroom door and switched on the light. The intruder—or intruders—whoever it was had entered here. The darkroom had been left untouched. Either from the intruder's haste, or possibly from a distaste for, or even fear of, chemicals.

"I think I will watch," decided the cop, following him in. "I'll stand over here. Don't try anything funny."

"Like what? Making a pass? Or making a break?"

"You'd regret either one."

Lowell grinned and went about setting up the trays. Pouring the chemicals, he switched on the enlarger. The old negatives were very dry and brittle, but with careful handling he might still be able to make a decent print and blow it up.

"How long will it take?" Bedrosian checked her watch, worried. "We're damn vulnerable here." After seeing the destruction, she wished they hadn't come.

"An hour or so."

"Well, hurry it up. You said you might be able to make some adjustments on those, bring up some of the features or whatever?"

"Maybe. I'll have to see. What I'd really like for that would be a computer."

"Christ," muttered the cop. "Now he wants a computer. Maybe you'll want a Concorde next, to fly to Paris. You can't do it here?"

"Somewhat. It takes time. This equipment is kinda primitive, but

215

it's still the best and only way to get a customized print. All that new technology of photo processing—all that one-hour shit—is based on taking an average exposure time, and then cranking the entire roll on a single setting. Fast, easy, and mediocre."

"So why do you want a computer?"

"Enhancement. It's like digital sound. A computer can break down the available information, shape, size, relative depth of shadows, and so forth, and give a best estimate of what a face, for example, might look like. Even if we can't see it. Sometimes it's uncannily accurate. Especially if you have another photo of the same person taken around the same time, for comparison. Which I do believe we have."

"You mean the courthouse photos," said Bedrosian. But that gave rise to another concern. "Look, let's say you can squeeze out an image that alleges to be Michael Folner from this. What would be your next move? You can't just go and have him arrested. You don't have a case."

That was a point. Once again, Lowell was suddenly unsure of his own motivations. Did he merely want to nail this judge, for political reasons? Did he really think Folner might be a murderer? Even a maniacal one? Was all this worth a lousy hundred bucks? Not likely. So what was he in this for? Justice?

"Let's just get our blowups, see what we've got, and worry about that later," he suggested.

Bedrosian nodded reluctantly. She was in this far. She may as well see how it turned out.

Lowell lined up the first negative under the camera stand, and printed a variety of exposures. Now for the enlarger. Bedrosian watched, fascinated and impatient at the same time, as he placed the photographic paper beneath the lens, set the focus, and switched it on.

"Well, we'll know more in a minute." Dropping the paper into the developer, they watched as the image slowly formed. It still seemed magical to Bedrosian, antiquated though it may be. The outline of a man's face formed, turned toward the woman, but his profile clearly visible, definitely more visible than before.

Lowell lifted the print from the developer, and dropped it into the fixer a moment. Then the rinse. The face of the man groping the woman on the boat was as clear as it was going to be. It was still indistinct. Too much shadow. But the hand cupping Julie's breast was now much clearer. This was no friendly chat.

"Interesting," she admitted, with a slight blush. "But that still could be anybody."

Lowell knew she was right. Maybe a blowup, with a little more exposure time on the face and a shorter developer bath, might be enough for the computer to work with. But would the cop go along with him? He doubted it.

"I can try again, but I think we're going to need that computer."

Bedrosian shook her head. "Try again. Do the other one."

Lowell could feel the pressure. He placed the second shot under the enlarger and pushed the image way down, until the face of the man holding Maureen's arm filled the frame. Quickly, he made the print, held the exposure time a moment longer, and dropped it into the developer. A few seconds less, this time. He checked his watch. Normally, he would take meticulous notes: of each enlargement setting, focus range, exposure time, developer time, and so forth. There was no time for that now. He would have to wing it.

The image formed. They watched it, faint, then darker, then darker. Quickly he pulled it out, and dipped it in the fixer. Then the rinse. He had set the enlargement so the two faces were approximately the same size.

Faintly, they could make out the ridge of bones, above the eyes— mostly shadows still—and the outline of a chin. The two men appeared to be the same man.

"I still can't tell from these. It does look like him, but . . ."

Lowell turned to the cop. "Can you get the other shots? I'd like to compare with them."

Bedrosian shrugged. "Okay to open the door?"

"Go ahead." She went out into the studio for the tube, slid out

217

the contents onto the coffee table, and found the two courthouse photos. She brought them back, doubtfully.

Lowell laid them out on the work table, and turned on the fluorescent lights above. Using a magnifying glass, he went back and forth, from Folner by the car, to the two men with Maureen. Back and forth, back and forth.

"Take a look. The ridge across the brow here. And here. The same bone structure. And the nose. Same shape. And chin. This is definitely him! In all of these."

Bedrosian wasn't convinced. "Still could be anybody to me." But she had to admit, an expert witness—another one, not this guy with a prejudicial viewpoint—might make a case here.

"We need that computer. It would clinch it, one way or another. I say we find out for certain."

They heard a sound. At the same instant they both spun and found the door blocked by Sgt. Allenson. Behind him were Deputy Pilchner and the two Feds—or whatever they were—Werner and Lefcourt, who had pursued them all this way.

"Find out what, Lowell?" Allenson wanted to know.

21

Lowell and Bedrosian didn't look at each other. The decision to make them a team had been made by others. They were in it together now, for the duration. Too bad they still didn't like each other.

"I hope you have a warrant this time," said Lowell. "Otherwise, you are trespassing. Which is against the law."

"Yes, sir. We have a warrant right here." Allenson held it out. "For your arrest on suspicion of three counts of murder, grand larceny, flight from justice, resisting arrest, and possession of stolen property."

"Stolen property?"

The sergeant nodded to Pilchner. "Get those negatives and prints, will you, Joe? And the ones outside."

"Is that what you refer to as 'stolen property'?" pursued Lowell, sarcasm building. He felt the danger but didn't care.

"Shut up, Lowell. You're in way over your head, pal." Allenson hadn't liked being dragged into this thing. But the two Feebes had been vehemently persuasive, had threatened massive intervention from Washington if they didn't cooperate and hinted at other unpleasantries, such as tax audits. So in he was, and damned if he was going to take shit about it. "You just come quietly, before this mess gets any worse."

"Where's Jeffries?" demanded Bedrosian. "I want to talk to him."

The cops turned to her finally. Lowell could tell they had very mixed feelings toward her right now. "He's busy, Lena," the sergeant finally answered. "Special Agents Werner and Lefcourt have taken over jurisdiction here."

"On what authority?"

"My authority," replied Werner, stepping forward, a small Baretta pistol in hand. "Will you two step out of that darkroom, please."

From the studio, Werner gestured for them to raise their hands and turned to Lowell. "That was quite a stunt you pulled out on the water," he remarked, an edge to his voice.

Lowell smiled. "Glad you liked it."

Werner pressed his lips tight. "I was watching your wake. I should've been watching the markers."

"I was counting on that," said Lowell.

Werner grinned slightly, then turned his icy gaze back on Bedrosian. "Just what do you know about all this, ma'am?"

Bedrosian looked at him warily. "It's 'detective,' to you. Those charges you mention are bogus and you know it. This man is a material witness to a murder under my jurisdiction. I am keeping him under my own personal protection until we go before a grand jury, for the purpose of investigating a possible conspiracy to murder Henry Hartley the Third, in January of 1966. So if you'll excuse me, you can tell that to the judge."

Lefcourt shook his head in admiration of the woman's grit. Bedrosian noted the location of Allenson as she spoke. Pilchner was a few feet away, examining some of the shredded clippings. Werner moved behind them. That left Lefcourt. The big man. Lowell stood, waiting for a clear signal. It came, lightning fast. With reflexes that belied her clothes-horse image, the police detective whipped out her police special and dropped to one knee in a single movement. Turning to one side so that all four men were in her peripheral line of sight, she fired once, and Werner's gun spun out of his hand across the room, glinting cold and blue, as it clattered against the far wall.

"You. Over here. Now. Next to your partner."

"Lena, come on—" protested Allenson, sweating profusely.

"Shut up. Move it!" she barked, as Werner slowly raised his hands, staring at her in wonder. Lefcourt tensed, unsure what to do. He made a slight move in her direction. Bedrosian warned him with her eyes. "I'm acting as a police officer in the line of duty, and you are interfering with the execution of said duty. Get next to your partner, hands up. Now!"

"Lena, we have orders—" began Allenson.

"Shut up, Bill. Move it!"

Lefcourt stood stock-still. He began to move as though to comply, then suddenly grabbed for his gun, tucked into his belt. Bedrosian calmly shot him in the shoulder. Everyone's hands went up immediately.

"Did you have to do that?" demanded Lowell.

"Sorry about that," said Bedrosian calmly. "I'll send a doctor, it's just a graze. Deputy. Get over here, don't try anything stupid."

Pilchner contemplated whether to try for his own gun. But for what? It wasn't his idea to be here in the first place, he'd been dragged along by Allenson. He'd just as soon stayed with Lorraine. Bad enough Denise had caught on and booted him out this very morning. His luck was definitely at a low ebb just now. Why push it for these jokers? Cursing women in general and women cops in particular, he raised his hands high.

"Lowell," ordered Bedrosian. "Get their guns, and put them on the table."

"Say please."

"Fuck you."

"Close enough." Lowell gathered up a small arsenal.

Werner watched, seething.

The guns were on the table. Everyone looked at Bedrosian, waiting to see what happened next.

Bedrosian seized the weapons and loaded them into her coat pockets. She looked like a bag lady, all lumps and sags. "All of you, into the darkroom. Move!"

"Does that include me?" inquired Lowell.

"You stay."

Bedrosian stepped aside as they moved past her, careful to stay out of reach of Lefcourt in particular. She knew the danger of a wounded quarry. Lowell remained at her side.

"All right. On your hands and knees. All of you. Now!"

They glared, and grumbled, and obeyed. Lefcourt was turning pale, teeth gritting. The wound was a minor flesh wound. He'd be all right. Bedrosian felt bad about it, but she'd had little choice.

"Lowell, get their cuffs," she commanded. "They'll be in the jacket pockets of those two." She indicated the two cops. "Hurry up!" Then she remembered. "Please."

Lowell dug them out, right where she'd said.

"OK, would you please cuff them to each other—hand to foot?"

"Sure."

Lowell did so—careful of hands he knew were itching to seize him. By keeping the prisoners down on all fours, as Bedrosian correctly had surmised, quick hand movements were precluded. As soon as they were secured, he fetched a strip of cloth and bound Lefcourt's shoulder.

Bedrosian approached the two Feds. Holding the gun at their necks, one by one, she reached into their jacket pockets with her free hand and extracted their wallets. She also took a set of car keys from Werner's pocket.

"All right," she snapped, searching for identification. "Now let's see who you two clowns are supposed to be."

She found the badges. They appeared legit. Which didn't mean jack shit, as she well knew. She read the names. "How the hell do I know these aren't phony?"

"There's a number on the card in the money compartment," snarled Werner, veins bulging in his neck. "Call it. They'll tell you."

"Call who? God? Carmen San Diego? J. Edgar Hoover?"

"They'll tell you."

"Tell me what? That you got a license to assault and shoot an unarmed citizen and a police officer doing her duty?"

"You're the one who shot somebody. We're just doing our job, Detective. Which you are obstructing."

"We'll see about that."

"We were trying to get you to turn back," insisted Werner, trying a new tack. "Nobody wants a firefight. We just want to talk."

"Who's 'we' supposed to be?"

"I can't tell you that," breathed Werner, straining at his restraints. "But we have authorization. Call that number. They'll confirm what I'm saying. You're in over your heads!"

"Then we're just gonna have to swim for it."

"Again," added Lowell.

Bedrosian pocketed the I.D. and turned to the open front door the four men had just walked in through. Stepping onto the veranda, she hurled the wallets out into the bushes. She then turned to Lowell, who was watching the entire performance in grudging admiration. "What're you lookin' at? Get your evidence, and let's go!"

"Say please."

"Fuck you."

"Close enough."

Leaving the four men shackled and swearing, Lowell and Bedrosian walked out the door, to where the Ford was parked in the front driveway. Lowell looked it over and frowned. She made a quick visual check of the area.

"No backups," she observed.

"That car. It's three years old. Feds don't drive three-year-old vehicles. They have sweetheart deals with the Big Three," said Lowell. "They buy new cars every year, with our tax dollars. Saves jobs, the argument goes. Good for the economy. Goes right along with 'Buy American.' "

"So?" She shrugged it off and opened the door, using Werner's keys. "Maybe they got budget cuts."

Lowell got in and unlocked the door on the driver's side. In moments, they were out on Mangrove Road, racing away.

Bedrosian glared. "You're still under arrest, you know!"

"You're the constable."

Ten minutes later, they pulled over to a phone booth in Gulfbridge. Lowell kept watch while Bedrosian made the call. The cop returned to the car, face grim.

"I can't get through to Jeffries. But I talked to the deputy chief."

"What'd he say?"

"He said come in. I still want to call that number on the card."

"What for? It's a setup. They'll just tell you whatever they want you to hear."

"Maybe." She turned, returned to the phone booth, and dialed a long series of numbers. He watched her face. She asked a question. The answer didn't please her. She returned to the car.

"So, are you going in?" he inquired.

Bedrosian shook her head, started the engine, and pulled into the road once again. "Nope. We are."

Lowell was silent, contemplating his next move. He then made a suggestion, to which the cop sullenly agreed. They made a detour, which took about three minutes. By the time they got to the station house, less than fifteen minutes had gone by. Speeding up to the front entrance, Bedrosian skidded to a stop in the red zone. They got out and casually strolled inside. Two patrolmen and a nearby meter person watched them enter, aware that something was afoot.

Baker and Shuler were just on their way out when they saw the two coming, and turned back to spread the word. Lowell and Bedrosian were greeted by a buzz of commotion as they walked past the desk sergeant—the briefest hello—and on down the hall to the squad room.

A reception was waiting for them, obviously hastily assembled. Their surprise attack had thrown the station into total disarray, just as Bedrosian had hoped. Better yet, there were no Feds in sight to pull strings. Not yet anyway.

"Well, well," spluttered the captain, Pete Carrera, face red as a

224

beet. He'd obviously had to run to get here ahead of them. "Look what the cat dragged in. The mouse and the rat."

"Who's which?" Lowell wanted to know.

Carrera was just back from his administrative leave over the accidental shooting of a prisoner, and in a foul mood for being thrown into the trenches. Especially so soon after a fishing holiday in the Keys.

"So, Captain. How was the fishing?" Bedrosian smiled cheerfully.

"Forget the fishing," snapped the captain. "What the hell you think you're doin', Detective? Where's my other men?"

"What men?" Bedrosian scanned the room quickly. To her relief, she saw that Jeffries was present. Looking exceedingly uncomfortable. Jeffries must be under the gun, she thought. That explained his tone this morning. Shit.

"Hey, what happened to Manatee City's best-dressed woman?" cracked Lee Hargrove, wrinkling his nose. "Jesus, Lena, you look like shit! You taken up mud wrestling or something?"

"Lena," inquired the lieutenant, with a grimace and a glance at the captain. "Where the hell are Pilchner and Allenson?"

"Sorry, Arlin. They're kinda tied up. Along with their two Fed buddies."

"What Feds?" blustered Carrera furious. "There's no Feds on this case."

Lowell and Bedrosian exchanged looks. "You sure about that, Captain?" she asked.

"Yeah, I'm sure, I'da heard. There were a couple suits hangin' around here last week, but—" He frowned, pondering.

"They're safe, don't worry. But I gotta make sure we stay that way, too. Right, Lowell?"

"It would be preferable."

"My partner here has reason to be concerned. On account of they shot at him, and he's a material witness."

"Who shot at him?" demanded Jeffries.

"The Federales."

"There was Feds with Allenson?" Carrera couldn't believe it.

225

"So they said. They had credentials."

The cops all stared at her, then looked sidelong at Lowell in disbelief.

"Anyone check with Washington about this?"

"You ever try and call Washington?" Carrera took a breath, let it out, and took another one to calm himself. He lit a cigar and blew a smoke ring into the air. Bedrosian hated smoke, and Carrera knew it. "They call you, you don't call them."

"Detective," he went on, in the calmest, most officious manner he could muster, "you are so far out of line you'll never carry a purse in this town again, not to mention a badge, I got any say in it. Just for starters, you been insubordinate, leaving this jurisdiction without checkin' with your superiors and without a partner."

"I got one," she said, not looking at Lowell.

Carrera looked confused, but Jeffries got it and grinned in spite of himself. "Maybe we should take a look at her report, Captain. Soon as she's had a chance to file one," he said.

Bedrosian looked at her superior sideways, reached into her bag, and pulled out a large envelope. "I think you should check out what's in here, Arlin. It's quite interesting."

Carrera glowered. "What the hell you got there, Lena?"

"I'm still workin' on it, Peter. But there may be evidence here that links the murder of Maureen Fitzgerald to Judge Michael Butler Folner, of the Hillsborough County Superior Court and possibly the Supreme Court of the United States," Bedrosian replied.

"All right. That does it. Cuff them shitheads, and call the Marshall," barked the captain to Hargrove, fed up to the gills and out for blood. Especially the blood of this cocky, insubordinate little cunt of a cop and the goddamn hippy P.I.

Hargrove pulled out his handcuffs and reached for Bedrosian's arm, with an apologetic look. He and Bedrosian were old friends and went to the same church.

"One thing," mentioned Lowell, in a casual tone. "Those are just copies, of course. The press gets the originals in two hours time."

Carrera turned purple. "You say what?"

"Do I have to repeat myself, sir?"

Carrera turned livid. "OK. That's it for you bozos. You're outa here. You got the fuckin' nerve to—"

"That'll do, Pete," cracked a booming voice. Chief Sturbridge had probably been waiting for just such a moment to make his entry. "And put that goddamn cigar out. I don't smoke, you don't smoke, got that?"

"Sure, Chief," fumed Carrera, stubbing his stogie. "But you heard what the goddamn—"

"I heard. Detective Bedrosian is just following good police procedures. You know how evidence has a way of getting lost around here at times. How are you, Lena?" He nodded at Bedrosian and turned an appraising eye on Lowell. "I don't think I've had the pleasure."

"Anthony Lowell, Private Investigator."

Sturbridge nodded, curtly. "The Huntley case. And that child molester in Bradenton?"

"The one and same."

"Sir," began Bedrosian, "I was trying to—"

"I know what you're trying to do. You're trying to create the goddamnest quagmire of speculation, innuendo, and libel since Irangate, and if you got a bone to pick with Judge Folner this is one hell of a time to bring it up."

"I know, sir," said Bedrosian. "I apologize. I feel the same way as you about it, but if you'll read the file and give me twenty-four hours, well, maybe you'll agree somethin's got to be done."

"Like what?"

"Like maybe call for a grand jury."

"Jesus. You don't ask for much, do you? What exactly is it you think you're onto here?"

Lowell took a chance. "Chief. Am I correct in assuming you haven't heard anything negative in the way of an investigation into Judge Folner's background?"

"You got that right. The man is Mr. Clean personified."

"We may be sitting on another Supreme Court hot potato, sir," said Bedrosian. "And this one involves homicide."

"Come on, you gonna sit there and tell me—"

"Twenty-four hours, sir. Read the documents. I think you'll see that there's something that isn't quite right, and I think the three murders of involved parties in the last three days raise some serious questions."

"This is the most cockamamie—" blustered Carrera.

"Shut up, Pete." Sturbridge worked his jaw. Avoiding Carrera's blazing rage, he turned to Jeffries. "What do you think, Lieutenant?"

"I don't know, Chief. I'd say it was a last-ditch political cheap shot, except that I know Lena. Even so, I'd have to know a hell of a lot more than what I've heard so far."

"That's what I'm saying, sir—" interjected Bedrosian.

"Quiet!" Sturbridge was dying for a smoke, and silently cursed Carrera for reminding him. "All right. Twenty-four hours. But we hold Lowell here. And you get a partner."

"No, sir. Mr. Lowell has special knowledge of this case. I want him with me on this investigation."

"She needs me," grinned Lowell.

Now it was Sturbridge's turn to lose his temper. "Dammit, Lena. You better know what the hell you're doin' here. OK, you got your twenty-four, with your—colleague here. But then you are lion food. Both of you. Agreed?"

"Yes, sir."

"Except the lion part," agreed Lowell.

"All right then. Get the hell outa here."

"Yes, sir. By the way, Sergeant Allenson and Deputy Pilchner are handcuffed over at Lowell's place out on Mangrove Road. With those same two alleged Federal agents you may have mentioned. The big guy needs a doctor, so you better send the paramedics."

Amid the ensuing stunned silence, Bedrosian and Lowell headed for the door, not looking back. The moment they were gone, Carrera slammed his fist on the table, with an explosion of invective. Sturbridge just shook his head, unable to conceal a grin of admiration.

228

"What's wrong, Pete? It's called balls, and she's got more than you." He put his hand out. "I'll take those papers or whatever they are, while we're at it."

Carrera ground his teeth and obeyed, seething.

22

_____

Lowell watched the left flank, front to rear, and Bedrosian the right, as they left the station. They weren't followed. Bedrosian started up the Ford sedan, and they got the hell out of there, not even bothering to remove the parking ticket from the windshield. If this was a Federal vehicle, no one would be looking for it yet, not until they picked up their two men.

About a mile out of town, Bedrosian made a sudden turn into a typical subdivision of tract houses.

"Where we going?" Lowell asked.

"I got a stop to make."

The cop pulled up in front of an ordinary blue ranch house, with tricycles and toys littering the driveway. She jumped out and hurried in. Lowell realized where they were. This was the detective's home. She was checking in with a family who hadn't seen her for days and didn't know if she was dead or alive. Funny, he hadn't thought of her in that way. People rarely bother to see each other as parts of intricate patterns of relationships, he thought. If they did, we'd all have much more love and respect for each other than we do. I'd have stopped too, he decided. Dangerous as it was. Anyway, it was her turn to freshen up. He couldn't begrudge her that.

Five minutes went by. Lowell began to consider evacuating the area on foot if the cop didn't return in another minute. They were sitting ducks here.

The door opened and Bedrosian came out, face washed, hair pulled back (no time to wash that), and wearing a clean beige linen suit. With her was a flustered young man, with pink puffy cheeks and a baby cradled in his arm. Behind them trailed two young children, girls around four and six, both crying. The detective kissed the children, and then the man. The little girls pleaded. Bedrosian took the baby for a brief moment, held it with a mother's tenderness, then gave it back. She kissed the man once again fiercely, hesitated, then turned away, blinking back tears. Lowell didn't need to ask. It was plain as day.

Signaling for Lowell to wait, she ran to the attached two-car garage, opened it up, and moved a wheelbarrow and bale of peat moss aside. The man went angrily back inside, dragging the wailing children with him. They never even glanced in Lowell's direction.

Behind the lawn mower gleamed a '65 Mustang GT fastback, badly in need of restoration. Lowell smiled in approval as he watched the detective get in and crank over the 289 V-8. So. Police Detective Bedrosian had a long-term project of her own. She also had a personal life. He could relate to that. A family. He should have guessed. He felt glad that he hadn't followed up on any of those fleeting urges he'd had, to put a move on her in his weaker moments. He couldn't help feeling a deep-down sadness and a new respect for this fiercely determined and independent woman who just happened to be a cop. She had a family. All he had left was the remains of a boat.

After several attempts, Bedrosian got the engine running and waved him over.

This heap is almost as far gone as my Chevy, Lowell thought with an inward smile, as he climbed into the passenger seat and buckled the frayed old seat belt. The car's paint job, which must once have been cherry red, had long since faded to a sort of dull orange. The pony upholstery was cracked and torn, the headliner ripped and sagging, dashboard cracked and oozing dried yellow foam. Valves worn, rings worn, probably gulps a quart or so of oil per tankful, blue smoke everywhere, cracked muffler, slipping clutch, synchros shot—my kind of car!

Bedrosian backed out of the garage, careful to avoid the various tricycles, skateboards, and other toys in permanent occupancy there.

"Put the other car in the garage," she ordered, handing him the keys. Lowell complied, agreeing it was a necessary move. The car was like a billboard, advertising their movements.

He quickly pulled it in, closed the door, and hopped back into the Mustang. She drove away, burning rubber, leaving a trail of smoke and surely tears from the watchers at the window. It didn't matter whether it was a man or a woman. A cop's family learned to treat every farewell as potentially their last.

"Don't say a word," she snapped, turning the corner.

Lowell didn't have to.

Bedrosian took a quick breath and released it. "This is all bluff, you know that, don't you?"

"You mean you don't have a foolproof plan?" he asked, in mock bewilderment.

"Real funny. We got twenty-four hours to pin a case on the tail of this donkey, or we're finished. My family included."

"They look like nice people. I hope you're wrong."

"Nobody's gonna touch them, physically. They'll just kick my butt in the gutter and let them eat dirt, is all."

"So, I vote we prevent that."

"Forget this 'we' crap," growled Bedrosian. "You're nothin' but a what-cha-ma-call-it—albatross—around my neck. I'm still in charge of this investigation, Lowell."

"Maybe you forgot. Back on the Island, you said I needed you to know what I know. Now you need to know what I know. I'm still your partner or it's no deal. Besides, those documents belong to me, and you haven't said 'please.' "

"Like hell," shouted Bedrosian. She pulled over to the curb and seized Lowell by the shirt. "Look. I agreed we work together, Lowell. But don't piss me off. Four days is about as much as I wanna know you."

"Five days," corrected Lowell, extricating himself from the detective's grip. "I just thought we oughta run 'em through the computer first."

She blinked. "Run what?"

"The photos."

She glared. "What computer?"

"At the college. Where I teach a class." Or, he thought to himself, where I used to teach a class. Prior to taking an unexplained leave of absence this week. The cop waited a long moment. Then shrugged.

"All right," she snapped, throwing the door open and getting out. "You drive, I'm beat to shit."

Lowell nodded, slid over, buckled up, and checked the gear-box. A familiar late-sixties four-on-the-floor. No problem. Another occasion, it would be a ton of fun.

Bedrosian got back in on the other side, ignoring the seat belt. She winced as Lowell threw it into first, ground away half of the remaining gear teeth, and took off, burning off what was left of the rubber on the two rear baldies.

"Son of a bitch!" Bedrosian simmered. "You're just achin' for me to pop you one, is what you're doing. Probably so you can yell police brutality and sue the county for millions."

"Good idea," nodded Lowell agreeably.

Bedrosian shook her head. Why the hell couldn't it ever be easy?

It took fifteen minutes to retrieve the photos and clippings from the copy shop where, for safety, they'd left them when they made the copies they'd given to the chief. Ten minutes later they were on the campus of Sun Coast College. Like most community and junior colleges in the South, it resembled a high-school campus more than it did the traditional East Coast college. There were no ivy-covered walls, broad, tree-dotted lawns, or gray stone arches; no Victorian bell towers or Georgian columns. It was entirely, fundamentally utilitarian: four one-story brick blocks, each with a covered walk-

233

way, and rows of classrooms with outside entrances. A fifth building served as combination administration offices and library, set off on the far side of the two-acre parking lot—the entire "quad" of the campus. Behind the classroom buildings were a baseball diamond and combination football-soccer field, with a cinder track, small field house, and grandstand.

Lowell pulled the Mustang into the student parking lot, unable to use the faculty spaces because they required a sticker. The Science Building was at the far end of the campus.

"There," he pointed.

"Lead the way, Professor," muttered the cop, tucking the now thoroughly bent and battered poster tube under her arm.

They approached the building, curious glances coming their way from passing students. Some knew Lowell, but couldn't place him, the way he looked now, with the new Navy crew cut.

"You sure this lady's gonna be here?" The cop asked, for the second time. Lowell had explained his plan. He knew the faculty advisor and head of the Computer Sciences Department. He didn't bother to mention he'd dated her twice, as an experiment in social awareness. They'd parted friends.

A young female student hurried past, threw them a casual glance and stopped in her tracks, staring in disbelief.

"Mr. Lowell? Is that you?"

It was Sheila Balfour. The young, would-be model from way back a couple of lifetimes ago. Three, to be exact. Lowell tried to go around her, but she stepped in front of them.

"What happened to you?" she gasped.

"Yeah. Sorry I didn't make the—meeting. Something came up." He glanced at Bedrosian, shuffling impatiently. "Listen, I have to ask you a favor."

"Sure, anything," Sheila replied, instantly wary, eyes shifting nervously to the detective.

"I need you to notify the department head and put up a note on the lab door that I had to take an unexpected leave on family business. Can you do that for me?"

She stared, not comprehending. "Sure, Mr. Lowell. But what about classes? When will you be back?"

"I'll let you know." He turned away, the cop right behind him. Sheila stared after them in dismay, and hurried away to tell her friends.

Entering the Computer Center, Lowell marched up to a bored student-assistant manning the receptionist's desk. Waiting for his shift to end.

"Hi. We'd like to access the Data Processing Interface."

"Sorry, that's strictly for faculty and research," replied the young man, glancing momentarily up from his copy of *Sports Illustrated* with unabashed insolence.

Lowell slapped his faculty card down on top of a picture of Cowboy QB Troy Aikman. "I *am* faculty."

The student-assistant blinked, totally abashed. He hastily reached for the telephone. "Sorry, sir. I just have to check with Dr. Meeker."

"Now there's a good idea," said Lowell approvingly. "You do that, Aaron."

Aaron Karpler had been in Lowell's Basic Photography class two semesters prior, and had failed to recognize him. Until now. Red as a beet, the student almost dropped the phone, stammering his explanation. "Mr. Lowell! Gee, I didn't recognize you. Dr. Meeker didn't say anything about you or I—"

"That's because she didn't know. Something just came up."

Moments later, a round-faced black woman, middle-aged, with a warm expression and bright, intelligent eyes, emerged from the inside office. She was dressed in a yellow jump suit.

"Tony Lowell! You old rascal, I thought I heard your voice!"

Playfully, she looked Lowell over, shook her head, and turned to Bedrosian. "You must be the latest star attraction. So delighted to meet you."

Bedrosian scowled, not knowing what to say.

"OK, OK, Luisa. I cleaned up my act. Dr. Meeker, this is Detec-

235

tive Bedrosian, a constable of police from our vaunted local gendarmerie. She made me do it."

"Do what?"

"Clean up my act."

She raised her eyebrows. "Well," she chortled, gripping Bedrosian's hands with hers, smiling happily. "That being the case, we here at Sun Coast College have much to thank you for, Detective." She turned back to Lowell. "And to what do we have the honor of this ever so rare visit, Tony Lowell? Another one of your freelance wild goose cases?" Luisa knew all about Tony's "other job," the one that always got him in trouble.

Five minutes later, after a brief explanation leaving out any damning details, they were inside the lab, and Luisa was personally tending to their intended business. It was obviously just the sort of hands-on project she loved: a combination of graphics with photo enhancement and global search into the media files. Fun, fun, fun!

The windowless computer lab had drab, pale green cinder-block walls and full overhead fluorescent lighting (which Lowell hated with a passion). The equipment consisted of a Macintosh Quattro with one-point-two gigabytes—the single most costly equipment purchase the college had made—with full interface into every national data service available, from Nexus to the *Encyclopedia Britannica;* together with six Mac S-X's, two SE-30's, various digital scanners and copiers, and a dozen other miscellaneous P.C.'s.

Luisa pulled up two extra rolling desk chairs in front of the main terminal and powered it up. She pointed to some peripheral equipment, while the big hard drive whirred into motion.

"This is the digital scanner, when you're ready for input," she explained to Bedrosian, switching it on. Bedrosian nodded, uncomprehending. She'd tried the computer at the police station a couple of times. But she couldn't even type, and had quickly left it to the collegiate crowd on the force.

"Don't worry, it's a snap," Luisa assured her, reading her discomfort. "You just slide the document in here, for scanning. It's a lot like a FAX machine. It also reads graphics, which includes photographic images, converts them into computer language, sort of a personal code of its own, and searches for similar coded phrases in the data bank."

"What about the what-ya-call-it, enhancements?" asked Bedrosian, anxious to get on with it.

"That's a little trickier, we'll have to wing it on that one." She looked askance at Lowell. "Unless, of course, Mr. Lowell here has used that feature without my knowledge. It's usually reserved for the police and F.B.I. For criminal investigations, not us local yokels."

"I know the program," Lowell informed them, avoiding her accusatory glare.

Luisa raised her eyebrows. "I should have figured on that one. All right, Mr. Private Eye. Lead the way. I'll just show myself out and—"

"Stick around, Luisa. We need your expertise."

They hadn't told her anything about the nature of their inquiry. Knowing Lowell, she hadn't asked. "Fine. Then let's get on with it. Ready when you are."

Lowell looked at Bedrosian. "You want to cut to the chase, or work up to it?"

"Give it your best shot," she asserted.

With a nod, he inserted the first photograph into the scanner. The blowup of the apparent abduction on the dock. It slid in slowly, and after a few moments, the photo image appeared on the monitor.

"You want color?" teased Luisa, checking the operations manual. "I always wanted to be like that Ted Turner. I'd colorize everything. Make everybody colored, like me!" She laughed heartily. Lowell laughed with her. Bedrosian scowled. Racial humor always made her nervous.

Slowly, Lowell selected the area around the man he believed to be Folner and built up the contrast, enhancing the man's brow, cheekbones, nose and chin. A profile began to take form. Bedrosian frowned. It did look a lot like the early photos of Michael Folner.

237

But not enough to be convincing. There was still a shadow of a doubt.

"This isn't gonna prove anything," muttered the cop finally, standing up.

"How about this," suggested Luisa. "Use the Photoshop and get as clear a picture as you can of your guy, then we run a comparison with one you know is him. If the shoe fits, it'll run like hell, believe me."

"I agree," said Lowell, reaching for the second photo—the one of the couple on the boat. "Let's do a matchup with this photo here."

Luisa nodded and went to work. In a few minutes there was a positive match. "Bingo," she said. With growing excitement, Lowell ran a third photo—of the couple in New York. Again, a match.

"You still don't know for sure it's him," objected Bedrosian. "That only proves it's the same man."

"OK," agreed Lowell. "Then let's match it to one of the courthouse photos, where we know he's recognizable." He selected one. The shot of Folner escorting a triumphant Julie into the Lincoln, with the older man watching from nearby. "With this we should be able to get an overlay that's about ninety-nine percent accurate."

Luisa looked from one to the other, wanting to help. "Is this person supposed to be a public figure?" she asked.

The two detectives looked at each other. "Why do you ask?" inquired Lowell, guardedly.

"Because if it is, you can access the media data base. It can cross-reference the image with all the published photographs of the last twenty years or more. Everything from the *New York Times* microfilm files to the U.P.I. archives."

"But it's not gonna—"

"Come on, what are you afraid of?" asked Lowell in a low aside, putting his hand on the detective's arm, willing her to sit down again. He felt a jolt of electricity at the touch. "Let's use the data bank."

Bedrosian shook her head. "That's fabricating evidence," she snapped. "You'd just be making something up to suit your expectations."

"No, it doesn't work that way," interjected Luisa. They both looked at her. "I've read the systems analysis. It only works if it fits. If the bone structure is even slightly different, for example, or the nose, you overlay new data on top of what you got, you just come up with a double image. Like a double exposure of two different faces, and the data won't register. This sucker is smart."

"Christ," muttered Bedrosian, not knowing what to believe. "Go ahead, then, but I don't think it'll prove anything, I'm telling you."

Lowell slid the courthouse photo home into the scanner, programmed the monitor for split frame, and zoomed in to the man's face as he escorted Julie past the reporters. He pushed the button. The wheels spun, the processor clicked away, billions of bytes of information processing the images into binary language codes, then digital signals, then back to the monitor with a burgeoning series of images. There was a match.

"Same face again," confirmed Luisa.

In a photo montage, the images began to click into place. The face on the boat. Unmistakable. Then another one. The same photo as the one by the courthouse. Lowell caught his breath, and Bedrosian let out a long sigh of regret.

"Why, that looks like Judge Folner," cried Luisa, in surprise. "This must be an ancient photo, he looks so young! And handsome!" she added, approvingly.

The computer didn't stop there. It kept going—matching frame after frame, building a block wall of photo images from the press—the same face, now a little older, its owner shaking hands with Miami Dolphin football coach Don Shula . . . another with Senator Grimm . . . more with the senator, another with Congressman Claude Pepper . . . now older, with Burt Reynolds, on and on, through modern history, the legacy of a public figure. The last images were ones seen recently in the papers, and on television. Of the new Supreme Court nominee. Judge Michael Butler Folner.

Finally, Dr. Meeker turned to them in all earnest innocence.

"You get what you were looking for? Judge Folner and his wife are primary benefactors here at the college, you know." Met with silence, she added somewhat defensively, "I do believe they donated this very computer!"

Lowell looked expectantly at the cop, waiting. Bedrosian had known deep in her gut ever since she stepped onto the twelve-meter that this was probably how it was going to turn out. But now she had to cope with the harshest of realities: what to do about it.

"If you're researching his background," continued Luisa, "the Poly Sci Department did it for a project about a month ago. It's all in the public record."

Not all, thought Lowell.

"Married an heiress from Palm Beach," Luisa was continuing, "no children, ran for P.A. in '68 and has an outstanding record as a judge and in public service in the Bay Area here, ever since."

"Yes. Thank you, Luisa," Lowell said. "You've been a big help."

"Thanks very much, ma'am," muttered Bedrosian. "Let's go," she snapped, getting to her feet. Lowell hesitated, feeling they'd overlooked something. He retrieved the photos from the scanner.

"Lowell?" Bedrosian pulled on his arm.

Luisa ignored them. Her eyes were glued to the screen. Something was happening. As Lowell got up to go, he'd flicked the graphics mouse back to full screen—while the data bank continued to run. The computer had picked up on another face in the second photo, matched it to one in the first photo, and had initiated its own search.

Meanwhile, Lowell took Bedrosian aside. "So, what are we going to do about it?" he demanded.

"About what?" snapped the cop.

"Come on! We got solid evidence now that Judge Folner was involved in the physical abduction of Maureen Fitzgerald. By her own words he took her when she didn't want to go."

"There's another one of your little revelations I haven't heard before," she snapped.

"You can't ignore it anymore," he insisted. "We got him on

240

kidnapping, plus positive I.D. of him in an intimate relationship with Julie before and during her marriage, at the scene of the drowning. This means there could have been a conspiracy! Lucretia Hartley may have been right."

"It proves no such thing, Lowell, and you know it. You got any idea what's going to come down, you start makin' noises based on this? Up till now you're talking child's play."

"You saying you intend to sit on this?"

Bedrosian shook her head, unable to think clearly. The fatigue was finally taking its full toll.

At the other end of the lab, Dr. Meeker continued staring at the monitor, trying to comprehend what it meant.

"Hey!" she shouted. "What's this all about?"

Lowell and the cop hurried over to join her.

Up on the screen, the computer had built a new wall of photo blocks and had connected it to another one. The match was of the man at the top of the courthouse steps with the one of the man in the car, helping Michael Folner force Maureen Fitzgerald to get in. Luisa didn't notice the abduction as such. She was busy watching the data fly by: more shots from the media, later, gradually older, balding, then bald, no more mustache. Similar political platforms, but many more. A national assortment of celebrity poses and handshakes. Then a political campaign. Hands waving in triumph. An election. Then another. Culminating with a very recent photo of both men together. Senator Bob Grimm and his friend and nominee. Together once again. A circle completed, and a final link.

"Holy shit," breathed Lowell. Bedrosian just shook her head.

"This gets more interesting all the time," remarked Luisa looking at the photo again more closely. She frowned. "Let me try something here," she said.

Neither detective made a sound as she punched in the enhancement software, selected the area around the man in the car and enlarged it. Then she began running a series of filters, removing shadows, enhancing lines, bringing out the face. What the computer had already determined, was now unmistakable to the eye. Moving along the computer rack, she switched on another machine: a digital printer. Punching some keys, she ran three copies directly off the screen: one of the abduction photo, a closeup of the judge, and another of the senator.

"Dr. Meeker?" a young woman had entered the room behind her. Luisa jumped, her heart pounding. She wasn't even sure why. But she knew there was something wrong with what she was looking at. Something screamed in her mind—no! Not another. Not another Supreme Court justice accused of impropriety.

"Mr. Lowell? What's going on?" the young woman asked, joining them. It was Sheila Balfour. In addition to studying photography with Tony Lowell, she'd been taking some of the brand-new courses in digital imaging with Dr. Meeker.

Sheila looked at the computer screen. Then at the prints. She looked at Lowell, eyes questioning. Lowell and Bedrosian exchanged glances. This was going to be tricky. Tony took Sheila aside. "Sheila, you don't want to be involved in this," he told her.

"What do you mean?" she asked. "Is something wrong?"

"Yes. You might say so."

Luisa took Sheila's elbow, and tried to usher her out of the lab. "You really shouldn't be in here now," she chided.

Sheila resisted. "I don't care." She pulled away and turned back. Picking up one of the prints, she looked more closely. "Isn't that Judge Folner? And—the other guy. Bob Grimm. That bastard! What are they doing to that woman?"

Bedrosian tried to deal with the situation. "This is police business, miss. You'd better go, and I'd strongly advise you not to speak to anyone about this."

"Or what?" demanded Sheila. "I just came in here to talk to my teacher, who hasn't been in class for days." She looked back at the picture, then at the other ones. "There's something wrong here." Images of her own began flooding her mind. Images of drilling on the bay and dead sea birds. She and her student activist friends knew of Folner's connection to Southern Oil. They also knew all about Senator Grimm's prodevelopment, antienvironment stands on just about every issue. To see the two of them together doing something obviously nefarious confirmed her worst expectations. She and her friends may have protested in vain at Folner's nomination. But maybe this she could do something about.

"Folner's another sleazeball, isn't he?" she said finally.

Lowell sighed. "It's beginning to look that way."

Bedrosian gestured furiously for him to join her outside.

"Excuse me," he said, and left with the cop quickly.

Sheila looked at Luisa and made a decision. "I'm going to stop them," she stated flatly. Luisa listened and tried to dissuade her. But the student was determined. "Just let me borrow these prints," insisted Sheila. "For half an hour. You don't even have to know what I'm going to do."

Luisa didn't like the idea of allowing a student to do something that could be dangerous. She shook her head.

"I'll do it," she decided.

"Then we'll both do it," said Sheila.

Luisa sighed and nodded. They took the copies, went over to the FAX machine, and loaded them in. Then Luisa picked up the telephone.

"Get me long-distance information," she requested of the campus operator. "For Washington, D.C."

23

Lowell was borderline elated as they drove out of the parking lot. Bedrosian, however, was glummer than ever, a black mood settling over her like volcanic ash. Lowell, still driving, turned off Bay Drive in downtown Manatee City, and headed east towards Route 19.

Bedrosian glared over at him reprovingly.

"You think you got all the answers now, don't you?"

Lowell shook his head. "I don't have all the answers. I know what our next move is, though."

"You planning on letting me in on it?" she said sarcastically.

"Let me ask you something first, Detective. What do you believe is happening here, now?"

There was a pause. Finally she answered: "I don't know. What do you expect? I hear what you claim poor old Ms. Fitzgerald said. I see what was in the files and on the screen. I—"

Lowell sat bolt upright. "Jesus Christ!"

"Now what?"

"What Maureen said. You mentioned what she said."

"Yeah, well, it just doesn't—"

"She said something, just before she died."

"Now what? This woman has more last words than Shakespeare."

"She said a lot. It's hard to remember everything."

"Yeah, sure. So what'd she say this time?"

"She said they forced her. She didn't want to go. And she mentioned something about politicians. Now it's clear who she was referring to."

"That does it." Livid, Bedrosian reached over and grabbed Lowell's arm again in an explosion of wrath, nearly causing a five-car accident. "One thing I really don't need any more of, Lowell, is damning testimony from a dead witness who nobody talked to except you!"

"Sorry. But I remember the conversation clearly now, and it finally makes some sense."

"Yeah, yeah. You know what? I don't even want to hear it."

"Well, maybe you'd better." Lowell extricated himself once more, and barely managed to pull the still-moving vehicle over to the curb. Bedrosian sat back, glowering, as he continued: "She said 'It was my—kill' something. I thought she had meant to say 'my killer' and didn't think anything more about it. She was ranting about Lucretia, and I don't know what. But what I think she meant to say was, 'It was Michael.' The boyfriend. Michael Folner. She was naming him as a murderer!"

"You won't quit, will you!"

"All right then." Throwing the Mustang into gear, Lowell yanked the wheel hard to the left, squashed the gas pedal as if it were a bug, and spun out into a squealing U-turn, polishing off the remaining tire tread. He barely avoided a collision with an onrushing semi, pulled around it nearly hitting a pickup head on, and took off like a slingshot in the opposite direction.

Bedrosian hung onto the edge of her seat for dear life. She quickly buckled up her seat belt.

"Slow down! Where the hell you think you're going?"

"Tampa. I think it's time we paid a visit to the judge. You can either come along and listen, or question him yourself."

"You serious?"

"Goddamn right I'm serious."

"You're crazy, Lowell."

Lowell kept his eyes on the road. The miles clicked by. The outlying suburban sprawl that heralded Tampa drew closer.

"I hope you don't think this means I'm gonna bust him for you," glowered Bedrosian after a while. "Whatever he says. And it sure as shit don't mean you're off the hook, got that?"

"Yes, sir. I mean, ma'am."

Hurling the old fastback north on Route 19, Lowell sped into the city. For better or worse, it was confrontation time. And while not wanting to admit it to Lowell, Bedrosian did have a few questions of her own.

The Hillsborough County Courthouse was on East Twiggs Street just off Kennedy Boulevard in the heart of downtown Tampa. They made it in a little under an hour, the Saturday traffic sparser than usual. As they pulled into the government center, they could see banners being strung and barriers set up for the big confirmation parade, scheduled for tomorrow after the reception.

"What makes you think he'll be there?" Bedrosian wanted to know. "This is Saturday."

"He works Saturdays. He made a big deal out of it, last election. 'A judge for all the people,' as he called himself, 'doesn't play golf on weekends when there's justice to be done.' Or some crap like that. You live around here, I'm sure you heard the campaign."

"Not actually. I hate TV. And I quit reading the papers right around the time you quit working for them."

"Can't say I blame you."

Lowell parked the Mustang next to a small city park and pulled the hand brake. "After you," he said, opening the door. "Superior Court's on the third floor."

"I know where the goddamn Superior Court is!" snapped Bedrosian, not liking this development at all.

Lowell marched up the marble steps, the police detective close behind. The building had two security guards at the revolving door, and two more in the lobby, possibly Secret Service. Bedrosian used her badge, and they went in.

Footsteps echoed loudly as they walked across the long lobby to the elevators and pushed the button. The elevator took forever to go up, and Lowell felt his tension rising with it.

Inside his chambers, Judge Michael Folner was feeling a keen

246

sense of frustration as he removed his robes for what he hoped would be the last time—in this venue, anyway—and hung them on the hook just inside the door. There had been a delay in Washington. He'd just gotten word that the Senate had postponed the vote until tomorrow. They'd scheduled a special Sunday session for right after church, just for him. But it still troubled him. Another twelve hours of waiting! Why? Why couldn't they have gotten it over with today and gone home for the weekend? It didn't make sense. Unless . . . he shook off the thought and went into his private washroom to freshen up, before signaling Rolfe.

At least he'd managed to clear his own docket. He'd just finished a special Saturday session to hear an appeal on a zoning variance for an old friend, who was fighting efforts to restrict development in the south county. He'd done his best but the mood of the county was changing, and he was glad he'd no longer have to be around to intervene in the future. Between the bank failures and the collapse of the real-estate market, it was a lousy time to be granting favors to developers as it was. He hoped this would be his last. Because after tomorrow, he was on his way to Washington. At last! A lifetime dream fulfilled, and he sensed his destiny looming, like the Washington monument itself, beckoning north. He had built the road that would take him there himself. And now his turn had come to travel its shining path.

His biggest regret was the drilling. As always, he'd done the best he could for the cause. Conflict of interest rules had precluded him from taking an active role. His controlling interest in Southern Oil was in a so-called blind trust. But too many people knew of the connection, and he'd had to lay very low. And it was a damn shame, too. He was a firm believer in the need to develop his country's energy resources to the maximum. That debacle in Kuwait had proven that, hadn't it? But those short-sighted Environmental Nazis (as he liked to call them), couldn't see beyond the snot hanging from their little runny noses. Now they'd foiled his plans, and those of many of his friends and colleagues. But he would not leave them empty-handed. There was exploration taking place at this very moment up in the Panhandle: an area ripe for exploitation, with little or no organized local opposition. It was a potential gold mine.

That reminded him. Before leaving tomorrow, there were one or two items to attend to over at the First Florida Tower office, where he ran the family business interests. Julie was titular head of Star Enterprises, as their joint partnership's umbrella company was called, but she was usually too busy with her charitable activities to come into Tampa and hadn't in weeks.

He just hoped his wife was holding up under the increasing pressure of their wait for the Senate's decision. She'd been on an increasingly breakneck schedule of late. In fact, days would go by without him seeing her at all, what with his appointment schedule, and her cluttered social and fundraising agenda. And there was that something else still bothering her as well, he could tell. That something to do with their distant past . . .

Tonight she had promised to be home. They were going to have an intimate little dinner together, just the two of them. As a private celebration of their achievement, Senate delay notwithstanding. He had never denied, certainly not to her, that she had helped him every step of the way. There was a fierce loyalty about her, he knew, which had lasted throughout their marriage. And well before. She must know he loved her in his way. And yet he felt sorry for her. Despite her busy schedule and ceaseless social activity, she must be a terribly lonely woman. And sometimes, in the wee hours of the morning, he knew deep down that she needed, yes, even deserved, better than he could give her. The very life they had constructed together so carefully—so lucrative and rewarding for both of them—stood on the verge of fulfillment. He would know for certain in a matter of hours.

As he went back to his desk to gather his remaining papers together (his secretary, Phyllis, had cleaned most of it out before she left), he heard the outer office door click open.

"Phyllis? Is that you?"

He snapped the gold-plated latches shut on his tooled leather briefcase, and stepped through the inner chamber door to see what it was she'd come back for.

Detective Lena Bedrosian and private investigator Anthony Lowell stood waiting for him. He stopped short, half-expecting a robbery. Damn those worthless security guards! And his gun was locked in the file cabinet, so much for self-defense. Concealing his alarm, he stood tall and firm and faced them down.

"How did you two get in here?" he demanded. "The office is closed, in case you didn't notice."

The woman showed him her badge. Folner felt a twinge of new worry.

"Sorry to bother you, Judge. We know how busy you are, but there's been a crime which involves people you know, and we need to ask you a few questions. If you don't mind. We won't keep you long."

"Well, I do mind. It's five o'clock Saturday afternoon, I've had a long day, and I have a reception tomorrow. What kind of crime?"

"I'll get to that in a moment, Judge."

Folner squinted at the badge, trying to read the name. Manatee City? This cop wasn't even from Tampa. What the hell was she doing up here? Unless—

"I brought this man with me because he wanted to meet you," Bedrosian continued.

"Meet me? What is this?" Folner glanced at Lowell and scowled.

"My name is Anthony Lowell. I'm a private investigator, representing Lucretia Hartley. You remember her?"

The judge froze, the air leaking slowly from his lungs in a long sigh, like a pinched balloon. He turned toward Lowell with considerable effort. A quick appraisal, recalling and noting the name. Maybe there was still time for damage control. Depending on the extent of the damage.

"Anthony Lowell. Yes, let me see. You were involved with the Friedrichs' divorce, isn't that right? He's an old neighbor of mine."

"Give him my best, sir. About Mrs. Hartley?"

"What? What's she done?"

"Nothing, sir." Lowell had to stop and think about that, though. It had occurred to him more than once that Lucretia Hartley had as much motivation for murder as anyone.

Lowell and Bedrosian had discussed how to approach Folner the whole way up I-75 and over the Crosstown Expressway. Lowell preferred the direct approach. Bedrosian, an experienced interrogator, insisted that was suicide. Especially when talking to a lawyer-turned-judge. But Lowell felt, in his gut, that his was the only way. And now the moment had come. Bedrosian watched him. Waiting for him to hang the both of them, by her look.

"Because of recent events, we have some questions regarding you and your wife's former husband," Lowell began.

Folner controlled himself, with some effort. This had to be a ploy, he decided. A last-ditch fishing expedition to pull me from my flight to destiny. I'll have none of it. But he glanced nervously at the detectives, wondering just what they did know, and how.

"Come into my office," he said, revealing nothing in his tone. "I'll give you five minutes."

They followed him in, Lowell reflecting on how these powerful people kept giving him deadlines.

The judge's inner chambers were an homage to elegance. Solid walnut paneling, a matching oil-rubbed desk the size of a billiard table, two simple Shaker side chairs Lowell suspected of once having been at Breezewood, and a huge reclining black armchair of pure buttery Connally leather were the only furnishings. Of course, Lowell and Bedrosian had no way of knowing about the treasure trove of period pieces that had only been removed this very morning.

The judge turned to Lowell, very direct. "Let's not play games. You're working for a famous family of robber barons who reaped what they sowed. So what do you want from me?"

"Well, you're right about that, Judge. But I gotta hand it to you, the way you targeted somebody no one could love—a waspish old woman with a lot of inherited wealth—I mean, why not? Go ahead, clean her out, live it up. Maybe you and your wife deserved it as much as she did. Except one thing."

"What would that be?" Folner inquired, humoring them.

"You resorted to murder."

The judge paled. "All right. That does it. You have one minute to get out of my office or I'll see to it you both find a new line of business. Do I make myself clear?"

Just then a voice called from the anteroom. "Michael?" A woman's voice, soft yet rich. The judge reacted in genuine surprise. They all turned as she entered the room. The air itself seemed to stop, motionless. She was ageless and stunning. "Michael, I was just in town and—" she hesitated in the doorway. Lowell knew her at once. She was an exact match for the one treasure left in the room that hadn't been moved—probably waiting until the appointment was confirmed. It hung above the solid Italian marble mantelpiece that overhung the real working fireplace.

Bedrosian saw her and the painting at the same time, and caught her breath. Lowell was transfixed. Like her portrait directly above them, she was larger than life. Her eyes were bluer than the sea itself, watching them from the doorway and wall. The portrait had been painted on commission by William Styler just before his death, in homage to his Character Study period. The woman was Julie Hartley Folner, formerly Barnett. The Judge's wife.

The police detective studied her in fascination, eyes particularly drawn to Julie's clothes. They were simple, yet spectacular. A brown tweed suit, hand-cut and stitched, a red silk scarf, and a plain white blouse.

Lowell forced his gaze back to the judge, now seated and waiting stonily in his power position behind his desk.

"All right, Mr. Lowell. You had something to ask about my wife's former husband. Maybe you should ask her, since she's here." He turned to his wife. "Hello, dear. I have visitors, as you can see. They have a few questions, it seems. Regarding Henry."

She didn't even blink. Lowell had to hand it to her.

"Sorry to trouble you, ma'am," he said, watching her face carefully. "Some very unfortunate incidents have occurred, lately, gravely affecting people related to your former husband."

251

"What sort of incidents?" snapped Julie.

"Three people who knew Henry Hartley have been killed in the past week," said Bedrosian.

There was only the slightest reaction, from either the judge or his wife.

"We were wondering if you or your husband were aware of any of this," added Lowell, "and whether you might consider it cause for concern."

"Are you a reporter?" Julie demanded after a moment.

"No, ma'am. Private investigator. This is Police Detective Bedrosian, of Manatee City."

Julie ignored Bedrosian and looked at her husband, her face a mask. Folner stared at Lowell in bewilderment. How much could this gumshoe know about him? And about Julie, for God's sake. He began to feel it all slipping away. He carefully placed both hands flat on the desk.

"I don't think she or I know what you're talking about."

Lowell risked a quick glance at Bedrosian, whose widened eyes indicated that he had her attention.

"You don't know about the murders? About Maureen Fitzgerald, and the people on the East Coast?"

"What murders? What people?" demanded Folner.

"Maureen Fitzgerald was murdered in Manatee County five days ago," interjected Bedrosian, taking the cue. "We have determined she was the former housekeeper of Lucretia Hartley. She stated directly to Mr. Lowell here that she witnessed a murder twenty-five years ago—of one Henry Hartley the Third, who we understand was married to Mrs. Folner here at the time."

Julie caught her breath, sharply. Bedrosian went on, without looking at her. "In the past three days, her former doctor and a museum director doing research on the Hartley drowning have also been killed."

The judge turned dark. "I think you'd better go. We have absolutely nothing to contribute to this matter, and you're upsetting my wife without cause."

252

"Sorry, Judge," said Lowell. "It's just that some questions have been raised about your past relationships by people who are now dead. It would really be helpful if you could put some of those questions to rest, before the public and media get wind of this."

"What?" Julie clutched her husband's arm protectively. He removed it, ever so gently.

Lowell reached into his jacket pocket and took out a large brown envelope, containing the computer digital printouts. The first was the shot of Julie and the two men on the boat.

"This is you two together, isn't it? You were both on board the boat the night he drowned. This is you, Mrs. Folner. Who happened, at the time, to be married to the man who's about to fall over the side." The room fell icily silent, as Bedrosian tensed, ready for anything.

Julie spoke up. "What is this? Some feeble attempt at blackmail?"

Folner was furious. "This is meaningless innuendo, and you know it. Now get out."

"I'm sorry." Lowell took no offense. Such accusations came with the territory. With a glance at Bedrosian he produced a second photograph. The one that showed the then-young lawyer forcing Maureen Fitzgerald into the car.

Lowell tapped the photograph. "This is you here, isn't it, Judge? And this is Senator Grimm. And this woman you are forcibly abducting is Maureen Fitzgerald."

"That's hogwash! How dare you—"

"You and the senator worked together back then. Didn't you?" Lowell persisted.

"We were law partners. But that photograph—"

"Partners in a lot more than law, looks like to me."

"You can't even prove that's him or me in that photograph. As for your allegations of abduction, we were simply—"

"You're wrong, Judge. We believe we can prove it's you."

The judge looked at the photo once more, then leaned slowly back in his chair. Julie remained impassive. So be it, he thought. He had

253

expected this might happen some day and had prepared for it as best he could. He wasn't former president of the Florida Bar and a Superior Court justice of ten years standing for nothing.

"She was out of control," he said finally. "As you may or may not be aware, medical and psychological services were in very short supply at Palm Coast Harbor. There was no time to get a doctor, we had to take care of her ourselves."

" 'We'?" interjected Bedrosian.

He faltered, just for a moment. "All of us. The crew, the captain, the other guests had to be taken care of. It was a very traumatic moment."

"Especially for my client," commented Lowell.

"Look, what would you have me do? I most certainly had nothing to do with any—crimes that have taken place, now or in the past. Nor has my wife. The woman was crazy. I called Bob from the boat to come and meet us, to help cope with her."

The judge went over and stood by his wife, who remained as though carved in stone. Her eyes had narrowed, however, and the corner of her mouth twitched upward, ever so slightly.

"Are you planning to press charges against my husband? Because if so, I'm going to call our lawyer now. If not, you'd better explain yourselves, or I'll have you arrested for harassment."

"We're not here to press charges," said Bedrosian. "At least not yet. Your husband and his partner may have had their reasons for forcibly placing Ms. Fitzgerald under confinement. However, I have a murder to solve. So I'm going to have to ask you what you know about it."

Julie's eyes narrowed, and then seemed to focus, as though a decision had been reached. She let out a long sigh and sat down. "The person you want is Lucretia Hartley," she said at last. "She's insane, you know. Worse than that Fitzgerald woman. She has had it in for Michael and me since my lawsuit. And if she is in fact your client, Mr. Lowell, then you've seen her, and you undoubtedly know that when I tell you she is insane, I tell the truth."

Lowell couldn't deny it. She faced him straight on. "She hated me

254

from the moment we met. Called me a gold digger and a whore. Called my husband worse things than that. I wanted him to stand up to her. But his biggest weakness was—weakness."

Without looking at Lowell, Bedrosian edged closer, probing. "Mrs. Folner. Is it, or is it not true that you and your current husband knew each other prior to your marriage to Henry Hartley?"

"We did. What of it?"

Lowell spoke up quickly. "I knew your husband Henry Hartley, Mrs. Folner. We come from the same town."

She gave him a dubious look. A curl of smile formed on her lower lip. "Oh. Well. Henry knew lots of people, I suppose. He was a bit of a gadabout, wasn't he?"

"Yes, I guess he was," nodded Lowell, agreeably. "That's how he met you, isn't it?"

She ignored that. "I gave him something he needed, which was respectability, and he did the same for me. Was that so terrible?"

"Profitable, anyway."

She shook her head. "You're wrong. He always felt all that money was the biggest handicap a man could have. It was as if he had a nipple jammed between his lips his whole life, and he couldn't shake it loose. And Lucretia—she was some nipple!"

"I wouldn't know."

"Mrs. Folner. Is it, or is it not true that you and Michael, with the assistance of attorney Robert Grimm, conspired to arrange a marriage between yourself and Henry Hartley in order to get access to the Hartley fortune?" Bedrosian demanded.

"Outrageous."

"Then why did you marry him? Or do you claim not to have known he was gay?"

"Of course I knew. I didn't love Henry, of course. I always loved Michael. But who could resist a Hartley? He was poetic—sensitive—good-looking—and filthy rich. Every woman's fantasy of a Prince Charming come to life."

"Except that Henry loved Michael too, is that right?" said Lowell. "So you had a little rivalry going there, didn't you?"

She shook her head emphatically. "Michael was Henry's friend. He introduced us, in New York. Michael knew he would never be able to keep me the way Henry could. That's why he agreed I should marry Henry."

"That was big of him," remarked Lowell.

"And your allegation of conspiracy is absurd. There was no need. We were all happy with the arrangement." She paused, pointedly. "Except for Lucretia."

Lowell frowned at the nearest wall, losing himself in the swirling images of Julie's portrait.

Bedrosian saw an opening and seized it. She turned to Mrs. Folner.

"Mrs. Folner," she called quickly. "What really happened that night. On the boat?"

"Honey, don't—" began Folner, but she brushed him away angrily and turned toward the police detective.

"We were all there," she began hesitantly. "Henry, me, that woman, and Michael."

Folner sighed and sat down, once again feeling it all slipping away.

"You'd better tell them, Michael," she said at last, turning to him. "Tell them about Lucretia."

He looked at her and blinked. "Julie, for God's sake—"

"She killed her own son," she said, almost with a sigh.

Lowell tried to picture the scene, altered, changed, as she spoke, as though narrating a dream.

"Lucretia had learned that Henry was gay that very day, and they were having this big fight. She was calling him the vilest names. And tearing me down, of course. We were there by the fantail waiting for him to join us, but she wouldn't let him go."

She stopped to catch her breath, and you could have heard a feather fall in the room. "Henry was drunk. And for the first time in his life, he stood up to her."

"Then what happened?" urged Bedrosian softly.

"Henry just stood there weaving and wobbling on the deck," she went on as they listened, each in his own visionary trance. "Then he sort of saluted her, and said 'Dear mother, is it my fault you took my manhood from me and kept it for yourself?' He told me once that he felt as though she had castrated him, personally. As a symbol of domination! And then—"she went on—"and then she went berserk. She gave him a shove—and he fell over backward—he couldn't stop himself."

She paused. Folner reached for her hand, with a reproving shake of his head.

"That's enough, Julie," he said.

"No!" she snapped. "Let me finish." She turned back to the two detectives. "And then it was that maid—Maureen—she was suddenly standing there. I think she'd come out of the galley. I think she saw it too, but she was too terrified to move. She just stood there, screaming and screaming, this terrible sound she was making. We couldn't shut her up!" She was fighting tears now, and had to stop to catch her breath. "And then everyone came running, and somebody dove in after him. But it was too late. It was too late!"

"We had to put Maureen in restrictive care," said Folner quietly, after a while. "She would have harmed herself."

Julie stopped, and her demeanor changed perceptibly. "It was an accident. But then she accused me. *Lucretia* accused me! She was the one who did it. She killed her own son. And she accused me! I had a right to take steps! I had a right!"

"Of course you did, dear," murmured Folner. "Of course you did. Now please stop." He cast a withering look at the others, as though noticing them once again for the first time.

Lowell shook his head, knowing that it could be true. Bedrosian was already nodding for them to leave. Bedrosian handed the judge her card. "Just give me a call if anything comes up that might be of help. Nice meeting you," she said to Julie, and started for the door with a warning look at Lowell.

"Just a minute!" the judge called after her. Something was clearly bothering him. "I want you to know my relationship with Henry Hartley was strictly friendship. Likewise mine with Julie, during her marriage to him. There's nothing wrong with that." It wasn't a question. Julie nodded in agreement.

Bedrosian stopped in the doorway. "I'm sure that's true, sir," she agreed. "But in light of the events that have taken place recently, in combination with your—friendships with these people, you understand why some questions might be raised."

Folner's black look turned blacker. "I think this stinks. The timing, the insinuations, all of this suggests to me an obviously politically motivated attempt to derail my nomination to the High Court. And I'll tell you one thing. When I get to Washington, I intend to order an investigation into this entire matter. Including how my name happened to be dragged into a murder investigation that has nothing to do with me, at the last minute like this."

Lowell turned back to the judge, ignoring Bedrosian's urgent gestures for him to go. "By the way, Judge, I didn't appreciate you sending those cretins with guns and helicopters to burn us down."

The judge stared. "People *I* sent? I'm sure you're mistaken."

"Come off it. They were F.B.I. We have photos of them too, and their I.D. Besides, who would've sent them, if not you?" He thought a moment, and it struck him at once. "Unless, of course, it was your pal, the senator."

There was just a flicker of a frown in Folner's expression, which Bedrosian noted. Julie remained imperturbable.

"I'm sure I wouldn't know. Perhaps you've been identified as a security threat. I think that's very evident actually."

As he spoke, the judge pressed a button beneath his desk. "The authorities are on their way," he announced. "I'd advise you not to attempt to elude them this time, or they will hunt you down like dogs."

"Then what?"

"Then you go to jail, and I go to Washington."

"Maybe you should reconsider. If you really have the interests of your country at heart, you really should withdraw your name from nomination."

"Why ever would I want to do that?" snapped Folner impatiently.

"My record is beyond reproach. And perhaps you've heard about the term 'slander'?"

"You're a public figure. And the public deserves full disclosure about your background. Wouldn't you agree?"

"Only what's relevant. And I'd strongly advise you not to pursue this little vendetta of yours any further, Lowell. Either against me, or against the senator. It'll come back to haunt you."

"It already has." Lowell turned away. "Let's go, Detective. Game's over."

They walked toward the door, waiting for the other shoe to drop. Suddenly Folner came after them, blocking their way.

"Listen! Listen to me! We knew someone would turn up some day, looking for retribution. Someone sent by Lucretia Hartley. Well, you're aiming the wrong way! I may be a lot of things, but did you really imagine I would set out to achieve a lifetime goal, to serve the cause of justice, to seek high office, by committing or condoning murder? That's insane!"

"Sometimes things just get out of hand," said Lowell with a shrug.

"Come on. That's nuts and you know it!"

"Besides, you wouldn't be the first," Lowell added, looking at him oddly. Folner turned away, somehow diminished. He had won, he knew. But it was a pyrrhic victory.

He looked at his wife. There was a bond between this pair, Lowell noted as he left. They had been through a lot together, and it showed. They clearly shared a fierce sense of loyalty and common purpose. Some might even call it love.

Lowell and Bedrosian stepped into the hall, and were met at once by two armed Secret Service men, embarrassed as hell at being eluded.

Bedrosian knew, at this point, that they were finished. They had played their hand and lost. She had no illusions about the consequences. Had David thrown stones at Goliath and missed, he would have simply been another bloodied battlefield statistic, forgotten to posterity.

Moments later the police arrive in force—a sheriff and three officers from the Tampa Police Department. Two more suits were with them: Federal agents Bud Werner and Cecil Lefcourt. Lefcourt was patched up with his shoulder wrapped in a heavy bandage, his arm in a sling—clean jacket sleeve hanging loose. He gave Bedrosian a look that offered a promise of future retribution of a most unpleasant nature.

Bedrosian regarded him evenly, with a shrug of apology. "Sorry about that shoulder. How is it?"

"I've had worse," grumbled the Fed, taken aback.

The cops handcuffed the two detectives while the judge and four gray suits looked on impassively. "You're under arrest for trespassing and harassment," the sheriff informed them, asserting his jurisdictional control.

"Sorry this happened, Judge," the first agent said. "We'll take care them." He looked at the sheriff. "If you fellas don't mind."

"I'm a police officer," Bedrosian said, as they pulled her arms behind her.

That seemed to startle the sheriff, who looked around for confirmation. "Is that true?"

"Check my wallet, and call Lieutenant Jeffries at Manatee. I'm on a case!"

Werner spoke up quickly. "She's been aiding and abetting a fugitive, Sheriff. It's in the report I filed with your commander."

The sheriff frowned, wary of the oddly charged atmosphere in the room. Like Bedrosian, like his counterparts down at Manatee—he'd have to call them as soon as they got back to the station—he was suspicious of federal interference in local affairs. Which, despite the presence of Secret Service protection, was what this was—simple trespassing, as far as he could see. When the judge's electronic alarm had sounded, these guys had popped out of the woodwork. It was late, and he wanted to get home and see the end of the Miami–Florida State game. But something told him he'd better stay involved. There was something not quite right going down, here.

"I'll handle this." he decided.

"Somebody read 'em their rights."

"This man is stark raving," interceded the judge. "Please get him out of here."

Jesus, thought the sheriff as he headed for the door. Why did this crap have to happen here in Tampa? Something didn't sit right at all. A cop and a crazy in the judge's chambers, talking about God knows what—everybody acting weird—no, he thought to himself. Whatever's going on was personal. Involving the judge and his wife. Gorgeous woman. They were holding something back. But that wouldn't surprise him. Rich people always had a ton of skeletons in the closet. Which is why he personally didn't think they should be judges.

24

The Hillsborough County Jail, located not far from the courthouse, was typical of most jails. It had windowless, cinder-block walls, pale green paint, dirt and the constant smell of sweat, fear, excrement, and urine. And this being Florida, the added element of mold, lurking in every dark corner.

The prisoners were the usual crowd—mostly young, mostly black, mostly in for drug-related offenses, mixed with the occasional murder suspect, drunk driver, or other oddball offender.

Out of professional courtesy to a police officer, and also for Bedrosian's own protection, she'd been given a separate cell. Not a small concession to anyone who knew what it was like to spend a night in jail, crowded into a block full of unwashed, uncouth, often rage-filled individuals who saw any newcomer as a threat.

As it was, word had leaked to the other prisoners somehow that one of the newcomers to Women's Block B was a cop. That had produced a nonstop torrent of taunts and verbal abuse throughout the night.

Lowell, for his part, was thrown in with the usual drunks, druggies, and felons. There had been little sleep for either Lowell or Bedrosian that night—exhausted as they already were.

Lowell couldn't sleep anyway. Not after hearing Julie's last charges—ones that aroused suspicions he'd been harboring for two days now. Could his client, his latest client, that is, be a murderer? Of her own son? Lucretia Hartley had been awful—shrewish, selfish, harsh, even cruel, uncaring—many things unbecoming to motherhood. But murder? And yet, it was possible.

A deputy brought breakfast—powdered eggs and Spam—at seven-thirty, and he accepted it gratefully. Lowell had no illusions about his predicament. He was an embarrassment and a threat to the entire federal judicial system, and he knew it. At seven thirty-five, a deputy came in and brought him to an interrogation room. The county sheriff came in a moment later, followed by a bailiff with Detective Bedrosian, who looked bedraggled.

"Morning, folks," said the sheriff, studying them with curious, insomnia-reddened eyes. "I'm Sheriff Pearson. I didn't get a chance to introduce myself yesterday."

Lowell mumbled a greeting. "You bring the firing squad?"

Pearson smiled, not finding the joke particularly funny. "I called Manatee, they're sending somebody up to talk to you. Maybe they'll post bail, I don't know. Her, they're pickin' up."

"Who's coming, did they say?" asked Bedrosian, suddenly.

"A lieutenant, uh—"

"Jeffries? He's my superior officer."

"Yeah, him. Don't expect him to be glad to see you, though. Seems since you and your buddy here started doin' whatever it is you're doin', nobody's had too much sleep around here." He studied them, waiting for a response.

Bedrosian was elated. Jeffries was her best chance of surviving this mess, she knew. And probably her only ally on the force right now. Or was he still an ally?

"If I give a statement, you promise to hear me out?"

Pearson thought that over. He didn't like to make promises when he didn't know what they were going to involve.

"Depends. Judge Folner has requested a psychiatric evaluation of you two. He doesn't seem to think anything you have to say is connected with reality."

"You buy that?"

Pearson thought that over as well. Bedrosian didn't strike him as crazy at all. For that matter, neither did the guy.

263

"I'll withhold judgment for the moment. But maybe you'd better give me a statement as well," he said, leaning back and crossing his arms. "I got Feds yappin' at the gate after blood, and I can only keep 'em out so long."

Bedrosian sat forward in her chair. "What did you do with our personal effects?"

"In the lockup. Why?"

"Lowell had some photographs in his jacket. There's also a key there, to a red Ford Mustang parked on Dale Mabry. You'll find a cardboard canister in the backseat, containing certain documents all of which lay something out I'm havin' trouble believin' myself."

That's what I was afraid of, thought the sheriff wearily. "What kind of documents?"

"Evidence of kidnapping."

"Against the judge?"

"That's right. You can ask my client, Lucretia Hartley," said Lowell. "It goes way, way back."

Sheriff Pearson pursed his lips and looked Lowell over dubiously. Mrs. Hartley of *the* Hartleys is this man's client? It would be easy enough to check out.

"You get the documents, you can read for yourself," said Lowell. "Lucretia Hartley is the widow of Henry Hartley, son of the founder of Southern Oil. Judge Folner and his wife took her to court and walked away with the family fortune. Back in 1968."

"Yeah, I know the story, it's old news. What about it?"

"This is the incredible part, Sheriff," said Bedrosian. "We have photographic evidence Judge Folner together with his old law partner, Bob Grimm, forcibly prevented an eyewitness from giving testimony against them by means of abduction and illegal confinement."

The sheriff's jaw dropped open. "You're talking about Senator Bob Grimm? Our Bob Grimm?"

"Yes, sir."

"They were law partners," Lowell interjected. "Grimm directed the slander suit against my client, based on an unsubstantiated accusation on her part that her son was the victim of foul play. Both Maureen Fitzgerald and Lucretia Hartley stated to me that Maureen—an eyewitness to the drowning—was physically prevented from either reporting to the police or testifying to what she saw. Physically prevented by Michael Folner and Bob Grimm. And we have that action on film."

The sheriff shook his head incredulously. "You're trying to tell me Judge Folner and Senator Grimm committed a capital crime? Now that is crazy."

"Yes sir," nodded Bedrosian. "And as you know, Henry Hartley was drowned."

"My client—my previous client, Maureen Fitzgerald—claimed she witnessed him being pushed overboard," stated Lowell. "Unfortunately, she was murdered this past week, in the act of hiring me to reopen the case. Which is where Detective Bedrosian comes in."

Pearson let out a long, soft whistle. "Well, all I can say is either you two are candidates for the funny farm, or you're onto something hotter'n spatterin' bacon grease." He paused. "If it's true. Which I ain't about to take on your word. Especially since Judge Folner obviously takes serious exception to your views on this matter."

"I can see how he might," agreed Bedrosian.

The sheriff looked at her and scowled. "I'll make some calls," he decided. "You two wait here." He turned to go, nodding at the deputy, who had been watching in silent curiosity. "Les, get that key and send somebody down to pick up the car." He looked back as he went out. "I'll be back." The deputy closed the steel door behind them with a hollow clang, and they left.

It wasn't until ten-thirty that Jeffries arrived. He'd had to wait for a briefing from Sturbridge and the Secret Service about the various crimes his detective and her alleged prisoner were supposed to have committed by invading Judge Folner's private chambers. Bullshit, he'd been thinking the whole time. Bullshit, bullshit, bullshit! Jeffries had a knot in his stomach that nothing would appease. It meant something bad was about to happen.

Bedrosian waved glumly as the deputy opened the door. "Hello, Arlin. Thanks for coming."

"Don't thank me yet," said the lieutenant. He looked at her sharply, then quickly scrutinized the suspect P.I. Or witness. Or whatever the hell Lowell was. "The press is outside. They're starting to smell a fart on the wind."

"Good!" said Lowell. "That's good. They won't be able to put this stink back in the bottle now."

"Yeah?" Jeffries turned a quizzical gaze on Lowell. "Seems they've added old lady Hartley to their hit list now. Something about a crazed murder binge."

Christ, thought Lowell. They must have planted that story last night. Bad enough they got her money. Now they're going to get her too.

Jeffries had news as well. "The Senate voted thirty minutes ago to approve Judge Folner as Associate Justice to the Supreme Court." There was silence. He sat on the edge of the table, looking fatigued. "Senator Bob Grimm is already on an Air Force jet en route to Tampa to personally congratulate his old friend. He should be here within the hour."

"I can get you out, if that's what you want," added Jeffries. "But to tell you the truth, you might be better off in here. Those people are in a foul mood."

"Fuck 'em," snapped Bedrosian.

The sheriff entered with a puzzled look. "I read your file, and looked at your photos." He looked back and forth from Lowell to Bedrosian. "Makes nice pulp reading, might make a good horror movie. But I don't know as you got any kind of case against the Folners, even if they did get all your client's money, Lowell. Especially when it looks like she may be a murder suspect. No offense."

"What about the kidnapping?" demanded Lowell.

"I talked to the judge about that this morning. He claims she was deranged and a threat to herself. They took her straight to the hospital."

266

"Where they kept her for almost thirty years, the legality of which I seriously question."

"What I think you need to look at," said the sheriff, "is what happened when she got out. Whoever killed her and those others needed a motive. Folner wouldn't be covering up a case he already won, like you're trying to pin on him. A much better case is revenge. In her own distorted mind maybe Lucretia Hartley might blame Maureen Fitzgerald for losing her fortune—for letting her down by not testifying—"

"But that wasn't Maureen's fault, they had her committed."

"No matter. Mrs. Hartley might still blame her. If so, she could've tracked her down, after she got out. She could be out to get the people she thinks are responsible for losing her fortune."

"So why didn't she do it years ago?"

"Maybe she just got crazier and crazier, pining away in that big house. Maybe it's like Mrs. Folner said. She was waiting . . ."

"You're trying to pin all this on Lucretia Hartley now?" demanded Lowell, his worst suspicions confirmed.

"There could be another motive, Lowell," said Bedrosian. "What if Julie was right, and Lucretia flipped way back then and did push her son. Maureen Fitzgerald was a witness!"

"OK, but what about Elliot? And the doctor?"

"Maybe they had access to the real truth, and she couldn't take the chance. Or maybe she just ran amok."

The sheriff broke a brief silence. "I got through to some people over at Palm Coast Harbor. They confirmed most of your story, Lowell. But we got a new problem."

"Now what?"

"Your client. We tried to call her house and got no answer. So we called the police, and they sent someone over to check."

Lowell tensed, sensing what was coming.

"She wasn't there. But the Reverend was there, the one who brings her food. He says she left this morning. By limo. For Clearwater."

Lowell shook his head, not wanting to believe it.

"She's coming for Folner," said Bedrosian. "That must be it. She's coming to—holy shit. The reception! At the Belleair Mido!"

Jeffries jumped to his feet. "Sheriff. The judge is in danger!"

"Not just him. What about the senator? They were in it together!" added Bedrosian. Jeffries just shook his head. The sheriff shouted for the deputy to unlock the door. "Bryson! Call Secret Service, and tell them to try and head off the senator. Then meet us in my office for a briefing. Ten minutes. Move it! And better alert the Pinellas Sheriff's Department and Belleair Police. Also security over at the Biltmore, to look out for this woman. And get a chopper ready, I'm going over there."

The Belleair Mido Hotel, formerly the Biltmore, was a famed nineteenth-century watering hole for Vanderbilts and such just south of Clearwater, across the bay on the Gulf. It had recently been bought and renovated by the Japanese, and renamed the Mido. But to Tampa Bay locals such as Pearson, it was still, and would probably always remain, the Biltmore.

Pearson turned back to his prisoners, feeling very old. "I just wish to hell you all coulda done this someplace else," he said with a sigh.

"Sheriff, this man can identify her. She's his client, remember? Take us with you," urged Bedrosian.

The sheriff hesitated but only briefly. "All right. Fine, let's move it. You too, Lieutenant. These two are your responsibility."

They ran.

The Belleair Mido was supposed to be the largest wooden structure on earth. Originally built by pioneer hotelier Henry Plant in the 1890s, it was a vast Victorian palace of clapboard (sided over with aluminum some years earlier) that covered some twenty acres or so, surrounded by a golf course on three sides, and Clearwater Bay to the west. It was only a few blocks from the Folner residence, and the perfect location for a political reception. Or assassination.

The building was one giant conglomeration of nooks and crannies. With a hundred entrances, fifty gables, and dozens of towers, crawl spaces (even an abandoned railroad tunnel), porches, verandas, five hundred rooms at least half of which were always empty—especially at this time of year—it was a security nightmare.

The Secret Service had warned the senator against such a location, but he had insisted. This was his friend Mike Folner's party. And it ought to be in Mike Folner's backyard, where he could celebrate it with his own friends and loved ones. Among which he certainly included himself. Besides, he loved that rickety old place—no longer so rickety—and had many fond experiences in those hallowed halls himself. He remembered how they had opened up one of the ballrooms, boarded up since World War II, and found hidden skylights—20,000 square feet of them, of solid, stained Tiffany glass. Those skylights alone, he had reckoned wryly at the time, could probably pay off the national debt. Except that now the Japanese owned them. And the rest of it. Purchased during a recessionary period, with Florida real estate at a standstill, for less than some houses might cost in, say, Beverly Hills.

The sheriff scrambled to mobilize, which first required coordination with Pinellas County and the Belleair Police (in whose actual jurisdictions the hotel was), under the overall umbrella of the Secret Service and the rest of the federal types who seemed to be everywhere. It was during that crucial period when no one seemed to be in charge that a long, black limousine pulled up at the wide portico entrance and a highly courteous young Japanese doorman opened the door, then escorted the old woman inside. It was easy to see she was Somebody. She was dressed all in black, and bedecked with diamonds.

Soon she was inside, mingling with the other hotel guests in the huge lobby. Moments after she'd passed into the hallway, two gray-suited Secret Service agents burst into the lobby. Word had just come over the police band that the senator had already landed in Tampa and was on his way over by helicopter. With walkie-talkies in hand, they ordered all access points to the Tiffany Room blocked off. They were to check everyone who entered the hallway or approached the banquet hall. All in all an impossible task.

Meanwhile, on orders from their own headquarters over on Ponce

De Leon, Belleair cops fanned out around the parking lots, having been told to be on the lookout for a "possible terrorist attack."

When the Hillsborough sheriff's helicopter sped over the golf greens and dropped unceremoniously onto the hotel's front lawn, it was greeted by a Belleair cop, who seemed unaware of any problems.

"Did you see her?" shouted Pearson, piling out, followed by Jeffries, Bedrosian, and Lowell.

The cop looked at the sheriff blankly, wondering what the sheriff from Tampa was doing on this side of the bay. "See who?" he blinked.

"Jesus Christ!" shouted Pearson in exasperation. "Didn't you get word? There's an old woman heading this way, and she is to be apprehended and held for questioning on sight!"

"What old woman?" blustered the cop. "The whole place is full of 'em!"

The two Secret Service agents sped up the same instant in their own Ford sedan.

"Any sign of her?" one asked.

Pearson shook his head. The other mumbled into his walkie-talkie.

"Nothing yet," he confirmed. They hurried off in the direction of the east wing, where the Tiffany Room was located.

"Anybody see Folner yet?" This question from Bedrosian.

Lowell wondered, in the melee of the last quarter hour or so, if anyone had even bothered to inform the Folners of Mrs. Hartley's impending arrival. They'll be in for quite a shock, he thought grimly.

Moments later the local sheriff arrived, confusion reigned, and time was running short.

Inside the lobby, Lowell scanned the crowd for any sign of his client. The Belleair cop was right. There was a sea of gray heads scattered around. Half the population of Belleair was retired, and they'd all come out to see their heroes.

Lucretia Hartley was by then wandering across the gardens on the far side of the hotel, walking alongside a retired couple from Bel-

270

gium, here for some golf and to see the American celebrities. Nobody paid the slightest attention, as they entered through the gift shop into the East Wing . . .

At the hallway entrance to the lobby, the Secret Service had erected a barricade, allowing nobody past without an engraved invitation, checked against a list and identification. That had created a logjam of reception guests trying to get in.

Down the hall a loudspeaker blared, introducing various local notables. There was a roar from the south entrance, indicating that the senator's helicopter had arrived from Tampa.

Pearson and Jeffries caught up with Lowell and Bedrosian at the rear of the pack of guests waiting to get in.

"Is there another way in?" Lowell wanted to know.

"Shit," muttered Pearson. "The old lobby. That's where they'll bring him in." He collared the nearest Secret Service agent and a puzzled looking Pinellas deputy. "We have to get to the ballroom," he snapped. "She may already be in the building."

"Who?" asked the agent.

Great. "Come on." Pearson turned back to the two detectives. "We'll go around." They hurried off, elbowing their way through the crowd, unknowingly by the same route Lucretia had just taken.

Inside the Tiffany Room, the mayor of Tampa was warming up the audience. The reception organizers were in a panic because the senator was on his way in, and nobody had seen Judge Folner.

"Ladies and gentlemen," shouted the mayor, amid the din of the ballroom, "may I have your attention please!" The crowd noise died down now, into a ripple and murmur of expectation. The guests were unaware that danger was present. "Ladies and gentlemen, please find your seats!" There was a rush of movement to the tables, and he went on. "It is indeed my great pleasure and honor . . . to welcome you today to this momentous occasion . . . The Chambers of Commerce of our combined Bay Area cities of Clearwater, Tampa, St. Petersburg, and of course our host city Belleair, together with the governor of our great state of Florida and our Japanese hosts, are all humbly proud, and deeply honored, to introduce to you without further delay our old friend and yours, our own former governor and yours, Senator Bob Grimm!"

The crowd burst into a frenzy of applause, necks straining to see where the senator and his entourage would be coming from. The band began to play "For He's a Jolly Good Fellow," and the crowd surged toward the east end of the ballroom.

On the authority of their police badges and P.I. permit, the three cops and Lowell had managed to get themselves past the security people into the room, just inside the hallway entrance.

"Here he comes," muttered Bedrosian, pointing. Senator Grimm, in a dark blue worsted suit, red tie, and carnation, his down-to-earth wife in a modest store-bought dress, approached the dais, almost smothered by a phalanx of security people. He was a very popular senator, especially in Florida, his home state. He had aged gracefully: certainly plumper, jollier, the last remaining wisp of hair thin and white. He wore glasses now. No wonder, Lowell realized, we didn't recognize him in the more than twenty-year-old photo he'd been staring at for days. How many people would anyone recognize, in photos that old, not knowing or suspecting who they were? He returned his mind to the task at hand.

The senator reached the platform and hopped up onto it with practiced ease, waving to the crowd, wife at his side. The mayor leaned over, whispering something in his ear. He frowned momentarily, then seized the microphone. The crowd died down. The senator began to speak, his voice firm, clear, and confident.

"Thank you for that kind reception, Mr. Mayor! Ladies and gentlemen. It's great to be back in Florida. Especially after some of the chills we've been experiencing lately up in Washington!" (Applause, and laughter.) "As a matter of fact, I look forward to some serious marlin fishing off the Keys this week. You didn't think I was just going to turn around and head back north empty-handed, did you?" (More laughter.) "You know, from my earliest days, my family and I have had strong ties to this part of the state. And nowhere are those ties better exemplified than right here in Pinellas County!" (Loud cheers and applause.) "And while I'm always happy to be here, I'm not the real reason we're here today." (More applause.)

A Secret Service agent joined Lowell and the two cops for a moment at the door, fretting into his walkie-talkie. "Where the hell is he?" he barked, then hurried off, speaker squawking.

One of the senator's aides reached up and tapped him on the elbow, whispering urgently. The senator nodded and continued, hardly skipping a beat.

"I am basically just here to welcome, or should I say reintroduce to you—since I'm sure you all know him as an old friend as I do—a man who like myself is a native son down here, a man who sure as hell has done good for us all," heads were turning and twisting now expectantly, "and a man who has just been confirmed to become one of the finest Associate Justices of the Supreme Court of the United States ever to sit on the bench. Mike Folner, come on up here!"

The crowd burst into a frenzy of applause. The band played another chorus of "For He's a Jolly Good Fellow." More heads turned. There was no sign of the judge. The crowd murmured, waiting. Wondering. Another urgent whisper from an aide, and more squawking of walkie-talkies.

The senator seized the microphone once again. "Ladies and gentlemen, I just got word Judge Folner is in the building. But it's so darn big, he lost his way!" (Relieved laugher.) "He'll be here in a minute, though." He shouted, gleefully. "Mike, where the heck are you?" Then, working the crowd, "If he ever shows up late to one of my parties again, I'm gonna tan his hide!" (More laughter.)

Almost unobserved in crowd, the judge came into the room. He stood for a moment in the doorway, nearly at Lowell's elbow before he was noticed. He was dressed in a simple gabardine suit, and seemed faintly distracted. He, too, had a retinue of Secret Servicemen around him. Hanging a little back were the two agents who had hounded Lowell for days, Werner and Lefcourt. Julie was at his side, and cast an odd look of recognition at Lowell. The judge saw him too and scowled, pulling her away. Werner gave Lowell and Bedroian looks that promised a future settlement of their differences. The

crowd parted, rippling with murmurs and cries of welcome, and th
Folners made their way forward.

The senator saw them at last, smiled broadly, and shouted ove
to them: "Hey, here they come, Ladies and Gentlemen, Judge—
mean, Justice Michael Folner and his lovely wife, Julie. Let then
through, folks."

It was then that Lowell spotted Lucretia, moving diagonall
through the crowd, at an angle that would intersect with the Folner
at the foot of the platform.

"Mrs. Hartley!" he shouted, rushing forward. Pearson, Bedro
sian, and Jeffries were instantly behind him, walkie-talkies cracklin
all around the room.

"Stop!"

She half-turned at the sound. Lowell saw her and the glint o
metal in her hand at the same moment. Next to him, he could hea
a Secret Service agent shouting: "Drop it!" Unwavering, she raise
a small-caliber pistol and fired a single shot. It sounded like a sma
balloon popping. It was answered almost instantly by a second sho
fired by Agent Werner, appearing out of nowhere. As Werner pu
away his small Baretta automatic and disappeared back into th
crowd, Lucretia Hartley crumpled like gossamer in a flame.

There was a moment of absolute silence in the vast ballroom
Then pandemonium, as someone shouted: "The senator!"

Lucretia Hartley had hit her target. Or at least a target. Almos
unnoticed in the bedlam, Senator Grimm lay on the floor, a sma
hole in the center of his forehead, staring blankly into his next realn
of conquest.

The judge and Julie were whisked away in an instant, under a
umbrella of gray suits, bodies forming a human shield.

Lucretia lay forgotten on the floor, the crowd giving her room:
circle of deathly solitude. Lowell reached her and knelt by her side
joined by Bedrosian a moment later.

"Clear the room!" someone shouted, and the cops and Secre
Service agents went to work, herding people to the exits—those wh
had not already panicked and fled—and none too gently.

She was still alive, eyes open, a trickle of blood at the corner of her mouth. She turned her head slightly and looked at Lowell. In her hand, she clutched a silver cross. The same cross she'd been holding when he had visited her a few days before. Karma. A small revolver lay close by.

"I got the weapon," Jeffries shouted, picking up a small, snub-nosed pistol. He checked the chamber. It had been fired once.

Werner edged toward the door, Lefcourt with him. No one paid attention to them, all eyes were riveted on the face of the old woman, trying to speak.

"Justice!" she murmured. Holding up her cross like a ward against evil, Lucretia died.

The room seemed to let out a long sigh of its own.

"So," breathed Lt. Jeffries at last. "You got your killer, Lena. An old lady. God help us all."

Pearson pushed his way forward. "Did anybody see who shot her?"

"I saw him," said Lowell. "It was one of the same two F.B.I. men who've been hounding us the past week."

Pearson conferred in urgent tones with one of the Secret Service people, frowned, and turned back to them. "That's funny. These guys say there are no F.B.I. here. It's not their territory."

"Then who the hell were they?" demanded Bedrosian, looking around. Lowell searched the room, Bedrosian along with him. The two men were long gone. Bedrosian and Lowell looked at each other. Neither one said anything. There was nothing to say.

25

Amid the pandemonium following the senator's assassination, Chief Sturbridge had quietly arranged for Private Investigator Tony Lowell and Detective Bedrosian to fly back to Palm Coast Harbor by commuter plane via Sarasota, to pick up their cars—Lowell's Impala and Bedrosian's unmarked police sedan. This also served, at least temporarily, to shelter them from the media spotlight. Lowell was shaven, cleaned up, and sporting a new outfit from J. C. Penney's. Navy blazer and gray slacks, and a plain gray shirt. He had the look of a man who had been scrubbed with a wire brush, as though to scrape off the scum and crust from his immersion into the mire, literal and otherwise. Bedrosian seemed subdued. Her designer skirt and jacket were gone, replaced by a simple brown tweed jacket and casual slacks from Macy's.

They had spoken of inconsequential things on their way out. Actually Lowell had spoken very little. His mind was on Caitlin, now that his thoughts weren't focused on immediate concerns.

To fill the void, the police detective had been unusually garrulous. Chatting about the meaninglessness of "Hollyween," as Lowell called it, and how it now seemed to blend, in a sea of pumpkin by-products, into Thanksgiving—which had already long since been coopted by Christmas—becoming a single, long two-month feeding frenzy of consumptive commercialism. Lowell nodded as he listened, eyes fixed on the clouds and Everglades below. He was thinking about justice. Also his fee. The one he never got.

Lena Bedrosian talked about her kids, and how hard it was to be a good wife and mother and a good cop. George adored her, she knew, but she rarely saw him; and the girls saw her more as a role model, to be emulated but not necessarily listened to. As for the baby, she couldn't help feeling guilty for not being there full time to care for him. Maybe it was a female thing. They were so dependent on their mothers for feeding, for nurturing, for their immediate needs (the only ones they knew) that there was little room for transfer of this role to fathers, despite the popular theories of the age. Mommy picked him up and he cooed. Daddy picked him up and he screamed. Mommies could always make it better. But daddies, it seemed, could only make it worse. Small wonder most men preferred to stay away. And yet George persevered, and the baby didn't seem to be doing too badly.

Lowell remained silent on the subject. During the forty-minute flight over, neither of them mentioned the case of Maureen Fitzgerald et al.

Lowell and Bedrosian shared a cab from West Palm Beach over to The Harbor and were waved through the gate by a duly respectful Harry Martin, who assumed they were a visiting couple. (He made no connection between them and the two separate strangers he'd admitted just over a week earlier.) Lowell had requested that no one other than Ernie Larson be informed of his coming. He wasn't ready to see or deal with anyone yet. That would come later. He had unfinished business here with Caitlin and his daughter. But first he must prepare. It would take time.

The cab drove past the gates of Breezewood. There was a new, tempered stainless-steel, half-inch chain and Yale padlock on the gate, put there by order of the local police to discourage the curious. They pulled down Pelican Street to the boatyard, where Lowell got out. The police detective shook his hand briefly.

"Take care," she said. And drove away. Nice woman, Lowell thought to himself, watching her go.

Ernie Larson was waiting in the shed, with the car keys and a pot

277

of coffee. He wore a brand-new pair of tortoise-shell glasses, and looked embarrassed as heck.

"I adjusted the valves on that piece of shit out there," he said by way of greeting, as he gripped Lowell's hand.

"Dammit, Ernie. Now I owe you one!" complained Lowell, with the first smile he'd mustered since the Mido.

"Tony, you worthless junkyard dog! What you owe me, aside from everything you got, which ain't shit, is a decent breakfast over at Hungry Charley's, with some proper damn grits!"

Ernie Larson cajoled and cheered Lowell the way no other person could have done, and they parted late in the afternoon with promises of another, happier reunion "real soon." Perhaps after the holidays and the onslaught of the blues they inevitably brought had passed. Then Lowell headed into the sunset and home.

The blaze was visible on the horizon, before he reached Gulf-bridge—a deep orange afterglow, like the Northern Lights. At first he thought it was a residual effect of the sunset over the Gulf. But at seven-thirty P.M. in early November, that was unlikely. Then, as he crossed the last bayou bridge on the coast road, with a clear view out toward Sandy Key, his pulse quickened.

The fire was somewhere in the direction of his home. Racing now, pushing the old Impala to the limit, he felt a burning of his own deep within. He heard the siren but didn't slow down. It was a fire truck, overtaking him fast. He pulled over to let it by, then followed close behind.

The flashing strobe lights in front of his property lit up the trees and mangrove in psychedelic flashes, pounding the inside of Lowell's skull with foreboding.

He skidded to a stop on the shoulder (his driveway was blocked by two pumpers) and hurried as though in a trance through the trees. To his relief, his house still stood, starkly outlined against the night sky. The blazing light came from beyond.

He heard voices. Shouts of fire fighters, a few neighboring snowbirds he didn't know—they'd placed the call probably—and picked out a few phrases. They had put it out quickly, with minimal damage. The worst danger had been the spread of sparks to the drought-ridden woods and marshes, and the house itself.

"What was it?" a latecomer shouted to a returning fireman carrying a length of hose. They had needed a lot of hose, because of the distance involved to the nearest hydrant.

"Just a boat," came the apathetic reply.

Lowell ran.

The old schooner was a total loss, all except for the keel. That venerable single piece of timber had somehow survived but for a little charring, its aging having made it harder than steel. The rest was ashes. Lowell perfunctorily answered questions and signed forms. Still in a dream. Except that boat had been his dream, his single most focused reason for existence for many years, and now it was gone. Maybe it was meant to be. Karma.

But he did need to know what had happened.

"Any idea of the cause?" he asked the fire chief, Leo Pappas. Lowell had known Leo from the time he'd moved to these parts. They were neighbors, of sorts, separated only by a couple of miles of bay and bayou.

"Yeah," growled Pappas, beckoning Lowell to follow. Over where the workbench stood was a can of kerosene and a box of matches.

"Whoever was playin' with matches, didn't bother to hide the fact," he commented. "And they left a message of some kind. Least, that's what it looks like to me."

Leo led Lowell to the foot of the tracks he had built, eventually to slide the finished vessel into the bay when the time came. There, where the dark bay waters lapped lazily at the shore, someone had planted a pole. An oar, actually, driven crudely but with great force into the sand. Waving gently, tied near the top, were two small flags. Lowell recognized them immediately. Red, with black squares in the center.

"Those yours?" Leo asked.

Lowell shook his head.

279

"They look familiar. What are they?"

Lowell almost smiled. It was another closure of sorts. "Hurricane warning," he replied.

Hurricane. The single most dreaded word on the Gulf. The Chief looked skyward, involuntarily. He hadn't heard anything about hurricanes. "Isn't it kind of late in the season?"

"Yeah," agreed Lowell. "Yeah, I would say so." And that was that.

Lowell had read somewhere, or heard it said, that when your enemies came for you, they came after the things you loved. Funny. And yet, as he assessed his inner feelings—still largely unexplored territory, but which he had vowed during this past terrible week to venture into—he realized that they had missed their mark. This project, for all the time, effort, and money he'd put into it, had been nothing but a diversion all along. His true love was elsewhere, he now knew. And with that certain knowledge, he was able to resume his life . . . almost. First, he'd had to withstand an onslaught by the media, because someone in Palm Coast Harbor had leaked word about the three killings and his connection to the Hartley scandal, which was dredged up anew. He had steadfastly maintained his silence, and the press had for the most part given up and gone away—turning their attention back to the assassination. And to a lesser extent, the Folners.

When it was over, he slept for three days and three nights. The college gave him a sort of postmortem sabbatical to get himself together, withstanding pressures from various quarters to dismiss him. Then he was back, good as new. Better, in fact, because his angry sixties rebel image, uneasily tolerated by his peers and associates as part of an artist's milieu, was gone. Lena Bedrosian had asked him, during their journey together across the Florida peninsula, why it was that he loved the sixties so much. Lowell's answer, popping immediately from the cellars of his subconscious, had been a revelation to both of them.

"I never loved the sixties," he responded, testily. "I just couldn't ever *shake* 'em!"

Bedrosian hadn't understood, of course. And Lowell didn't care to explain. In any case, it was over. Life would go on.

A week later the surprise had come. Broke, he'd gone to the bank to withdraw the remainder of his savings account. And there he discovered what he had least expected, in the last place he would ever have thought to look. Someone had made a deposit in his name. An elderly woman, he was informed, when he tracked down the teller, who remembered. The deposit had been made on the day she'd called—before he'd even agreed to take the case. It was as though she knew even then how things would turn out. It had been her life savings, she'd told the teller, which she wanted the young man to have. For the amount of ten thousand dollars.

He was rich! So why couldn't he sleep at night?

Three weeks after the death of Lucretia Hartley, Tony Lowell rose at dawn, and went downstairs to resume the task of restoring his life and his home. He had decided to take down all the prints and mementos of the sixties from the gallery walls, and store them in his file cabinet. He was determined to put that decade to rest at last. Even the poster he had so carefully carried and preserved during that long day and night of flight remained untouched—still battered and rolled up in a corner where he had left it.

Instead, his journalist's instincts and training had pushed him in another direction. A direction of more recent concern. And closure.

He had made a single major purchase, partly from the insurance money he'd gotten for fire damage, and bought a nearly new Macintosh CX. Using this, with graphic animation and software of his own design, he'd begun experimenting with negative processing and computer enhancements again. Just for the hell of it. Perhaps to incorporate into a more advanced photography program at the college. Or perhaps for something more. He worked up a complete set of prints of Mike Folner and his old senator partner. Poring through the college library and newspaper microfilm, he found two other

281

photographs of the two of them together. He'd even tried to approach their old law firm, still doing robust business in Miami, but not surprisingly, had been given a cold and emphatic brush-off. And then, in an old issue of *Town and Country* magazine, he stumbled across the pièce de résistance—a society function photograph of an art opening in New York's Greenwich Village. Dated in the spring of 1965—many months before the wedding of Henry Hartley and Julie Barnett. And there they were together. Hartley looked boyish and happy, his arm wrapped around the shoulder of his friend Michael Folner. And Julie was there too, merrily kissing Michael on the cheek. A third man stood back from the group, looking smug and slightly aloof: a youthful Bobby Grimm. The sprightly caption read:

"Oil heir Henry Hartley cavorts with unidentified friends at the new Village Gallery."

Some friends, Lowell had thought, smuggling the magazine home in order to get the best possible reproduction.

And so, this morning he'd gone out and picked up the paper—the *St. Petersburg Times* (another new addition to his life was deciding it was time to rejoin the world of the informed)—and the headline struck him like a thunderbolt: "JUSTICE FOLNER RESIGNS."

The shock wave was widespread, the reactions in political circles predictable, and the explanations vague. The judge, who had not yet even assumed his seat on the bench, had "after agonizing and sleepless deliberation, decided for reasons of personal and family nature, combined with declining health, to resign from his newly appointed position as Associate Justice to the Supreme Court of the United States."

A few of the more canny and skeptical journalists, from the *New York Times* and *Washington Post* particularly, had raised questions regarding his relationship with the senator and the assassination in Belleair, Florida. The response from the White House had been brief and diplomatically regretful. Some media cynics even suggested that with Grimm out of the way, the President was off the hook.

The reaction of Anthony Lowell, P.I., was far more complex. Certainly, he felt that the judge's resignation was in the best interests of the nation. Personally, he could not deny a certain satisfaction of sorts, although the fact that Mike Folner was a self-important megalomaniacal pompous SOB was beside the point. He had never really cared one way or another about the outcome of the Hartley vs. Hartley case. He'd never cared much for Lucretia, certainly, but had cared even less for Senator Grimm and the Folners. Nor did he have any interest in wealth and its burdensome accoutrements. He had no reason to feel differently now. The issue for him had always been justice. Period.

But he had been having increasing doubts, the last few weeks, as to how well justice had been served in regard to the death of his cousin Elliot. And Lucretia Hartley, and her housekeeper, and her doctor, for that matter. They deserved better than to be swept under some tightly woven political rug, in the aftermath of the assasination.

That, and the fact that he felt he owed Maureen Fitzgerald and Elliot Dupree more than a little, had been his motivation for resuming his own quiet inquiry. Now, with this new development, he was beginning to feel a glimmer of vindication. And with it, a new, cloying, clinging ache in his gut. Was it doubt?

For the hell of it, after finishing the papers, he went into his darkroom, hung up his new series of photo creations, and, carrying the phone extension in with him on its twenty-five-foot line, placed a telephone call.

Things had returned to normal down at police headquarters in Manatee City. There had been a few hard feelings, especially between Lena Bedrosian and a couple of her male colleagues—Allenson and Sheriff's Deputy Pilchner—who had made several pointed threats on two different occasions. Jeffries had quickly interceded, warning them that any harassment in his department would mean suspension on the spot. The sheriff had backed him up—especially when a check with the F.B.I. confirmed that no agents had ever been assigned to the Fitzgerald case. Allenson and Pilchner had been

283

bamboozled. But then again, so had everyone else. The Manatee Police Department came up empty as to the identity of the two men. They had come from nowhere and vanished the same way.

All in all, it had been a tough situation, and everybody eventually agreed that Lena had simply been doing her job. The sergeant, who personally liked Lena and her family, quickly let bygones be bygones, and the matter was soon forgotten.

The news from Washington had been duly discussed at Manatee P.D. over morning coffee and donuts, with lots of speculation. Bedrosian, as resident expert on the subject, had politely deflected questions, however, and taken shelter in her own office.

Bedrosian was pondering the news, a Styrofoam cup of coffee in one hand, a piece of baklava (that succulent Middle Eastern pastry with nuts and honey) in the other, when the phone rang.

Popping the remainder of the baklava in her mouth, she grabbed the receiver with the freed hand, annoyed. "Yeah?" she spluttered, mouth full.

"Bedrosian? It's Lowell."

She swallowed, almost coughing the oversized bite back up again. "Lowell! Son of a gun! Whaddya want, I got it up to here already with questions about our friend Folner. Not to mention our late, great senator."

"Hey. I just missyntle sweet sound of your voice, that's all."

"Yeah, right. What else?"

"Well, actually, I've been thinking about Maureen Fitzgerald." Bedrosian sensed trouble. "What about her?"

"I've been thinking about who killed her."

"What? Come on, Tony. The case is closed. I know it was a lousy thing. But let it rest in peace."

"I can't. Not until I know Maureen Fitzgerald and the others can rest in peace."

"Look, to be blunt, old Mrs. Hartley went off the deep end, rightly or wrongly. There's a legal name for it: 'diminished responsibility.' Maybe the senator and Folners did burn her, maybe she had reason to flip. Thing is, she did. And those people paid the price, and that's it."

"No, that's not it. I've been thinking about it, and even if you could make a case for the Fitzgerald woman, Lucretia Hartley had no reason to kill Dr. Morton, or Elliot Dupree. This just doesn't follow. She was practically an invalid. Granted she made it to Clearwater to shoot the senator, and probably intended to hit the Folners as well. But running all over the place knocking people off—I just don't believe it. And why would she want to suppress those files? If anything, they implicated the Folners."

"Look, I'm telling you, you're blowin' smoke down the chimney. It's liable to start a fire under your own ass, all over again. You gotta be crazy!"

"No. I know who killed Henry and probably Maureen. And it wasn't Lucretia. Maureen had said something before she died—"

"There you go again!" shouted Bedrosian.

"No—she said something about a jewel. I never could figure what she meant, until—" Lowell heard a sound and froze. Behind his back, the darkroom door had creaked open, a narrow crack. And a figure like an angel appeared, beauty incarnate. But it was an angel of death.

"Just a minute, I thought I heard something." He turned in his chair, and found himself face-to-face with a startling transformation. Almost a mocking remembrance of what so recently had been, life's epitome, all that beauty corrupted and turned inside out. The judge's wife. The late Henry Hartley's widow. She was reaching for him, hands extended, oddly pleading. Outside, she was as beautiful as ever, though her eyes were red from sleeplessness and grief. All Maureen had been trying to say when she died—as he now belatedly realized—was "Julie."

"Hello, Julie."

"Hello, Lowell."

"What brings you way out here to the boonies? Or were you just in the neighborhood?"

"I asked around. Said I needed a private detective."

"So. Was it just you? Or was he in on it too?"

She ignored his question. "My husband's gone mad, Lowell! He's throwing it all away, and all because of you!"

"Me? How so?"

"Someone sent him that photograph of yours. Making all sorts of wild threats about telling the media. Calling him a kidnapper. Calling him a polluter and unfit for the court. You should have minded your own business, and that wouldn't have happened."

"Sorry about that. I don't know who sent it, but I can't control what others do. And whoever sent that had a point."

Bedrosian's voice crackled over the line, questioning. Lowell knew he had to think fast.

Julie seemed to notice the telephone for the first time. Reaching out suddenly, she seized the receiver and threw it across the room.

Bedrosian winced at the clattering noise and strained to hear, at the other end. "Lowell?" she called out. "You there?"

Too late he saw it coming. Out of nowhere, she produced the small .22-caliber handgun and fired. But he was just slightly quicker and ducked. The shot missed, and she aimed again. "Life is so fragile," he heard her saying, as though from across the universe. "So brittle, don't you think? We have all these parts, cells, fibers, organs, a brain! All those years of thoughts and feelings and experiences stored in our beings. And one little hole—one tiny little hole, destroys everything. That's what you are, to me and my husband. A hole in our being!"

They stood, staring at each other for a moment, each catching their breath, pumping a new supply of adrenalin for what must happen next. "So," he said finally. "Is this how you did Maureen and my cousin? And Maureen's doctor? Were they holes in your being, too?"

She seemed momentarily taken aback. "No! I didn't do those things. They didn't need to be done, only little warnings."

"Storm warnings?"

"Yes! Bobby promised me they'd take care of everything."

"Bobby? Senator Grimm? You mean those phony F.B.I. agents were working for him?"

"He planned everything. He always did. He said they were professionals."

"I'd say they were definitely professionals."

"They let us down. I hope they don't think I'm going to pay them, just because Bobby's gone."

"They might not agree." No wonder they burned my boat, he thought, with a flash of irony. Guess I burned a hole in their beings, too.

"So now," she went on, "I am going to put a very small hole in you. It won't hurt much, they tell me. But it'll stop you cold. It's only right. A life for a life!" Her voice was oddly deep and gritty.

"If you say so." This time he wasn't quick enough, and the bullet struck him in the shoulder. He dropped to the floor and dove across the room.

"Lowell?" Bedrosian heard the shots, and didn't have to be told what was happening. "Lowell, you all right?" No answer. Cursing herself for her slow reactions, she jumped to her feet and ran for the door . . .

Inside the darkroom, Julie Folner had Lowell cornered. His shoulder was bleeding, but he ignored it, eyes on her and the barrel of her gun. He hadn't made it out the door. Body still in shock, he felt no pain. Yet.

"You persecuted my husband and me with your selfish vendetta, out of pure spite and politics." She looked around at the new photos hanging up to dry, and began tearing at them in a frenzy.

Pulling himself to his feet, he tried to lunge for her. She spun and fired again. The bullet struck him on the hand. Now he felt the pain. "Who are you to bring him down?" she screamed. "A man so great, who dedicated his life to serve the public? You dare?"

She followed his motion like a sunflower following the sun. She would finish him now. Retribution time.

"What was it, Julie? The money wasn't enough? You got the

money. You got the power. You got Southern Oil. Look, if your husband wants absolution from me, he's out of luck. He's a ruthless, unprincipled—"

"*He doesn't know!*" she shrieked. "He doesn't know a thing about what I've done!"

He stared, stunned by the words.

"What are you talking about?"

"Henry knew about us. Michael loved me, and I loved him. He was all I had! He promised to take care of me forever. But we needed money, I had to push Henry! And then that Fitzgerald woman appeared, threatening to spoil everything. I had to protect Michael, damn you!"

One thing about smart, unprincipled people, reflected Lowell, with a touch of sadness. They can rationalize anything. Even murder.

Now she was poised for the kill, sensing he was weakened. This time, she would not be denied. He watched the gun swing toward him once more. And then, with one sudden, last surge of energy, he dropped to the floor in a wrestler's takedown and kicked her feet out from under her. She fell with a piercing shriek, hit the floor hard, and the pistol skittered across the room. He fought his way on top of her, struggling to evade clawing nails and fingers, then slowly, gradually, straining to his utmost limit, pain searing down his right side, his hand aching agony, and yet hanging on, using his superior weight, until finally, at last, he had her pinned.

The fight was out of her instantly, and her eyes went dead. Like in the portrait, he suddenly thought.

Twelve minutes later, Bedrosian arrived with Lt. Jeffries together with officers Baker and Peters. They came by helicopter. Bedrosian had burst into Jeffries's office, where he was in the middle of a meeting with Chief Sturbridge. With unheeded coffee spilled all over her new blouse, she'd shouted:

"She's killing Lowell!"

Sturbridge could only stare, uncomprehending. But Jeffries,

knowing they could discuss the who's and what-fors later—God bless him, for all his sluggishness—moved quicker than Lena Bedrosian had ever seen a man move. Inside ninety seconds they had commandeered Baker, Peters, and the Hughes 300—about to depart on traffic patrol.

Arlin'll make a great captain, Bedrosian thought, as they sped over the bayous and out onto Manatee Bay. Baker, a pilot in Vietnam, manned the controls.

Lowell heard the chopper coming, and it gave him the strength to hang on. She was stronger than he now, he knew. His shoulder tendons must be cut, disabling half his arm strength on one side. And his other hand was crippled. But she no longer seemed to care.

"Please let me up," she finally said. "I won't run. I'm too tired. I'm too tired to care anymore."

He wanted to believe her. He stretched, fingers crawling across the dirt-crusted hardwood floor to reach the .22, and grasped it in his good hand. Tucking it in his belt, he scrambled free and stood. She lay there a moment, breath coming in gasps, not moving.

"All right. You can get up. Slowly."

She obeyed. They could hear the engines, pitch whining down, as the chopper landed next to the carcass of Lowell's schooner.

Bedrosian, Peters, and the lieutenant ran for the house, fanning out. They were inside faster than a SWAT team, guns drawn. And that's how they found them. Sitting quietly in the living room, for all the world like a couple of Quakers at Meeting.

Then they saw the blood. The second shot had severed an artery. Lowell had left a trail of blood from the darkroom to the kitchen, and back to the studio. He seemed oblivious. So did Julie Folner. Bedrosian tore a white silk scarf from her neck and tried to stem the flow.

Peters, who was also a paramedic, raced back to the helicopter for the first-aid kit.

"Tell me, Anthony," Julie was saying, sounding so sweet and thoughtful. "Did you ever love someone?"

He replied, voice fading fast: "Once upon a time."

289

"You see?" she said, as though that explained everything. "You *do* understand!"

"Love is good," he agreed. He stopped, winced, and waved at his friend the cop, who had just entered with help.

"Yes. If only we wouldn't mess it up so!" Julie said.

Peters returned with the kit. In moments, he had fashioned a tourniquet for Lowell's shoulder and bound up his hand.

"Hold still a sec'," he ordered, and gave him a shot of morphine.

"Thanks for getting here so fast," murmured Lowell, hanging on. Bedrosian sat next to him and held him, wishing she could do something more. At this moment, she loved him as a friend and felt no shame or remorse for it. It was just a simple fact.

"No problem. Hang in there, babe." She looked around, bewildered. Julie had moved away, and was singing softly to herself in the corner. Desdemona's "Willow" song. "What in hell happened?" The detective asked, keeping her voice low.

"Just a misunderstanding," murmured Lowell, fighting the pain and now fighting the painkiller. "She thought I should die. I thought not."

"We'd better get him to Bayfront Medical," said Peters. "He's lost a shitload of blood."

"I'll call ahead, get him ready." Bedrosian picked up the telephone and dialed 911. It was busy. Lowell leaned back in the sofa and smiled, dreaming of billowing spinnakers.

Jeffries came out of the darkroom, carrying a stack of photographs. He knew the whole story and understood instantly what they meant. And in that moment he made what amounted to his first, and possibly his ultimate, executive decision.

"I'm gonna have to confiscate these," he informed Lowell. "This has gone far enough, for God's sake. We can't undo the past. It's like pulling a thread in a tapestry. You affect everything. It'll all come apart. Let it be!"

Lowell opened his eyes once more, gazing up at the spot where his John Lennon blowup had once hung. He'd taken it down in deference to a need for new beginnings. "Let it be," he murmured.

Bedrosian helped him to his feet, assisted by Peters. "Let's go. We're getting you to the hospital."

Lowell tried to stand, weaving.

"I'm fine," he said. "Never better."

Then he collapsed to the floor . . .

Epilogue

Spring in Florida is usually best noted for its massive influx of hormone-charged adolescents, bent on releasing their oversupply of libidinous energy built up and suppressed in their (presumably) studious confinement, during the winter months.

For Floridians, it mostly amounts to little more than staying away from the beaches and spreading some fertilizer on their gardens.

Out on Manatee Bay, a fine spring morning found Tony Lowell working feverishly on his new schooner. A lovely breeze, laden with the scent of hyacinth and hibiscus, a touch of salt and shellfish, wafted in from the Gulf. He had his shirt off, enjoying the sun on his back and shoulder. The scars had healed nicely, and the discoloration had greatly receded. It would remain a part of him, though, for the rest of his days. Another battle scar for an old warhorse, as he laughingly called himself.

A year had come and gone, during which he'd been content to let the old boat rot away, the last vestige of wasted years. Knowing that he had other priorities now, other duties. And loves.

It was his former student, Sheila Balfour, who had convinced him to reconsider. She'd stopped by the bungalow, not having seen him since the Folner affair and his return to the college.

"You'll never guess what we saw coming over the bridge," she'd exclaimed in breathless excitement.

"What?" he'd asked, humoring her.

"A manatee. A real, live manatee! They still exist!"

So, he thought. Still an environmentalist at heart. And why not? He had guessed who had sent Folner the damning photograph. Sheila might have done more for the movement with one FAX than whole organizations had managed to accomplish. The fact that she'd dropped out, and gone off to New York to become an instant success on the fashion circuit—strongly boosted by the strength of his unorthodox portfolio of stills—was therefore quite forgivable.

She wanted to thank him and show off her new status. Then, upon seeing what had happened to the schooner, she'd boldly suggested that he should either remove the old hulk, eyesore that it was, or restore it once again. He congratulated her on her new career, and listened noncommittally.

A few months later, after disposing of a couple of run-of-the-mill, low-stress investigations—a divorcee who wanted access to a high-rolling ex-husband's hidden wealth for back alimony; and a routine workmen's comp fraud case—he made his decision. He would go back to work. His "real" work. Using the good keel as a solid foundation for a new beginning. Sheila had loved the symbolism and approved wholeheartedly . . .

His hand still troubled him, though. Especially during manual labor. It probably always would. But he persisted, working out diligently with grip strengtheners and a prescribed rehabilitation program.

He had planed away the charred surface and sanded the keel smooth in just a week. Then he'd begun the search for new wood, suitable for ribs and keelsons. He had wanted white oak. But it was too scarce and the cost too prohibitive, and he no longer had the strength or flexibility in his hands to bend and shape it. He'd finally settled on three-quarter-inch birch plywood, five four-by-eight panels he'd painstakingly glued and clamped, cross-layered to a thickness of four inches. The resulting boards were strong as steel, and he'd sealed them tight with multiple coats of water seal, then urethane. Next, he'd cut them into the U-shaped ribs—notched for the keel, keelsons, and stringers—from a template, using a new band saw. He'd made that concession to technology from necessity, unable to proceed further with hand tools.

Today he'd begun mounting the fifth new rib onto the keel, glued and braced until dry, and bolted through top and sides into the massive wooden beam beneath. As he wound the large hand wrench—one hand tool he insisted on using to further strengthen and rebuild the tendons and flexibility in his hands and arms—a white VW Rabbit convertible entered the driveway. He heard the wheels on the crushed oyster-shell drive, and thought nothing of it as the visitor parked up toward the front of the bungalow. No longer an isolated place of refuge, comings and goings were now commonplace on Mangrove Road.

A young blond woman in crisp white slacks and a neat button-down pink blouse came walking down the drive, heading straight for the water's edge and the boat. She knew the way.

Lowell looked up and flashed a broad, surprised smile. He waved her over. Ariel was home for spring break, and had come over from the Atlantic coast for the weekend. She wanted to introduce him to her boyfriend—an event no father is ever quite ready for, he realized.

Other events had preceded this moment, of course . . .

It began with a long overdue reunion with his father, at a nursing home in Citrusville. He'd arrived one day in the spring and spent a memorable two hours with the old man. Chief Lowell didn't remember him. Which is probably why they managed to have the nicest afternoon together of their entire lives.

Tony arrived at the admiral's door late that same night, still bandaged and hand in a sling, leaving his Chevy idling in the circular drive. The same Chevy he'd bought new, the admiral remembered oddly, when Tony and Caitlin had first dated. Lowell had brought a bouquet of red roses, which he held in his good hand, dressed as though for a prom.

The admiral had answered the door and just stood there, too shocked to react.

"Evening, Admiral," Lowell had said with a grin. "I'm here to thank you for caring for my daughter. And to pay for the damages to the *Wellington.*"

The admiral had accepted the check, still speechless, so Tony went on: "I've also come to see them."

And that had been that. That very night Lowell drove to West Palm Beach Airport with the two of them, mother and daughter, and they all flew off together to Bermuda. For an unforgettable two weeks, unmindful of the spring chill and rain.

Ariel and Tony had circled each other warily, not daring to approach. Finally tears flowed, there were regrets, and recriminations. Then reconciliation, more tears, and finally the wonders and pleasures of sharing and discovery.

Then Ariel had met some boys from Princeton (she herself was planning to enroll at Duke in the fall) and had gone off on a spree of sailing, tennis, scuba, and windsurfing, leaving Tony to come to terms with a new emotion—paternal jealousy.

He and Caitlin were finally alone together again. They made love, awkwardly, and talked. And talked. Tony had been prepared to propose a long overdue marriage. But somehow, it hadn't quite happened. Too much time had passed. Or something. Too many new tricks for a couple of old dogs, was how she jokingly put it, in the end. Instead, they decided to stay friends. They'd see each other now and then. It would be nice.

The big change was father and daughter. Tony took to parenting like a spinnaker to a Gulf breeze, and soon he and Ariel became close confidants and best buddies. She came over to the Gulf whenever she could, and he even visited the Gold Coast. They saw each other over Christmas, and she came down from Durham during exams. He had told her to consider Manatee Bay her second home, and she'd taken him up on it.

And now here she was. Boyfriend and all.

"Guess what, Dad!" Ariel announced, after a warm hug and kiss on the cheek.

"Tell your friend it's safe to get out of the car and come on down here. I can use some help with these planks."

"OK." She turned and waved in the direction of the car. A long, lanky form with a reddish shag haircut began the seemingly endless process of unwinding itself from behind the wheel. "Dad, I've got news!" Ariel exclaimed, dancing in front of her father.

He stopped work and looked at her warily. "What?"

"I've chosen a major. I've decided to go into photo journalism!"

Lowell winced. Oh well, he thought to himself. At least she didn't choose criminal justice. . . .

ROBERT LEE HALL'S BENJAMIN FRANKLIN MYSTERIES FROM ST. MARTIN'S PAPERBACKS

BENJAMIN FRANKLIN TAKES THE CASE

When Ben Franklin rushes to a printer's shop on London's Fish Lane, he finds the old proprietor murdered and a ragged servant boy with blood on his hands. But Franklin knows the lad is innocent, and together they set off to find the real killer . . .

_____ 95047-0 $3.99 U.S./$4.99 Can.

BENJAMIN FRANKLIN AND A CASE OF CHRISTMAS MURDER

A prosperous London merchant, entertaining guests on Christmas Eve, collapses and dies. At least one of those present—Ben Franklin—knows there's more to this than meets the eye . . .

_____ 92670-7 $3.99 U.S./$4.99 Can.

MURDER AT DRURY LANE

The constable labels a fatal plunge from a theater gallery a mere accident, but when a number of suspicious incidents begin plaguing the playhouse, its premier actor engages Franklin to investigate.

_____ 95112-4 $4.50 U.S./$5.50 Can.